MARTIN CAIDIN is a pilot and former
consultant to the air surgeon of the
Federal Aviation Agency. He has written
over seventy works of fiction and non-fiction
utilizing his broad experience in aviation.

Cyborg
Martin Caidin

Mayflower

Granada Publishing Limited
Published in 1974 by Mayflower Books Ltd
Frogmore, St Albans, Herts AL2 2NF

First published in Great Britain by
W. H. Allen 1973
Copyright © Martin Caidin 1972
Made and printed in Great Britain by
Cox & Wyman Ltd, London, Reading and Fakenham
Set in Intertype Times

For Big Milty

CHAPTER ONE

Lonely mountain took the first harsh whisper of naked sun. Far beyond the ridges of the San Bernardino, the San Gabriel, and the Shadow Mountains, the peak the Spaniards long ago named Soledad glowed against desert morning sky. Earth's horizon dipped lower to cast Lonely Mountain with increasing brilliance. It was a clear sign of blistering heat to come during the day.

Many miles distant from the stone-hard, baked, desert floor of Rogers Dry Lake, the sight of the faraway peak brought eyes flicking to wristwatches. The events of the morning were to be measured as a race against a wickedly hot sun and its enervating temperatures. Not so much the heat itself but its thermals wavering in the desert air could snatch dangerously at stub wings already teetering on precarious balance. The time to get things done in the California desert was early in the morning, and that was now.

From the floor of the dry lake, sunrise began with the flaring upthrust of Lonely Mountain. As the men glanced up from their work the sawtooth edges of near mountain ranges were yielding to light. Silhouetted ramparts in deep shadow rang brightly with the fireball impact of the sun. Etched by early-morning dust, sunlight stabbed through crevices as huge glowing shafts across the vast desert floor. There was now that magic transition between dawn and day. With the sun angle still so low, there was stark contrast; clumps of scattered tumbleweed hid their brambled surfaces in the form of soft puffballs glowing along one side, casting long shadows behind the other. Along a nearby ridge, midget desert flowers shone in purple and yellow. Sagebrush seemed to glow, but above all there rose from the flat tableland the oldest denizens of this desert nowhere, the great cactus trees known as Joshua trees. Some of these grotesquely crooked giants of their kind reared fully thirty feet above the flatness at their base, frozen in some ancient torment, and it was difficult to realize as they accepted the

7

morning sun that they had stood here as long as the towering redwoods had stood farther to the west. Against the hazy blue of dust already shrouding the distant peaks, charged with a mild electrical glow by the ascending disk in the sky, they set a somber mood of stark contrast against the newcomers to this forsaken flatness.

Through most of the night there had been other light here in the Mojave. Along the western rim of the floor of the dry lake, a blue-white incandescence showered upwards. These were brilliant floodlights and under their harsh glare there had been created a small oasis from which night was banished. Great generators howled and thumped and whined through the long hours to power the lights, and their exhausts and vapors, rising slowly, had added to the feeling of an outpost on another world. There were other vehicles; long trailers gleaming whitely beneath the lights, identified in glowing signs and blinking panels of their own. Several large-bodied trucks displayed thick red crosses. Other vehicles were tracked, coated with armor and asbestos, and studded with hand grips and thick hatches. Still others were a garish red, knobbed from bumper to bumper with the protuberances of nozzles and hoses; each of these could instantly be transformed into a dragon foaming from half a dozen nozzles and spouting flame-depressing liquid from half a dozen more. A great crane on sixteen massive wheels stood silently by on the perimeter of the island cluster of lights and sound and movement. Long, yellow trucks with cylindrical bodies and chains dragging behind to eliminate static electricity waited patiently to move kerosene fuel into metal-enclosed tanks. Other fueling vehicles were present; these were painted dazzling, international orange, splashed with warning signs, glowing beneath lights flashing the unmistakable signal of danger. There were sedans and station wagons, some Air Force blue, others the white of the National Aeronautics and Space Administration. On the latter the blue insignia circle of NASA was displayed prominently. Communications vans extended wispy and curving helical antennas high above their bodies. And there were, finally, several personnel trailers, long-bodied enclosures sealed so completely from the outside, air-conditioned and humidity-controlled so carefully that they were literally spacecraft on wheels to sustain their internal environment.

All these, the screaming generators and flashing lights and trucks and cars and vans, were present to meet the needs of two other machines. At first glance only one of these was visible, and not until the sun rose high enough to bathe its vast spread of wing was its true size apparent. It hulked along the dry desert floor, a brooding monster of many hundreds of thousands of pounds, a technological vulture with wings sagging at their tips nearly to the ground. It was a football field of metal shaped and angled into its present form of wing and body and towering tail, all of it balanced on tandem sets of tires, the far edges of the wing tips teetering in impossibly silly fashion on stick legs of outrigger gear.

Standing close to the right wing the observer had no view of the second machine, which was the reason for this great assembly of machinery and more than two hundred people. This second and smaller machine nestled closely to the underside of the left wing, a blunt dart beneath a great spread of metal, sandwiched in between jet engines and long, external fuel tanks. It *appeared* to be a thing intended for flight, but rather than wings it had stubby appendages jutting from a rounded body shaped like a bathtub. Three flaring fins marked the aft section, sharply angled metal quivers, ending a ridiculously short and stubby metal arrow. The nose of the strange machine, marked with black lettering that read M3F5, revealed a shaped glassy enclosure that gave it the appearance of a whale with a transparent snout.

Two men wearing bright-orange jump suits and white helmets with fluorescent stripes stepped back from a final inspection of the finned bathtub. One glanced at his watch, then turned to study a long, white trailer bearing the rounded NASA insignia. 'About that time,' he noted. His companion nodded, saying what they both knew. 'Any minute now.'

As if on cue a door in the trailer side opened, a man stepped out quickly, turned about, and stood expectantly by the steps, looking back into the trailer. He appeared nervous, as if wishing that whatever was scheduled to happen would do so quickly. Moments later another man appeared in the doorway, moving with greater deliberation, almost shuffling clumsily within the constraints of a white pressure suit, his face obscured by a gold-opaque sun visor. He might have been an astronaut stepping

9

from a trailer at the foot of a launch pad on Cape Kennedy; he wore much the same garment as the men who had voyaged to the moon. He had been one of those men, a member of the last crew to make the voyage between earth and its desolate satellite a quarter of a million miles distant. His name was Steve Austin; he had been a test pilot before his weightless traverse of vacuum and he was now, again, a member of his former profession. No shifting lunar soil awaited this journey, but still, the flight he anticipated to a height of some sixty miles above the floor of the desert held far more danger. The path to the moon had been well established with mathematical certainty before he watched his planet fall away during Apollo XVII. The machine into which he was soon to be sealed lacked such certainty, and in its area of unknowns were dangers unpredictable but predictably lethal. It was a simple rule of thumb. No one had ever been killed on his way to or on his way from the moon. Every year at this sprawling center of test flying in the California desert, every year for the past twenty years, an average of eight good men had been killed.

Austin stood for a moment in the doorway, looking out past the jumble of vehicles, studying the huge winged shape with its wicked little machine suspended beneath the left wing. His gloved hand lifted slowly to slide the opaque visor away from the plexiglas bubble before his face. Then, satisfied, he nodded his head, an acceptance within himself that it was time to move on. He had worn this clumsy garment often enough to know its restrictions, and he moved his left foot forward, crabbing his body as he did so, leaning into the step in a practiced maneuver. The man waiting at the foot of the steps reached forward anxiously to support Austin at the elbow, for the test pilot was encumbered with a portable air conditioner in his left hand. Even at this early hour, being sealed within a suit designed for survival in vacuum guaranteed immediate severe perspiration without internal cooling air flow. Steve Austin took the steps carefully, stopped for a moment as if to test the fit of his heavy garment, then moved off steadily toward the huge airplane. Directly behind him walked his suit technician, a cold-eyed fussbudget connected by swaying telephone wire to the radio headset in Austin's helmet.

Austin's appearance in the trailer doorway was an unspoken

10

signal for almost all activity in the area to end. It was, of course, a story familiar to all who were there. Austin could not move an inch into that waiting black sky far above the earth without their co-ordinated efforts. But they would remain well within the comfort of earth-surface gravity, while he was the one to attack the unknown with its inevitable dangers. So they stood, by some unspoken signal, to watch him take his final steps before commitment.

All but one. *'Steve!'* Her cry caught everyone's attention but his own. Within the pressure helmet he heard only the voice of the man walking behind him, but that man grinned into his headset.

'Colonel, I think someone wants to say good-bye.'

As the girl ran to Austin's side, her brown hair flowing from her movement, the suit technician was lifting his headset from about his ears. He cast a swift approving glance over the lithe figure standing before Austin, then handed her the headset and boom mike. Austin smiled down at her as she fitted the equipment. It was almost impossible not to smile at the sight of Jan Richards.

'Steve, I – I didn't mean to, you know, interfere, but I just had to say something before . . . before you left.'

The smile broke into a broad grin. 'Say it, then.'

She glanced about self-consciously, edging closer to him, whispering the words in the microphone. 'I love you, Steve Austin.'

He gestured with an easy laugh. 'You sure must like privacy.'

'Is that all you're going to say?'

She saw his head move inside the helmet, tilted slightly to the side as if appraising her. 'Same here.'

She thrust her arm about his, glanced behind her at the suit technician eyeing them both. 'Can I walk with you to the plane?'

His gloved hand patted her arm. 'Sure.' He glanced at the suit technician. 'Charlie's already having his fit so I guess it doesn't matter.'

She moved as close to him as his bulky covering allowed, matching his shuffling pace, the suit technician staying immediately behind with quick, short steps. Jan did her best to keep her words easy.

11

'It's hard to believe this is the last one for a month, darling.' She squeezed his arm, suddenly hating the thick material separating them. 'And starting tomorrow . . .'

'Save your strength,' he told her. 'You're going to need it.'

'Breakfast in bed, right?'

'Breakfast and lunch *and* dinner.'

'You'll never make it to dinner. Not when I get through with you.'

'Got it all planned?'

She nodded. 'I intend to wreck you, my love.'

'God,' he laughed, 'what a way to die.'

She glanced at the flying wedge suspended beneath the huge machine. Oh, God, I hate that thing, she thought suddenly. I've been here too long and I've seen too many of them . . . She refused to think deliberately of the word die. She turned her eyes from the gleaming metal back to the man at her side.

'I'm afraid I love you more than you deserve.' Quickly she removed the headset and microphone and handed them to the suit technician trying unsuccessfully to remain at a discreet distance. If she stayed with Steve any longer . . . It wouldn't do to cry, for God's sake. She hurried away without turning back until she was far from the metal that frightened her. When she stopped, finally, she knew Steve would be only a figure in a white pressure suit. She turned as a bearded man approached, and quickly she wrapped his arm in hers. He glanced at the sudden tears.

'Steve see that?'

She shook her head angrily. 'No. Just you, you old bastard.'

Rudy Wells patted her hand with open affection. 'If it makes you feel any better, Jan,' he said, 'as his flight surgeon I can tell you that Steve Austin is in perfect shape for this—'

'That's how I want him back.'

'That's how you'll get him back,' he said confidently. 'My God, Jan, I've never seen you with jitters like this. That man has walked on the moon. The *moon*,' he emphasized. 'This is just a little hop around the old meadow in comparison. You of all people should know that.'

'I know it, I know it,' she said, almost hissing the words. She pointed to the blunt shape beneath the wing of the giant plane.

'But that thing is, well . . . Oh, dammit, Rudy, you know what I mean.'

'I know.' He didn't need to say any more. Not on that subject. Time to turn to one that was' safer. 'Everything set for tomorrow?'

'All set. Twelve noon at the base chapel for the marriage ceremony and time for a party afterward. A damned brief party,' she added.

She studied the winged machines. 'Thank the Lord,' she whispered aloud, 'this is his last one.'

He looked at her with affection. 'For a month, anyway,' he said gently.

'You didn't need to remind me,' she said. Her arm went rigid against his. The figure in the white suit was climbing into the swollen belly of the finned dart. They watched in silence.

He paused for a moment, one foot still on the ladder, the other within the cockpit of the M3F5. Paused for that final scan of the horizon, for the telltale signs. Even at this early hour the air, cool and still at sunrise, had changed its temper. The hazy-bright horizon was gone. Now that horizon had fuzzed, thermals dragging dust and vapors from the ground, building a miragelike effect that made the peaks and ranges appear higher and closer than they really were. The long shadows from the Joshua trees had diminished; soft gray had become intense black greatly foreshortened on the ground with the climbing of the sun. And there was still another sign to his practiced eyes; the most certain of all omens that the heat of day was blistering the desolate land and casting back its writhing heat. In the distance, picked out by his keen eyesight, the black shapes of buzzards casually riding the thermals, soaring in wide, sweeping circles higher and higher above the desert floor. Buzzards this early in the morning. It was going to be a bitch with updrafts on the way back.

He half turned for a glance at Jan, standing with Doc Wells. For a moment he thought of that splendid body and the wonder they had found in making love – Steve Austin cut himself short. Get your ass in the cockpit and your head out of your ass, he snapped to himself. The fastest way in this business to get killed, and it was by God *the* fastest, was to let your mind roam instead of paying attention to what was at hand. When you drifted between earth and moon in that delicious zero-*g* fall that went on day after day, you could mess up your thinking all you wanted to. Three guys in the cabin, and autosystems to take care of everything but the laundry. But not in one of these vicious little things. They had hidden reefs and all manner of nasty surprises up there in the sky, and this chunk of angry metal was intended to chart a safe path through those lethal mantraps. Which meant keeping your nose to it. He allowed himself one more extraneous thought. The lights; the sun was up. What the hell did they need the lights for? A quick smile; the lights went out silently, the pressure helmet hiding the sounds of heated metal shrinking back to normal size.

He grasped the handholds, slid into the contoured seat. For a moment he sat quietly, not moving, allowing his mind and his body to *feel* what might be wrong. You look for the things that don't fit. The mind has been trained so that whatever is normal, whatever is right, snaps into place and rings no bells, makes no clamoring warning. What doesn't fit, what's slipped out of the pattern, then jars you. No bells, no lights; it was all there, in place. He waited a moment as a technician leaned over the side of the cockpit, took hold of the air-conditioning hose. Austin nodded at him, held his breath. The technician unsnapped the hose, stabbed it into its proper receptacle inside the cockpit to resume the cooling flow of oxygen. Austin glanced at the gauges, gestured with his raised thumb. The technician slid from view and another face appeared in place of his. They began the long checklist. Austin checked out his communications circuits with the B-52 pilot, the drop officer, and radar control, and made a final test of the link to the chase planes that would be with him during part of his flight. It was all terribly familiar, as close to home as brushing his teeth in the morning, and yet every step was critical. It went quickly enough, a mechanical, rote procedure, and then it was time for the last man leaning almost into his lap to disappear. Austin took the hand signal to button up, confirmed with the drop officer in the bomber, closed and locked the canopy. There was now little for him to do; he would wait out the engine start and climb to altitude, becoming progressively more concerned with

14

different gauges as he approached that moment when he would be released from the mother ship.

'Relax.' He breathed deeply, slowly. Plenty of time later to be afraid.

She could never watch that huge damned thing moving along the desert floor without feeling her lungs were going to explode. She couldn't help it. Some silly thing in the back of her mind told her that if she held her breath through the long, pounding run on the desert she would be able to help the giant claw its way into the air. Whatever the cause, she was never able to remind herself to breathe. She waited until the thunder rolled slowly down the long desert strip; no movement yet. The giant sat poised, black strength and fury, the engines howling, throwing back swirling plumes of kerosene smoke that built into a great cloud rolling over hard and dusty sand. Then came that bare shift in sound, the signal that brakes had been released and metal was dragging itself ponderously forward. From this distance she could not see the tiny silver dart beneath the wing, had no view of the terrible little machine her lover was strapped and sealed into. But at such moments, as the giant rushed closer and closer, she held her breath, sucking it deeply into her lungs, her nails biting into her palms. This time, only one palm would show the signs of her inner strain. Unknowing, her other hand holding the arm of Dr. Wells, she would make him the victim of her gouging nails.

Jan Richards watched the monster rush toward them. She saw the great wings flexing, the upward bend of metal that told of lift changing the forces on the wing. She knew the signs, had watched this same scene many times before, but no matter how many times, it was always inner torment, with her breath held until she needed desperately to breathe, and did so explosively, her heart pounding.

The takeoffs were *almost* the worst; only the landings were worse. The seconds dragged on and on, and the great machine seemed to take forever in its sluggish early motion. But now it had speed, and she knew enough of the world of flight to know that at such times speed was everything. It was control and lift, it was life, and she wished speed – *Godspeed!* – to the great black shape, and then it was almost on them, malevolent in its

15

suddenly swooping approach. Then it was alongside, directly before them, and she saw two things at the same moment, the silver shape of the tiny aerospace machine, with a glimpse of the pressure helmet within – she saw that and she saw the nose wheel of the B-52 rise away from the desert, and the breath rushed out of her. The nose rotated higher, and then daylight showed between the clumsy main gear and the desert floor. Now the thunder crashed back against them, shaking their bodies, and she turned to bury her head in Dr. Wells's shoulder as the stink of kerosene washed over them. When she looked up again the black cloud stretched high into the bright desert air, a winged destroyer at its head. Two black minnows flashed into view, cracking the morning wide with their own thunder. The chase planes on their way to ride tight formation with Steve Austin until he would outstrip them and arrow away from the planet itself.

'Checklist complete. Over.'

Austin nodded to himself within the helmet. 'Okay,' he said. 'Stand by, Roadrunner. Cleaning up the office.'

'Roger.'

Austin stuffed the checklist into its enclosure by his right arm, pressed on the velcro seal. One last, careful look around the office. Everything in the cockpit was clean. Just about that time.

'Cobra to Roadrunner,' he called the drop officer in the bomber. 'Ready for final count.'

'Right, Steve. Three minutes coming up. Please call off your tank pressures and qualify valves armed.'

They went through the final predrop checklist quickly. As they moved down into the last sixty seconds the personal tones faded away. Crisp, no-nonsense exchanges now, broken by a personal touch only when the man in the wicked little M3F5 led the way.

'Cobra,' they called Steve Austin. 'On my mark, one minute.' A pause for five seconds, then: 'Mark! Sixty seconds and counting.'

'Roger, Roadrunner.' Steve Austin flicked his eyes over the gauges, glanced again, swiftly but steadily, at every control and lever and dial. He didn't bother to glance to his sides to check

16

the position of Chase One and Two. The big, black SR-71 jets would be sitting well to each side, slightly higher and behind the B-52; the moment he dropped away and lit up, they'd be on him like faithful sharks. Until he left them behind.

'Thirty seconds.'

'Okay,' he said. The bright-orange hand swept around the timer. At ten seconds the drop officer called it out. At the count of zero he would—

'*Drop!*'

'Right on the money,' Austin said easily, feeling the old gut-sinking feeling as he went from solid gravity to that momentary free fall of dropping away from the giant ship above him. There was a brief glance at the earth nine miles below, a scan of mountains flattened out by height; the scratch-pen pattern of roads and a quilt of irrigated farmland. Only the reassuring glance to orient himself. The M3F5 dropped away at angels forty-five. He'd allow himself only a drop of one mile. By then he had to have everything on the stove. He hit the final pressure switch with his left hand, moved it to the throttle. Big bastard of an engine back there. Same design they had in the lunar module. Reliable and gutsy. He moved the throttle forward into ignition phase. It came instantly. The invisible hand threw him back against the seat. He nodded in approval, pulled back on the stick just slightly. No need to lose more altitude. Good; he'd dropped only three thousand feet so far. The stick came back some more as the throttle moved inexorably forward under his left hand. Then he had full power and the thunder howled freely behind him, riding a long flame studded with diamond shock waves. He arrowed the nose higher and higher, taking up a slant of seventy degrees, booming up and out of atmosphere, and he knew everything was in the slot and behaving when he heard the sound of his own breathing in his helmet. Other sound was far behind him now; he felt the vibrations of controlled thunder. And he'd lost the sky. Vanished; gone. Snap your fingers; just like *that*. No more blue. Not even dark purple. *Black*. The black of space. No stars yet; hell, he was still sun-blinded. There was only that velvety, impossible black.

'Cobra, this is Tracker.'

'Roger, Tracker,' he said easily.

'You're right on the money, Cobra. Smack on.'

'Okay.'

He was too busy for chatter. Not yet. He still could see only sky. Or what had been sky. He crashed upward into blackness. A moment for a glance to his left. His eyes drank in the sharply curving horizon. God; that sight! He forced himself back to the instruments. No time for sightseeing here.

At 280,000 feet he eased the nose down, began coming back on power, brought her to minimum thrust. Control with the small rocket ports in the tail section and the bow; spatters of energy to move in vacuum. That, and the big engine on its gimbals. Just enough to change the flight path, as he began now, a clumsy but effective turn, a wide sweep above and almost beyond the planet, practicing what other men would soon be doing when they flew the big Orbiters of the shuttle program back from beyond the edge of space.

The fuel alarm light spattered red at his eyes. Right on time. Quickly he eased the throttle back full; shut her down evenly before she could sputter. The latter could tumble him up here like an insane cartwheel, so precariously fine was his balance. He was prepared for *anything*. No fun in being a skateboard on sheer ice going out of control. He tensed as a great hollow bang behind him signified clean shutdown. Good; he hit the nitrogen-pressure switch to flood the tanks and dump the volatile fuel through the lines. He was flying now strictly on centrifugal force. He could modify his attitude but it didn't mean a thing if he flew sideways or backwards. Until he hit air, that is. Then he had to be in exact position – the nose up, just so; the silver wedge positioned and balanced in such a way the nose and belly would act as a heat shield to slough off the fiery touch of friction.

But for a few moments, now, a precious interlude in the midst of flight-plan demands, this mission was for him. He topped the great parabolic arc at 328,000 feet, more than sixty miles high, and as he brought the nose down steeply to command the world before him, the horizon curved sharply away on either side to remind him he was back home where he belonged. At the edge of the world and far beyond that. He was light-adjusted now and the brighter stars invited him. Familiar, too; stars by which they had navigated precisely to another world a quarter of a million miles distant. Low over the

18

horizon, a silver of promising crescent, he saw the edge of the silent rocky globe he had once walked on. The awe returned to him, seeped through his bones and brought the taut feeling. The cosmos itself . . .

Something tugged at the metal outside.

'Christ!' That damn sightseeing again. It was a drug from which he had to tear himself free. He could get in trouble quickly up here; the silver wedge was feeling the first wisps of atmosphere, heating up now. The lights were on. Time for a brief check with the ground before he'd be in the communications blanket, the silver wedge surrounded with a fiery sheath of stripped atoms.

'Cobra to Tracker. Over.'

They were sitting on the radio. 'Roger, Cobra. Go ahead.'

'Confirm start of reentry. Got the heat light on, and the zero-zero-five-g light is also on.'

'Roger, Cobra. We confirm start of reentry.'

He permitted himself the small luxury. 'I'm bringing this mother home.'

Regrettably, the horizon began to flatten.

CHAPTER TWO

He had to imagine the silver wedge as a machine slicing its way from orbit back into the atmosphere. That was the whole idea of the mission, to test the equipment and the procedures for the big Orbiters that would be flying at the close of the decade. He lacked the speed of an orbiting ship, but everything else was phased into his flight. Enough to make it an acid test, anyway. Which is why NASA wanted an experienced astronaut for the flight program. You can't beat the attitude of the man who's been there, and Steve Austin had come back into the atmosphere once with a speed of seven miles a *second*.

But slamming back into air with the Apollo took less out of you than handling this tricky little bastard. In Apollo you flew a ballistic entry with some lift to control where you'd screw your way down through atmosphere before going to the parachutes. The lifting bodies had to handle both assignments. Function as a spacecraft out of atmosphere, but function as an aircraft when the air became dense and nasty with decreasing height. It called for more than simply surviving reentry. He had to *fly* the thing down, work his way through great descending curves, pick an airfield and then grease the mother back onto unyielding ground.

A neat trick to carry off, but if it worked, all the way from out there in vacuum, it meant the future spaceships wouldn't splash down into an ocean, they wouldn't need huge recovery forces, and they could pick home plate. Any runway a few miles long would do. In fact, they were really pushing him against the wall with the M3F5; the wedge would land a good fifty miles an hour faster than the big ships being prepared for orbital operations.

He used the small control rockets to bring up the nose, measuring every inch of his attitude against the lighted globe on the panel before him. Sharp lines against the golden sphere told him degrees of attitude above or below the horizon, and indicator lights helped him keep the nose pointed on a line directly along that of his flight path. Coming in with a sideways crab could demolish the ship and incinerate it with unexpected friction. That sort of nonsense could ruin your whole day.

The glow came before he expected to see the heat ripping away from the ship. At first it was a bare hint of pink, deepening swiftly to orange and then to fiery, bloody red that left nothing to the imagination. Shock waves pounded through the metal by his feet, and Austin laughed silently as he felt his toes curling within the pressure boots. As if that instinctive, helpless human gesture would alleviate two thousand degrees of hell should the epoxy resin of the shield fail anywhere! The heat would come through the ship like a bazooka shell and with all the explosive results of an actual blast. But the heat shield held, as Austin expected it to do, and the automatics held the attitude right where it belonged. The ship rocked and sometimes it shivered to hammering blows, and if he hadn't once seen pieces and chunks of heat shield streaking past the window of Apollo, he would have had the living hell scared out of him. He was tense enough; he would never have claimed he wasn't always afraid, but experience with Apollo and years of test flying managed to keep the pucker factor down to a level he could live with.

Then he was through the heat pulse. He breathed a sigh of relief, for from this moment he was master. He cut the automatics and went back to manual control; now the stick in his right hand and the pedals beneath his boots worked familiar flight controls, even if he lacked even a smidgin of power. He kept the nose down, the silver craft plunging earthward with supersonic speed. A hell of a ride; not an ounce of thrust and he was still well above the Mach, the machine honey smooth to his touch. It might not be the same when he went transsonic. Sometimes the plunge back through line center, from supersonic down through the transition range, went smoothly. Sometimes it didn't.

Like right now. The wedge slid abruptly, a crazy yawing motion that came out of nowhere. No wings, really, to lock her steady with lift, to bring a wing up or down. No ailerons out there with which to play instinctively. Just that triple-damned bathtub shape and the three flaring fins, and somewhere, somehow, a shock wave streaming off the bathtub shape hammered against one of those fins, or locked its movable surface in a steel vise, and she threw her nose to one side, a sickening yaw that caught even his swift reflexes by surprise.

What had been smooth as honey became a washboard increasing its violence with every second. He hoped the ship would stay glued together until he dropped down to subsonic speed, but for the moment it was touch and go. Behind him he heard the three flaring fins buffeting, the forces acting upon them sending a thrumming sound through metal, a discordance picked up by the entire metal shape. The harmonics went through metal and through his seat and grated on his teeth. He couldn't see the fins but he knew they were twisting and flexing, and he thought of the ejection seat that could punch him away from this suddenly savage little beast. He pushed that from his mind; he brought his ships home unless they shredded on him in the air. He tried to fight the controls but this was no longer an airplane; he was a prisoner in a rounded metal coffin giving explosive birth to shock waves that both astounded and frightened him. From the curving prow, bands of gray, gleaming light streamed stiffly back, a ghostly pattern streaking to each side. Curving around the nose, reaching up and back, were broader bands flowing out and intersecting those from the sides in a ghostly, flickering procession. They were knife-sharp, crystalline, weird, impossible.

They were terrifying.

He knew that the shock-wave vise hammering the little machine could dissipate, or the waves might flow together and—No more time to think. She snapped over on her side, the horizon straight up and down before him, and he knew he'd lost her. She was berserk, a demon running wild. Despite the harness strapping him in he felt the forces hurling liquids about within his body. The wedge spun nose over tail, the horizon cartwheeling insanely. She spun flatly, inverted. He was mashed to one side by the alternating g-forces as she stood on her nose and whirled. He felt like a rag doll, the pressure oscillating, hurling him to the edge of blackness from positive g, then exploding his brain in red as reverse acceleration gorged his brain and eyes with blood. He knew his blood sloshed back and forth, breaking small veins, distending his main system dangerously. Instinct kept his hands working the controls, instinct that had always

22

brought him through before but was worthless at this moment. How long the hellish ride went on he couldn't know. No sense of time. He realized seconds were racing by, time was building – and running away from him – because he was starting to hyperventilate. Pure oxygen in his system. Fighting the punishment, he was breathing in short, jerking gasps, flushing the carbon dioxide from his lungs, almost on the brink of passing out. A sudden savage blow, slamming his head to the side of the canopy. He lapsed into a gray world, hazy, fighting for coherency. He was struggling to raise his right hand back to the stick when the silver craft broke free.

Subsonic. Shock waves behind him. He listened to his hoarse, gasping breathing. Habit, instinct, training – blind memory – moved his right arm and his legs. He brought her out of a careening dive, transformed a bulletlike plunge for the desert floor into a swooping, controlled curve. He studied the altimeter. Thirty-two thousand. He had room. Plenty of room, but where the hell was he? He couldn't see that well yet. Spots went through his vision, through a red film hazing his eyes.

Then he heard the voice, insistent.

'Do you read, Cobra? Chase One calling Cobra. Do you read? Come in, Cobra, come in. Do you—'

He gasped out the reply. 'Chase One, uh, Cobra, ah, here. Read you. How—'

'Have you got control, Steve?'

'That ... that's affirmative. Chase. Better give me a ... a fix. It's been a hairy ride.'

'Steve, we're about ten miles behind you, closing fast. Take up a heading of two six zero. Got it? Two six zero.'

'Okay, Steve. We're coming up on you now. You've got plenty of room. The field is now about twelve miles dead ahead.'

'Uh, Roger.' He peered ahead, trying to see through the red film. He could barely make out the long, black line painted on the desert floor. 'Uh, Chase, I think I've got it in sight. What's the wind?'

Radar Control broke in at once. 'Radar to Cobra. Wind is fifteen knots from two two zero, gusting to twenty knots.'

Not good. Where the hell were the smoke flares? He wished he could rub his eyes to clear them.

'Cobra from Chase One. Can you see the smoke?'

'Negative, Chase. No sweat.'

'Roger, Cobra.'

A blessed moment of silence. He pegged the air speed at two hundred forty knots, holding it steady, maintaining his rate of descent, planning ahead for the moment when he must flare, when he would bring up the nose. Damn his eyes. He—

'Cobra from Chase Two. Please lower your gear, Steve.'

Christ, he'd forgotten. He mumbled acknowledgement, hit the lever. The ship rumbled as the tricycle gear banged down in the slipstream, quieted a bit as the doors closed. Three green lights came on before him. 'Three in the green,' he called.

Chase Two was directly to his right. 'Roger, confirm three green,' the pilot replied.

The mountains were higher on the horizon now, the world flattening out even more on all sides. A broad band of water shimmered to his right. He shook his head angrily. Mirage, but enough to screw up his depth perception. He forced his eyes back to the black line on the desert floor now swelling swiftly before him. Things were happening too fast, he was behind his procedures.

'Cobra from Radar, you are now four miles out, that is four miles from the edge of your landing strip.'

'Okay, Radar.'

'Do not reply, Cobra,' the Radar Controller intoned. 'You are above your glide path.'

He nudged the stick forward a hair. 'Returning to proper glide path, now three miles out, maintain your speed and rate of descent.'

They were talking him in like the old GCA. Right now Radar was a blessing.

Desert features rushed by. He glanced at the airspeed – down to two fifty, dropping again. Even as Radar told him he was slightly above his planned glide path he nudged the stick forward again. What the hell was wrong with the trim? He nudged the trim control on the stick. *No response.* Something was screwed up in the electrical system. It would be even nastier than usual.

'You are one mile from end of runway. Slightly above glide path, coming back to glide path nicely. You are coming up on

24

runway. Prepare for full visual takeover. You are now over the edge of your landing run.'

The voice went silent. The back line stretched away to infinity as the ship trembled from thermals smacking up from the desert. Damn that crosswind; it was edging him to the side. He corrected with rudder but the ship felt sluggish, and he was holding hard forward pressure on the stick, and—

'Bring her to the right, Steve.' The voice of Chase One. His foot went down a bit harder on the rudder pedal and he compensated with the stick. Time to bring her around now, flatten out the glide, set her down on the main gear.

'*Watch it, Steve!*' The voice roared in his headset even as the side drift brought one gear to touch. Too fast! The silver machine bounced, wobbling through the air, the speed playing off rapidly, the precarious lift bleeding away. Without wings out there to— He felt the impact as she rocked on the left gear, bounced again, then the nose was coming up, and without that trim to compensate for—

He stopped thinking then because he knew he'd lost her – there wasn't any more lift, and control sloughed away in his fingers, and what had been a beautiful aerodynamic machine became a lump of metal going its own way, and there was a sickening gut feeling as the horizon tilted crazily and the earth came up with terrifying speed to meet him.

He'd seen it happen before, maybe a dozen or more times through the years, and memory shaped its own patterns in his brain, and the warning motions were enough to trigger the sequence of events he knew *must* happen. Dr. Rudy Wells for a moment felt Jan's nails digging into his arm and then he felt nothing because he was, gratefully, numb from head to foot, his mind separating from his body, throwing total concentration into the impossible scene taking place before them. Numb through his limbs, rooted to the desert floor, mouth open like a fish, he knew what would happen even as the ship went through its inevitable motions.

At that instant Steve Austin was condemned, for the ship was now slave to inertial forces over which he had no further control. Even with an engine behind him he would have been behind the power curve, the ship slewing along with its nose so high that only a huge rocket could have blasted him away. There was one chance left and because he had not seen it happen already, Wells knew that Steve Austin in his desperate attempts to save the machine had ignored completely the ejection seat. It could have punched him free. It could have hurled him up high enough for a rocket slug to boom open the parachute. It *could* have saved his life, but it didn't have the opportunity to do that, because Austin was a conditioned test pilot first and last.

There was that sickening swerve of the nose, the yawing, nose-lifting motion that flashed reflected sun into the eyes and sounded the first mental shrieks of warning. A gear stabbed the ground, much too hard, and a stream of dust snapped into being, trailing the still-speeding, lurching coffin. The yawing motion and the dust trail froze Wells's senses where he stood; there was the momentary sensation of nails digging into his arm. Maybe he heard the gasp from the girl clinging to him, maybe not, but certainly he heard the noise of tearing metal. First the one gear, then another wallowing motion; the ship rolled drunkenly, her lift gone, taken away from her pilot, and the other gear snapped down, hard enough this time to crack metal and send pieces of the gear screaming off at an angle.

There was a long, breath-sucking moment before the next impact, a moment filled with rustling wind, the last sighs of the machine about to destroy its pilot. Other sound filtered through to Wells's mind; the banshee wail of the chase pilots overhead, and the reflex action of a man on the ground stabbing the disaster button. In that moment, mixing with the sound of the jets overhead, began the strident waver of the crash siren.

She came down hard, slightly to one side, taking most of the impact through the center line of the rounded belly. Wells heard a bone snapping, a bone of metal structure moving before his eyes. She caromed back into the air, a crack showing her innards, spewing debris and liquids from pressure bottles – a growing spray of destruction. This time the nose went higher; she twisted through her length and came back down partially inverted, stabbing a fin into hard desert. More dust, a bubbling torrent mixed with metal, and the new sounds, a gnashing and tearing roar as the ship began to disintegrate. When she hit again she broke into huge chunks, methodically chewing herself

to pieces, and bright-orange flame licked through the tumbling
mess as the liquid-oxygen tanks went. Wells knew what must
happen next. Hydraulic lines rupturing, the sudden fiery lash
feeding on the oily mixture, and a growing blossom of fire that
seared through her innards. Pounding, breaking up, hurling
forth a sputum of debris, mashing what was left of the nose
section, now trailing metal, smoke, flame, dust and other junk,
the ship died. The noise changed, a staccato growling unreal,
terrifying to hear, pierced through to his mind above the roar of
the chase jets banking hard, returning to the scene, the pilots
agonized over their helplessness. Other sound now – sirens,
thin voices from all sides, and the roar of engines. Wells saw the
crash helicopters moving in from the side, the meat wagon and
fire trucks pounding to what had come finally to a stop nearly a
mile away. The first choppers were on the scene, big ugly
Kamans, working in a team. He saw the downwash pounding
flame away from what was left of the silver machine, saw
another Kaman pouring foam from its nozzles at the wreckage.
Asbestos-clad men dropped to the ground, rushed in.

But he couldn't move. Startled, he realized Jan was standing
by his side in shock. Wells tugged to free her grip from his arm.
'Dammit, let go!' He finally pulled free, left her sagging to her
knees as he signaled to a crash wagon moving by. They slowed
enough for him to leap onto the running board, clinging to the
door as the driver raced for the wreck.

He had a moment of lucid thought that all this was a waste,
that no man could survive what he had just witnessed, that
Steve must be dead. And if he's not, thought Wells, then he was
even more unfortunate.

He was off the truck and running before it screeched to a halt.
The crash teams were swift and effective. Someone had cut
open the canopy with an axe, even at that moment was in the
midst of torn metal and rising steam, trying to get the straps
free of the body. Wells didn't waste time asking questions. No
one could know any more than he could see with his own eyes.
He moved as close as he could to the wreckage, checked for the
medical teams standing a few feet away, and found himself
waiting to do *something*.

Someone shouted a warning about the ejection seat; the crash
teams were trying to keep the arriving technicians back from

the smoldering wreckage. If the rocket tube in the seat went it would erupt with renewed violence, hurling the heavy metal seat through the men milling about the scene. To hell with that, Wells thought. He had to get in closer, and he motioned the medical team to move in with him. If by some miracle Steve were still alive then he would need whatever help they could give him immediately.

Heat washed over him. The wreckage crackled ominously, but there were qualified people to worry about that. Wells wanted to remove Steve from his shattered metal coffin. At long last one of the asbestos-clad figures began moving backward, the man's legs clumsy in the foam-sprayed twisted metal. He motioned with one arm, and the medical team rushed forward with a lightweight stretcher. Wells pushed even closer, wanting to call out to the men to be careful, to take it easy, that whatever might be alive in there could only be a perilous moment away from death.

They lifted a smoking form from what had been a cockpit. The pressure suit was torn and seared from flames. Someone had had the sense to pull open the faceplate so that air could reach Steve, if he were still breathing. The body was limp, the arms and legs askew. Wells moved over sharp wreckage and felt as if he had been stabbed between the eyes.

Steve's left arm was gone.

Wells rallied his shocked senses. He motioned to the medical team to move to his side, barked instructions. Moments later he secured a tourniquet outside the upper arm of the suit. It might not do any good but it must be done. He noticed, then, that both legs were twisted badly, one crushed almost completely. *My God, my God* . . . The words spun through his mind, but his hands moved of their own accord, felt the face, saw the bruises and lacerations, the unmistakable signs of a jaw broken in several places, the signs of severe shock.

He was alive.

The rest was a blur of instinct. They moved the basket stretcher away from the wreck. The team moved swiftly as they worked with Wells. Plasma, right there on the spot. Cortisone to keep the heart pumping. Oxygen through a lightweight mask held over his nose. Gently, gently . . . he's bleeding there. Make sure he doesn't choke on his own blood . . . All right, now, get

him into that chopper at once. Careful, goddammit, careful . . .
As if they needed to be told. They moved the broken form to the
turbine helicopter, slid the stretcher inside. Wells and the team
were in, waving for the pilot to move out at once. Wells clutched
the side of the stretcher to keep it from sliding as the powerful
machine boomed into the sky, already swinging toward the
emergency room at the base hospital. Wells didn't need to tell
anyone to radio ahead; the word had been passed and a crack
medical team would be ready and waiting to do whatever was
possible for the man closer to death than to life. There were
things to do in the meantime. Learn what he could, cut away the
tough pressure suit now, plan ahead to those moments when
their hands and instruments would decide whether or not this
man would ever see another day.

The chopper banked away, turning steeply, reaching for all
possible speed. Wells had time for a brief glance through the
open door. The last he saw of the crash site was Jan Richards,
her face a white mask.

CHAPTER THREE

They were a hair-trigger medical team second to none in the world. They knew who was flying, of course. Every time a flight test went onto the schedule, the pilots were identified on the large notification board in the emergency medical building. Dr. Milton Ashburn, head of the emergency teams, insisted on this procedure. The pilots were identified and their medical records were copied and placed on immediate availability. Blood type, possible blood donors, and other vital information were thus right there, and not somewhere else, when needed.

Every member of the medical team understood that Colonel Steve Austin was up today in that little bastard of a flying abortion they called the M3F5. Hard not to know when a man who had walked the surface of the moon would be scheduled. You got just a bit tighter, then. Just a bit more shipshape, if that were possible. And when the alarm stabbed their ears and jangled their nerves and brought them bolt upright from beds they thought of Steve Austin. Only for the moment. They thought also of the pilots and radar navigators in the SR-71 chase planes. Of the crew in the huge B-52 that would drop Austin at 45,000 feet. Of the helicopter crews, also. It could mean *any* of them, but it was important for them to know as quickly as possible just who it might be.

Dr. Ashburn hit the medical-request switch on his desk. In the control tower, in Radar Control, in Helicopter Control, in every control facility active that day, the request light flashed on and off, and would stay flashing until medical was advised. It didn't take long. Radar Control was monitoring the chase pilots, of course, and they had listened to the agonized cry of Steve Austin's friend as his voice told unbelievingly of the carnage splashing across the dry desert floor.

'Medical from Radar.' The speaker box on the wall in the emergency building rasped the words.

Dr. Ashburn answered immediately. 'Go ahead. Any identification?'

'Yes, sir. It's Colonel Austin, sir. Crashed on touchdown. Pretty bad from what I understand.'

'Details?' Ashburn said.

'Only that the ship broke up, sir.' Radar Control hesitated. 'I can patch you into the medical chopper. They're starting to lift from—'

'Do it,' Ashburn snapped.

He waited impatiently while the radio line went into the central switchboard, patching him directly to the chopper.

'Colonel Ashburn here. Rescue One, do you read?'

'Rescue One. Go ahead.'

Ashburn recognized the voice of the copilot. He knew every member of the rescue teams personally. 'Jackson, what's the status on Colonel Austin? Keep it tight.'

'Yes, sir. It's not good, colonel. From what I saw he's lost an arm, and I understand his legs are pretty bad. Dr. Wells is with us. They're giving Austin oxygen now. He's unconscious.'

Ashburn cut away from the patch line, punched three digits for the control tower, told them the rescue chopper was coming straight to the medical building, to get everyone else the hell out of the way. He knew the Air Police were monitoring the line, that within seconds they would start out for the medical building to clear the immediate area for landing the helicopter. Ashburn glanced up, saw several of his staff standing by. He banged the telephone back to its cradle.

'Get ready in the hyperbaric chamber,' he ordered. 'Everything we need in there at once.' The men disappeared with his words. He rose and walked quickly to the corridor. Seeing several medical technicians in the hall he ordered them to drop whatever they were doing. 'Get every door between the emergency entrance and the hyperbaric chamber open,' he said. '*Hold* them open until they bring Colonel Austin through.' He didn't wait for confirmation but went straight to the chamber where his assistants would be waiting for him. He had less than one minute to prepare himself.

Ashburn and the medical team waited inside by a surgical breakaway table in the hyperbaric chamber. 'Put him on there,' Ashburn said quietly, his nerves stringy-cold now, the emotional response dismissed as the surgeon's mind took over his thinking and actions. Wells was there to help, hands under the twisted, flopping legs of the unconscious pilot. They moved Steve Austin from the stretcher to the surgical table and Ashburn stepped forward, studying, seeking information before he moved. Wells paused by the table, his face contorted, hands trying to find something to do. Quickly he sketched in what had happened, his immediate findings. Ashburn nodded. 'All right,' he told Wells, 'I'd like you to stand by, please.' He glanced at the dust and soot caking the doctor. 'Use the room to your left to clean up.' That was all; no time for anything else. Wells hurried to the scrub room, where a nurse waited to assist him.

The first step had already been taken in the opening moments of the struggle to retain what little life remained in Steve Austin. That was the decision to bring him into the hyperbaric chamber. As Austin was placed on the surgical table, technicians sealed a heavy steel door. Oxygen poured into the sealed chamber, and the technicians kept it at maximum flow until the air became much denser, several times the air pressure on the other side of the chamber. This eliminated the need to feed oxygen directly to Austin. He was now breathing the equivalent of full oxygen flow from a mask, but without the encumbrance to the medical team of such equipment. With the atmosphere so heavy, his tissues would also become saturated with life-giving oxygen, and would remain so as long as the hyperbaric chamber pressure was maintained. This would be, for that period of time required for his body to stabilize, the only environment Steve Austin would know. Dr. Ashburn was determined to keep Austin unconscious throughout this period when his life hung by a precarious thread. It would not do for Austin to emerge from shock into the horrors from which he might never escape.

The medical team cut with difficulty through the tough, multiple layers of the pressure suit. With the garments clear of the body there began the immediate steps to assure continued survival. They almost ended before they could begin. Rudy Wells was just returning from the clean room when he heard from Ashburn: 'He's dead. Heart shock, at once. Move!' They did. Two doctors responded instantly with an electrode against the upper axis of the heart. Seconds later the beat was resumed, stronger than before. The team kept a shock apparatus at hand.

Another doctor cleaned out Austin's windpipe. Because complications of shock made it impossible to determine immediately the respiratory-system damage, standard procedure was followed. An intubation tube was moved carefully down through the trachea into the lung sac to assure continued oxygen flow and the exchange of gases within the lungs. It would be kept there as long as was possible.

Austin had suffered the outright loss of his left arm, as well as the mangling of both legs. Skin ripped away, compound fractures, severing of blood vessels, internal injuries. The medical team, of course, immediately clamped all exposed vessels, but there was another reason why Austin had not bled to death despite the terrible mauling of his body. The answer was in the unique nature of the forces tearing at him in the tumbling, flaming crash.

His arm and leg muscles, subjected to violent acceleration forces as the lifting body broke up on the desert, also received extreme twisting forces because of this shearing, twisting motion. In effect, startling as it seemed, it saved Austin from profuse bleeding. As his body took its battering, the limbs torn open and mutilated, the femoral arteries snapped shut. It was a matter of body defenses instantly going into play. Moreover, that action established a time frame of lifesaving. The femoral arteries literally self-sealed themselves, and they would remain in this condition for some four hours after the body gave its biological alarms. Four hours and no more, but four hours in which his own body mechanisms assured he would not bleed to death, and it was barely sixteen minutes between the time of the crash and the moment when Austin was placed on the surgical table in the hyperbaric chamber. The exposed vessels were clamped as quickly as more critical matters allowed them to be. But the body had protected itself. Plasma had been used at the crash scene, but Wells had done this more as a safety precaution than because of fears of fatal bleeding. Major blood loss, despite body and head damage, had been essentially restricted to the limbs that were severed or mutilated so badly they had to be removed. In effect, then, Steve Austin retained nearly the fully required blood quantity of his body because he retained the blood in the still-functioning parts of his system.

Cortisone injection was continued to assist the heart. A doctor inserted a catheter into the vein of Austin's right arm. Intravenous fluids would be kept moving through the catheter. It was essential that fluids be kept circulating through what remained of his body.

There were, of course, uncounted other items to which the medical team attended. Some of these were considered peripheral, such as cutting away skin hanging in flaps and shreds. The pressure suit had provided an excellent thermal barrier between Austin and the fire that swept the cockpit; fortunately, at that moment, the integrity of his environmental control system had been unbroken, and he suffered no intake into his lungs of fire or even extreme heat. And the suit, as it had been designed to function, kept the flames from his body. By the time the suit began to yield to direct fire the rescue team had split open the canopy and doused the slumped figure inside with fire-quenching foam. Steve Austin's burns were therefore minor, a factor of major importance in the labors of the medical team to keep him alive.

There was other, critical work. A piece of metal had snapped off somewhere in the cockpit and penetrated the helmet visor. Penetrated it deeply enough to stab through into Austin's left eye and, from all preliminary studies, deeply enough to have destroyed the optic nerves and eye structure to such an extent that no one in the room doubted he would be forever blind in that eye.

The list of injuries grew as the medical team moved from the immediately critical to the attentions that had been held aside. His jaw had been broken in several places. Several ribs were crushed, and an angry laceration along his left side, from the same tearing chunk of metal that had severed his left arm, had penetrated deeply enough to provide suspicion that several ribs were not only fractured but reduced to dangerous and separated pieces of bone. A skull fracture also was suspected, and the head injury, producing fracture of both the skull and the jaw, had broken perhaps half the teeth in his mouth.

The instruments placed tenderly on his body – the same monitoring instruments developed originally for medical monitoring of men in space and then adapted to hospital use – led Dr. Ashburn to believe that there had been some damage to the heart-valve structure. But the heart continued beating strongly enough to allow that examination to be held for the 'second phase'.

Ashburn's plan was to keep Steve Austin under hyperbaric conditions for at least three to five days. It was essential that this time be provided for the body to stabilize, to adjust to the drastically altered conditions of its existence.

There was the other immediate need – to be certain that Austin remained unconscious as long as possible before shock and unspeakable pain intruded. And also while emergency treatment and surgery continued. For this Ashburn used an electronic device already distributed to most of the Air Force's emergency wards – the electrosleep machine, an instrument the Russians had long used successfully and which only recently had found widespread acceptance in the United States. Electrodes were applied to the skull while Austin remained on the surgical table. With the connections inspected carefully, an electronic pulse was generated directly to the skull, transmitting through to the brain in impulses that matched the alpha rhythm. In effect, Austin's body began to resonate to the impulse, and as long as the current was maintained he would remain within a deep sleep, oblivious to pain. He would remain this way for days free of any gaseous anesthesia, of barbiturates or narcotics.

It was many hours before Ashburn stepped back from the surgical table to wipe his tired eyes. Until he could say two vital words.

'He'll live.'

For the next several days, with full oxygen saturation and body stabilization the two prime requisites for his continued life during that period, the medical team would take its X-rays and would attend to the secondary survival requirements to sustain Austin's life. He would remain there, in the hyperbaric chamber, until his tissues sealed off, and body stabilization was assured.

Lieutenant Colonel Chuck Matthews slumped in his easy chair, holding the empty glass in his hand. He stared vacantly across his living room, his arms and legs leaden. It was his third drink and it wasn't doing a bit of good.

'Another?' His wife gestured to the mixer.

35

Matthews sighed. 'No, I guess not.' He let his arm hang over the side of the chair, the glass forgotten. 'It's not doing much good tonight.'

She nodded. 'You keep seeing it, don't you?'

He shrugged. 'Hard not to see it.' Hard? *Impossible.* From the pilot's seat of Chase One ... he'd see it for a long time to come. The flash reflection of sun off metal as the lifting body twisted and yawed with its nose too high in the air, the plunge into desert floor, the ship breaking up, the flame licking through ...

'Where's Jan?' he asked suddenly.

'With Marge,' his wife said. 'She's under heavy sedation.'

An awkward pause followed. 'Chuck, I'd like to go to the chapel.'

He leaned back in the chair, pain screwed into his face, his eyes closed tightly.

'If you love that man like I do ... then pray that he dies.'

Dr. Rudy Wells glanced again at his watch. Jan Richards would be here in a few moments. She would walk through the door to his office in the main hospital building. Well, there wasn't any way out of it. Steve for years had been a special favorite of his. Now they were, and would be, even closer.

He crossed his office and opened the slats of the venetian blinds, staring into the rippling heat waves covering the concrete flight lines and the desert beyond. He looked out of place in the midst of the most advanced flight-test center in the world. A picture of thundering jets and razored wings did not include this man. Wells stood six feet tall, nicely thick in the shoulders, the indifferent owner of a rounded bay window that reflected years of exceptional dining and staggering quantities of Japanese beer. But in his presence you forgot such details almost at once and your attention returned insistently to the salt-and-pepper beard, a surprisingly thick shock of dark hair, wrinkles about his eyes. And the eyes themselves. Wells was a man with a gaze so penetrating as almost to be hypnotic. His eyes commanded attention and with acute discomfort would often lock the gaze of another person. They seemed constantly to move, to flick back and forth, piercing those before him, and it could be unsettling indeed to be a victim of Rudy Wells when zeroing in on target.

He was either hyperactive or nearly somnolent, with no comfortable middle ground. When hyperactive he exuded energy, a bustling figure of staccato motions and nervous gestures and his eyes almost illuminated from within. Then, without preamble or transition, he could become a bearded Buddha, a paradox of a doctor, chain-smoking the cigarettes his peers adamantly condemned. That, and the aura of knowledge about him, quickly suggested that here was a mind that held far more than was ever learned from weighty tomes or direct experience as a doctor and a flight surgeon.

Wells had never been able to sustain a civilian practice. Oh, he had tried. After years in Japan and Korea with the Fifth Air Force, he shed his uniform, hung the necessary papers on his office wall in Indian Harbour Beach in Florida, and nearly drowned under the rush of afflictions assailing the good people of that small coastal town. If success were to be measured by the immense popularity he enjoyed as a general practitioner, as a modern M.D. with an old-fashioned bedside manner, then Wells was an astonishing phenomenon in a time when the public derided medical indifference. For Rudy Wells *was* in many ways an adherent of yesteryear. His philosophy was that while things changed and society went through its head-bumping, the human body, and individual fears of a body failing itself, had changed not one iota.

Above all else, even his professional skills, Rudy Wells discovered he had a talent recognized by a minority, rejected almost wholly by his contemporaries. For years this *thing* he had had been called the laying on of hands, a startling intuitive sense of the ills of his patients. Startling because he found little explanation for it. But it was there, and it was real. Wells could learn much from a simple verbal exchange with a patient; revealing words rolled from them, and he gained this inner *feeling* of what was wrong. Every time the sense flowed through him, his medical examination confirmed his intuitions. There had been times when diagnosis contradicted feeling – and in the long run, diagnosis had proven in error.

The explanation, he suspected, to some extent manifested itself through his fingers. They were extraordinary. His fingertips were so sensitive that they might have been sanded down. It had proved almost impossible for him to have clear fingerprints taken, and the necessary fingerprints during his military career were a record of smudges that baffled security officers. But to patients whose ills he identified quickly, he became known as much more than a doctor. He was a healer.

Several years passed pleasantly enough, despite calls through all hours of the day and night, in the small coastal town in Florida. Then Wells began to suffer from his own form of malady until it was no longer possible to ignore the itch for which no medicine could be prescribed. He missed the challenge of his former role as a flight surgeon. He missed the thunderclap of machines splitting barriers of sound and heat, of watching

38

pinpoints of flame pushing their tiny silvered darts away from a planet. No pilot himself, he had nonetheless spent many hundreds of hours high above the earth with pilots and scientists, studying, charting, planning, testing. Twice he had been forced to bail out of aircraft. Once, from a lumbering C-124 with three engines burning. Again, when he ejected from a jet bomber with frozen engines and equally frozen solid controls. He had also survived a half dozen crashes, these unusual moments all prompted by his determination to be in the thick of testing. The pilots and aircrews knew him to be a magnificent flight surgeon, a little nuts, and one hell of a man.

The siren call proved finally too heady to ignore. There was also a felt responsibility compelling his return. He knew intimately the dangers to which the young men of the flight test programs were subjected. There was, he reasoned aloud with his wife, Jackie, a need for the best men available on the ground to assure that those who paid for flight testing with physical injury and disfigurement would be given every opportunity to return as whole as possible to the society to which they'd paid such extravagant dues. Wells's intimacy with the human body under extreme stress, through the gamut of atmospheric and space environments, and his ability to relate closely to the men who flew the dangerous machines, had always made him welcome at the test centers.

The daily ministrations to ailing housewives, whining children, grumbling old men, frightened youngsters, and those who knew they were dying and concealed such imminence in loud complaints, all these, and more, at long last piled up like the bow wave of a speeding vessel. Phlegm and fractures, obesity and bladders, venereal diseases and worms and lungs tortured by drugs and – well, enough. He packed away his shingle and with a sense of growing pleasure that they were, and far overdue, returning home, rushed back to the sprawling flight center in the California desert.

And now he waited for Jan Richards.
To whom he must be not a friend.
Because it was necessary to be cruel.
To avoid the greater, later cruelty.
She came into his office with more control than he had

expected. Four days had elapsed since she stood with him to watch the savage mutilation of her fiancé.

Correction, he told himself. Of what had *been* her fiancé. Don't forget the past tense, doctor. It will help in here with this girl.

He rose to greet her. 'Jan, thank you for coming,' he said quietly, his voice flat, almost mechanical. It would do no harm to establish from the outset this would not be pleasant for either one of them.

He motioned her to a chair.

'How is he, Dr. Wells?'

'He's alive, Jan.'

'Alive? Is that all . . .'

'That's all,' he told her. 'How much do you know?'

'I know that Steve has been badly hurt. He . . . may lose a leg, from what I understand.' Her face colored suddenly. 'But Dr. Ashburn won't *say* anything. He talks around the subject, as if something unspeakable had happened to Steve. Rudy, you know I've been around this business for a long time. I've seen airplanes crash before. My father was in a very bad accident. I saw what the burns did to him. I am not a child, Rudy, and yet you're acting like Ashburn. You have—'

'Been in an operating room with Steve Austin almost every hour of the day for the past four days and nights,' he said.

'I know that,' she replied, her voice suddenly subdued. 'That's why I wanted so much to speak with *you*. Now, will you please answer my questions?'

God help me. 'Yes,' he said.

'Why haven't I been allowed to see Steve?'

'He's unconscious.'

'Something's happened, then? I mean, just now?'

He shook his head. 'No. He has been unconscious since the accident.'

'You mean he's been in a coma all this time?'

'No, no, not that. We have kept him unconscious. Deliberately.'

'But *why*, for God's sake?'

'Because we have been afraid of the shock if he were to regain consciousness at this time. Not only the physical shock,' he emphasized carefully, 'but also what could happen to his mind.

40

Steve . . .' Quickly he forced out the words. 'Steve is a triple amputee.'

She stared at him. *Now,* he thought, now while the shock is on her.

'He lost his left arm in the crash, and both legs were crushed. We had no choice but to amputate.' He rushed on, not wanting to look at her. 'You're going to have to get out of here, Jan. You're going to leave him.'

'You're crazy,' she whispered.

'The man you know as Steve Austin is no longer living,' he said in the same affected, mechanical voice. 'This is what I want you to understand, what you *must* understand. If you leave him now, it will be just one more shock to his system. It will mix with the rest. But if you stay with him, what is now love and devotion and loyalty will change as you face the everyday sameness of the horror of what Steve—'

'Stop it!'

Not now; there was no stopping now. 'If there is even a chance that he will live, that he will – recover is hardly the word, of course – that he will survive, your leaving him at a later time could kill him. It could finally destroy whatever man may come out of all this. There's something else you should think about.' He waited until she calmed a bit. 'Do you believe Steve would *want* you to be with him now? You know the man, you must know how he will feel.'

'You still can't just write out your little prescription, Rudy, and tell me to disappear. My God, how could I do—'

He gestured impatiently. 'Will you hear me out? Steve will come to hate you. He is no longer a man as we knew him. Oh, I know, it's what's inside a man, it's fortitude and the rest of that, and it's all true enough, but this has transcended anything within your experience, *or his.* You will not be able to avoid pity. He will never believe, *never*, that pity is not your chief motivation.'

'You're a cold, heartless bastard,' she said, grimly quiet now.

'I wish I were,' he replied. 'Are you ready for the rest?'

'The rest? I don't—'

'I told you he is a triple amputee.' He watched her stare at him. 'He is also blind in one eye. He is a man with one arm,

41

without any legs, with only one eye.' *Get it over with, doctor,* he said in a scathing lash at himself.

'He has a multiple fracture of the jaw and has lost most of his teeth. We do not know, at this time, if he will regain full articulation for speech.' Her face was getting whiter and he forced himself on. 'He has a skull fracture, and there is every chance of pressure against the brain. At this point we cannot tell if we can avoid complications, or if there will be some brain damage on a permanent basis. There was some inhalation of gases within the cockpit, and we are still uncertain of their effect on the brain.'

He lit a cigarette. 'Several ribs were crushed. Not just crushed, but broken off in pieces that have damaged his lungs. There appears to be injury to the heart; perhaps the valves. It will take some time to determine exactly what, but heart surgery appears inevitable. We're concerned about injury to the spinal column. If the main nerves are affected, he may not be able to use even his remaining arm.'

He didn't bother reciting the other injuries, the pelvic fracture, his left ear mutilated, the internal bleeding they suspected, the growing conviction there might be more serious pressure on the brain than the first X-ray had indicated, and – oh, Christ, why repeat it all to himself now?

He no longer looked at Jan Richards. He couldn't. He looked through her. He had talked with Ashburn, they had spoken with the nerve surgeon in Colorado, Dr. Michael Killian, they were planning and hoping to do *something* for Steve, something drastic and unprecedented, but this was nothing to build a future on.

Wells was sure Steve Austin, if he could, would thank Wells for doing now what he would do himself with this girl.

Her life was to be lived. He found himself on his feet, looking down at her. 'Do you love this man?'

'Oh, God . . .'

'Then do the one thing he would ask you himself. Leave him, and *don't ever come back.*'

He pushed past her, through the door, walking down the corridor like an automaton.

CHAPTER FIVE

'We are prepared to support this project with whatever funds may be necessary. We understand this may run to a high figure, of course, but the implications, which I'm sure you gentlemen understand as well as Mr. McKay, lead us to accept whatever cost is involved.' Oscar Goldman, representative from the Office of Special Operations, leaned back in his seat, one arm resting on the chair, the other stretched forward so that his hand could toy with the ashtray in front of him. Goldman wore a dark suit, pale-blue shirt, and thin, dark tie. But Dr. Rudy Wells, Dr. Michael Killian, and other Air Force officers and officials were far less interested in Goldman's appearance than in the offer of extensive financial support he'd brought with him. The fact that he mentioned Jackson McKay, the director of OSO, was also encouraging. McKay, who had cut his teeth through several decades of undercover operations for the United States, was involved personally in the decision to send Goldman with the offer of money.

Dr. Michael Killian, a distinguished surgeon and head of the Bionics Research Laboratory in Colorado, leaned forward to rest his weight on his elbows. 'I have some experience with Mr. McKay,' he said carefully. 'He has never been one to commit frivolously to a project of this size. I find this both heartening and also the basis for some suspicion.'

Oscar Goodman smiled. 'I was told to expect this reaction from you.'

'My reaction is not the issue. You are talking about years of work, Mr. Goldman. What is involved here concerns the active participation of much of my laboratory, both the public facility, and, of course, our secret center. You are talking about dozens of skilled doctors, engineers, technicians, the use of at least one and perhaps two computers, critically needed in other areas. We can promise you no real measure of success, and—'

'May I break in, Dr. Killian?' Goldman asked quietly.

'Perhaps I can bring things to a head. What do you estimate would be the financial requirement for this program? More specifically, as it involves Colonel Austin.'

'Two million the first year, perhaps. After that it is difficult to tell. I would say from a half million to twice that much every year for some time to come.'

'Doctor, tomorrow by this time there will be placed within your fiscal control – nonreturnable so long as this project is under way – six million dollars.'

'I presume you are serious?'

Goldman barely shrugged. 'You may confirm my orders, Dr. Killian. If you place a call to Mr. McKay's office it will go through immediately.'

'Mr. Goldman.' They turned to Dr. Wells. 'How much involvement do you foresee by OSO?' Wells said quickly.

'Minimal, Dr. Wells. We will not interfere with the basic construction. We will not interfere for a number of reasons, the first of which is that we are not qualified to do so, and the second is that you would not tolerate amateur meddling.'

'At what point would you become involved?' Wells asked.

'We would like to have one of our people assigned to the Colorado laboratories. We will provide an individual well trained and qualified either simply to observe or, depending upon your own feelings, to be used as an assistant or in any other capacity. He will not, I repeat, *not*, interfere. He will, however, maintain a meticulous record of all that takes place. We hope he would be in a position to have his queries responded to in order to meet our needs. Should this person we select prove to be unacceptable, for whatever reasons, he – or she – will be replaced at once and someone more suitable will be assigned to Colorado. You people will make the final decisions regarding Colonel Austin.'

Goldman moved his gaze about the table, studying each man present. 'We would like to assure you, each and every one of you, that we fully understand the unprecedented nature of this matter. To us, this is an investment in an area where we hold grave responsibility. If the promise of this new – let us say development – is sustained in your work, then several things will happen simultaneously.' One by one he held up his fingers. 'First, we at OSO will gain what may be an extraordinary new

44

capability in carrying out our assigned tasks. At the same time, this means, of course, the nation benefits to a considerable extent. Second, you people will be provided with the means to carry out your hopes for human research, involving as it does a total application of bionics and cybernetics. Third,' Goldman said, suddenly very sober, 'there is the matter of Colonel Steve Austin. The *man*. Every business, his or ours, suffers its casualties, and he has been struck down by the odds. Until now we had no special interest in Colonel Austin. Now we have an overriding concern with his future progress, and above all, as you all well understand, with what he becomes. Your offices will—'

'Mr. Goldman—' They turned to Rudy Wells. '—there's the matter of Steve Austin. As you say, Mr. Goldman, there is the matter of the *man*. No one has yet asked him what *he* thinks about all this. It can hardly go through without *his* acceptance, don't you agree?'

'I should think,' Goldman said, 'there wouldn't be any question on the matter one way or the other.'

'But there is,' Wells persisted. 'It's his life. He may decide to end what's left of it rather than to accept your elaborate schemes for, as you put it, reconstruction. Re-creation would be more like it. Perhaps Steve won't like playing the role of the phoenix. I am not prepared at this time, Mr. Goldman,' he said carefully, 'to second guess Steve Austin. Such a decision really belongs to him.'

'Do you have any idea how he will decide?'

'He is still unconscious, *has* been unconscious, for that matter, ever since the crash. We are keeping him that way,' Wells added quickly, 'for reasons I'm sure are obvious.'

Goldman had to push and he did. 'Dr. Wells, do you believe in this program, in what we propose for Steve Austin?'

'Of course I do,' Wells replied, his surprise evident. 'There's no question but that—'

'Will you recommend this program to Austin?'

'Yes.'

Goldman's head almost snapped, he moved it so swiftly to confront the other doctor. 'And you, Dr. Killian? Are you prepared to push for our proposal? Will you recommend to Austin, whenever he is conscious, that he go ahead?'

Killian nodded slowly.

They could almost see the man shifting gears. 'All right,' Gold-man said briskly. 'I will preface my remarks by stating that they may offend you. My position here is strictly as a messenger. I am a mechanic in our organization, gentlemen. It is the policy of Mr. McKay,' and he nodded to Dr. Killian, 'and you, doctor, know this from your own association with this man, not ever to give you reason to suspect we are holding back on you. Feel free to be insulted—' with a wry smile '—but believe that we are at least completely honest with you. First, Steve Austin. Why is it *this* particular man we are willing to invest so heavily in? And the investment is comparatively minor in terms of dollars, but extraordinary in terms of personnel, genius, and facilities.' They accepted the obvious compliment in stony silence. Goldman had set the rules for candor and they were willing to let him carry the ball.

'There are plenty of men who have been torn up physically as bad as Austin,' Goldman continued, 'or even worse. You both know that. So it is not simply *a* man in whom we are interested, but specifically a man so unusual, extraordinary, in fact, as to command our attention. Dr. Wells, here, knows Steve Austin personally. He knows him so well he has come to regard this young man almost as a son.' Goldman flicked his eyes in the direction of the doctor sitting like a statue, then nodded and turned to Killian. 'You, Dr. Killian, are the scientist, and Austin means something entirely different to you. Vindication of theory, for one. Proof of years of experiments, for another. Opportunity, for a third. The opportunity to establish that physical mutilation need not be a living death for a man. Also, as a spin-off, there will be the opportunity to expand your own research into restoring physical movement to paraplegics.

'We all know Colonel Austin's background. Test pilot, as-tronaut, a man who's been to the moon. But there's more. There's an extraordinary rounding out of this particular indi-vidual. Physically an outstanding specimen. A great athlete. An advanced student of the military arts. At the same time, a man with no less than five degrees. Steve Austin breezed through his masters and his doctorate.'

Goldman again glanced at Dr. Wells. 'There is another ad-vantage, one we had not counted on,' he said slowly. 'Austin has no immediate family. His father died in Korea; in fact, he died in a Chinese prison camp. His mother passed away some four years ago, and he was an only child. The closest relative is a distant cousin, and there has been no family contact with Steve Austin for many years. There was one potential complication in this area, but it has been, well . . .' Wells's face remained frozen but his eyes were alive and they stabbed straight at the OSO man. 'It has been . . . resolved,' Goldman said carefully. 'We have no comment one way or the other, being unqualified for any involvement. Our only interest is that there is no family to create undue complications.' It was a dangerous reef and at least they were all beyond the barrier. At least for the moment.

Dr. Killian listened in silence. He did not like Oscar Goldman. Too damned sure of himself. Made a habit – a career – of meddling in the affairs of others. Killian slipped back into the reserve for which he was known in his profession. To the public at large he was a man who inspired awe for the minor miracles he worked daily with the human system. He even looked the part that had been created for him by a properly impressed media. The clichés moved around him – tall, stately, dignified, brilliant, genius. In truth, Killian was an extraordinarily respected and distinguished figure not only in the United States but throughout the international community as well. He was now sixty-two years of age; his name had become synonymous with daring, brilliant surgery, and he was as much the pioneer as he was the surgeon, with his revolutionary procedures and research efforts involving transplants and transplanting nerve sheaths from one individual to another. He had turned upside down the procedures for electrical stimulation of body systems; he had returned 'dead' limbs to an astounding new life. He had brought controlled movement to the legs of paraplegics by routing the still-living nerves of the newly dead into the bodies of paraplegics, by-passing the spinal-column block to perform what had been – until he began his new program – medical feats considered impossible.

Now he sat in a small room on the edge of the California desert, held captive by the promise of the financial rainbow offered by this strange man from an undercover organization in

Washington, and feeling ill at ease because of this unaccustomed role. A national recession had taken its toll in research funds slashed by the watchdogs in Congress and the Air Force, which funded the lion's share of Killian's work at his Colorado laboratories. And just at the time when his research called for a larger staff, increased use of computers, for more elaborate facilities. At the doorstep of new success so great he was almost breathless with the thought, the fiscal axe had cut him down in midstride.

Killian had flown to Edwards Air Force Base in California in response to an insistent telephone call from his old associate, Dr. Wells, and he had found enough to justify that sudden flight, not the least of which was the assurance of millions of dollars from the OSO, through this man, Oscar Goldman. That, and the miracle they might still perform with the shattered body of the unconscious Steve Austin.

As well as this irritating monologue from Goldman. With mounting surprise and annoyance, he listened to the recital by Goldman of his life in a manner that had never appeared in any newspaper or magazine.

'What has most impressed the media and the public,' Goldman was saying, 'is the sensational, such as your success in returning sexual capability to paraplegics. If I recall, Dr. Killian, you instituted this program through direct electrical stimulation to the nerves of the ejaculation nerve center, which lies approximately in the center of the spinal column, and by experimental routing of nerves past, or around, this ejaculation center. This success, and the intense public interest, and, perhaps,' here Goldman smiled, 'the age of Congressmen involved in appropriations, brought you some unprecedented funding to continue your work. In the last year, however, those funds have been reduced drastically, and you are now, to say it frankly, hard up to continue your more advanced experiments. To be even more blunt about the matter,' Goldman said with a direct stare at Dr. Killian, 'you will have to eliminate some sixty percent of the programs you now have in their beginning stages.'

Goldman rode the issue without letup, not permitting Killian to break in. 'You are better known, doctor,' he said, not without respect, 'in Japan and the Soviet Union than you are even in this country. The work you did with the medical scientists of those

48

two nations in limb grafts and organ transplants is astonishing. Dobrovolskii, in Russia, especially has the highest praise for you, and often refers to that period when you worked together with him as perhaps the most productive time of his career. If I recall, it was Dobrovolskii, in fact, who demonstrated to you the ability to restore sexual capability to men whose organs had been damaged by gunfire or other forces. This was work he had begun as a young medic during the Second World War. And Vasilov worked with you in optics, I believe, in performing what many people consider to be near miracles in restoring sight to damaged or diseased optical systems.

Goldman shifted in his seat and, again, Killian and Wells had the distinct impression he was shifting mental gears as well, homing in more directly to the issue at hand. 'Now we come closer to home,' Goldman said quietly. 'The Air Force, because of the freedom it was enjoying in basic research, provided you with an elaborate medical laboratory and associated facilities just north of Colorado Springs. That medical center is, of course, well known. One of the reasons for its fame is that the Air Force has gone to great trouble to publicize, especially to appropriations subcommittees, the benefits accruing to the entire nation from this military program. So your facility, your Bionics Research Laboratory, has ridden a high crest of financial support. Your bionics lab and, of course, your somewhat more secret lab that is buried in the mountain behind the public façade.

'From our point of view, gentlemen,' he said, 'the bionics laboratory and its hidden offshoot, your cybernetics systems, when combined with what we in OSO have to offer in the field of subminiaturization in electronics and related fields—'

'What your office has to offer, Mr. Goldman? You seem to forget the Air Force's own work in what we could properly call microminiaturization. Or that of NASA, or any of the technical and military services, for that matter.'

'Of course, Dr. Killian,' Goldman said. 'No argument. OSO is fully aware of developments in these fields. My point is that OSO also functions as a clearing house; we keep tabs, shall we say, on all work done by every other agency and organization in the country. We co-operate fully with them, and they with us. Through this clearing house, you can be assured that whatever new advance has been made, anywhere, in this country or elsewhere, its results will be provided immediately to you. Microminiaturization in the electronic and mechanical fields, combined with what you have done in bionics, all of which can be welded into a wholly new discipline through computer systems, well, that is what this is all about, isn't it?

'One of the purposes of OSO, I should add, is to eliminate the sort of charade that developed through interagency competition over the years. I'm sure you're aware of what has been going on when all our security and intelligence organizations must fight for their own piece of the appropriations pie. OSO doesn't fit in there. We're actually subordinate to the needs of the intelligence community. We work *for* them. Being non-competitive, we give and receive absolute co-operation. We function as a, well, you might call us the Switzerland of our intelligence factions.'

Rudy Wells gestured to the OSO representative. 'Mr. Goldman, would you be good enough to get on with it.'

Goldman did. Office of Special Operations had something special in mind for Steve Austin. Killian was to supervise directly, participate intimately in a program to create out of the mutilated human wreck not only a new man but a wholly new type of man. A new breed. A marriage of bionics (biology applied to electronic engineering systems and cybernetics. A cybernetics organism.

Call him cyborg. The words rang through Killian's mind, pushed aside the humanitarian issue of whether they could alter and modify Steve Austin's body without his total co-operation. But would they *try*? Killian admitted to himself that he would not only accept this OSO effort but would grab at the opportunity. And *what* an opportunity! Goldman was right. Steve Austin was the most perfect of all candidates for the bionics laboratory in Colorado. It was far more than a matter of a human body to experiment on. Human bodies in every degree of damage were always available for his research programs; the people brought in in wheelchairs and basket stretchers could receive help from the research programs beyond anything available at the 'normal centers' for amputees and other maimed patients. Not a man or woman brought to the Colorado laboratories had ever come through his doors without full consent. And Killian stuck to one ironclad rule; at the first indication from any patient that he might feel himself being used as a guinea pig for medical experiments, all work, including the direct medical procedures created solely for the patient's own benefit, was halted at once, and reassignment of that individual was made to another, more conventional facility.

Killian without qualification was consumed in his work, a trait much approved by Goldman and his boss at OSO. And he had enjoyed his life, starting his medical career in the Second World War as a brilliant combat surgeon. He had been a concert pianist (his long, strong fingers were an asset), an astonishing avocation for any man, especially one so steeped in his medical and research work, but those who encountered the intensity of his dedication accepted the unusual as usual. His children were long married and scattered around the world, and with his wife delighted to have settled down in the Colorado hills, he found virtually nothing to interfere with wholehearted dedication to his work.

He could not deny the truth. Steve Austin represented an extraordinary opportunity. Killian was perfectly aware that OSO hoped that as a consequence of its support Killian would transform the one-limbed torso stump of Steve Austin into some kind of super-being. To be utilized for their own rather unique requirements, of course.

Except that when that day came, were Killian to be fully successful, then Steve Austin *could* make up his own mind, and Killian would be free of involvement.

Killian glanced at Rudy Wells, then turned his attention once again to the OSO man.

'Mr. Goldman, I will accept OSO under the conditions you have presented, but my acceptance could well be irrelevant.' He gestured to Rudy Wells. 'There is the only man, I believe, in whom Steve Austin will place complete trust and faith. That man is Dr. Wells. It is my opinion as a doctor, Mr. Goldman, that unless Dr. Wells can persuade him otherwise, Steve Austin will take his own life. And if Austin does accept Dr. Wells's thinking, he will come in many ways, for a period of time we cannot yet anticipate, to depend almost wholly on Wells, for the decisions that will so drastically affect his life. So either Dr.

Wells involves himself totally, or there is no use proceeding any further.'

Heads turned to Rudy Wells. Oscar Goldman withheld the obvious question. He sat erect in his chair, studying Wells, waiting.

Dr. Rudy Wells had long before made his decision about involvement. There could be only one way to go. But there was another decision to be made.

'There is an immediate problem,' he said. 'Someone must decide for Steve Austin. The program must begin without his agreement. This is necessary because Steve is in no position now, and will not be for some time to come, to make a judgement we might consider logical, or, perhaps, even sane. I don't want to make this decision for him, but I'm closest to him and I don't want anybody else to bear that responsibility if we ... fail.'

Goldman spoke with great caution. 'Have you decided, Dr. Wells?'

Wells sighed and nodded. 'Today is Friday. I recommend that no later than Tuesday morning we transfer Steve Austin to Colorado.' He glanced at Killian, who nodded in confirmation.

Goldman leaned forward. 'I would like to speak with Colonel Austin. There are—'

'When do you propose to do this?' Wells interrupted icily.

'Perhaps next week. The end of the week,' he added hastily.

Wells glanced at Killian, who nodded. 'Next week? Mr. Goldman, you have no idea what is involved here. Let your education begin *now*. You will not be able to speak with Colonel Austin for several months, perhaps as long as six months, and you will speak to him only when I so decide.'

Wells rose to his feet.

'Don't call us, Mr. Goldman. We'll call you.'

The sense of unreality was almost overpowering. Rudy Wells stood before a thick, glass window, an oval shape in a thick metal door. Beyond this first barrier, bathed in the warning glow of red light, lay another, similar door. The two doors, tightly sealed, formed a pressure-airlock barrier to the chamber beyond, the hyperbaric world within which they had imprisoned Steve. The pressure airlock cast its red glow into Wells's eyes, adding to the unreality of the sight beyond. The special overhead lights, casting off little heat but an intense illumination, targeted the unconscious form beneath.

He waited for the inside door to be locked by one of the doctors inside before the airlock door would slide open. A green light flashed; an instant later the hiss of air escaping through the sliding door began. Cool air, enriched with oxygen, washed against Wells as he stepped inside the chamber. He stopped, turned to his right, pressed a flashing switch. The door through which he had entered closed behind him and he heard the inrush of air. He looked up at the pressure reading. One dial showed the heavy pressure within the hyperbaric chamber, the other, the airlock in which he stood. The two finally matched and another green light flashed on, this one over the entrance into the final chamber. As quickly as Wells stepped through, the door closed to seal off the chamber.

Steve's body lay partially exposed. The oxygen was rich in his system. His tissues were almost sealed off by now. The internal barriers to destruction were compensating, rerouting, rebuilding, changing, and adapting for their unconscious host. Wells studied him with professional care, noticed the even movement of the chest, the barely discernible flaring of nostrils. A metal frame held the sheet above him but let the air bathe the naked form beneath, and brought a slow oxygen flow against the angry, red skin where there had been legs and an arm. Steve existed at this moment as the terminal of wires and tubing. His shaven skull, resting in a molded receptacle to prevent undue movement, sprouted wires from electrodes held against the skin, the alpha pattern coursing through his brain, his body responding to the subconscious beat, holding him safely within whatever darkness flowed through his mind. Whatever might be. Rudy Wells knew it could be only infinitely better than what awaited Steve this side of consciousness. They had kept the tubes leading through his nostrils into the trachea. The intravenous bottle suspended above his arm sustained the flow into Steve's system.

Electrodes placed around the heart measured every movement, every sound, every pulse and coursing moment of that magnificent pump; measured what went on within the body and flashed its signals to a battery of instruments. Oscilloscopes, recording graphs, a battery of lights, even a buzzer that would clamor its warning should the heart falter. The same instruments on this body that Austin had worn walking the desolation of the moon – they were here again, this time sending their messages barely a few feet instead of a quarter of a million miles. At least now they could respond to failure, and do so instantly; they were constantly at his side.

The doctors had performed emergency surgery. Enough to assure his body would stabilize. Wells looked at the battered face, the swollen lips, bruises along both sides of the face; yet, even in this moment of studying the mauling of that splendid man, the strength he had known showed clearly. Wells needed no movement of his own, needed no survey of Steve Austin, to know the other wounds and mutilations. He closed his eyes and thought of the work that must be performed. *Work*. A common word for uncommon efforts to sustain the animal creature so that the mind, that wondrous vessel inhabited solely by man, might survive to continue its wonders. They must teach Steve Austin to want to sustain the animal that hosts the mind. Rudy Wells understood that before Steve might win his own torturous battle for life, he must hate the man who would guide him through the dark shadows. Understanding that now would make it more tolerable later, Wells told himself.

He had spoken with Ashburn of the decision to be implemented this Tuesday. Just a few more days. The journey to Colorado was essential. It was, in fact, critical. Steve could recover here, might be shipped later to a veterans' hospital,

54

where the most advanced prosthetics science would be available to him, promising him the glorious future of a broken doll that has learned to imitate some order of co-ordinated movement. And that would be it. He'd kill himself first, Wells knew. Here was a man of two worlds, and the future had to hold more than the posturings of a clever marionette.

Rudy Wells was prepared to give him every chance.

The research lab was known simply as The Rock, a facility within which Killian and his brilliant associates enjoyed the sanctuary of government support and, to some extent, the isolation of government security. The Rock had been named long before the appearance of either Dr. Michael Killian or even the United States Air Force. Doubtless some miner or hunter had had good reason to curse the high sheer face, the jagged outcroppings, and almost numbing sterility of its higher reaches. Despite the lush timber growth along the lower flanks and the stunningly beautiful land stretching away from the eastern shoulder of the Rockies, it was unmistakable to the viewer. In winter, with the world swathed in the heavy snows expected in high Colorado land, the black face of the rock jarred the view. No trees, and a sheer face kept it free of a white blanket. Below that blank granite, however, there shone glass and metal, and lights gleamed through the night. Here nestled the twin laboratories run by Dr. Killian, of which only one presented its face to the world – the bionics lab, called by its occupants, The Shop. The second lab, in which cybernetics was of paramount interest, lay deeper within the mountain and officially it did not exist.

If Steve Austin had to face horrendous months ahead, at least there could be few more beautiful geographic settings for it. The Rockies did not form a single line of peaks, their own serration of jagged ramparts, but rather a grouping of ranges, a thick cluster of mountain barriers separating the eastern and western parts of the nation. Pike's Peak, abutting Colorado Springs, overshadowing the community, was almost the height of the Matterhorn. And forming the thick skeletal backbone were many other peaks higher than Pike's. The land directly east of the mountain foothills was a gently rolling plain of a rich green-and-yellow carpet, sliced and ravined by water streaming violently down from the Rockies so that the grassy realm was grooved with gullies and buttes, with deep streams and sudden outcroppings of rock. Then, approaching the Rockies from the east, the green carpeting yielded to stands of rich timber.

There would be more than enough facilities to support whatever Steve and his team of specialists would need for the years ahead. Near the town of Colorado Springs itself was Peterson Field, the only major civil airport in the area, convenient not only to the community, but serving also the needs of the sprawling Air Force Academy, which lay northward along the mountain's flanks. There was also the activity created through the presence of Fort Carson, an Army camp that had stood as an area fixture for decades; this was served by its own airport, Butts Army Field. For Carson had long been secured within a restricted area so that when it became necessary to fly in security-labeled materials or personnel, it was simple enough to do so in a military aircraft that would attract no special attention at Butts. Helicopters or Army vehicles completed the trips to the labs.

The country sprawling around the mountains and along the high rolling hills to the east of the Rockies carried the colorful names affixed by trappers, hunters, and miners, along with the Indians, of course: Texas Creek, Black Forest, Cotopaxi, Shawnee, Silver Cliff, Buffalo Creek, Shaffers Crossing . . . And the two laboratories, bionics and cybernetics, used the code name of Slab Rock, which became the official name of the post office.

Colorado Springs, with its plush Broadmoor Hotel, lay about eighteen miles from where Slab Rock jutted from its mountain. You drove north from Colorado Springs, and then northeast, picked up a road that drifted back to north and northwest, and then began curving up the mountain foothills. There was no attempt at concealment; quite the opposite, since the hospital design took every advantage of the breathtaking scenery through huge windowed areas. Coming down from the mountain road, which ended at the laboratories, a side road led directly to U.S. Highway 87, which in turn worked its way southward to the Air Force Academy and resort ranches sprinkled through the area. Denver lay about one hundred miles north of Colorado Springs.

One additional organization provided a tremendous flow of traffic and resources when needed, especially since it operated on both sides of its own security wall. This was NORAD, headquarters for North American Air Defense Command, residing within great tunnels and caves gouged from the deeper bowels of Cheyenne Mountain. As the electronic nerve center for space tracking, detection, and surveillance system by the United States throughout the entire world, and as the command center for alerting the nation in the event of enemy strategic strike, NORAD functioned as a multibillion-dollar iceberg. Its purpose and its location were known, deep within the mountain, but it showed little of that face to the world.

The bionics and cybernetics laboratories, under their code name of Slab Rock, benefited directly from the gargantuan construction task that created the complex NORAD facility within Cheyenne Mountain. Tunneling an entire mountain could hardly have been kept a secret, and the thousands of engineers and construction workers raised dust that drifted for hundreds of miles. When they were through, assembly groups moved in, and a throng of electronics specialists went to work to establish the intricate substance of NORAD. It was, essentially, a complex of electronic linkage to the entire world and beyond the world, the whole of it run by banks of massive computers to whom their human masters were essentially servants tending their electronic oracles.

Slab Rock came into being as an offshoot of the construction within Cheyenne Mountain. It was a matter of official convenience. Construction of the NORAD center required extensive laying of cable between Cheyenne Mountain and main trunk terminals in the Denver area, and the engineers built what were known as booster stages along the cable lines. One such stage, on the road leading to a substation officially identified as Slab Rock, called for blasting deep within a mountain. Later, much later, that same area was selected as the site for the Air Force's bionics laboratory to be run under the direction of Dr. Michael Killian. As the outer shell of the hospital laboratory slowly assembled, the cybernetics laboratory, concealed entirely within the mountain, also came into being. Thus a normal flow of traffic, of personnel, supplies, and equipment was carried out in completely open fashion to the bionics lab, which functioned both as a research center and a hospital. It required little additional effort to distribute further whatever was necessary for the inner, secret laboratory after it arrived at the 'outer office'.

No small measure of miracles had emerged from Killian's bionics research. His goal was to substitute for what nature had provided, and had then been removed, for those who suffered amputation and severe disfigurement. This was not simply a matter of plastic surgery or prosthetic limbs. That constituted the most piddling of goals compared to what Killian and his staff sought. To Dr. Killian, an artificial leg was a *real* leg. Not flesh and bone, but intended to be fully as articulate as the original, and capable of rendering the same flexibility provided by nature. It had to extend far beyond a fancy stump or appendage with flesh-colored plastiskin and hairs embedded in the material. The idea was to create a replacement for the original that could not be distinguished by an observer as artificial, and this demanded a test of movement.

The new leg had to be as good or better than the real thing. Indeed, it must *be* the real thing, with the only difference being that the replacement was fabricated rather than created through original living tissue.

Rudy Wells would become in many ways the alter ego of Steve Austin. For some time to come, until shock eased from that young and impressionable mind, Wells would have to think for Steve – function not only as an intelligence center, but also supply the patterns of reason and logic that would for some time be missing from Steve's thinking. Steve would need to be sustained, protected from himself, so to speak, until shock eased and he regained complete control of himself once more. Wells also knew that the same levels of thinking might never again be achieved. In this he could only hope for the best and work.

There were two keys to the work in which Wells would immerse himself in the program for Steve, and both were peripheral to medicine as that word is commonly defined. Cybernetics was known as the science of computers or electronic brains, but that was rather the restrictive term. To the laboratories at Slab Rock, cybernetics covered a wider gamut of activity. It involved the computers, of course, meaning in the broader sense any artificial instrument – a sensor that received an input, examined it, made a decision, and initiated an action – that added to a cybernetics system. A device that functioned as an automatic pilot to hold an airplane on the proper heading, course, and altitude, and could be slaved to a radar or radio-homing system, to follow that system through turns at a certain time and space, and would even initiate a descent and carry it through to a landing, utilizing pressure altimeters and radar altimeters, and compensate for temperature and humidity and the effects of crosswind – this was wholly an automatic pilot that must be considered a computer.

Or the other way around: The cybernetics laboratory under Killian developed such systems on a scale far below their application to the everyday world; they were more akin to the sub- and microminiaturization techniques of military electronics systems and those developed by the space agency, where reliability and light weight were as vital as the ability to perform. Understanding the nerve patterns of the human brain enabled one to perfect artificial nerve patterns as well, which in turn gave one the advantage of superfast artificial brains to break down in the most exhaustive detail the nerve patterns of living creatures. It was a mutual activity, and Killian's utilization of cybernetics extended in both directions – from the large brains that could squeeze a century of tracing nerve patterns into only a few minutes of computer operation to the creation of small servosystems that functioned much in the manner of living systems.

The benevolent despot who ran the bionics and cybernetics laboratories, Dr. Michael Killian, was preeminent among the medical researchers in human systems. Much of Killian's work involved the nerve circuits of the human body and the brain. The thousands of billions of cells that involve message transfer and reaction throughout the body do not necessarily follow repetitive pathways but vary greatly, and take up strange and unexpected nerve tributaries throughout the body. To analyze the potential number of pathways was a numerical task beyond the lifetimes of a thousand mathematicians. But *not* beyond the capacity of a great computer, the macro part of the cybernetics laboratories that could produce within minutes an answer that would have taken a thousand human lifetimes. Thus the electronic brains functioned as superfast detectives to trace the almost infinite number of neural avenues within the brain and the body. The answers they provided enabled Killian's staff to design their man-made counterparts.

And so the second key – *bionics*. It was in this area particularly that Rudy Wells was no stranger. His own association had evolved from a combination of research disciplines – both basic and applied – and the rehabilitation programs in which he had for years participated. In the earlier days, when doctors and scientists were still trying to define their new areas of research, the Air Force explained bionics as the 'science of systems that function after the manner of, or in a manner characteristic of, or resembling living systems'. A bionics arm, then, would be an artificial limb that functioned much as did the original before its loss to the owner. But in their early research, when they were even adapting the biological systems of beetles to create artificial indicators to judge the speed over the ground of aircraft, they felt they were mixing the craziest part of biology with the most outlandish of concepts in electronics.

The term itself, bionics, still found ready understanding within only a limited area. Originally it was coined by Major Jack E. Steele, who had been a research psychiatrist at the Aerospace Research Laboratory in Ohio. Dr. Steele was a combination electrician, engineer, medical doctor, psychiatrist, pilot, *and* a flight surgeon. He created the word bionics as a combination of the Greek *bios*, meaning life, and the suffix *ics*, meaning after the manner of, or resembling. Steele taught his coworkers that the scientific goal of bionics was to acquire specific biological knowledge, then reduce that knowledge to mathematical terms (again with the indispensable computers) that would be meaningful to an engineer, who would then produce what the doctors, or the bionicists, if the term was preferred, requested. As Rudy Wells came to participate in the revolutionary field, bionics represented a remarkable step forward because it adapted biology to a new dimension. Until bionics studies came about, biology was mostly a descriptive science. It sorted and labeled the parts of living systems. With bionics, biology advanced to an analytical science that dealt with the specifics of the chemistry and physics involved in the biological processes.

Now Rudy Wells knew he would be reaching the culmination

of his several decades of work as a medical doctor, flight sur-geon, psychologist, and bionicist. It all centered in Steve, and the experience would introduce to Wells new dimensions of re-sponsibility. On him would be all the weight of physiological and psychological agony that Steve would know. If they proved successful with Steve, they would open new worlds to thousands of others. Oscar Goldman had come to them from an agency dealing internationally in deceit and secretive terror, and from such an agency's interest in Steve Austin there might emerge unprecedented hope for many savaged by the violence of acci-dent.

God help us, Wells thought, especially Steve Austin.

CHAPTER SEVEN

'I don't want you in the room when it happens.'

Wells studied her carefully, trying to judge the woman, to measure her steel. 'Understood, Miss Manners?'

'I understand, doctor.'

'Good.' He wanted to be absolutely certain of this woman. Jean Manners, RN. On their arrival in Colorado, Killian had brought her to the hyperbaric chamber personally, saying that Miss Manners was the best nurse he'd ever known. Killian simply didn't offer accolades. Nor did he bother to explain that much. 'I am assigning her to you full time,' he added. 'If you need anything, Rudy . . .' He let it hang, then turned and left the room. Killian would not be involved for some time with Steve. Not until they began surgery. That disturbed Wells. He wanted the program begun as quickly as possible. He had already made up his mind to move ahead faster than anyone expected.

She stood tall and willowy, and his appraisal took in small but firm, high breasts, the straw-colored hair, and a face on which freckles had run their wild course. But there was more; much more. He shook his head. He would make his evaluation later. He would *not* accept any nurse on first meeting. Not for Steve. This was going to be a long haul, and no matter that Killian broke his own rules to offer her with what was, for him, a stunning recommendation. That would do for the moment. He would decide later.

Her initial conversation impressed him. She was already fully conversant with Steve's case. She explained it quickly; Killian had notified her of the decision to bring Colonel Austin to Colorado. She would be assigned to the case, as direct aide to Doctor Wells. She had already checked out Steve's records, obtained the details of the crash, received the medical records.

She knew. That went a long way with Wells. He wasted no more time.

'Colonel Austin will have a full staff with him in the

hyperbaric chamber. I would like you to rest during the day. Tonight at approximately eleven o'clock, I'll bring Steve Austin back to ... awareness. I would like you to be with me during the preparatory stages. We will maintain the hyperbaric condition for an indefinite period. After we attend to the initial stage, I would like you in the adjoining chamber. I assume there is a microphone pickup in the main chamber. I want you in that adjacent chamber. I want you to listen to everything that goes on, to observe what you can. However, I *don't* want you in the room when it happens. It could be far worse that way. Do you understand that?'

She said she did. It could be vital.

She was with him well before eleven that night. He made a thorough examination of Steve, forcing from his mind as much as it was possible to do so the personal relationship. He must be both doctor and psychologist now. Together they strapped the unconscious form to the surgical table. Impossible to predict a physical reaction, what might happen. Steve had that right arm. He could move with it, apply leverage. The straps went across the chest, his groin, the lower one just above the knees where they had amputated. There would be an awareness of those straps. It would help.

They adjusted the lights carefully. It wouldn't do for the lights to be streaming into his eyes. Better for low-keyed lighting. A side-lighting effect would be best, would illuminate Wells's own face, provide a point of immediate recognition. That was important. Comprehension could come in fits and starts.

Wells had Jean Manners prepare a hypodermic of paraldehyde for immediate injection if it proved necessary. He noticed her brows arch when he specified the drug to knock him out.

'It's old-fashioned,' he said to her unspoken question, 'the sort of thing you use for belligerent drunks. It applies in this instance,' he said with a sudden ill-temper. 'It's nondepressive in terms of the respiratory system.' She nodded, placed the hypo within easy reach of his hand should it be needed.

Then it was time. God, he needed a sedative for himself. She saw it, too. She hesitated at first, then decided candor was best.

He didn't appreciate her question but he respected her intent when she asked if she might get him something. His response was curt, even nervous. She felt with him, accepted his mood.

'All right, Miss Manners,' he said finally. 'Time to start.' They stopped the trickle of alcohol into his system. They waited a while as Wells examined his patient. Finally he nodded to Jean Manners, told her to carry out the next step. Her hands were firm, skillful.

She administered the thyroid. Intravenous. Time again to wait. The thyroid would burn up the alcohol. As it did, Steve would emerge from the deep well of unconsciousness.

Wells glanced at the wall clock. Twenty minutes to go. Wells imagined himself emerging from that sodden stupor. Steve's last memory was of the crash. He would remember, first of all, the yawing, sickening motions. Maybe none of the impact. Impossible to tell. But he would remember that he was, or had been about to enter, into a crash situation.

He had a brain. He would think; he would try desperately to think. A skip-and-bounce process as he emerged from his protective cocoon. Then, within the next half hour, more cohesive thought would follow. It had to be set up by the time when Rudy Wells must tell him. No kick in the head, but no dragging it out.

Just about there. Wells stared at the face, waiting for the first signs of returning awareness. The muscles moved, twitched slightly. Any moment. He nodded to the nurse and she left silently, taking up position in the adjacent chamber.

He turned back to Steve.

His eye moved.

At the last moment the thought came to him. Rudy Wells reached for Steve's hand, held it in a firm clasp.

Steve stared at him, not yet comprehending. Wells knew he saw with blurred vision, a matter of mental groping, of not having the reference points of depth perception with both eyes. The doctor moved slightly to his left, to adjust his position so he was closer to Steve's right ear. The left was still swathed in bandages.

'Steve.'

Just the name at first. It would be difficult for him to talk at all. His jaw was wired shut. The teeth ... so many of them gone. Keep talking to him, give him reference points.

'Steve, it's me. Doc. Doc Wells.'

The eye closed. A long moment of ... pain? Something there, something deep and with the first signs of pain reaching him. The pain will be good. He—

Steve stared at him.

'It's Doctor Wells, Steve.

A sudden, cruel pressure against his hand. The eye opened wider. 'Steve, listen to me carefully. You're in a hospital. A hospital. Don't try to move. You're strapped down in your bed. You—'

'*Uh ...*'

'Take it slowly, Steve. Very slowly. You can't talk very easily. Do you recognize me, Steve? Just nod your head if you recognize me. That's all. Take it very slow, just nod your head.'

The eye closed. Wells held his breath.

The head moved ever so slightly. Steve had closed his eye, but his head moved. Several times Wells felt Steve's hand pressure increasing, then slowly decreasing.

'Listen to me carefully, Steve. It will be difficult to talk. Can you open your eye – eyes, Steve? Look at me if you can, fella.'

A man stared at him from the depths of his soul. The thought processes were running faster now, joining together.

'That's good, Steve. Can you understand me better now?'

'Y-yuh ... I ... I—'

'Slowly, slowly,' Wells said soothingly. 'Don't take it too fast. Can you understand me better now? That's good, son. Take it slowly. I'll fill you in. Take a deep breath. Try to relax. That's better. Breathe deeply. Some more. Good, that's good.'

The thyroid had taken its full effect now. The eye looking up at Wells was clearer, almost sharp. Lines had returned to the face. He was experimenting, feeling. Wells saw the tongue moving within the mouth, against the jaw, feeling the slight space between the teeth.

'Do you understand now? Your jaw is wired. It was broken. You can talk, but do it slowly, carefully. Do you understand me, Steve?'

'Y ... yes.'

'Good. Don't try to move anything but your right arm. Only your right arm or your head. That's all. Take it very slowly. You've been out for a long time, son. But you're coming out of it. You're ... What? Say that again, Steve. Slowly, slowly.'

'Where, doc? W— where are we?'

'In a hospital, Steve, in Colorado.'

'Colorado?' It came out muffled, forced through his teeth.

'That's right. We flew you up here yesterday from the test center.'

'Why — why Colorado?'

'Special facilities.' Wells took a deep breath. Time to get into it. Dragging it too far with this man could be worse. Give him enough to let him start drawing his own conclusions. 'We didn't have what we needed for you at Edwards.'

The eye widened, closed for a long moment, opened again. Then Steve Austin found himself, and the questions came faster and harder.

'How bad, doc?' His hand squeezed.

'Bad.'

Again he retreated, came back with his own growing fear as he fixed his eye on Wells's face, tried to read what hadn't been said with words. 'Tell me.'

'Do you remember what happened, Steve?'

His brow furrowed with sudden concentration. 'I ... yes, I think so. I flared ...'

'That's right. You flared right on target, but the wind got under you. Remember? She rocked pretty badly and you dug in a gear. You—'

'Yeah. Remember now.' The face grew vacant as he slipped away, back in time to *the* moment. 'Yaw ... that's it. She yawed. Nose went up high and ... and she got away, she yawed. I remember. Nothing I could do—'

'Nothing anyone could have done without wings, Steve.'

'Yeah. Nothing. I ... I remember her when ... hit. When I hit. How ... how's the ship?'

The test pilot coming out in front. 'Sorry, Steve. I'm afraid you totaled her.'

'Yeah.' He started to experiment. He released his grip on Wells's hand, lifted the hand before him, brought it closer to his face, flexed the fingers, balled them into a fist, flexed them

66

again. 'Looks pretty good,' he said finally, forcing the words through his wired jaw with greater strength. Wells waited for what must come next.

Strain showed on Steve's face. 'How ... come ... I can't move ... other arm?'

'You're strapped down.'

'Can't move my legs, doc.'

'I know, Steve.'

He looked up at Wells. 'You ... *know?*'

'Yes.'

'They're ... okay, aren't they?'

He shook his head slowly, extended his hand. Steve didn't take it. His face hardened.

'*Spill it.*'

'Your legs were crushed, Steve.'

It took a few moments.

'Crushed?' He was bewildered. Wells knew he was going back in time. He'd seen other ships go in, knew what had happened to the people inside.

'You mean ... can I walk, Doc?'

'I'm sorry, Steve. We had to amputate.'

For an instant Steve struggled wildly. Wells glanced to his right, to the needle with the paraldehyde. The muted thrashing lasted several seconds. Steve looked wildly to his right and left, his head snapping back and forth. He fell back from the straps, then, knowing he was helpless.

'What the hell did you let me live for!'

Wells held his silence. He was strong. He'd come back by himself.

Suspicion grew in Steve's eye. He tried to roll his vision to his left arm. 'My arm ... its not strapped down. *Where the hell is my arm?*'

'It was crushed when you hit.'

'Crushed?'

'You lost your arm before we got you out of the ship.'

'Both legs ... my arm ...'

'Yes, Steve. You've lost both legs and your left arm.'

He stared up at Wells, disbelieving. Again his mouth hardened. 'There's ... more, isn't there?'

Wells nodded.

67

'Get it over with, you bastard.'

Wells didn't even feel it. 'You're blind in your left eye, Steve. A piece of metal, the same thing that took your arm, severed the optical nerve.'

And then he gave it all to him, in a desperate rush . . . internal injuries, broken ribs, pelvic injuries, possible damage to the heart valve, slight concussion, jaw broken and wired shut, making speech difficult.

'I'm one arm away from being a basket case and you let me live.'

'Steve, we brought you to a special hospital in Colorado. The bionics laboratory. You know about it, we've talked about it before.' Wells groped for the other man's hand, gripped it. 'Dammit, Steve, I promise you, you'll walk, as good as you *ever* did. I don't mean just prosthetics. It's something entirely new. You'll walk and run and you'll *fly*, as well as if not better than before. You—'

'*Get away from me.*'

Well he had expected it. There wasn't any other way. It had to come out. Better here, now.

'Don't come back, doc.'

Wells leaned back in his seat, wrung out. He couldn't leave. Not yet. There were things to do. He wondered about the paraldehyde. Too drastic. Yet he knew Steve would never let him do what was needed. Not now. Not until the fire burned through his brain. He looked up, where he knew Jean Manners would be watching him, could hear his voice.

'Sparine,' he said. She was sharp; he knew that already. She came in moments later, walking as quietly as she could. But Steve heard her. He opened his eyes, looked up at her. He went white.

'*Get out!*'

'Quickly,' Wells said, grasping his arm. She moved as swiftly as he hoped she might. In an instant the needle went into his arm, the plunger moved, and the sparine was in his system. The mild hypnotic would calm him within seconds, start to send him back to sleep. He had to hold Steve just long enough for that. He stayed with him, Jean Manners watching closely until the spasms subsided.

Her voice came from a great distance to Wells. 'He's

68

asleep. Doctor Wells.' He released the pressure, stood on shaky feet.

'What doctors are on duty now, Miss Manners?'

'Doctors Horowitz and Baker.'

'See if they can come here immediately.'

'Yes, doctor.'

She moved out of sight. Well, no other way now. While he was under they must start to rebuild his strength. If they didn't get into surgery quickly Steve would retreat even farther into his mind. It could be too far for him to return. Wells made his plans. They would keep Steve under, at first with the sparine, then back to the electrosleep equipment. No question but that Steve would refuse to eat, even if he could with that jaw wired shut. They could get a straw through his teeth but it wasn't enough, because he would refuse it. They would need to get him high protein intravenously. They would use steroids; use the male hormone in the steroids. He thought about the effect on protein metabolism. It would be wise to go to tubal feedings, a tube directly into the stomach. They could use foods of zero residue to prevent the need, for a while, anyway, for bowel movements. He disliked having to leave the indwelling catheter for urine disposal, but there was no way out of that for now.

Doctors Horowitz and Baker were there within minutes, and Wells discussed with them and Miss Manners what had to be done in the next several hours. He planned to meet with Dr. Killian in the morning. Whatever must be done ... well, time was now critical in the psychological sense. He looked back at Steve, tossing fitfully despite the sparine. Almost impossible to prevent even subconscious disturbance now without either massive drugs or the electrosleep machine. But the sparine would hold him for a while.

Wells left soon afterward. He could no longer help Steve with his presence and it would be necessary to start the more detailed plans for immediate corrective surgery, and, as soon as possible after that, the recovery and ... the rebuilding phase. Thank God Steve was as strong as he had indicated tonight.

His strength nearly killed him.

Dr. Horowitz called shortly after four in the morning. Wells was instantly awake. Jean Manners had gone off duty at three, and Horowitz and Baker, the damned fools, had left Steve unattended. Just for a few minutes they said, their voices shaken when it was all over and he had personally attended to Steve.

Wells had only two or three times in his career cursed another doctor. He did it this morning, slowly, bitterly, with a fine cold rage. For Steve had very nearly succeeded in his one great overwhelming desire.

He had emerged from the calming effect of the sparine. They had not yet placed the electrodes on his head for the electro-sleep machine. Just a time span of a few minutes. Steve came awake, saw he was alone, somehow, incredibly, with one arm and hand, unstrapped himself, dragged his body from the surgical table. He fell heavily to the hard floor, nearly battering himself unconscious again. Somehow he hung on to his wits. Using his one hand, hard against the floor for friction, he had dragged himself across the floor to reach a cabinet. He smashed the glass, grabbed anything with steel within his reach. He had managed to wound himself in the stomach region only superficially. But inside his mind . . .

Steve was never to be left alone again, not for an instant, no matter *what* was being done, had to be done, no matter how personal. Not until Wells could judge that Steve's most devout wish was something other than death.

CHAPTER EIGHT

For a long time Steve never saw her as a *person*. Except in rare moments, and few of those were pleasant enough to be willingly recalled. She was an efficient, crisp worker, a nurse to delight her associates. Steel nerves and a bitter history of her own had molded her to her present level of control, and it was not something she would yield easily. Jean Manners had a devastatingly effective smile. You just couldn't get through it to discover whether she was personal with that smile or simply courteous.

They knew her inside the laboratories as a woman of rare intelligence. She also had an understanding, an empathy that established almost an electric bond between herself and her patients.

Except for one man. She could not reach Steve Austin.

At first she made certain *not* to attempt this contact of *feeling*. It would have been both foolish and useless. For a long time after that first night when Steve tried to kill himself in an incredible display of courage – and it *was* that – she held herself almost as a nonperson in all her contacts with the man. Her presence mattered to Steve. Not her; not Jean Manners. Only the nurse. There were things to be done, and Rudy Wells had decided it was infinitely better for Steve to become accustomed to the sight, the sound and feel, the repeated presence, of this one woman rather than a group of nurses or medical attendants. Lost in himself, enduring a new kind of shock with the continual, incessant realization of what had happened to him, Steve never truly *saw* Jean Manners but was in some remote fashion simply aware of her presence. She was a shadow moving barely within the limits of his restricted awareness. During those moments in between the almost weekly surgery, she tried to reach down to him, to offer her hand even as a faceless guide. When he responded it was wholly instinctive, as if the subconscious found it necessary to link with human warmness what the conscious had rejected.

71

And then, as he moved away from the numbing sameness of repeated excursions into the stupor of drugs and the electro-sleep machine, as the surgery to restore his internal systems passed, he could not prevent himself from examining what he had become. Whatever Jean found in him before, this was worse; he no longer showed even the bitterness she was so familiar with. He had become utterly indifferent. He could not fight the surgery being conducted on his person. So be it; he went along because there was no way for him to resist. But Jean Manners and Rudy Wells feared most of all that at the first opportunity, when he had regained strength and his wits, Steve would do whatever was necessary to end his life.

The months passed, and he became her life, day in and day out, with relief for her from the caring for him only when he was in electrosleep or beneath drugs. Those periods of relief were her rare moments of trying to find herself again, for the world had four walls, close about her, and in their center lay the maimed body of Steve Austin.

Who finally broke through his own indifference. It was the first, long-awaited sign, the opening wedge in forcing himself back into life. It could hardly have been more personal for Steve, more impersonal for her.

'Get out of here. I'll do that myself.'

The sound of his voice caught her completely by surprise. Her hands stayed where they were, at his groin. She looked up, startled. He had never spoken to her before, not a good morning or go to hell or anything. Not for nearly four months. As he emerged from each session in surgery, numbed and withdrawn, she had resumed the care of his body in the personal as well as the medical sense. For months he had used the catheter for urination. Irritation to the sensitive skin was of course impossible to avoid and now at the moment she was exercising particular care in removing the device.

'You can let it the hell go,' he said angrily.

She took a deep breath. 'As you like, colonel,' she said smoothly.

'And I'll do it myself from now on,' he went on with the same tone. 'I'm old enough to go to the bathroom.'

'If you won't take offense, Colonel Austin,' she said, her voice

72

deliberately calm, 'that hasn't been the case for the past several months.'

He dropped his head back to the pillow. 'You the one?'

'Yes.'

'Just you?'

She nodded. 'No one else. Dr. Wells's orders.'

He watched her. My God, it's . . . it's like an explosion inside him, she thought. Like someone threw a switch and he's back to life. He cares. He actually cares again . . .

'I wondered about that,' he said. 'Somehow it doesn't seem so bad now.'

'I don't understand, sir.'

'Don't ever call me "sir". *Ever*, understand? That's past history.'

'Do you prefer "colonel"?'

'I have a name. Use it.'

'Delighted to. First or last?'

He looked at her as if seeing her for the first time, which was most likely true, she judged. I've been only background all this time. He raised himself up on his one elbow, grunting with the effort. For a moment he squeezed his eye shut tightly, fighting the sudden dizziness. Then he opened it again.

'You didn't try to help me just then,' he said.

'You didn't want me to.'

He nodded. 'Yeah. I guess you're right.' He rested on the elbow, awkward, trying to find his balance points. 'Am I that goddamned clumsy?'

'No, St—' She shook her head. 'I still don't—'

'Steve will do fine.' He glanced at himself where he was still exposed to her. 'A first-name basis seems to be in order. What's yours?'

'Jean. Jean Manners.'

'Jean all right?'

'Yes. It will do fine.'

'You've been, uh, taking care of me, everything?'

'Yes.' She wanted to say more, tell him it was her duty as a nurse, but she held back the words. Why say what he must certainly know?

His face was going white slowly. 'I'm weaker than I . . . thought . . . whew. Dizzy. Wow, that came on quick.'

She was by his head immediately, cradling it in her hand, pressing him firmly down with the other. 'Please. Lie back. It will take a while.' His head sank down against the pillow.

He stared at the ceiling as she finished carefully but quickly and moved the aluminum frame over his hips, drew the sheet to his chest.

'Thanks.'

He chewed on his lower lip. The surgery to his jaw had been a marvel. Thin white lines were the only marks of the special wiring and braces they had needed. A month ago Dr. Wells had ordered dental work. He felt false teeth as vital to Steve's attitude as it was to his system for chewing. There was no evidence that the jaw had been smashed and most of the teeth on one side broken free. Killian decided for plastic surgery as a concurrent activity and it had paid off well.

His hair had grown back sufficiently to give him the crewcut he'd always worn, and a single dark patch replaced the heavy bandages that had obscured not only his left eye but nearly half his face. Along the side of his cheek there were still the thin white lines of scar tissue but these were leaving slowly. Within a few months they would be gone entirely. He—

'This bed raise up?'

'No. But we can take care of that if you like.'

'I . . . I think so,' he said.

'Water?' He nodded, and she brought him a glass with a straw. 'Take that thing out of here.' He struggled to a sitting position, half crouched, using his leg stumps as balance counterpoints. He managed the glass in his hand, drinking slowly, closing his eyes as if this was the first time in months he had actually tasted liquid. He gasped suddenly for air, extended the glass to her.

'What about food?'

'Most of the time you refused to eat,' she told him. 'Your intake has been largely intravenous, and also some direct tubal feeding. That's introducing the food directly to—'

'You the one who's bathed me?'

She nodded.

He laughed without humor. 'Closer than a damned wife, aren't you?'

'Yes.'

'I don't believe it,' he said suddenly, 'but I'm damned if I'm not hungry.'

She moved cautiously. 'Anything in particular?'

'Uh, yes. It's crazy. Steak. Steak and orange juice. *Fresh* orange juice. I suddenly feel as if I could drink gallons of it.'

'It's been a long time,' she said.

'Uh, yeah. Just how long, by the way? I mean, since they brought me here.'

'Four months.'

'*Four mo—!*'

She sat with him in silence as he digested the loss of time.

'Let me ask you something else,' he said, breaking slowly from his reflections. 'This bed. You said I can get something that will let me sit up?'

'Of course. Power bed's the answer. Just about any position you want.' She glanced at the flat sheets where his legs would have been, then up at him. 'There's no use pretending anything, is there?'

'Christ, they're gone, aren't they? What's there to pretend? Then there's something else I'll need. Some way of my being able to do things for myself.' His expression was fierce as he concentrated. 'From now on, if you please, I'd like to go to the crapper by myself. I'll need an overhead brace bar of some kind. Leverage, that's the answer.' He bared his teeth in a mock smile. 'Simian leverage. Have to do with one arm. Tricky but I think I can hack it.' He ignored her for the moment, moved his right hand about the stump of his left arm. 'Not too sensitive. Surprised at that,' he murmured, as much to himself as to her. He looked up suddenly. 'Can you get me a large drawing pad and some pencils?'

'You need rest.'

'I've been dead for four goddamned months!' he shouted suddenly. 'As long as I'm still alive, quit fighting me, for Christ's sake and get me what I need, or get the hell away from me completely.'

He closed his eye, lost to her. 'I'll get it for you. Just as soon as I get someone in here to relieve me.'

He reacted slowly to her words, to the sudden catch in her throat. 'Relieve you?'

'Yes. I – I'll get Miss Norris. Kathy Norris. She's a nurse, but she's been working on ... your case as a lab technician. She's—'

'Why the hell do you need someone to relieve you?' He made a sweeping gesture to take in the stumps of his legs and his arm. 'Do you think I'm planning on going anywhere?'

'No, it's not that. I—'

She couldn't hold it down. 'It's not a *game*,' she said, far more sharply than she intended. 'Orders.'

'From who?'

'Doctor Wells.'

'Doc—' He was honestly perplexed now, his expression showing the pained confusion. 'But why would doc . . .' He let it trail off, almost completely exhausted, staring up at her.

'You want me to be honest with you,' she said. He nodded, his face vacant. 'We did that ... some time ago ... right after Doctor Wells first brought you out of it. You tried to kill yourself, Steve.'

'I don't believe it.'

He stared off at the ceiling, into space. His voice came from far away. 'Do what you have to,' he said. And she knew he was lost to them again.

Kathy Norris was there a few minutes later. By then Steve was fast asleep. 'Watch him closely,' Jean told the other woman. 'Don't leave his side for a second, understand?'

Kathy looked at her in surprise, held her question. 'Of course,' she said.

Rudy Wells found her in the nurses' lounge, face buried in her hands.

'Just like that,' she said, the disbelief still evident. 'For months he's had his mind turned off, shutting us all out, and now, my God, now he's shouting and giving orders and ... it's too much, Rudy. I'm sorry. I didn't mean to go on like this, but he's been *dead* all these months, and now he's alive and demanding and wanting, and he's planning on how to make things better for himself, and it just doesn't seem possible, does it? I mean, well, do you know what he's doing right now? This minute? This same man who's been so withdrawn he's been the same as unconscious ... he's got Kathy holding a drawing board for him, and he's making engineering drawings. He's—'

76

For the next hour Wells questioned her, grateful it was Jean in the room when he snapped out of his withdrawal and plunged back into living. There could have been no other way for Steve Austin to have made the return journey. There was still danger, however. Steve would soar to new heights of promise and adaptation, and then there would come, inevitably, the plunge to black, when he would become so morose with the realization of his shattered body that self-destruction could again become a serious danger. It was imperative, then, that he begin the next phase of Steve's rebirth. Sit with him, spend hour after hour with him, fill his waking moments with a complete backward journey into the last four months, let him know every detail of what had happened, and from the near impossibility of medical miracles they had already performed, there could be created a belief that more miracles lay within their grasp. That was the key. Steve was starting to ride high now; he would stay that way for a while. But when he realized the surgery that lay ahead, the crippling, enervating tests, when he was made aware of the pain, the heartbreak, the experimental nature of things, the specter of one failure after the other – they would be pioneering – well, he might go either way.

Everything depended on Steve's accepting what lay ahead as a challenge. If he succeeded, he would become a man, a being far beyond the wildest reach of his imagination. . . .

'Tell me about the drawings he's making,' he said to Jean Manners.

She looked up. 'It's a frame,' she began. 'Oh, I'm not an engineer, Doctor Wells, but I get the general idea.'

He told her that would be fine. He would get the details later; right now he wanted to know how it came about.

She explained his reaction when she had been removing the catheter. 'Was there any direct sexual response?' Wells asked.

She looked at him in surprise. 'No. Nothing I could detect,' she said uncomfortably.

'Jean, no wife could be closer to that man than you are right now.'

'That's almost exactly what he said.'

He nodded. 'Steve at this moment is impotent,' he told her. 'Nothing physical. For Steve Austin, at least right now, masculinity is linked irretrievably with his limbs. His arms and legs,

77

Jean, were the key to his flying, to going to the moon, to his athletic prowess, and they highlighted his appeal to women. I expect it to get better until there will be a shocking realization of what I've just passed over lightly. At that point Steve will be absolutely convinced that no woman will ever want him, and impotency will become just as absolute. From there on it's an uphill battle all over again.'

'That certainly will be a challenge to some people,' Jean said.

'Oh?'

'Not *me*,' she said quickly. 'Kathy. Her feelings are obvious.'

'Well, Kathy is a beautiful girl, and—'

'Kathy is *stacked*, Dr. Wells.'

'What about his reaction?'

'He looks right through her. She isn't even there.'

CHAPTER NINE

Rudy Wells watched, fascinated, as the man in the bed demonstrated, without the attempt to prove anything, the marvelous flexibility of the human being. Technicians in the bionics machine shop had followed Steve's engineering drawings to the letter, and among the items he requested was a modification of the wheeled hospital bed-table that can be placed across a bed directly before the patient. Steve's table was that, and a great deal more. From left to right it featured a series of vises and clamps to give him the gripping or clasping ability now denied to him through the loss of his left arm and hand. At the moment he was preparing a cigar, which he had clamped in a rubber grip. He sliced off the end of the cigar with a razorblade, then removed the wrapper with his right hand. He gripped the cigar in his teeth, lit up with a butane lighter, and blew a cloud of blue smoke in the direction of the doctor.

'Brandy?'

Rudy Wells nodded, but made no offer to help. Steve reached to his left by crossing his arm over his body – he refused to keep his supplies and equipment entirely to his right – to withdraw a bottle from a cabinet. The bottle went into a clamp and he withdrew the cork, placed two glasses on the table, and poured. Wells held up his glass in a silent toast, sipped, and returned the glass to the table by his side.

'All right,' Steve said behind another smoke cloud, 'I guess school's on.'

'If you feel up to it.'

'Up yours, doc. No games. You know you're anxious to fill me in so you can pitch your next program to me.'

'Worked it out that well, have you?'

Steve's one eye held his gaze. 'How many years do we know each other?'

Wells shrugged. 'You had just gotten your wings the first time we met.'

'Uh huh. And you were there holding my hand when I went

79

through flight-test school, and – hey, you know the story. So I know when and how you fidget, and it's time to get on with it.'

'The liver is as good an example as any,' Wells began, 'to get it through your thick head that you've enjoyed a succession of miracles. Almost as if you were meant to survive the—'

'Can the sermon, Rudy,' Steve interrupted, more serious than his expression indicated.

Wells gestured lightly to dismiss what he had started. 'The miracle, then, is that you suffered no more damage than you did. You know what happened to you. There's grim evidence of that. But internally you went to the wall. You had some liver damage. I want you to understand that. Just some. To the very limit that we could do something about it. I say the limit because had it been any more severe we would have had little hope of bringing you through. The organ is simply too complex for us even to understand its makeup or function as well as we would like to. It handles something like five thousand body functions. No way for us to take over what nature started. Not permanently. But we did take over for a while. It cost us an excellent chimpanzee—'

'A what?' The cigar stopped midway to Steve's teeth.

'A chimpanzee. You owe your life to the animal.'

'Are you crazy?'

'We kept you alive for two days, about forty-three hours, while we used a chimp's liver to fill in for yours. Process we call perfusion. We anesthetized the animal and removed his liver, and placed it in a special glass container. Then we made a series of connections between your body and the liver. We needed three of these. They're cannulas. We attached and inserted them into the vessels of the chimpanzee's liver, and then we connected the whole shebang to you.

'Actually, the liver has marvelous powers of recuperation. Almost regeneration, in fact. If, that is, it can have its workload removed for a while. This really is what we did. We took the load off you and your body had the chance to take care of itself. The liver virtually carried on its own regenerative program. We—'

'How the hell did I live through the liver of a chimp?'

'After the system was set up,' Wells said a bit more slowly,

80

'and the tubes were ready, we connected the tubes to an artery and a vein in your arm. Your blood was kept pumping by your heart, although we gave it some assistance. It was pumped into a glass reservoir. There we added anticoagulant heparin, and the blood then went to the liver of the animal. There nature took over, doing whatever it does to purify your blood, to rid it of undesirable elements. It went from the chimpanzee's liver to another reservoir, where the heparin was neutralized, and from there back into your arm and through your system again.'

'You kept this up for *two days*?'

'Two days.'

'Jesus Christ.'

'No sermons, remember?'

Steve studied Wells carefully. 'Don't I recall you saying something about a heart operation?'

'Not quite that,' Wells said. 'We talked about a heart-valve operation. Not the same thing.'

Wells seemed to withdraw into himself.

'There was something else, wasn't there?' Steve pressed the doctor.

'Yes. I've been debating whether or not to tell you.'

'Rudy, you can be goddamned exasperating, do you know that? Of all the stupid times to play coy, I—'

'It was back at Edwards,' the doctor broke in. 'It's what I meant when I said you seemed, well, destined to survive all this. Your heart failed on the emergency table.' He paused, then said, 'You were dead, Steve. There's no other way to say it.'

'For how long, doc?'

'Seconds. No more than that. We anticipated it and we were ready. We shot a jolt of electricity through you. If we hadn't . . .'

'It might have been better if you hadn't.'

'I wish you'd knock off that crap, to put it bluntly.'

'Sorry about that,' Steve said, unconcerned with the doctor's mood. 'But there was more. I mean, right here in the labs, wasn't there?'

'There was. When the ship broke up around you, a lot of things became unglued,' Wells said. 'A piece of metal – we don't know what it was – ripped open your rib cage and punctured the area around the heart.'

Steve waited in silence for Wells to continue.

'The mitral valve sustained damage. We didn't know how bad it was until we had you up here. It became progressively worse, in fact. You had barely enough pumping energy to keep up a proper blood flow. To get things back to normal, Steve, we had to replace a part of the cardiac system.'

'Replace? Another chimp?' He waved the cigar at the doctor. 'Or did some other animal, maybe a giraffe or something, get creamed this time?'

'We wanted a human donor but it didn't work out that way. There was no opportunity to set up a transplant. We went to an artificial replacement.'

'I'm all ears.'

'The first thing is to reassure you that your heart is as sound as ever.'

'Hooray for our side.'

Wells ignored it. 'We – Dr. Killian, that is; I only assisted – performed open-heart surgery. We decided on using a Hufnagel disk valve as a replacement for your own damaged valve.'

'You mean the damned thing is inside me *now*?'

'It is, and it does a better job than the original.'

'What the devil is it?'

'It's made up of a ring of metal rimmed with Teflon, and in the center, within a metal cage, it's got a white silastic disk that floats around. It's—'

'Silastic?'

'That's silicone rubber. It's fastened by sutures. We placed the valve within the left ventricle of your heart. Like I said, it works as well if not better than the original.'

'Jesus.'

Wells laughed at the other man's expression. 'We shut down your heart during that operation, by the way. Used what we call the pump. It's a heart-lung machine. It substituted the pumping action while we took your heart out of the system. I'm sure you know the basic routine. We wired you up—'

'Wired up what was left of me, you mean.'

Wells paused. Steve was suddenly on a downslide, his mood altering rapidly, moving into depression. No way out of it, Wells told himself. He went on quickly. 'We wired you to monitor the vital functions. Oscilloscopes – it's all familiar to you from the astronaut program. Then we inserted a tube at the hip into the main artery and used this to return the blood to your body from the heart-lung machine. The pump. You still with me?'

Steve had been gazing vacantly into the distance. 'Yeah, doc. Don't quit now. I'm all ears for the next thrilling chapter.'

'We cut open your chest and—'

'That should have been easy. Plenty of holes there already, right?'

'We spread several ribs to – I'd better interrupt myself here and tell you we took care of your rib cage at the same time. You now have five vitallium ribs. Special kind of metal. Better than the original . . .

'We placed two tubes through your heart wall to collect the blood delivered from the main veins of the heart, which was then carried to a blood-oxygenating chamber. Here it picked up oxygen and was pumped through a rather complicated channel system back into your body. Now, when we removed all the blood from your heart, we opened it, removed the damaged valve, and replaced it with the artificial—'

'Maybe I ought to change my name to Steve Hufnagel.'

'—valve, closed the heart, and sewed you up.'

'Very decent of you.'

'Then we restored circulation. Only one bad moment. Some fibrillation. Quick electrical shock to—'

'The old ticker must have been used to that by then, right?'

'It wasn't unexpected, Steve,' Wells said patiently. 'As far as your heart is concerned, you're as strong and healthy as you ever were.'

'Boom, boom, boom.'

Wells didn't respond. Steve toyed with the cigar, brushed off the ashes carefully, lit up again. 'You said Killian did the operation?'

'Killian and seven other doctors.'

'I'm flattered.'

'He's the very best.'

'Three loud cheers for—'

'And your attitude stinks.'

'Maybe I just don't like being a freak with your shiny new Hufnagel—'

83

'No one considers you a freak because of a mechanical heart valve, for God's sake!'

'And why the hell not?'

'Because,' Wells told him quietly, 'Michael Killian, to name just this one surgeon, has performed this same heart operation on nearly a thousand people. *Before* you showed up. If you're a freak, you've got a great deal of company.'

It wasn't nearly that easy when they got down to the matter of two legs and an arm. Wells tried to stress the body adjusting to new balances, new tolerances. Steve's expression promised a difficult period.

'Few people realize the adult male has more than two hundred bones in his body,' Wells said. 'In childhood the number is something over three hundred. These fuse together, become the basis for larger bone networks. And despite common belief to the contrary, there's less fragility with increasing age. Of course there's no identical pattern. Like everything else in life it's a matter of variables. When—'

'Doc, if you don't mind, just what has all this to do with me?'

'Bear with me a bit longer. It will fit. I was saying that the bone structure follows a basically similar pattern in the adult male. When the bones don't fuse, for example, you can end up with an extra rib. Out of every twenty people you've met in your life, Steve, at least one of them has an extra rib. This simply reflects on the great flexibility in body construction. Actually, it's one out of every twenty *men*, because with women it's one in sixty. Why, we don't know. Maybe God is apologizing to us for Adam's loss.

'Now, getting closer to home,' Wells continued, 'is the specialized bone structure, and medicine's ability, through bionics, the cybernetics systems, electronics, prosthetics, plastics, all these put together, to duplicate and in some cases to *improve* on the original.

'You lost bones, Steve. You lost your legs and an arm. You had other bones damaged. All right. It happened. No way of undoing it. But the human bones were designed by nature to do more than to articulate or function simply as a framework from which to hang the rest of you and create a skintight container

84

for the liquids in your body. Nature designed your bones to act as a buffer, a shield, for your vital organs.

'And by and large they did their job. The flat plates of your skull, for example, took a terrific pounding. Some pieces were chipped out, and we've already replaced them. Then—'

Steve looked at him coldly. 'That's a new one on me,' he said slowly. 'Got any more surprises?'

'Yes, I do. We've been using vitallium as a bone replacement for more than twenty years. We didn't experiment with you. There are more than a hundred thousand people in this country alone with vitallium now permanently a part of their bone structure, and—'

'Everybody just clanking right along?'

Wells leaned forward, looked directly at Steve. 'Self-pity? You're certainly entitled to it, but it's not very useful. Still—'

'You go to hell.'

'More than likely. Steve, what I'm trying to do is to establish the groundwork for what comes next. For example, Steve, your spine was – is – curved. No more and no less curved than it was before we did some repair work. To anyone who flies as a test pilot and pulls the positive g-forces you know so well, anything even a bit out of variance with the spine is of utmost concern. For a while your spine was *straight*. Think about the spine, what it really means to the body. The thick cables of nerves and muscles and tendons, the architectural bridges, the whole of the incredible structure. Then think of it as being straight instead of its curvature.'

Steve's expression was wary. 'No one ever said anything about that,' he said slowly. 'What happened?'

'I've been trying to make the point that the body adapts, changes and conforms. Your spine, and that of every human child born, is straight at birth. It curves only with growth. And it adapts to modification, whether that alteration is natural *or artificial*. We did work on your spine; it was necessary. We added elements of vitallium and cerosium, but we went only far enough to return the spine to its shape before your accident. You'll never know it from the way it acts or feels, and if I hadn't told you about it now, you might never have known what we did. Again, Steve, the point is adaptation of the body. All this will have relevance when I get to more specifics about

85

you.' Wells turned to the intercom. 'Miss Norris? Could you bring some coffee to Colonel Austin's room? Yes, the works. Thank you.'

When a side door opened and Kathy Norris came in with a tray holding a coffee pot, a creamer, sugar, and cups, Rudy Wells couldn't help breaking off his thoughts about Steve to look at the lovely woman who had just entered. Jean Manners was right. Kathy was stacked. A classic body: Great legs, slim waist, firm, proportional breasts. Wells turned to Steve, who was merely looking at *him.* Steve hadn't reacted in the slightest to the presence of this beautiful girl. Except to motion to her to place the coffee on the table that crossed his bed. Wells noticed also that Kathy crossed the room into the adjacent laboratory, making certain to leave the door open. Good, he thought. Let her learn as much as possible. It would take a benumbed man not to see her reaction to Steve. Which was Steve's condition at the moment.

He drank slowly from his cup. One eye peered at Wells over the rim.

'Steve, what you do with the opportunities we'll give you is entirely in your own hands—'

A stump of an arm moved above Steve's shoulder. 'If you don't mind, Dr. Wells. Singular, please. Let's be accurate.'

'*Hands,*' Wells insisted. 'It's not attached yet. That's all.'

'It *still* makes it one hand. A prosthesis does not a hand make.'

Wells shook his head, slowly, firmly. '*Hands,*' he said. 'Plural. I've seen it. You haven't. But you're going to.'

The sessions went on for hours. They broke for dinner, Wells leaving for home. He hoped Kathy Norris would share the time with Steve. Not even Steve could be indifferent to her for long. But when he returned, Kathy was gone, and Steve made no mention of her being in his room during Wells's break for dinner. The doctor handed him a long cigar. 'Jamaican,' Wells said as Steve sniffed the tobacco. 'If you behave, I might even be talked out of a box of them.'

Steve lit up, leaning back against the angled bed. 'Okay, get on with it. It's obvious you can hardly wait.'

86

Wells leaned forward. 'Pay attention. We're going to crawl inside you a bit. Specifically, your left hip bone.'

'I'm all ears.' He brought his hand around to the left side of his face. 'Ear and a half, anyway.'

Wells ignored it. 'In some ways, Steve, you are already an artificial person. In *some* ways, and your pelvis is one of them.' *That* woke him up, thought Wells. 'You took some damage to your left hip, where the upper part of the femur joins the pelvis. We had to go in there. It's the joint between the hip and thigh, a ball-and-socket joint. The cartilage was damaged. In future years, if we hadn't taken the corrective measures now, you would have ended up with excruciating pain. Think of it as a latent and unavoidable stiffness of movement. So we replaced some of the cartilage with molded cerosium, a form of ceramic. Matched the cartilage and cerosium. Not too easy, because natural cartilage is as smooth as glass, and it's made free from friction by applying synovial fluid to the flexible parts of the joint. That's your internal lubrication system working. All we needed to add was the cerosium. If I didn't tell you about it now you would never know we were in there, patching and adding pieces. There was no damage to the femur itself, by the way, and you can be thankful for that.'

'I'm overjoyed.'

'You should be. The femur, as I'm sure you know, is built like a hollow cylinder. You're an engineer, Steve. You can appreciate a design that's cross-hatched internally. It can take two tons of pressure per square inch, even more at times, because the hatch lines within the bone will actually shift depending upon external pressure. The bone is *alive*. Not many people realize that. With everything we can do in here,' he gestured to include both the bionics and cybernetics laboratories, 'we haven't found a way to improve on the thigh bone. In your case, fortunately, we needed to repair only certain elements of the ball in the socket.'

'Jesus, doc, you sure got a bedside manner about you. You make me feel like a goddamned Oldsmobile.'

'All set for the next thrilling chapter?'

'Shoot.'

'Five of your ribs were crushed.' He studied Steve, the blank look the other man gave him.

'They knitted, I assume,' Steve said slowly.

'No.' Wells shook his head. 'They were literally *crushed*. Splintered. Bits and pieces, Steve. But they did what they were supposed to do by keeping you alive. The thorax, your rib cage, collapsed where the ribs themselves failed, but they functioned long enough as a cage, a barrier, to protect the organs inside — the heart, lungs, liver, spleen. You took some damage there, as you know, but not enough to write you off.'

'You said the ribs *didn't* knit? Then what . . .'

'We built you new ribs of vitallium and joined them with artificial tendons. Your metal ribs are as flexible as the originals and considerably stronger, and almost impossible to break. They'll bend more than double before they give way. We used what we call memory vitallium by giving them a magnetic memory so that after bending, or other movement, they always return to their original curvature. In the front of your body we used silastic, a form of silicone rubber, to join the ribs to the breastbone.'

Steve took this in silence. Rudy Wells didn't feel that it was the time to tell Steve Austin his new ribs had more than magnetic memory. They were also embedded with extremely fine wire and could function as part of an electrical system through an external power source. His ribs were an excellent radio antenna. But that would come later.

They spent several days in this fashion, Rudy Wells reinforcing his explanations with X-rays, detailed photography from the operating room, films showing the special materials of vitallium, silastic, and cerosium in their development and undergoing stress tests. Wells wanted Steve to have as extensive a working knowledge as possible of the alterations already performed upon and within his body. The hope was that as he went more deeply into the details Steve Austin would come to accept, as naturally as he accepted the electrodes he had worn as an astronaut, the modifications to his own system. Wells wanted them to be common to Steve's sense of his own body. Samples of the materials they'd used to modify his skeletal and internal systems were left with him, tossed about casually on a worktable with samples of bones and tissues, preserved in large jars. It became 'a bit ghoulish', as Steve said one morning to the doctor, but the deep association had been planted for the future.

Steve learned of repairs – his own term now after picking it up from constant usage by Rudy Wells – to his skull. Wells had Jean Manners discuss the various operations with Steve, feeling that she would be a welcome change. The nurse went into exhaustive detail about Steve's cranium, explaining its function as a powerful defense for the brain – armor plate made up in eight sections.

'That must have been some crackup,' Jean observed, studying the films with Steve of the lifting plane's last moments. They had watched the scene a dozen times and were now running it once more in slow motion, with the exaggeratedly deliberate breakup of the machine.

'Must have been.' He shook his head. As the accident un-folded once more, Jean explained that his skull repairs had been made not with metal or ceramics, but with human bone fitted surgically into place. 'Then,' she said briskly, 'over the cranium bone went a thin layer of silastic to act as an extra buffer. It also works as a cushioning element beneath the skin, where it's been heavily repaired and grafted, along the top of the head.' A manicured finger tapped the side of his skull. 'Like, right there,' she told him.

'How are you so sure?'

'I was the OR nurse.'

'You mean . . . you were there the whole time?'

'Why not? If I could take care of your body functions for months, what's wrong with taking a look inside your head?'

Wells hoped the association with Jean Manners would have another important effect – help Steve to recognize this woman's acceptance of him as a man. Kathy Norris had her part to play, too.

If only Steve would pay more attention to her . . .

They tried to assure Steve that the loss of his limbs had not affected the pumping and circulatory system. The normal body – in healthy shape, as nature created it – has some sixty thousand miles of tubes moving outward from the heart. Most am-putees feel that anything substantially interfering with this mass circulatory system will be disastrous. Every day the adult heart pumps ten pints of blood through a thousand complete circuits. 'That's about six thousand quarts of blood every twenty-four hours,' Wells explained. 'It's changed with you, of course. But instead of the circulatory system being all screwed up, as you seem to believe, *your* system is to a great extent simplified. Just the opposite of what you believe. Thousands of miles of ducts in both directions have been eliminated. Your blood requirements have been reduced. But your heart still has the same pumping capabilities as before. In effect, under stress this will raise your blood pressure, as your body needs it. It also improves oxygenation in the brain, where you need it most under stress and, something even closer to home for you, it makes you more resistant to acceleration. Your *g*-tolerance has actually improved instead of being reduced. I'm not suggesting you be grateful. But at least you might as well know the few plusses along with the minuses.'

Wells went on, explaining that Steve's fist-sized heart, no more than a pound of muscle, was able to increase its output to eight times normal, to twelve gallons every minute. 'And if the demand persists,' he said, 'the heart chambers enlarge and it can actually double its size to increase blood flow. But essentially all this is to increase many times the oxygen saturation of your system. So in effect you are now somewhat superior in circulation, pressure, and oxygen saturation than you were before the crash.'

Wells flicked the lights in the room back to bright after projecting a film on system circulation. 'Steve, it's not always easy to remember just how extraordinary your body is. And in your particular case we have *not* been fighting nature. We've worked *with* it. That's our purpose here in these labs. When you lost your three limbs you lost, of course, thousands of miles of capillaries. And yet everything still works perfectly where circulation is concerned, and without our help. The body reroutes, changes currents, adapts its systems of valves in order to compensate for its new conditions. Your system shifted whatever was necessary to a new – well – call it the new network of traffic. Everything works perfectly. We're not guessing about this, Steve. No one is doing any handholding. We *know*. You have been studied more intensively than any human being I know of, with every instrument and device known to science.

'Including,' he added with a wry smile, 'an old-fashioned faith healer.'

She brought the tray to his bed, then sat at his side. 'Do you mind if I stay here a while, Steve?'

He studied her expression. She watched him in return. She bent low over him, fussed with him. He ignored it all.

'No, I don't mind.' She settled herself in the chair, waiting, making certain she didn't stare while he ate. She wanted to stare. She wanted *him* to stare. 'There's something I've been wanting to ask you,' he said in the abrupt manner they'd all become accustomed to. Could he finally be—?

'Of course,' she said, leaning forward.

'You do the lab work on my case, right? Okay, then. Doc Wells was talking about something I didn't understand, and I thought I'd bring it up while I had it in mind.' She nodded, trying not to show her disappointment. To hell with her lab work ... 'Rudy,' Steve continued, 'said something about millions of blood cells dying all the time in the body. Is that true? I mean, is this normal?'

Well, she thought, if you can't beat 'em ... 'Sounds crazy, doesn't it?' She laughed lightly to hide the disappointment. 'But it's true.'

'*Millions* of cells?'

'Let me think a moment. Gotta remember the books.' She looked up. 'Okay, the recall is working. It's millions, all right.' She nodded vigorously. 'In fact, it's about eight million blood cells that die every second.'

'Eight mil—' He stared. 'Every *second*?'

'Know what it works out to? Every single week something like five trillion blood cells die in the body. It's sort of spread out. The distribution, I mean.' She was rattling off numbers and details as if Wells had suddenly inhabited her mind. 'Most of the work goes on in the bone marrow, the lymph glands, and lymphoid tissues. These are all shoved into your intestines, tonsils, spleen, and the thymus. In your case, despite the, well, the—'

'Dammit, Kathy, it adds up to two legs and an arm. For God's sake, this is no time to get uptight.'

91

'*I'm* not the one who's uptight, *Colonel* Austin.'

He couldn't believe the outburst, the way she suddenly turned away from him. He started to reach out his hand, drew it back.

'What the hell is the matter with you?'

'Nothing.'

'Dammit, look at me.'

She turned and he was stunned by the sight of tears.

'You want your numbers? All right, I'll give them to you. You have twenty-five trillion red corpuscles in the bloodstream and you've got thirty-five billion white blood cells and nearly two trillion platelets, and everything is always dying and being reborn all the time, and your heart pumps like mad, but the only thing wrong with it is that it's colder than hell!'

For the first time, as she ran out of the room, he noticed she had a well-rounded ass. Now why the hell, he wondered to himself, did I think about that now?

'You wanted to talk to me, Steve?'

He nodded, working the small control stick on the right arm of the wheelchair, gliding into Wells's office. He spun the chair about and slammed the door in the face of Wells's secretary. 'Damn biddy,' Steve muttered.

Rudy Wells looked at him with sudden concern. 'Anything wrong?'

Steve motioned him to relax. 'Nothing's wrong. It's just that I've been noticing things, that's all.'

'What sort of things?'

'It's not important. Crazy broads,' he muttered. Wells made a mental note to check with Jean Manners and Kathy Norris as soon as Steve left.

'I want to discuss my eye. Or rather, the eye I don't have any more.'

'All right, Steve.'

'Don't patronize me with that syrupy voice, you belly-thumping old bastard. I know your routine by heart.'

'Shot down in flames,' Wells said. 'Okay, let's have it.'

'Tell me straight out, Rudy. Can I get back my vision?'

'No. We can never hope to replace the eye you lost. We can't even begin to try. Despite how far we've come, in so many areas, at this stage of the game the eye remains far beyond us. It's so incredibly complex. The male adult eye is normally about an inch in diameter, in the shape of a complete sphere. It's extraordinarily well protected, and—'

'But it wasn't in my case. Why not?'

'You took the equivalent of a spear thrown into your face,' was the immediate answer. 'The nerve endings of the retina lie at the back of the eye, where they're insulated within a deep, bony socket. Except for diaphragm openings for protection against severe glare, this system is the way the eye protects itself. The metal – most likely a piece of the canopy – tore through the soft part of the eye, slammed into the bony socket and crushed the nerves there. We're helpless to restore your sight, Steve.'

'No favorite theories?'

'No theory, I'm afraid. Your eyes contain something on the order of a hundred million neurons, which are layered in the retina at the back of the eye. What happens back there we still classify as a miracle—'

'You keep using that damn word. Why?'

'Because with all we know, we can't tell you how it all works. We simply don't *know*. We know that the light from the front of your eye focuses at the retina. But how do the neurons in the retina convert light waves into electrical signals? We haven't any real idea. We know they send an electronic-signal interpretation of a light wave to the brain. There, again by some unknown process, the signal gets translated into what the brain accepts as a visual image. We know about the cones that define colors and the rods that aid in seeing in dim or scarce light, and we can tell what the eye does and the process it follows, but not *why*. No one can explain how the rods of the eye can pick up light as faint as a trillionth of a watt.

'There's nothing we can do to replace that vision. Oh, we can build microwave receptors, or infrared sensors and all sorts of wonderful things, but we cannot give you vision where you lost your eye. Of course, you still have superb vision in your right eye. Twenty-fifteen, in fact, and you'll learn quickly to compensate for the depth perception you miss so much at this point.'

'That's a crock and you know it,' Steve said with sudden heat.

'There's a world of difference between depth perception for the ground, and what a man needs to fly a . . .'

Wells kept his voice gentle. 'Steve, I'd like to make a promise to you. If you'll work with me, with Dr. Killian, I can promise you something.' He paused, the spacing of his words deliberate. 'In six months you can fly again.'

On Steve's face a mixture of desire to believe, and bitter disbelief. Then he slumped again. 'Only a son of a bitch would make a statement like that,' he said at last.

'Then consider me a son of a bitch. But if you want to, you can fly in just about six months from now.'

CHAPTER TEN

'He's under.'

Dr. Killian nodded. He studied the oscilloscopes and glanced back to Dr. Wells. 'Under, but not really out. Look at the wave. The subconscious is working overtime.'

Wells studied the glowing scope. 'He's got a lot to think about.'

'We all do,' Killian said.

'I wonder if that was a wise decision, Michael.'

'Taking him into the cryogenic chamber?'

'Yes. It seemed to upset him, seeing pieces of himself laid out like so many parts of an automobile.'

'It had the shock effect we wanted.'

'You playing psychologist this morning?'

'Don't we always?' Killian glanced at the unconscious form of Steve Austin. 'The next several months are going to be trying – for him, for all of us. Austin will spend much of his time reflecting on what's happening to him. There's no way he can avoid chewing over the fact that foreign objects now hold him together. You were absolutely correct in making certain he understood what had been done to him. Now he knows we're patching him together with himself. That will go deep. It was the right move. It will help.'

Rudy Wells looked down at Steve's face. A muscle in the right cheek twitched. 'I hope so,' he said. 'He'll need all the help he can get.'

Never heard anything like that before. The way he brought it up. Didn't understand. Whole thing's impossible. Dream, that's all. One more nightmare on top of another. Christ. Too much to hope for. Gotta face it. All there is to it. Face it, Stevie, old boy. No legs. Both of them right above the knees. They're playing God. No other way to do what they're talking about, right? Hey, God, you listening? Ol' Doc Wells is all mixed up. Thinks he's you. You listening up there? You better listen. Doc Wells is

*gonna push you right out of your job. Him and the other one,
Killian. They both think they're you . . .*

He drifted, formless, no legs or arms or even a body, only one
eye, a cyclopean view of everything and nothing, an infinite
spiral winding downward. Voices came to him, and faces ma-
terialized from a space different from anything he'd known, even
on the trip to the moon. He saw the face of his friend and
doctor; and Rudy Wells's voice drifted down the spiral after
him, circling him until it hovered before him, held him prisoner
until Wells's face could catch up to them both, and the face and
the voice joined, and the scene came to him again . . .

'You lost both legs. Fact.'
Steve looked at him from the bed. The strict diet of medicinal
liquids for a week had him on the thin edge. He didn't need
nonsense cooked in philosophical crap. It was all rather grotesque. He didn't answer. One hardly needs conversation with a
gargoyle, he decided.
'Now, then,' Wells continued, 'a question. How long should
the legs of a man be?'
'You've flipped, Doc. You're hypoxic. Better have Jean bring
some oxygen.'
Wells shook his head. 'A long time ago, Steve, someone gave
the only real answer to that question. His name was Abraham
Lincoln. He said the legs of a man should be long enough to
reach the ground.' Steve would be unconscious for two weeks to
a month. No way to tell yet. Better to get as much said now as
possible. Killian was right. Give him the answers before the
questions clog his mind.
Steve wouldn't reply.
'You can't shut me out that completely, Steve. I won't be able
to talk with you for several weeks. You know that already.
I—'
'That will be a *relief*.'
Wells sighed. 'Look, Steve, can't you understand this has
nothing to do with prosthetics? They're artificial, certainly. But
prosthetics is as much vanity as it is utility, *and these will be
living limbs.* We—'
'What the hell are you going to do? Graft someone else's legs
onto me, for God's sake? What are you waiting for? Some poor

96

bastard to die so you can cut off his legs and rush them here to stick onto me? Rudy, will you go away and leave me the hell alone? Stick the needle in my arm and put me out so I won't have to take this shit any more.'

Patience, Wells ordered to himself.

'Steve, a bionics limb has the type of feedback that you will be able to sense. Not sensations as you know them. But you *will* feel certain things. We're not copying nature; we're going to duplicate the processes and you'll have full, and I mean full, mobility. You'll be able to—'

'Dance? How about that, Doc? Think I can make it with the now generation? Looka him go, folks, old Bionics Bob to the center of the floor! Looka how he—'

'*Goddam you, Austin, I didn't push you into that cockpit!*'

Instantly Wells was sorry. He was here to ease the way for Steve, and instead he lost control over the bitter words of a man who—

'I owe you an apology for that,' he said stiffly, 'but this isn't a social exchange. If you and I are going to discuss this as equals, instead of as a doctor, and a patient who's afraid to face reality—'

'Screw you.'

'—then we might as well know how it really is. Your body's been torn up but your psyche is undamaged. A bit twisted, I admit. Maybe more than a bit, and sometimes deliberately savage. But still undamaged, and undaunted. You can be quite a son of a bitch, you know.'

For the first time in days there appeared the trace, the barest trace, of a smile on Steve's lips. 'Touché, doctor,' he said quietly.

They had prepared for weeks for this moment. For weeks they refined, checked, and adjusted for the thousandth time. They knew every line, every nerve, every sinew, muscle, tendon, bone, every feature and detail of his legs. They had built – no, that wasn't the word for it. They had created, lovingly, with infinite attention to detail, a bionics and electronics duplicate of what had been the legs of Steve Austin. Elaborate medical records were available on this man since as a test pilot and an astronaut he had undergone exhaustive medical tests and their results had been recorded. Every detail, down to the electrical resistance of his system, the salinity of his liquids, the thickness of his muscle and nerve fibers, all these things were known, and now they added to that knowledge through the extraordinary examinations and tests of their own.

For weeks they had prepared the man. They anesthetized his leg stumps so that they could get in there, remove the skin that had stabilized. They had to by-pass, to cut, to reroute the tubes and the systems through which his body fluids coursed. This they did, sometimes using his own body units they had saved in supercold storage since the crash on the California desert; and where revascularization was not possible, they used plastic and cerosium and Dacron and silastic and whatever else was necessary. Several times it was necessary to measure the electrical currents, the feeble but life-supplied charges that flashed through the body, that ran from the brain down through the thick cabling of the spinal column to his extremities. During such times, Steve Austin slipped into the deep unconsciousness of the electrosleep machine and was gone from the world, either suspended in timeless space or burdened with the dreams that suffused his subconscious. And while he was gone, Dr. Killian and his staff were exposing the critical elements of the legs. They were opening nerves and tendons and preparing bone. They were on the brink of a new world of the human and bionics, of joining living flesh and bone to electronics and steel and vitallium and plastic and tiny, powerful units of nuclear energy.

When finally they were ready for the ultimate moment, the joining of the two worlds through the person of Steve Austin, he was placed even deeper into his unconscious state. For there would be pain now, where there had been none for many months. Where the body had stabilized, they must destabilize. They must open the cables and wires of the human body that carry messages of awareness and pressure and feel, and, of necessity, pain. That was the price. Steve would not have been capable of withstanding the surges of energy, the spasms of twitching, jerking, the convulsions as these elements of his body came alive. Human and human-made were brought together, connected, spliced, wired, sealed. Raw flesh was treated and joined with what was not flesh so that the two might function together as the human entity had performed before the limbs were mutilated and severed.

As he slept, he came back to life. As he swam deep in blackness, electrical probes were applied to his system. His body twisted, his body snapped, as the men attending him worked with feverish anticipation and brooding concern. As he slept they applied pressure to the soles of his bionics feet, and side pressures, twisting forces. They measured the flow of electrical energy from his brain down through the intricate nerve networks. They studied with their sensitive instruments how the feeble electric charge was received at the junction of human and artificial. It was there that what was being transmitted through a living system which had grown now was sensed and picked up by a living system that had been fabricated. The signal was terribly weak, but whisper-sensitive instruments in the bionics limbs picked up the electrical ghosts. The instant the instruments detected the incoming signals they flashed on the word for the signals to be amplified one thousandfold. The boosted signal went down to intricate, articulated joints that could bend, twist, and flex. A need for power was flashed through the system. Small motors spinning with nuclear energy received the signal, and in their response sent greater energy into the joints. It was the same signal that the legs Steve had been born with received and by which they functioned. The legs moved. The limbs flexed, bent, twisted, articulated. As he slept, his limbs came to life. Then the tests were done.

Nothing more could happen now until the raw connections had time to heal. There could be no movement until fusion became fact; until nature and man's products joined as one. They blocked off the flow of energy to the limbs. They kept him unconscious. When he awakened he would not be the same man. He would still be missing an arm, still be blind in one eye. But he would no longer be a man without legs. How useful those legs would be was unknown. The doctors had done their best. The bionicists and technicians and scientists had done their best.

The rest would be up to the man. All the others could do now was to wait.

'Jean, you'll have to be with him almost constantly.'
'I understand.'

'Of course, you'll need standby help. The technical group will always have somebody here twenty-four hours a day. They'll be monitoring the instruments.'

She nodded. 'Will they have to work directly with him? I mean, with—'

'With his body?' Wells shook his head. 'No, not unless something goes wrong.' He made a sour face. He was dog-tired, beaten physically, as were the others. 'And that would be a full emergency. No, they won't have to touch him.'

'I feel better about that.'

He looked at her. Like the others, she was nervous, overtired.

'It's a feeling doctor. He needs some privacy, for God's sake. I've got to attend to his needs, and for his sake I'd rather not do that with a bunch of gawking spectators,' she said.

'They're hardly that, Jean. You've got the right feeling,' he said. 'Who did you pick for your relief?'

'I thought there'd be no question about that.'

'Kathy?'

'Who else? She won't let anyone else near him, except me.'

He nodded. 'Tomorrow we'll start to bring him out of it. Only partially, however. We don't want his system coming full tilt into his rebuilding. The shock could be so severe it might undo everything we've accomplished.'

'Kathy says it would be a super short-circuit.'

He saw it again. A simultaneous look. From the cockpit and from the eye of the camera, the zoom lens slamming in tight so he could see every detail, see himself in the cockpit. He could hear it as well. The scream of metal and that gutting cry of flame out on the California desert. A finale at over two hundred miles an hour, with metal churning – and himself right in the middle. Thirty-two years come to its sky-tearing, earth-thudding blossom on a hard desert floor . . .

He was the youngest astronaut to walk on the moon. They had great plans for him. He would be one of nine men to spend up to two months aboard Skylab II, the big space station orbiting the earth at three hundred miles. While the station flight was being readied he went back to test flying. What better program

100

than the wicked lifting bodies preceding the flights of the Orbiters for the shuttle program? Because that put him right in the lead group to go back into space in the late seventies and the early eighties. He'd be younger then, and with far more experience, than was Al Shepard when he touched down on the moon's dusty surface in Apollo XIV.

People looked for something different in Steve Austin. Something different from what they found in the other astronauts. They looked for it and they were disappointed, because what they discovered was only more of the same. Individualistic as he might be and was, Steve Austin was still outwardly a product of the mold from which test pilots and astronauts were formed. You didn't earn your qualifications by straying from the hard line of training and necessary experience. If you were that eager to catch the public eye in being artistically different, then you could kiss the moon good-bye, and fast. Deke Slayton, who ran the astronaut office, was interested only in the mission and the best men to fly the mission, and your ass was on the way *out* when you didn't tack to the winds required by the astronaut office. The difference that mattered was being a little bit faster, smarter, and better than the best.

One of the keys to success was keeping your individuality concealed from the public. The astronauts *were* different, one from the other. The seats available to the moon and the Skylab were limited and they fought each other like wildcats and pulled every trick in the book – honest and less so – to shove some other guy out of the way so that they could slap ass into the seat they wanted. That was the name of the game. But to the world you showed the same bland expression. Those were the rules. If you took the records of fifty men who qualified both as test pilots and astronauts you would find an astonishing sameness of the breed. Individually every man would be different, and their variations at times were wide gulfs of personality and type-casting. But not in their professional traits. Their health was excellent (it had to be) and their physical coordination and capabilities no less so (they had to be). They had the basic social amenities. It's just as easy to pick a man who pleases you as it is a snarling lone wolf when both men are essentially of the same caliber. Screwing up socially under the eyes of the news media could get you bounced from a moon ride. It wasn't worth being a character – even if you were one.

Among themselves, where it couldn't hurt, Steve Austin's fellow astronauts considered him close to a genius. Predictably, Steve had earned his masters in aerodynamics and astronautical engineering, but raised eyebrows with a third masters in history. The eyebrows went higher when one considered the time he had to spend away from his intellectual pursuits to manage his levels of skill in the physical activities he favored. He was a star athlete in most sports, but found his greatest challenge, and satisfaction, on the mat – wrestling, judo, and aikido were his favorites. He had applied himself with such energy to these that his trophies included black belts in both judo and aikido. Aikido especially taught control over mind as much as discipline of body. To steel his body with the fluid motions and speed of aikido, he also took up boxing and fencing and rounded things out with acrobatics.

He came to test flying and the astronaut corps along a unique route. Rather than the Air Force, he had selected the Army so that he could become skilled in both fixed-wing and helicopter flight. He flew a gunship in Vietnam, sickened himself with the bloody carnage worked by the hellish firepower of his cannon and rockets, and almost welcomed the burst of machine-gun fire out of a jungle thicket that shattered his rotors and sent the gunship whirling crazily into the trees. Steve had himself the million-dollar wound. Three broken ribs and assorted lacerations that would heal without problem bought his ticket back to the States.

He transferred to the Air Force, breezed through the cadet programs, and slipped into the heady stuff of flying along the edge of the world. Special training, overseas duty, pressure, and good luck carried him into the cockpit of the SR-71, a great razorlike black beast that cruised at two thousand miles an hour twenty miles above the earth – on the edge of it; high enough to see the world curving away its horizons to right and left. The black spaces beyond were seductive, and he slipped into the last selection as a member of the backup crew for Apollo XVII. Lucky break in more ways than one. The lunar-module pilot broke his arm two weeks before liftoff, and Steve Austin was shifted from backup to prime crew and became one of the two

102

of the last men to walk the featherweight gravity of the moon.

There was a question about his returning. But the moon was being abandoned by his country, and until the United States was ready with nuclear engines and a whacking big budget to start the first permanent lunar base, there wasn't any use holding your breath. You could get awfully blue in the face in ten or more years. The concept of manned flight to Mars tugged at him, but the red planet lay a good many budgets and national priorities away. Still, men would be returning to space and he knew he *must* one day be in the environment he had found so much to his liking, so completely natural; the incredible weightlessness, the surging marvel of seeing the glowing planet as a dazzling jewel suspended in velvet black. Well, flight testing the lifting bodies was the best answer, and he went after the toughest assignments in the program because that was the only way for him. He slid along the edges of space once more in the vicious aerodynamic bathtubs that skittered like fidgety waterbugs on a shifting lake of thin atmosphere. It was rough. It was the best chance of punching his ticket for the big ride back into vacuum.

There was the 'other' Steve Austin. The man the public recognized as a past combat pilot, a test pilot, the youngest of the astronauts, a man who'd been on the moon, who stood six feet, one inch tall, with eyes deep blue; a lean, muscled frame, almost rangey; a laugh filled with warmth; and an animal attraction about him.

His bachelor status brought much conversation and considerable plotting by large numbers of leggy, busty, anticipating women. Not bad; not bad at all. Even the barracudas zeroing in weren't bad; cool sheets may have been their hunting grounds, but Steve was adept in that territory and elusive beyond the bedroom door.

Until he returned to the flight test center in the California desert. The moon was now behind him. He had proved a good deal to himself. Now was time for a different perspective.

Jan Richards came into that perspective, and ready as he was, the fall was fast and marvelous.

And then ... that terrible fiery stalk blossoming across the desert. It came back to him again, that shifting veil of memory, and through the unwinking eye of bloody flame he heard his name being called. A deep booming summons, far off, rushing closer and closer to him. Steve, Steve, Steve . . .

The faces swam in a blur before him. He blinked his eye, tried to focus. One face moved, a sickening reel to the side. He closed his eye, forced the world to stop spinning. *Try to think,* he ordered himself. *C'mon, let's get with it . . .*

'It's me, Steve. Rudy Wells.' He recognized the voice. Something to hang onto. That'll be better. He opened his eye again, waited for the blurs to dissolve and melt into one another. There. Good old Doc Wells. Clear now. And who . . . sure, Dr. Killian. Steve turned his head to the left. Something gold there. Hair. Jean, looking down at him.

'Take it slow, Steve.' Doc's voice, calm enough. He looked again at the faces. What . . . He voiced his thoughts.

'What is this? A wake?'

Doc smiled. 'No, Steve. Anything but. Can you remember what's been happening?'

He tried. It was like slogging through mud but he was getting there. Sure. The long preparations, then going into that deep, deep sleep.

'Yeah,' he said weakly. 'I remember. Nothing different. Just you and me having one of our fireside chats.' He was amazed. Weak; damn, he felt weak.

'Strange,' he murmured.

Wells leaned closer to him. 'What was that, Steve?'

'Strange thing, doc.' He groped for the words. 'I – I feel heavy. Crazy, isn't it?' He held the words back for a while, trying to think.

'Heavy, Steve? That is strange. What do you mean by that?'

'Don't know . . . Like I said, crazy feeling. Heavy. I mean heavier than before . . . before sleep . . .'

His face went white, as if they could see the blood draining away. Killian signaled a doctor who stood by for any emergency. Steve saw none of this, saw only Rudy Wells's face.

'What's the matter, Steve?'

He was completely white now, his body rigid. His arm came up, grabbed Wells's wrist.

'Doc!'

The sweat poured from his forehead. Jean Manners started forward with a cloth to wipe it away. Dr. Killian motioned her to stay back.

'Doc, I—'

'What is it, Steve?'

'My God . . . doc . . .

'*My . . . feet . . . hurt . . .*'

CHAPTER ELEVEN

'Mr. Goldman, you are forcing me to repeat myself.'

'I apologize, Dr. Killian. You said that the major surgery has been accomplished?'

'That was in my report. Yes.'

'What stage is Colonel Austin in? I mean right now.'

Dr. Killian consulted notes on his desk. 'It is what Dr. Wells calls orientation. Their relationship is remarkable. The legs and the arm have been attached, as you know. We have already gone through a series of adjustments. Electrical feedback, servomotor trim, as we call it. There have been difficulties in the interface of the two limbs, the natural and the bionics. None of these was unexpected. We have not yet applied the full pressure on the joining interface. That comes soon. What we are doing now, what Dr. Wells is doing, I should say, is going over detailed transparent models of different systems. With Colonel Austin, of course. We have prepared full working models, assemblies and subassemblies. Dr. Wells feels it is imperative for Austin to understand every last element of his bionics reconstruction, and this understanding is expected to assist his control.'

'I agree with him,' Goldman said.

'I'm sure he will be pleased to hear that.'

'I'm just as sure Dr. Wells doesn't much give a damn whether or not I agree,' Goldman said. 'How are these sessions set up? Between the colonel and Dr. Wells, I mean.'

'They meet in Colonel Austin's room. It's really a large chamber with movable walls. All the equipment we need is therefore within easy reach.'

'Anyone else with Dr. Wells?'

'Miss Manners, of course. And Miss Norris is often there.'

'She's the lab technician, isn't she?'

'She is also an RN, Mr. Goldman.'

'Yes, sir. I was aware of that. She's also much taken with the colonel, isn't she?'

'You seem to have your sources of information, Mr. Goldman.'

'Doctor, as you know, Smythe is our representative. He needed to go no further than listening to conversation in the dining room to know that. I assure you we have no spy ring in your hospital here. As I explained before, Dr. Killian, we will not interfere. But I would like to sit in on several of these sessions – I presume they're preliminary to the actual walking tests? – so that I can get a feel for how things are going.'

'You are not a member of the staff and *that* is interference. What if a question is directed to you?'

Goldman smiled. 'Then I will answer it, Dr. Killian. Between us – and I would like this to go no further than yourself or Dr. Wells – I have my masters in electronics and computer systems.'

Killian nodded. 'You are rather an unusual man, Mr. Goldman.'

'Yes, Dr. Killian. I am.'

They were surrounded by transparent models of human systems – torsos, limbs, the head, and brain. Different models for nerve networks, alive with flashing lights representing in slow motion the path of electrical currents. Others indicated muscle fiber, tendons, sinews, bones. Still others were two and three times normal life size to emphasize particular areas of the body, the switching points, articulated joints, points of flexibility and where extra loads were born. The walls were hung with charts and diagrams. There were individual models of knee and wrist joints, ankles and elbows, all several times life size, all intended to bring out certain specific areas and methods of operation.

There was another group of limbs. These differed from the representations of the human anatomy. These were the bionics systems, and they too were broken down into separate units and enlarged. Where there were diagrammatic representations for the human limbs, the bionics units seemed to be from the guidance systems of missiles or the electronic innards of spacecraft destined for distant planets. Working models of sensors, wire connections, solenoids, amplification systems, cables and pulleys; they were all there, the bionics equivalents to their predecessor limb.

The models, working systems, charts, diagrams, and stacks of manuals and schematics were placed in a wide semicircle around the long, wide room, which had been expanded to its present size by removing ceiling-to-floor partitions. In the center of the room was Steve Austin in his special bed. There was a difference in his appearance. The man who had lost both legs and his left arm now showed the full limbs of a normal person. A dark patch still covered his left eye, and his hair remained cropped almost to the point of a shaven skull. Otherwise there seemed little resemblance between this man and the same Steve Austin who had been here months before, with only a single limb to his body.

Several tables had been placed about the bed, and behind these sat or stood a dozen men. Dr. Rudy Wells was one. Oscar Goldman, introduced as an electronics specialist in sensing systems, was another. The others were specialists in bionics systems, stress equipment, mechanical drives. They were all members of the team that had spent months working together in the attempt to make the quantum jump into the future. The man about whom they stood would be the measure of their success or failure. Moments earlier the room had been dark, the assembled group watching an animated film following the passage of electrical signals through a human system into a bionics system. It had been a film intended to show one man what he had become.

'All right,' Wells was saying, 'let's consider this a working review. Question-and-answer time if necessary. Set?' Steve acknowledged with a curt nod. He had become unusually quiet, not so much withdrawn as deeply involved in his own thoughts, as if he were working overtime to assimilate the staggering changes to his system that one day might be commonplace, but which at this moment were unprecedented.

'We could have replaced your arm with a human graft, could have effected nerve and other connections, regained circulation. Aside from the rejection factor, of course, but that's really the least of it. The point is that we would remain within far more unknowns than are presented by the bionics systems. At this point, to add this on to the other factors, whatever we could do

108

would be partial. I said we could have restored circulation, but not full circulation. The arm has thousands of tubal connections beyond our capacity to handle. We can't match millions of years of evolution. We're talking about billions of living cells, an extraordinarily complex venous and arterial network, capillary action, of interfacing tendons and bones, of assuring red blood cell manufacture, of natural articulation and sensitivity of arm and hand hairs for kinesthetic sensing, of temperature measuring devices nature prepares for all parts of the body. We would have had to assure the proper functioning of thousands of intricate nerve sensors in the fingertips, of the ability to perspire or to close off pores as internal and external conditions allow. Success would have been partial. Dr. Killian and his staff are extraordinary. They are not supermen.'

Wells pushed aside a thick manual before him. He was nearly exhausted; the mental strain had been far worse on him than the others, and he had found little time for sleep or physical rest in recent days. But it was essential that he get these points down to Steve before the next several days, which would be the most critical hours in his 'rebirth'.

'At the same time, when we consider everything we've discussed for the past several weeks, Steve, it is vital to remember you are an adult human being with the most extraordinary computer ever known – your brain. You have, also, the values of experience, and logical paths to pursue based on that experience. All these factors, everything we have talked about,' Wells gestured to include the paraphernalia piled about the room, 'combine to make possible a living limb created by artificial means.' He pointed to the left arm that had not been there six weeks ago.

'That limb will not do all the things which your own arm could do. It will never be able to match the extraordinary flexibility given you by nature. At the same time, because of our advances in bionics, because of your intelligence and experience, because of adaptability, it provides enormous compensations. In some ways it can be a superior limb. Let's try an example.'

He paused long enough to drain cold coffee from a cup before him, then went on. 'For example. Let's say you study a flat, white-paneled sheet with several dark objects placed on that sheet. Let's look at what nature has enabled you to do, when you decide to do it.'

He looked at Steve, who nodded slowly.

'The light falling on that sheet is absorbed or reflected in the pattern formed by the objects. This reflection is what your optical system detects. Your eye is both a biological sensor and an electrochemical transducer. The system generates a barrage of nerve impulses through the optical network, passing it into a specific area of your brain.

Steve gestured to interrupt and Wells waited. 'How is this message, the nerve impulses, passed on?'

Wells turned to a man at his left, an electronics-systems expert. Steve had come to know Art Fanier well in the past several months. Fanier knew Steve even better. He had created the nerve networks for his bionics limbs. 'Art, you want to handle that?'

Fanier spread out his hands, palms up. 'We don't know, Steve. No one really knows. We all know that the system works, but we can't tell you *how*.'

'We can follow the process all the way through the system, but its specifics still elude us,' Wells said, and motioned to a technician. 'Let me have the optical system chart, Harry. Here, Steve, you can see how the pattern works. When the message arrives at its destination, the brain cells immediately trigger a feedback. New nerve impulses go out, here,' he tapped the chart with a pointer, 'and they direct your eye muscles to focus on the pattern of objects placed on the sheet before you.'

'How does the brain trigger the feedback?'

'That's the part that we don't know,' Art Fanier broke in. 'We've measured the electrical output, the pathways followed, the speed of signals. But how all these messages go back and forth is still a mystery.'

'Okay,' Wells said, 'we're at that point where your eye muscles have been told to focus on the objects. We now have a secondary feedback, a constant feedback system that now triggers the computer part of your brain to carry out an immediate search of your memory banks. Do you recognize this pattern you're studying? Is it familiar to you? If it's not familiar, can you correlate it with some other experience? Can you determine what it is?

'The feedback that continues throughout all this activity is electrical. You have now determined what you're seeing. It is *not* familiar. But there's enough associative memory here for you to figure out what it is. By now you have studied, researched, computed and decided. What has been an incredible, complicated, coordinated effort is to you but a single instant thought.

'Now,' Wells said, tapping the chart, 'it's time for your brain to shift into another gear. Do you want to pick up one of those objects for closer study? This triggers a vast chain reaction within your brain, which in itself directs a flurry of orders and institutes a vast system of electrical impulses through your nerve system. You commit. You make the decision to pick up one of those interesting objects.'

Steve waited in silence. 'This is where we get into the ball game, Steve,' Art Fanier said. 'Until this time your own system has done everything. But yours is no longer the same system we all have. You lost that, and we've brought it back to you, we hope, in a new way.' Fanier looked troubled. 'If things work out, if the theories are true . . .'

'We'll find out soon enough, Art,' Steve told him. He didn't like the sudden turn of conversation. He would be activated, which was a hell of a word to use about a human, and yet it was the only word that applied. He'd be activated and they'd find out if theory would work. He turned to Wells who was waiting to continue.

'It's decision time,' said the doctor. 'The brain sends out a new wave of signals. This is the implementation of your decision. The electrical signals flash down a tremendous splay of nerve networks.' The pointer in Wells's hand moved along the body pathways on the chart. 'All this time, of course, you're burning energy to produce electricity – this is the electro-chemical process – and the electricity is causing muscles to react on command. By react, well, perhaps I should use the term, selectively contract. The muscles in your forearm tighten. This in turn stretches and contracts the tendons of your wrist and your fingers. Your fingers send back their own messages – this is the steady feedback operating – relating to sensitivity and the grasping pressure necessary for you to overcome gravity, the mass of the object, by lifting that object.'

111

The pointer dropped on the table. Wells rubbed his forehead. 'As you pick up the object the signals rush back and forth. You bend your arm, twist your wrist, bring the object closer to you, change your optical focus, relate what you see and feel to past memories and new impressions, and all this time you're storing away data in new memory banks.

Wells paused again, motioning to an assistant for a fresh pot of coffee. 'We can't duplicate this system. We wouldn't even try. But what we can do, what we have done, in fact, is to use this science of bionics. We've reduced to mathematical symbols the events we just discussed. The engineers converted those symbols into tools and they produced the bionics limbs. But it's much more than building an arm or a leg that looks like the original. Everyone in this project has worked on the miniaturization level and below. A few years ago all of this would have been impossible. What these people have done under Dr. Killian,' Wells gestured to take in the group in the room, 'is to carry out a many-faceted process. It's a matter of connection, fusing – fusing is the best word I can think of, really – the bionics system with the same elements that existed where your arm was amputated. This is the real key to everything, Steve. When you look at an object, and decide to pick up that object, the signals that leave your brain must transfer to the bionics limb as if it were your own.'

Steve glanced to his left where the bionics limb – the living arm, they called it – was strapped to his side, waiting to be tested. He heard Wells's voice as if from a distance. 'The processes must duplicate what went on before. The operations of your optical system, brain input and output, sensory signals, feedback ... they must all work as if there had never been any gross alteration to the limb.'

Wells had a new chart brought to the table and started using the pointer again. 'Let's follow this routing, Steve. Your brain sends down its signals in the form of electrical impulses. These travel through the nerve network of your body. While your arm remained a stump ...' Wells paused, decided against any niceties, and went on, 'the signals terminated where the limb was severed. But now the wires in your bionics limb are connected directly – fused, as I said – with those of the stump. They have literally become a single unit. And the elements of the

112

bionics limb have been programmed to respond in direct proportion to the electrical signal that is sent out by your brain. They are also programmed to respond in the same manner as did your entire arm. This is the computer aspect of the bionics system. It's basically the same system for man or machine.'

'A good analogy, Steve,' Art Fanier said, 'would be the power-control system of an aircraft. The brain sends out a signal for a right turn. Your right arm and leg move the proper controls. When you move the controls you send a signal to a system that detects what you want, and moves the controls through hydraulic boost. So long as your hands and feet are on those controls you're a bionics system, with feedback and the rest of it.' Fanier glanced at Dr. Wells.

'It's a good comparison,' Wells said. 'When you think to pick up an object, what happened before with your original arm is repeated. The electrical impulses generated by your brain command everything. The electrical current – call it voltage or resistance or anything that fits – works the same way. The artificial muscles – Art, let me have that model there, please. The muscles, which in this case are silastic and vitallium pulleys, then contract, twist, and tighten. Everything your own arm did. You can even sense with your fingertips.' Wells tapped the model fingers. 'Your arm, your new fingers, have vibratory sensors. They detect pressure; they send the pressure signals back to the brain, precisely as before. The feedback system is the same. We can't quite match the flexibility of wrist and forearm and fingers that nature gave you, but where you lose you also gain.

'Your arm should have – and we'll find out soon enough now – on the order of ten times the gripping and handling strength you once had. The same applies, of course, for your fingers. Objects you could never dent with your natural fingers before, well, now you should be able to crush them like an eggshell. Your brain, Steve, will carry through every function with which you're familiar, except pain.'

He paused, an instinctive reflex. How could he forget what Steve had said when he regained consciousness after the long weeks while his new limbs fused to his body? *My feet hurt . . .*

He looked up to see a bemused smile on Steve's face. 'I had some thoughts about that,' Steve said.

'Some people call it psychological carry-over,' Wells told him. They had discussed it before.

'I know,' Steve said. 'It's a familiar syndrome. Man loses his legs, he still feels pain. His brain is really lying to him. You can also call it psychological compensation. A way for the ego to refuse reality. But that's not what happened to me, is it?' It was more statement than question.

'No,' Wells said. 'We're in an unknown area here. One can argue the very existence of pain. It doesn't exist, if you take one particular viewpoint. Pain is simply a survival message, instinctive protection signals transmitted with tremendous energy from the brain.'

'That's bullshit and you know it, Rudy.'

Their audience remained absolutely silent. To the bionics and cybernetics teams the exchange was critical. Steve Austin at this moment was the only true cybernetics organism living. *Cyborg*, they called him in the laboratories. And whatever his reaction, it was a measure, successful or otherwise, of their theories and labors. Whatever they heard in this room from this man, whatever he did in the following weeks and months and, they hoped, years, was the beginning of that new science of theirs come to life.

'It is not, as you say,' Wells mildly protested, 'bullshit to me. It is an area open to question. Subjectively, pain is real. So long as the nerve endings are functional there can be pain. When the nerve endings are blocked, physical damage results but there is no signal sent to the brain. Instinctive protection no longer exists. In your case you now have nerve endings *of some sort*. Whether or not the brain will accept the signals as they did before is open to question.'

Steve said no more, waiting for him to go on to the legs. Wells looked at Steve.

'The legs are simpler than the arm. The articulation is less complicated. The knee itself has minor sideways articulation. Fore-and-aft movement is mechanically simple.' The pointer moved along the chart. 'The ankle fits in the same category. The fore-and-aft articulation is much the same. Both elements, of course, have some sideways motion, but this is restricted by the limitations built into freedom of the ball-socket, or hinge, joints. In terms of opting for greater strength, we restricted the artificial tendons to provide the limited elasticity needed for, as an example, rounding through a running turn.'

Steve gestured impatiently. 'Let's get to the power amplification, Rudy.'

Wells nodded, shifted to new charts. 'All right. The energy for articulation – the electrical impulse sent along the nerve network by brain command – isn't great enough to cause the bionics limb to react through muscle contraction and movement. The voltage is far too low, and we can't avoid the fact that we're working with different systems. Different materials, in fact. The body provides electrochemical reaction throughout the entire system. That's impossible with the bionics elements.

'So we compensate for this.' He held up a model of a leg section. 'What the electrical impulse originating from the brain must do, then, is to trigger another energy source within the bionics limb. In this case we provide additional energy. The best way to do this is not through solenoids, which could result in a staccato or jerking movement, but through the latest advances in electrical motors. Art?'

Fanier moved closer to Steve and held up a metal cylinder barely an inch long by a half inch in diameter. 'This came directly from the stabilization system of a military-reconnaissance satellite TV system, intended for long life. Necessary to maintain a specific attitude over the earth's surface for the cameras. There's nothing else in the world like it. Once it's brought to speed, it spins at better than thirty thousand revs per minute. The sealed environment is as close to being free of friction as you can get. Of course, we've got to be able to sustain the inertia of spin and we use a plutonium isotope, but with something less than the half-life of ninety years. The cardiac pacemakers that have been used for a couple of years now use the longer-lived isotope. We needed to alter the system and, well, you can break down the details later if you want, Steve, but the main point is that we have this tremendous frictionless spin. There's enough inertia in this system to provide immediate translation of the energy to what we need to move. In your case, the bionics limb. I mean, this provides energy for articulating whatever part of the limb is involved.'

Fanier moved the small motor housing into a breakaway model of the bionics arm that was now a part of Steve's body.

'This has a pressure-sensing system, of course. When the message is received to grasp or to pick up an object, the motors apply energy to the pulley system of the arm. This makes rigid certain areas of the limb, applies pressure to the fingers—'

'How?'

'Well, the amount of pressure is decided by the electrical impulses that originate from the brain. These are fed the pressure from the sensory pads in the fingertips – the pressure is converted to an electrical signal, the intensity of which varies with the situation – and we have a constant feedback. The result of this feedback is exactly the same as with a natural arm. It's translated into energy demand, energy supply, and motion.

'This means,' Fanier said, 'that the body itself isn't being called upon to provide the constant energy. It couldn't do it. We could implant dissimilar metals in tissues of your body that contain salt water and the metals would function as batteries. A lifetime source, I guess you could call it, since the body provides a natural source of fresh electrolyte. But the body produces only about one-half volt, and even the simplest instruments implanted in the body, such as the pacemakers, need at least one and a half to two volts. But the nuclear sources change everything. With these power sources, Steve, a man can run – a steady, pacing run – just so long as he remains conscious and his other body systems are working. If his heart and circulation and brain and respiration are working, a man could run for days and nights. His legs are – *your* legs – are motivated simply enough through the minuscule electrical charges of the brain's impulses. But the key, the driving energy, comes from these internal power systems. Internal to the bionics limb, I mean. It's ... it's really incredible.'

He came to with his heart pounding, the perspiration streaming down the sides of his face. What a dream ... Something almost psychedelic. He saw a figure silhouetted against a horizon. The foreground absolutely dark, above the horizon line a gleaming, pale orange, intensely bright glow, and that running figure stark against the orange. The figure was running, a methodical pounding beat, breathing deeply and evenly. Tremendous breath control ...

'You've been having a nightmare,' Jean said quickly, to bring him back to the moment. 'You're strapped down, Steve. You must have been trying to turn and you had this nightmare.'

He sank back in the pillow, nodding. It was cold, soaked from his sweat. He was already back into the dream.

Nightmare? Or wish fulfillment? He didn't know. If the legs worked. He laughed at himself. If the legs worked as advertised . . . the key to long-distance running is breath control. Enriching and keeping the system saturated with as much oxygen as possible. What had Rudy Wells told him? 'Your legs won't be consuming chemicals, electricity, or oxygen. Your blood flow is reduced because the circuitry has been so drastically altered. Where you need oxygen now you'll get it, far more than you ever had. There isn't even any way for us to guess what your endurance will be. You'll be a superior man, a super normal man. You may even be the start of a whole new breed . . .'

They'd find out.

Starting in the morning.

He didn't know whether he wanted that morning ever to come. The thought of failure, after all these months, would be too much to take. He—

He told himself to shut up. Sleep came quickly.

CHAPTER TWELVE

'How about under the arms?'

Steve Austin lifted his arms, flexing the biceps, straining against the nylon webbing that passed beneath the armpits. He strained forward, bunching his back muscles, then leaned from side to side.

'It's okay,' he said curtly. 'Let's get on with the rest of it.'

'Take it slow,' Rudy Wells told him. 'We've waited a long time for—'

Steve was almost snarling. 'Drop it,' he snapped. 'Let's just get it going.'

Wells didn't reply. Instead he walked about Steve as he hung suspended in the harness, a close replica of the parachute harness with which Steve had been familiar for years. Wells stepped back several paces for a final examination of the harness and suspension rig. Steve was not only familiar with the webbing straps that encased his body, but he was experienced with the suspension rig. In his astronaut training he had used a variation of this same equipment to test his balance and walking capabilities under the one-sixth gravity of the moon. It would help; there was nothing here that was strange to him.

Wells glanced about the former gymnasium, converted to the testing center for Steve. He had cleared the room of all but a few people – himself, Dr. Killian, Art Fanier, Jean Manners, and two technicians. More than that would change a working team to an audience of gawkers. Besides, they had concealed cameras to record every moment. Steve's bionics limbs as well as his own body were loaded with strain gauges and instruments. They would have a complete record of temperatures, pressures, strains in every bending, twisting, pulling motion. It would all be recorded for later study and the beginning of the test profiles for the first cybernetic organism. The parachute harness and suspension rig went up a ball-socket travelway that followed the path on the floor that Steve would follow.

'Art, we're ready,' he said to Fanier. The technician nodded, looked at Steve.

'Start at thirty percent,' Fanier said.

'Right.'

Fanier worked the controls and the harness lowered. Steve stood with his legs slightly apart, braced for the best possible support. The harness lowered until the gauges showed thirty percent of Steve's weight resting on his legs. Wells watched him like a hawk, saw the perspiration beading on his face. He glanced at the medical console. Heartbeat, respiration, the other signs. All way above normal, as expected. Jean would monitor the console so that he could keep his attention on the man.

Steve rocked slightly and Wells felt a moment of panic as he saw the slight teetering. It was a false alarm. Steve was swiftly altering his own mood, once again becoming the test pilot, checking out his equipment, regarding everything with the finely trained senses and feel of the engineer. No one said a word or made a sound as Steve stood, stiff-legged, regaining balance, swiftly learning certain key sensations denied to him now for so many months. He leaned forward again, letting the harness take up the strain, then twisted from left to right, and back again the other way. He nodded to himself, judging, testing, ignoring them all. Wells felt a tremendous satisfaction and a sense of relief. At this moment Steve was the equivalent of a man back in the cockpit, the test pilot on his own.

'Give me fifty percent.'

Fanier was startled. 'Too soon, Steve. The schedule calls for an hour at thirty and—'

'Fifty!' He leaned forward in the harness, twisted about, glared at the other man. 'Now, Art, damn you, *now*.'

Fanier licked his lips, uncertain. He turned to Killian, who exchanged glances with Rudy Wells. Wells nodded and Killian moved his hand. 'Fifty,' he said.

Fanier moved the controls. The harness lowered. Steve now had half his body weight on the legs. He stopped his twisting motion, taking in the feel. He was searching now, getting the sensations down pat, learning quickly the vices he might find, the differences he felt now that clashed with memory. Wells waited for him to move the legs. But not yet. Steve knew what he was doing, was going by instinct and experience combined.

119

Steve looked to his left and slightly down. Silence. They watched the muscles bunch inside his jaw.

The arm bent at the elbow. Steve watched the limb with hypnotic fascination. It came down again. He rested for a moment, brought the arm forward and slightly across his body to his right. He bent the arm again at the elbow, added a twisting motion, continued the arm movement. He brought his hand – his new hand – to several inches from his face. His eye stared. Slowly the fingers closed into a fist. He held it that way, opened the fingers, spread them stiff and wide, closed and opened them again. He turned his hand through twisting motions. The arm went up, then backward. Abruptly he stopped, the arm straight at his side. Suddenly he snapped out the arm, straight out to his side, the fingers extended stiffly. Then back, forward. The arm went up, slowly, until it extended above him, as far as the harness would permit. He looked up and grasped the webbing. The fingers closed into a tight grip. He began to add pressure.

'Steve! Don't! You're not ready yet!' Fanier's voice. Wells started forward, checked himself. Leave him alone, he told himself. It's his life. He's got to gamble.

It didn't matter, anyway. Steve wasn't listening. He wouldn't have heard a bomb going off next to him. His concentration was total.

The fingers closed tighter. They watched, hypnotized, as Steve's bionics arm brought his weight away from his feet. Then, slowly, Steve lifted himself completely from the floor. His body turned slightly, swaying, as he kept the grip.

'The gauges,' he called to Fanier. 'What do the gauges show?'

'You're more than a hundred percent over the test criteria,' Fanier told him.

'To hell with the criteria, give me the reading on the arm.'

Fanier looked nervously at the others, saw Wells urging him on. 'You're . . . only thirty percent.'

There was a sudden shift of tone in Steve's voice. 'Tell me again,' he said, half shouting, disbelieving.

'Thirty percent.'

'It turns out,' Steve grunted with sudden effort, 'you're a pretty smart son of a bitch, after all.' Fingers knotted about the nylon, Steve pulled himself up even more, a slow and deliberate movement until his face was even with his hand. There was a flash of a smile and he lowered himself, still slowly and with control, back to the floor until the harness released half his weight again to his feet. He stood quietly, breathing deeply, the need for oxygen more psychological than physical. He forced himself to relax, and Wells, studying every move, was grateful for the superb self-control of this man. He had thrown away their test schedule, substituting his own, but it was still one of rigid self-discipline.

'Doc?'

'Right here, Steve.'

'Water, please.'

Wells brought the glass to him. A good sign. The way Steve was perspiring, they'd need salt tablets soon. He held out the glass, instinctively extending it toward Steve's right arm.

Steve grinned at him. 'Wrong hand, doc.'

'You sure?'

'Hell, can't you see me flying?' Steve laughed. He reached out for the glass, closed the fingers of his left hand. A sudden *crack* went through the room. Steve stared at the liquid splashing away from his hand, the glass hitting the floor.

'How about that shit?' he said to no one in particular.

One of the assistants hurried forward with a towel. Wells took it, wiped away the water, picked pieces of glass from Steve. 'That's what I meant,' he said finally. 'It will take some time to fineness of control.'

'You should have told me.'

'I *did* tell you.'

'But not loud enough,' Steve laughed. Wells was thrilled by the spirit in his voice. It had been a very long time.

'Get me some metal glasses next time,' Steve said. 'Then we'll go to plastic.' He used his right hand to hold the glass now brought to him, and handed it to Wells.

'Hang in there, doc,' he told Wells. 'You look awfully worried.'

'Take it slow, Steve,' Wells cautioned him.

'You ever hear that new saying they got, doc? Something about today being the first day of the rest of your life? It's time to walk.'

It wasn't as easy as he thought. The electrical patterns stayed almost precisely where predicted. But this was much more than a matter of simply assuring that the equipment would function. They were sure of themselves in that area. It was biological feedback that held the uncertainties. How would the body receive the feedback *from* the bionics limb? That was the big question mark. The built-in safeguards, the flexibilities of the electrochemical systems of the body, couldn't be duplicated wholly in the bionics equipment. This was the major unknown. But Steve had been going into the unknown for a long time.

He motioned for the others to step back, to give him room. And again, as he had done before, he slipped away from them into that special chamber of his mind where he became the expert technician, the engineer.

He stood with his bionics feet spaced well apart, one slightly farther forward than the other. They watched, fascinated, as he brought his hands to his hips, braced them, and began the movements that – Wells realized suddenly – he had been planning all this time. First he bent forward from the waist. His body jerked suddenly as the weight shifted and the knees tried to adjust for the change in mass. He pulled himself back quickly, weaving, fighting for balance. Then, forward again, back; forward and back a dozen times. Next he began to bend backward, tilting his head and shoulders behind him slightly. A rotating motion followed, with his hands bracing him, the half-weight of his body in the harness greatly reducing unexpected shift and balance changes. He turned and twisted with slightly greater speed than before, motions fluid in their start, sometimes becoming erratic, exhibiting a sudden snapping movement, as he fought to carry his returning balance down through the legs. Finally he stopped, looked straight ahead.

'Art?'

'Right here, Steve.'

'Take the pressure off.'

'It's already at fifty percent.'

'I know that. Take it down all the way.'

'It's coming down,' Fanier called to Steve.

Silence again. Steve stood rock still, feeling the pressures. He kept his feet planted solidly to the floor and began moving the right knee. Slowly, bending it back and forth. Then, more carefully now, to the right and to the left. Again he stood still, reviewing in his mind the sensations. He repeated the motions with his right knee.

'There's some pain,' he said finally, not turning around, knowing they would hear him and that the instruments would pick up every word. 'It appears to be at the juncture of my leg and the plastiskin. I think you'd better take a look.'

He stood patiently as Killian and Wells examined the area where they had grafted the artificial skin to his own living tissue. Steve wore shorts so that the juncture remained exposed for such examination, and also for the cameras. Killian's fingers kneaded the skin. 'Feeling?' he asked Steve.

'Finger pressure.'

'Pain?'

'No.'

'Where was the pain before?'

'Along the back. Where the skin would bunch with full bending.'

Killian probed. 'Nothing shows,' he said finally. 'That's a good sign.' He half turned. 'Miss Manners, was there any anomaly in the readings at that time?'

She scanned the readouts, nodded. 'Yes, doctor, it appeared to be a current surge.'

Killian went to the monitoring console, Wells at his side. He returned several minutes later.

'It appears,' he said carefully, 'to be in the electrical flow. You are picking up a mild shock in your leg. Not the bionics limb, Steve. Something is feeding back out of control and giving you electrical shock.'

Steve nodded. 'That shouldn't take much of a fix.'

'No, but we will have to study the correlations. It will take some time.'

'Still got to try to walk.'

'That would be foolish now,' Killian argued. 'It could become much more severe.'

'Only one way to find out.'

He did. Violently. He leaned forward slightly, lifted his left leg, poised the limb above the floor, feeling the sensations, then brought it down very slowly, easing pressure onto the limb. It held.

The right foot came up, a leg seeming to move in snow, the movement deliberately exaggerated. The knee hinged, and Steve brought the leg forward and down, going for the same careful contact with the floor.

'That's one,' he said through clenched teeth.

They could hardly breathe. He went through a dozen steps the same way, a miracle before their eyes, the joining of man and machine into a single living system. He walked twenty feet, then thirty.

'Doctor!' Jean Manners, calling to Wells. He hurried to her side, saw the needle oscillating wildly.

'Steve! Hold it! Don't—'

Too late. A sudden spasm of electricity slashed through the left leg. The limb snapped straight out, the knee locking, the signals mixing wildly. Steve spun sideways, his body helpless from the sudden upthrusting of the leg. Then he went limp, sagging in the harness.

'He's unconscious,' Killian said. 'Fanier, fifty percent. At once. Take the pressure from him.'

The harness lifted slightly. Moments later they strapped him to a stretcher, started back for his room.

CHAPTER THIRTEEN

'You're expecting too much too quickly,' Wells said for the tenth time that same morning. 'You're pushing too hard. It's understandable, I admit, but—'

'But what?' Steve interrupted him. 'The arm is coming along fine, isn't it? Then what the hell's the matter with the legs? Why can't they work out that feedback problem?'

'They *are* solving the problems,' Wells said patiently. 'They're not doing it fast enough to suit you, that's all. You're forgetting the experimental nature of all this. But even more, you're forgetting just how much progress you have made.'

'Damned little.'

'That's unfair and untrue. Look at your performance on the treadmill yesterday. You ran the equivalent of five miles. Perfect pacing. Your entire system worked like a charm. You did five miles and—'

'And then fell on my ass because that damned feedback went haywire again. I was like a clumsy kid who—'

'You *are* a clumsy kid. Can't you understand that? Biologically, that happens to be the fact. Oh, for God's sake, Steve, you *know* the score. Physiologically, much of your body is that of an adult child. Your system is learning things all over again at superspeed. But it's still *confused*. The problem isn't in the bionics limbs. It's in your own nerve network. If it was a matter of modifying the limbs, we could do that. You're an engineer; you understand remote sensing. But the controls don't exist in the bionics systems, and your body has got to build up its own memory banks of the new data feeds. That's what takes time.' Wells gestured with barely controlled anger of his own. 'You've been off the harness now for three weeks. We didn't think that would be possible yet for another *month*. Can't you consider just how fast you *have* come along?'

Steve looked at him. 'Are you patronizing me, doc?'

'No, you son of a bitch, I am *not*.'

'Well, you damn well are acting like it!' In a sudden burst of rage he swept the table clean of all objects; ashtrays, manuals, coffee cups went crashing to the floor. 'I just wish to hell,' he grated, 'we could stop all this damned testing and testing . . . it's driving me up a wall, Rudy. All those people hovering around like moths and I'm the damned candle. I am damned sick of it!' He curled his fingers into fists and his left hand slammed against the table.

Wood splintered as his fist crashed through the top. For an instant the table remained where it was, then collapsed with a bang against the floor. There was shocked silence as they stared at one another.

'Oh, hell. I didn't mean to do that, doc.'

Wells rose to his feet. 'I know,' he said finally. He forced a smile to his face. 'Feel better?'

'Not really,' Steve said. 'But I would like to try the maze again. How about it?'

Wells shrugged. 'It's your ass you fall on. Do you know you've got bruises there that have bruises?'

Steve rubbed his buttocks. 'Don't I ever. C'mon, doc, nothing ventured, nothing gained, and so forth.'

The test room showed the signs of progress. The suspension harness was gone. Steve insisted on taking his bruises as payment for progress, and the room had been modified to his requests. Much of it was now a specially designed maze with winding pathways, steps, undulating surfaces, chairs, and ladders, artificial pathways with gravel and rocks, all to test the legs under a wide variety of conditions.

Rudy Wells took a chair high above the running area for a clear field of vision as Steve went through his paces. For more than an hour he hammered through the obstacles, his body working flawlessly, the bionics limbs no less so. Then the erratic pattern began. It came only in moments, but it threw him off stride. Steve ran and dodged with deft agility when, suddenly, rounding through a sharp turn, he stumbled and fell headlong to the surface.

Wells started forward to assist the fallen man, thought better of the instinctive move. He gripped the chair with his hand, waiting. Steve lay in a heap, his right fist beating slowly against the floor in barely controlled anger. Moments later he rolled about and moved to a sitting position, looking up at Wells. Technicians in the testing chamber, always present, took their cue from Wells and made no move to interfere.

'Rudy, it's *got* to be the potential,' Steve said angrily. He struggled to his feet, working his left leg carefully. 'Look at this thing,' he complained. 'It's like you said. The signals go into the leg,' his hand slammed with a wallop against the bionics limb, 'but they're all messed up coming back. I can almost *feel* it happening.'

Wells kept his silence. Steve was groping. He turned suddenly, started moving at a trot, working his way through the course. Several times he stumbled, fought for and regained his balance. Steve wasn't aware of what was becoming clear to Wells and the others. The legs were improving, and rapidly. He could punish the bionics limbs now for more than an hour without difficulty. It was as if a time block existed for operation without fault. At that time his system began to tire, as would any man's, and a flow of erratic nerve messages was the result. According to their own calculations, in several weeks Steve would be through the worst of it, and his endurance would be measured not by the feedback of signals through the bionics limbs and his own system, but by his own ability to endure. The bionics limbs would have nothing to do with it. They were dealing with a superb athlete who knew better than any of them the extent to which he might abuse his own body.

Their superb athlete, unfortunately, also suffered a hair-trigger temper, considerably aggravated at this point by his frustrations. During one run through the testing maze, Steve was pressing hard ahead with fifty pounds strapped to his back. The bionics limbs did not fail but Steve, operating now under an altered center of gravity, stubbed a toe and sprawled helplessly. He clambered to his feet with an expression of anger and disgust and let fly with a well-aimed kick at the rock that had caused his tumble.

The rock took off like a rifle bullet, tore through a plate-glass viewing window, scattering observers in all directions, went on to penetrate a wall, and came to a stop in the next wall beyond. A sheepish, slightly stunned Steve Austin balanced himself on one foot, lowered his body carefully to the floor, and stared ruefully at the mangled end of his right 'toe'. The toes were crushed inward, and the sudden heat of compression had fused the material.

Rudy Wells sat down beside him and they watched Art Fanier leaping obstacles through the maze to reach their side in his own record time. 'How,' Fanier asked, pointing at the battered foot, 'does it feel?'

Steve looked up. 'You're kidding.'

'Hell, no, I'm not kidding. How does it feel?'

'It's not *my* leg, dammit. You guys built this thing here in your candy factory.'

Fanier shook his head. 'You're wrong,' he insisted. 'It *is* your leg. And you'd better start thinking about it that way, because you sure can't keep on doing *that*.'

Steve glanced up at Rudy. 'Maybe Art's got something there. It *does* feel sort of strange, at that.'

Wells raised an eyebrow. 'Well, it does, dammit,' Steve said. 'How? Any pain?'

'Not pain. It's more like a tingling sensation. It doesn't *hurt*, but it's annoying. If I look away from the foot, it reminds me something's wrong. It feels like that, anyway.'

'You mean that?' Fanier asked.

'Yeah.' Steve looked at the other man. 'What the hell is the matter with you?'

Fanier pointed again to the leg. 'What you just said ... we had theories about it, but this, well, I mean ... it's more than I ever really hoped for. It's compensation,' he said with near awe in his voice. 'Compensation beyond any level we ever thought possible.' A rising tone of excitement came into his voice. 'Do you know what this *means*? Good God, the two systems, the bionics and the physiological, are proving their total compatibility. And I mean *total*.' He rubbed his hands briskly together. 'The body, Steve ... it can't provide a pain sensation because you haven't those types of nerve endings any more, so it's compensating. It's substituting a new feeling, a new sensation as a warning. It's a pain indicator without pain!'

Fanier gestured to Wells. 'We've got to get him back in the lab, check out the readings. If I understand what's going on here, the end is in sight.'

Steve's arm shot out like a piston, grabbed Fanier's wrist. He had a scowl on his face. 'Explain that.'

Fanier squirmed. 'Hey ... you're hurting ...' His face had gone white.

'Steve!' Wells shouted. 'You're going to break his arm. Let go, man!'

Steve withdrew his hand. 'Oh, hell, ' he said softly, his words almost a moan. 'I'm sorry, Art. I didn't know ...' It had been his left arm. The bionics limb. Steve stared at it as if he were seeing it for the first time.

'No ... no sweat,' Art Fanier gasped. 'What I meant, Steve, was that compensation on this order means another month, maybe two and no problems anymore ... I—' He was white. He turned to Wells. 'Doc ... I think it's broken.' He cradled the arm against the other.

Steve stared at him, his own face white.

'Just when everything is going so beautifully with the project, too.' Art Fanier used his left hand in a clumsy effort to handle his coffee cup. He spilled some, put it back to the table. 'The bionics part is more than we could have hoped for. What's gone wrong with Steve?'

Wells looked at Fanier and the others in the room.

'He thinks he's becoming a Frankenstein. You can't argue him out of it. We know it's not true. He doesn't.' Wells rose to his feet. 'We'll just have to see who has the last word.'

'You may feel cosmetics is hardly the word for what you have in mind, but it is as necessary as the other surgery that has been performed. Yes, cosmetics surgery is as vital to—'

'Shut up and get on with it.' Steve made no attempt to disguise his impatience with the fluttering, talkative man.

Arnold Dupre was his name and he was the walking revival of Ichabod Crane, a gaunt, spare giant who bent strangely at all angles through his knobby frame.

'He operates a rather special kind of beauty parlor,' Wells said with a laugh. 'No advertising, and the price is right. He's an expert. Not a surgeon, of course, but he might as well be one.'

'Where's he from?' Steve growled.

'CIA.'

'What?'

'That's right. *They* think he's the best in the business. And it *is* important.'

When Dupre got down to business, even Steve was impressed. 'They made a mistake with your new arm and your left leg,' Dupre announced without preamble, managing to astonish everyone in the room. Steve, Rudy Wells and Art Fanier stared at one another and turned their attention back to the knobby figure. 'Notice,' Dupre said imperiously. 'The left arm is now of the same dimensions as the right. That does not occur as a natural growth, so? This man is right-handed. So his right biceps, his forearm, his wrist, would all be better developed than his left. But the, ah, replacement? Aha, the replacement matches the dimensions of the right arm.' He grasped Steve's wrist suddenly in bony fingers. Astonished, Steve offered no resistance. 'See here? The mark of a fighter pilot. Even if I did not know of Colonel Austin this is clear to me. The musculature, eh? See? Where he has spent years gripping a control stick. Fighter pilots have this characteristic.'

Steve pulled his arm free. 'How the hell do you know all this? You hardly seem the type. I mean, you—'

'Tut, tut, colonel,' Dupre said, 'you of all people should not make assumptions. Perhaps you should have looked at *my* wrist.'

They did, and Steve saw what had missed him before. The right wrist of Dupre *was* more heavily developed. 'Are you telling me,' Steve said in open disbelief, 'that you—'

'Thunderbolts, Fifteenth Air Force. Four thousand hours, single-engine fighters, colonel. I also shot down eight German fighters.'

Steve sat in silence through the rest. 'I imagine you had some difficulty becoming accustomed to your legs, so?' Dupre swept on. 'Obvious. The weight is the same, approximately, I imagine, as your own legs. But the mass balance? All wrong. That changes the inertia, so? The body mixes up the signals. It takes time to adapt. No, no, Colonel Austin, no need to answer. I am familiar with such problems.' They stared at the gaunt figure who had just stated in a few words what had escaped them all. Fanier's mouth was open in disbelief.

'But,' Dupre shrugged, 'other factors, right? Here, see where

130

the flesh joins the plastiskin. We need a permanent dye. More hairs. Oh, yes, much more hairs. If the skin is exposed to the sun, the skin will darken, but not the plastiskin. We will create some scars along the limb. It will cover the junction, right? And the hairs will make pigmentation differences more difficult to see. Yes, it must have water resistance. Salinity must be considered. We can also supply you with a dye, a lotion, that will closely match any change. It will function for both legs and the arm. Now, are we ready for the tests?'

Steve was frozen, baked, and immersed for hours at a time while Dupre fussed about him like an old maid. The specialist recommended injections to darken the skin, were that necessary, and Steve wondered at such attention to matching the plastiskin with his own. But finally Dupre ended his sessions.

'What now?' he demanded of Rudy Wells.

'Your eye,' the doctor told him. 'You're getting to look too much like Moshe Dayan. Time we changed that.'

'A glass eye? I might as well—'

'No, not a glass eye. Something better. Tomorrow morning. You'll see.'

Steve felt uncomfortable in his presence. The man with the balding head waited patiently in the optical chamber, wearing a white tunic, standing behind a wide table cluttered with plastic models of skulls and eyeballs. He extended his hand as Steve entered with Wells and Jean Manners.

'Oscar Goldman,' he said to Steve. 'My pleasure, Colonel Austin.'

Steve shook hands cautiously. 'Did you say Doctor Goldman?' Steve asked.

'No. Not doctor.' He nodded to Wells. 'That's his department. I'm a specialist in ceramics and plastics. Also, some familiarity with electronics.' He gestured to a leather chair. 'Would you sit there, please?'

'Maybe I should have explained more, Steve,' Wells told him. 'Mr. Goldman is a specialist in his, well, his field. He'll help you decide on types of equipment.'

Still suspicious, Steve took the seat. Centered in the table, directly before him, was an exact replica of his own head. Only this model was of lucite, plastic, and other materials, was transparent, and came apart in sections. There were also over-sized sections of the eye, the socket, and the optical system. Steve studied the display, turned to Goldman.

'My business extends somewhat beyond the cosmetic,' Goldman said abruptly. 'We both know your vision cannot be restored. There are different methods, however, for a replacement eye to function. It can be glass or plastic, and it simply fills the socket. Its effect as a cosmetic is illusory, for the eye does not move with the eye muscles. The so-called vacant stare straight ahead is its fault.'

Steve did not make a sound, and Goldman paused long enough to pick up a large eyeball. 'This is what we propose for you,' he continued. 'The weight, the weight distribution, match your eye. Color is the same, but this has added properties. We have developed a refractory ceramic that not only matches the cornea of your right eye, but will shift color depending upon light intensity and angle. More than that, it contains light-sensitive materials that will enlarge and decrease corneal size, again matching your right eye. The pupils will approximate one another as they change. Dr. Wells, here, and Dr. Killian will explain to you how the eye will be placed in your socket so that it moves when you alter your point of visual reference. As your right eye moves up or down or to the side this eye will do the same.' He placed the model back to the table.

'Lets me do everything but see, won't it? Steve picked up the model, studied it more closely.

'No one can replace the eye. Not yet. The Russians are doing amazing things with transplants but even they haven't gone that far yet. Only God can give you back your sight. My office can provide, however, a certain insight.'

'Get to it.'

'There are different ways for an eye to be useful,' Goldman told Steve. 'We propose one of these for you.'

'Mind identifying the "we"?'

'Your government.' Goldman turned to the model of the head. 'Here is what we have in mind. Please watch very closely, Colonel Austin.'

Goldman leaned forward with a small suction disk in his hand. He placed it gently against the lens of the eye in the model head, pressed in, and then twisted the disk to the left.

132

Steve watched intently as the lens turned. And Goldman carefully withdrew a cylindrical tube from the eye. He placed it on the table beneath a huge magnifying glass and bright light, motioning for Steve to come closer to him. Goldman's fingers worked deftly as he brought a tweezers into view beneath the glass. Two minutes later Steve stared at a tiny, disassembled camera.

Goldman took the chair across the table. 'It takes its pictures with regular or infrared film. It operates up to two-hundredths of a second. Anything over four feet is automatic infinity focusing, and light-sensitive cells handle exposure readings. You're familiar with Tri-X film? This will operate with twice the speed on the ASA rating. It can handle twenty exposures per microcartridge. It's not perfect,' Goldman said, the first personal tone in his voice, 'but it really is rather effective. It would be easier, of course, to build the entire eye as a camera. But then we couldn't make the eyeball a permanent installation – or Dr. Killian couldn't – and the eye would not move in a normal fashion and, except to an expert, be indistinguishable from a normal eye. It could be a dead giveaway.'

Steve glanced from Goldman to Wells and back to the strange man across the table. 'A giveaway to *who*?'

'I can't say.'

'Who the hell are you, mister?'

'Somebody doing his job. Like you, Colonel Austin. You're still on active duty.'

She stood on the edge of the board, a superb body, bikini covering a minimum of flesh. She stepped back two paces, went forward and up, came down neatly on the edge of the board and into the air. A perfect swan and her arms came together for her to cut the water like a knife. She went the length of the pool underwater, searching him out at the far end where he was testing scuba gear. They broke the surface together. Kathy tossed her streaming hair away from her face and smiled at him. 'Get rid of that junk and I'll race you to the other side of the pool,' she said.

He studied her for a moment. Then the interest faded from his expression. 'Maybe later,' he told her. 'Too busy now.'

'Even for a short race?' she pressed. 'Loser gets a whack on the ass.'

'I said no,' he told her, more sharply than he intended.

She stood motionless, beads of water glistening on her skin. Suddenly she shook her head, spun away from him, and swam to the opposite side of the pool, where she took the ladder quickly and left. Silence filled the pool for several moments.

Fanier took in the scene, then walked to where Steve stood quietly in the water. 'Okay for test number three,' Fanier told him. 'You ready for four?'

Steve turned slowly, as if he still held an image of the beautiful girl in his mind. 'Yeah,' he said, looking up at the technician, his eyes resting briefly on the plaster cast. 'Let's get with it.' He disappeared beneath the water.

'Everyone here?'

Art Fanier nodded to Dr. Killian. 'Yes, sir. Mr. Goldman was the last one in. We're all ready.'

Killian took the seat next to Rudy Wells. Jean Manners was next to him. The chairs around the oval conference table all faced to the far end of the room where a motion-picture screen waited to come to life.

'We'll keep this as tight as we can,' Wells started. 'Steve Austin, as you all know, at this time is undergoing performance tests so we can establish the parameters of his physical abilities. Those tests will be finished either late tonight or by noon tomorrow. At this moment, in fact, Steve is in the Sangre de Cristo area. The sand dunes, to be specific, testing his ability to work through that sort of terrain, and especially so under low-oxygen conditions. The terrain elevation there exceeds nine thousand feet, so it constitutes a rather severe test. From what I understand, and this is from a radio report late this afternoon, he has left his competitors far behind.'

He gestured to an aide and the room lights darkened. 'We have edited the film records to bring all of you the highlights of the tests. We'll start with the short track events.' The projector came on and they saw Steve and several athletes poised at the start of a hundred-yard-dash competition. Wells waited until the men flashed through the race, and there was a stirring in the room as they saw two men beat the man with the powerful bionics limbs. 'From these tests we were able to remind Steve that a dash run is determined not only by experience and skill, but also oxygen saturation. In the first runs Steve lost regularly. Two days later – as you will see now – there was no longer any competition. Oxygen control, experience in handling his altered body mass and changing center of gravity ... all these were now controlled by him.' He paused again as they watched Steve almost launch himself from the starting board and continue pulling away until he hit the tape. 'In that last run, Steve broke both the world and the Olympic records.'

Wells hesitated; the film continued and a chalk board showed the words, 'Endurance Runs.' A telephoto lens shot of Steve in the far distance appeared; at the bottom right corner of the film was a timer. They watched Steve running in perfect form, his legs kicking up dust as he ground up distance, getting larger and larger, the foreshortening effect of the camera bringing out every detail. 'Notice the timer in the lower right,' Wells told his audience. 'Steve has been running for four hours at this point. Four hours,' he repeated, finding it unnecessary to say more as Steve came closer and closer to the camera, finally passing the lens. The camera swung about to follow him and they watched the same nearly flawless grace of movement as

Steve moved away from their point of view. 'We ended this test, which was more for pacing and endurance than it was for speed, after six hours. As an indication of what he was able to do, for the entire six hours he averaged a mile in five point three minutes *for the entire run*,' Wells said.

'He was fully wired, of course?' Goldman asked Wells.

'We have excellent telemetry. His heartbeat remained steady throughout, and only slightly over normal. If we had not observed the tests personally *and* had these films for corroboration, we would be hard put to believe the biomedical recordings.'

For the next hour they studied films that depicted an exhaustive variety of grueling performances. They watched Steve racing with tremendous power and agility through obstacle courses. Approaching high walls he ignored knotted ropes and hurled himself against the wall, his legs pistoning him high enough to reach the top with his hands. 'Notice how he favors his bionics arm when brute strength is required,' Wells told the others. 'His legs take the initial requirement, he grasps with his left arm, the bionics limb, balances with his right, and then pumps himself over with the bionics arm. It's really quite something.'

The scene changed to a large swimming pool. 'You'll notice,' Wells said, 'that where the swimming begins without a hard dive, Steve is being beaten, not by much, but still he is being beaten by some excellent swimmers. In the short dash performance he is on their level but no better. Where a dive is involved, well, look for yourself. He is twenty feet along his channel *before* he hits the water and he already has so much speed ...' No need to elaborate further. Balanced on the edge of the pool, Steve's legs shot him forward in a long, flat, hard dive. He hit the water with a hard, flat splash, and disappeared at once behind a churning explosion in the water. 'His legs, of course,' Wells said with a smile. 'He's like a propeller. Once he gets going, well, the other men refused to compete any more.'

The scene shifted to a lake, and they watched an outboard cruiser moving steadily toward the camera. To its right the water foamed steadily. 'The boat is coming toward us, as you can see. That churning effect to its side is Steve Austin. He's

136

wearing webbed fins. With those tireless legs of his, well, again you can see for yourselves.' The boat and Steve rushed toward the camera lens, expanded in a sudden rush of spray, and were gone.

'There is one more water test, gentlemen. In this scene you will see a closeup of the interior left thigh, just above the knee. Notice how an access panel in the bionics limb comes loose. There, that's a good closeup, and you can see Steve extracting the oxygen tube.'

'I didn't know about this,' Goldman said.

'One of our surprises,' Dr. Killian answered. 'Within the limb we managed to leave room for a curving cylinder. It contains oxygen under very high pressure, and we have worked out the system to either constant flow or demand.'

Wells glanced at Goldman who was leaning forward, his expression intent, watching Steve uncoil the thin line. He placed the grip between his teeth, closed his mouth firmly, and slipped beneath the water. 'Please notice the timer,' Wells said after several seconds had gone by. 'We will cut the film here except for several underwater scenes.' They watched Steve swimming leisurely beneath the surface and then the camera cut back to the timer.

'Twenty-five minutes,' Wells announced. The rest was obvious. A man had just remained underwater, swimming, for nearly a half hour with an oxygen supply contained *within* his own person. Wells could almost hear the wheels turning inside Goldman's head.

The OSO man turned to Killian. 'Do you have any other surprises like that one, doctor?'

Killian toyed with a pencil. 'Several, Mr. Goldman.'

They waited in semidarkness as the projectionist changed the film. 'We have been running a series of tests,' Wells said to pick up the theme, 'for resistance to shock loads.' As he spoke the screen came alive and they found themselves looking at a parachute training tower. 'We consider this to be one of the more revealing. Notice the figures at the top ramp of the tower. The first man to go off on the cable, which, by the way, simulates the opening shock of a parachute of a man leaving a C-130 transport at a true airspeed of one hundred twenty miles an hour, will be an instructor. We obtained full loads from his drop and

137

chute opening, after which – you can see the first man jumping here – after which,' he went on, 'Steve will make the second jump. There was some concern here about the legs being able to take the deceleration.' They watched Steve pause a dozen paces back, then start out at a run for the edge of the platform, where he threw himself outward. His body twisted, then pulled sharply as the static line drew taut. A moment later came the simulated chute opening, and Steve's body snapped to one side and upward. He slid down the guide cable toward the ground. 'The landing impact is the same as that for a parachute,' Wells explained. 'Note Steve's position. He is executing a perfect PLF, or parachute landing fall, as is prescribed.' Steve's legs were together, his knees barely flexed when he struck the ground. He immediately allowed his body to bend in the direction of his fall, and crumpled perfectly to the ground, springing to his feet a moment later.

'The next jump speaks for itself,' Wells said. Steve came off the tower again, went through the opening shock, but this time, instead of executing his landing fall, he hit hard on both feet and remained standing. 'There was some minor damage,' Wells told the others. 'We hadn't prepared for such severe loads or this sort of activity. I'm pleased to say that several days after these films were taken, Steve repeated these jumps with a forty-pound backpack and still landed on, and remained on, his feet. A meticulous examination of his system indicated no injury or damage.'

They watched the films of Steve in the huge climatic hangar at Eglin Air Force Base in Florida. There Steve was subjected to bitter cold, down to seventy degrees below zero. Outfitted in arctic gear, he plodded for hours in the teeth of howling winds, fierce blizzards, and fought his way over icy hummocks. He was next seen in a tropical setting, the temperature at one hundred and thirty, perspiring profusely, hacking his way through thick jungle vegetation. From here he went on to desert conditions and, once again, endured the severe privations of the climatic extremes.

'It was important to associate Steve with the surroundings in which he has spent so many years,' Wells explained as they waited for another reel. 'You will see him in a Link trainer that simulates instrument flight, that reproduces almost perfectly the

138

conditions of flying without reference to a visual horizon. This calls for excellent coordination, and not the least of his problems are, of course, sustaining depth perception with only one eye. But other men have managed it, including some rather outstanding fighter aces in the Second World War.' The screen flickered and they studied Steve in the trainer, sealed from the outside world, 'flying' as if his life depended upon his performance. For a while the coordination was sloppy and even ineffective. But only for a while. Steve's system and his mind compensated rapidly. 'Within forty-five minutes,' said Wells, 'he was handling the instrument trainer with virtually his former skill. You will next see a test carried out in an Air Force JC-135, a modified 707 for zero-g training. Steve trained in such an aircraft before his moon flight, as you may know. We were able to achieve nearly sixty seconds of uninterrupted weightlessness for each parabolic arc of the flight path . . .' And there was Steve again, lifting weightlessly through the cabin with attendants watching every move.

'One would be inclined to believe,' Wells continued, 'that Steve was even more at home under weightlessness than he is under normal gravity.'

'I'd say the same thing for his performance in the water,' observed Oscar Goldman.

They met later in Killian's office. Oscar Goldman wasted no time getting into the subject. 'I know you have anticipated Austin's moods. That seems to be the best word for it. But this latest phase,' Goldman shook his head, 'amounts to a positive withdrawal. He hardly speaks to anyone or works with them—'

'That's not true,' Wells broke in. 'He works with anyone necessary to his testing.'

'Yes, *testing*,' Goldman agreed, 'but there's no personal relationship. Except, perhaps, with you and Miss Manners. But not with anyone else. What's causing this? We feel this is absolutely vital, Dr. Wells. If our program is to succeed then we must—'

'Mr. Goldman,' Killian interrupted, 'your program, I must remind you, is secondary to this project. Even you will agree with this? No, please let me finish. I know you have done everything possible not to interfere. I've told you before, and I'm pleased to repeat it now, that you have been, well, based on my experience in government, Mr. Goldman, you have been extraordinary in your conduct. But you seem to be pressing more than usual. Why?'

Goldman nodded slowly. 'In my business, Dr. Killian, the weakest point in any link is never the equipment used by a man, but that man himself.'

Killian studied Goldman carefully. 'I gather you have specific plans for Austin?'

'I would be foolish to lie, wouldn't I?' Goldman said bluntly. 'Of course we do. But those plans, and they are most specific, are worthless without the cooperation, without the desire to work fully with us, of the man. And Steve Austin right now,' he said, 'acts like a man who would rather go off in a corner and sulk. Dammit, I hate to say that, but it's true. What's gone wrong with him?' He turned to Rudy Wells. 'I've heard your theories on this, Dr. Wells, and up to a point I agree completely. The matter of fighting his way out of a morass, and then not knowing quite what to do with himself when he wins. But even that doesn't account for this present . . .'

Goldman turned to Jean Manners. 'Next to Dr. Wells, you are closer to him than any other person. Can you help us?'

'We've discussed it, I mean, among ourselves,' she said. 'I've talked about it with Dr. Wells. I've also talked about this with Kathy. That's Miss Norris.'

'Yes, I know,' Goldman said. 'Please go on.'

'It's that he doesn't feel he's a complete man. You must know that Steve believes he's impotent. Kathy is in love with him and he completely ignores her. It's not the disfigurement, any more. This used to bother him. Now he considers himself as much machine as he does man. That's all right in a masculine world, when he's with men, among men, competing or working with them. But when it comes to women . . .' She shook her head.

Goldman turned to Wells. 'Is there a problem in the physical sense?'

'Absolutely none. And Steve *is* fond of that girl. Much more than anyone realizes, including himself. He's afraid of being rejected, Oscar,' Wells said. 'He's so afraid of rejection because of his half-man and half-machine condition that he doesn't dare expose himself to the possibility of a woman turning away from him. So he has only one person left to fight. Himself.'

'Are you saying that he pities himself?'

'In a harsh and rather brutal manner, yes.'

'Any suggestions?'

'Yes, get him back into the element he misses most of all. The sky. Get him back into a cockpit. Turn him loose in a jet fighter. Let him—'

'Isn't that taking an awful risk?'

'What do you want, Mr. Goldman? A psychological wreck or a whole man? Steve's entire life has been flying. He does not believe, at this point, that he will ever fly again, which is to say, be himself. Let him fly again, and he will whip this thing.'

'All right,' Goldman nodded. 'I'll make the arrangements.'

'And if what Dr. Wells says is true, and I believe it is,' Jean said, 'arrange for Kathy to be with him when it happens.'

'Wherever did you dig *her* up?' Major Marv Throne-berry leaned far to the side of his chair, following as long as possible the departing view of Kathy Norris.

'Will you simmer down, Marv?'

'Okay, okay.' Throneberry held out his hands, palms facing Steve. 'I'll behave.' The smile faded from his face and he studied the other man. 'Time to be serious?'

'Time,' Steve nodded.

Throneberry went to the door and closed it. He came back slowly, eased into the swivel chair behind his desk, went through elaborate motions of slicing the end from a cigar and lit up. He pointed the cigar at Steve. 'Um, lots of questions.'

Steve nodded again. He and Marv Throneberry had flown together when they were lieutenants. Marv was now the training officer for the squadron of F-4C fighters at Davis-Monthan Air Force Base on the outskirts of Tucson, Arizona. He was physically a very big man, and in the cockpit he was a very good pilot.

Under the effective urging of the Office of Special Operations in Washington, the Air Force had cut temporary duty orders for Colonel Steve Austin, USAF, to report to the 433rd Fighter Squadron for 'refresher training' in the big Phantom II fighters. There had been a brief phone call to Steve at the laboratories in Colorado, clearing Throneberry with him. And before his arrival, Throneberry also had received a telephone call, from the director of training for the whole Air Force. 'Give Colonel Austin whatever he wants, answer no questions from *anyone,* major, and keep everybody off the colonel's back.' Throneberry had looked at the telephone in his hand as if it might turn into a snake. He said 'Yessir' into the phone and hung it up slowly and carefully. And now Steve was here in the room with him. He showed up with a ravishing beauty for company, and sent her packing to arrange for motel rooms and rental cars, and Marv

Throneberry was beside himself to find out just what the hell was going on.

'The official word was that you got tore up pretty good at Edwards,' he said carefully.

Steve smiled. 'That's close,' he acknowledged.

'After which you disappeared. Helen and I tried to find out what happened, Steve. We heard Doc Wells was on the case.'

'He still is.'

'How is the old boy?'

'Big beard, big belly. Great as ever.'

'How,' Marv said cautiously, 'is his patient?'

'Been a long time since I was in the air.'

'Uh huh.' Throneberry opened a folder on his desk, waved some papers at Steve. 'Your orders in here. *My* orders too. One of which says you are not, repeat, *not* to be given a flight physical. Which is sort of crazy, know what I mean?'

Steve tapped his fingers against the attaché case he had brought with him. 'The physical is in here. Given personally by Doc Wells.'

Throneberry nodded. 'My orders also say all your flight gear is to be kept with mine. During your stay, no other person, including the commanding general or the flight surgeon or the flight safety officer, is to be permitted access to that room. They've got *their* orders too. They're on my back wanting to know what gives.'

'Did you tell them?'

'Tell them *what*?' Throneberry showed his exasperation. 'All I know is what these papers say. That,' his eyes narrowed, 'and that you're going to tell an old friend, strictly off the record, you understand, what the hell goes on here.'

Steve walked to the window, looked out at four fighters cracking skyward in tight formation. It had been a long time since he'd done that.

'Okay, Marv. But you can't tell anyone.'

'Agreed.'

'Not even Helen.'

'That bad?'

'You could say so.'

'The grapevine said you would never fly again, Steve.'

He nodded.

143

'They also said, ' Throneberry continued, 'you wouldn't even *walk*. A lot of people said you were . . .' He couldn't go on, hoping Steve would help.

'A basket case?'

'Yeah, but you sure don't look like it.'

'They were almost right, Marv. Steve turned to face him. 'Want it all?'

'I don't really know, Steve. But I guess I should know.'

'I guess you should. You're the one who's going to turn me loose up there.'

Throneberry waited.

'I lost a couple of things in the desert, Marv. My left arm, for starters.'

The pilot stared at him.

'Both legs.'

'Steve—'

'I'm blind in my left eye.'

Throneberry was chalk white. 'I don't *believe* it.'

'Broken jaw, fractured skull, ribs caved in, heart valve torn up. Some other things, but that'll do.'

'Man, are you really standing there in front of me?'

Steve laughed. 'You better believe it.'

'But . . . I don't understand, Steve. Really, I—'

'I'm the first of a new breed, Marv. They're rebuilding me. It's called bionics. I'm half man and half machine, old buddy.'

Throneberry took that in silence. He stared at the wall, then turned slowly to Steve. 'Can you fly?'

'That's what we're going to find out.'

'I can't even figure out how you can *walk*!'

Steve walked to the desk, rested his hands on the top, looked directly at the other pilot. 'Listen to me, Marv. I don't want to have to repeat this, so I hope the first time sinks in. I can walk, run, climb, swim, and fight better than any man you've ever known in your life. I'm also going to prove I can still fly your ass off upstairs. Now, how about the first thing tomorrow morning? Say, oh six hundred?'

'I'm numb.'

'You'll get over it.'

Throneberry gestured helplessly. 'The girl . . . what's her name?'

144

'Kathy.'

'Does she know?'

'She knows. She's part of the project. That's why she's here. Official observer. She'll take notes, that sort of thing.'

'Nothing else, Steve?'

'Knock it off, Marv.' The tone had changed, was cold.

'Okay, okay,' he said. 'What do you want to do first?'

'Flight manual tonight. I want to study it from beginning to end. Catch up on things.'

Throneberry nodded, grateful to concentrate on business. 'You've got some time in the F-4, don't you?'

'About twelve hundred hours. But it's been a long time.'

'Okay. I'll get the manual. What next?'

'Cockpit check at six sharp. I'll have breakfast before I get here.' He hesitated. 'Kathy will be with me.'

'Six sharp,' Throneberry confirmed. 'Want to have dinner with us tonight?'

'No. I . . . I don't think I could hack that, Marv.'

His friend nodded. 'Anything else, Steve?'

'Yeah. I'd like to check out my flight gear now.'

'Right *now*?'

'Birds gotta fly, Marv.'

The sun lanced in from just above the mountains, casting strong, black shadows across the flight line. Throneberry lowered his visor, saw Steve doing the same. 'Ready to start,' came his voice from the front cockpit of the big fighter. 'Go, baby,' Throneberry told him. He had the feeling he was along just for the ride. Steve went through the procedures mechanically, smoothly. He brought the two powerful engines to life, checked out all the systems, signaled for the chocks to be pulled by the ground crew. The tower cleared them to taxi, and as they eased away from the flight line with a muffled boom of thunder, Throneberry looked to his left. Kathy Norris stood there watching. Steve didn't even glance her way. He rolled the plane expertly to the end of the taxiway, ran her through her checks, switched to tower frequency. 'Cobalt Six ready to go,' he called. 'Roger, Cobalt Six. Taxi into position and hold.'

Steve booted her out to the runway, swung the nose around, and locked the brakes. Clearance came a few moments later.

145

Steve eased the throttles forward. Marv Throneberry's fingers itched to grasp the stick but he held back as thunder boomed behind them.

'Marv,' Steve's voice came through his helmet, 'you still think I can fly?'

'Let's find out, old buddy.'

He heard Steve laugh for the first time since he arrived. 'Okay, let's see if this bear still has it.' The brakes came off and Steve pushed the throttles into full afterburner. The sudden explosion of power kicked her free and the Phantom bellowed and rushed forward. Three thousand feet did it, and the nose wheel came up, and then she was off the runway and into the air. Steve hit the gear and it banged solidly into place with the doors slapping tight with them. The nose came higher as Steve let her run, the power throwing them steeply into the sky. A wing rocked sharply and Throneberry almost grabbed the stick. Instead, he kept his hands in his lap and spoke quietly. 'You're fighting her, Steve. Ease off the pressure. She'll behave.'

He breathed easier when the motions slowed down. Steve was feeling her out. Departure control cleared them to angels forty over the bombing range and the sky was all theirs. Steve leveled her off, played with her for a while, and little by little, becoming as one with the machine, forgetting he was strapped into a cockpit, he started to *wear* the airplane. The master's touch was there and he pointed the nose up, away from the sun, and rolled her viciously until the speed fell off, and he brought her up and over on her back, a mighty, soaring loop through the sky. Coming over on top, he was barely over stall, but he made her hang and he played power and gravity as though they were strings on the end of his fingers, tickling the brute forces out there as she fell through, the nose coming down just where he wanted it, the power easing off. It was with real regret that Marv Throneberry, who hadn't once touched the controls, finally had to remind Steve that the fuel warning light was on and it was time to go home.

'It's time to *land*,' Steve told him. 'I'm home *now*.' And Marv couldn't argue with him because it was all very true. And he wasn't surprised when they taxied back to the flight line and he saw the girl standing there, waiting for them, as if she hadn't moved at all the whole time they were gone, and somehow he

146

believed that to be true. He raised his visor as Steve parked the Phantom, and he looked at the girl again, and was sure he saw tears on her face.

She locked the door behind her. Steve turned in surprise as Kathy gestured toward the magnum of champagne in an ice bucket on the dresser.

'There's no question any more, is there?'

He thought of the sky and the fighter beneath his fingertips. 'No.'

'Then champagne is in order.'

'I – I don't know.'

'I watched you today, Steve. *I* know.'

He didn't say anything.

'I watched a man come back to himself. Back where he belonged.'

'I'll open the champagne.'

He had his back to her, opening the bottle. He filled the two glasses on the dresser. He heard her voice behind him.

'Steve.'

'Right there.' He turned, holding a glass in each hand.

'I want you to make love to me, Steve. *Now.*'

He stared at her. 'Kathy, I—'

'For God's sake, *shut up.*'

Before he knew what was happening they were together, and she was crying.

It had been a long time, but he was really home now.

They stayed at Davis-Monthan three more days and then it was time to return to Colorado. Kathy talked him into canceling their airline tickets and renting a car. It would be a beautiful drive back through the desert and the mountains.

At dusk they were looking for a motel. Traffic moved slowly ahead of them, winding carefully down a narrow mountain road, following a yellow schoolbus filled with children returning from a picnic. They were three cars behind the bus, and when it happened it came in agonizing slow motion. It sounded like a mild *pop* when the front right tire of the bus gave out. For a moment it seemed as if the driver would be able to hold the suddenly careening vehicle. It swerved right, then

147

wildly to the left, but there was oncoming traffic and the driver had no chance but to pull again to the right. There he lost control, the front right wheel edging along slippery gravel, and the bus tilted. They could hear the thin screams from the open windows as the front end slid, dragging everything with it, and then it was rolling over, crashing through the brush along the steep slope, sliding and banging before it came to a stop against a tree. They were holding their breath, Steve slamming on the brakes of their car, when the flash soared out from the trees and they heard the dull, booming sound of the fuel tank igniting.

Steve slammed to a stop and in almost the same motion was out of the car and hurling himself down the slope, being able to see by the licking flames, urged on by the cries of screaming children. They had the emergency doors open, and shrieking children, cut and bloody, were struggling out and up the hill. But there were others pinned inside, tormented by the spreading flames, and Steve dimly remembered kicking in a window as the screams grew more shrill. The wreckage had folded over; metal trapped the children inside, and he went crazy as he pulled and tore at metal, hurling it aside, grabbing at bodies either limp or writhing in pain. He passed children through the shattered window, other hands grasped them, took them away from the flames, and then they were all out.

There came one last cry and he went back into the wreckage, pulling at seats, feeling metal grate against him. The flames reached at him but he found more metal and he was using his left arm as a club, flailing away at the imprisoning seat; metal gave, he wrenched it clear, jerked the child free and stumbled through the smoke. They were safe, the child in his arms. He looked down at the little girl, placed her on her feet, and watched as her eyes widened, her hand pointed, and she screamed.

He looked to where she was pointing and saw a ghastly skeleton of metal and wires showing where the plastiskin had ripped free. The child's screams went on, driving into his brain, and as others approached, he turned and ran up the slope, his legs pistoning him along, gouging clumps of dirt and rocks free as he made the road. He rushed to the car, where Kathy waited. She moved impulsively to his side when she saw him holding the

148

arm close to his body, covering it with the other. 'You drive,' he said, climbing into the right front seat.

'What ... what happened? Are you all right?' Words she couldn't hold back.

'Just drive, dammit!' he shouted.

He refused to let her stop at a motel, demanding she drive all the way through, stopping only for gas. He had a jacket over him now, hiding the arm. He told her what had happened, how the child had screamed, the look of horror on her face when she saw what she thought was a living skeleton. And then he sat cold and silent, a monster in his own mind, running from the shrieking, frightened youngster.

'All right, Steve, even my patience has run out. I'm not even going to talk about Kathy. You once had a girl who couldn't take what happened to you and she blew town. Now you've got a girl who's in love with you and you're so damned wrapped up in misery and self-pity you can't recognize the greatest thing that's ever happened to you.' Wells gestured angrily to cut off the shouted interruption he knew was coming. 'I'm not through, goddammit,' he said through clenched teeth. 'Kathy is your business, not mine. What I care about is the project, and that means I care about you. But I've had it, right up to *here*.' He drew his finger across his forehead. 'That far. Okay, colonel. You're quitting? Well, so the hell am I.'

Steve was shocked at the outburst from a man who'd been transformed into a total stranger. The stranger wasn't quite through, as he discovered. 'You can walk out of here any time you want to,' Wells said, now more in control of himself. 'I'm through killing my own life because of you. There are plenty of veterans' hospitals that can take care of you. They can fit you out with the best prosthetics limbs made anywhere in the world. You've seen them on other men. You can wear them like anyone else. And it'll be exactly what you want, right? You'll be free of this whole rotten place you've been complaining about. You won't be tied down to us any more; you won't be a freak, a Frankenstein. You'll be just another guy fate crapped on who has to make his way the best he can. There'll be thousands like you, Steve. No more miracles. No more special case. You can lose yourself in the army of legless and armless men.

149

'We can't work with you like this, not knowing from one day to the next whether you're going to wake up spitting mad and refusing to cooperate, or whatever. It's impossible. This project needs more than your body. It needs your absolute cooperation, your willingness, your drive, to make it all work.'

He turned and faced away from his friend. 'You can pick the rehabilitation center you want. Anywhere in the country. You won't be able to retain the bionics limbs but that doesn't matter since you hate them so much. So it's *finis*. You will, however, get the best that medical science provides for our combat veterans. And I guess that what's good enough for a man who's won the Medal of Honor should do for you.'

A long silence followed. Wells pushed himself into the chair behind his desk.

Finally Steve spoke through the office gloom. 'You through?'

'No,' Wells said wearily. 'But what's the use? You've made up your mind. Besides, if I kept talking I might hurt your feelings. Well, I wouldn't want to do *that*. At least you'll make Jackie a happy woman again. I haven't been a husband to her for months.'

'Spill the rest of it.'

'Don't tell *me* what the hell to do, *colonel*. That's behind us now.'

'I'd still . . . I still want to hear the rest of it.'

'Why? Let it drop. It's all over.'

'I've never heard you like this, Rudy.'

'You never will again. All right, you really want to hear it?'

'No. But maybe I should.'

Wells dragged himself away from his seat and walked to where Steve stood in shadow, his left arm covered by a long-sleeved shirt. 'A few days ago, mister, you saved the life of several children. They would have died. Burned to death if you hadn't been there. That means you've paid your debt to society – in every way. We here in this center represent that society and we no longer have a claim on you. You're home free. No obligations. But I'll tell you, personally, because we've known each other for so many years, that I am damned, damned disappointed in you. What's happened to you can never be undone.

150

It's happened. Period. But I never thought I'd see you go under in self-pity.

'You better remember something, Steve. Nobody here ever forced you into an airplane. I told you this once before and maybe I should have said it more often. You volunteered. You went into test flying fully aware that these things do happen. So the shitty hand was dealt. But then you were given a miracle in this place, in the bionics program, and it doesn't seem to matter at all to you. So, we'll find someone else who'll grab at this opportunity. There are more people torn up, busted, burned, and ripped in this country than you could imagine. We've got a whole war full of them and we won't be wanting for volunteers. It's a shame we have to lose your particular qualifications, but we'll muddle our way through. We'll make out. And like I said, starting in the morning you can pick the VA hospital of your choice.'

Steve rolled up his sleeve, extended the skeletal arm toward Wells. 'You wouldn't be saying a word of this if you had seen the face of that child. If you'd heard her screaming at . . .'

Wells shrugged. 'I know what happened. Children scream when they see people who've been burned. When they see compound fractures. Or lepers. Or a whole variety of people mutilated in different ways. So a child who was upset, terrified by fire, in shock, who was going to burn to death if you hadn't saved her, screamed when she saw your arm. She was screaming before, she got another shock, she screamed some more. I'm not impressed. I'm disappointed that you could be so blind.'

'Me? How can—'

Rudy Wells hammered the point. 'You were in a burning bus and you went through flames and you never felt pain. It didn't stop you. You saved lives, quite a few of them. You're blind to the fact that you have an arm that can be repaired and made as good as the bionics limb it was before. What an incredible thing life has given you. We can fix the arm without pain, without removing anything from your body. We could fix it even if you'd crushed it beyond all possible use, and make it even better than it is now. If you weren't so wrapped up in your damned private misery you'd understand you're being offered a third chance, where most men never get more than one.'

Wells moved toward the door, praying silently to himself. 'I've talked myself out. Dr. Killian will attend to your transfer. There's no need for us to see each other again.' He was almost through the door when it happened.

'Doc.'

Hoping, keeping his face a mask, Wells turned. He didn't trust himself to speak.

'You said something about a third chance.'

'Past tense.'

Steve hesitated. Finally: 'I'd like to have it.'

'Why?'

'I can't argue with what you've said here tonight.'

'Isn't it a little late for that?'

Steve's voice was calm. 'I hope not.'

'You broke something off inside Kathy.'

'I know that.'

'You did it to me, too.'

He nodded. 'I know.'

'If we forget what was said in here tonight, Steve, it's got to be all the way.'

'It will be. My word.'

'All right. I'll talk with you in the morning.' He turned again to leave, but was stopped once more.

'Doc, do you know where she is? I – I'd like to see her.'

'God's truth, Steve, I don't know.'

'All right. I . . .' He reached his limit. 'Good night.'

'Good night,' Wells said, and walked down the corridor. When he arrived home, Jackie watched in silence as he went to the telephone and dialed a number directly to Washington, D.C.

The phone rang five times before a sleepy voice answered.

'Oscar? Wake up. Rudy Wells here. In Colorado. Yes, yes. You can call Jackson McKay. Tell him Steve is ready.'

CHAPTER SIXTEEN

He looked nothing like the man one expected to find directing the subtly concealed activities of the Office of Special Operations. Jackson McKay presided over his office from a huge leather swivel chair, a brooding Buddha of huge physical bulk, sustained by a diet of excellent food and quantities of dark beer. The man enjoyed life, was committed to its luxuries, but his bulk belied his excellent physical conditioning. Those who knew him well understood the relationship between Jackson McKay and the Sumo wrestlers of Japan; they were great and heavy men with astonishing agility, layered with fat beneath which were coiled muscles of extraordinary strength.

If McKay well concealed his robust health and strength beneath his gross appearance, he performed as well in disguising a mind of extraordinary strength and precision. Extending over nearly thirty years of intelligence and espionage work, McKay's record included several dozen men dispatched at his hands; he had worked with British Intelligence and Interpol and dealt intimately with the security agencies of perhaps a dozen governments throughout the world. He was also a veteran of the military-security groups of his own country, had been an early member of the wartime OSS and its CIA successor. His penetrating knowledge of international intrigue, and the techniques required to survive in those roily waters, made him a natural selection as the first director of OSO. He was a master of the art of innovation, of introducing the wholly unexpected into his operations, and of keeping the opposition off balance.

He was the man responsible for funding the project they knew as Steve Austin. To Jackson McKay, Steve was not a man but an implement, a device, a weapon. A force, to be applied when and where it would exert the greatest possible effect in the shortest possible time. McKay enjoyed no status as a scientist, but he was a connoisseur of its handiwork, having, during several wars, used 'gadgets' both to assure the demise of the enemy and his own survival. Imagination, McKay devoutly believed, was the single greatest weapon one might possess.

OSO maintained a training camp in the hills of West Virginia, where it developed a force of special agents with the derring-do of Ghurka soldiers. Results were good but casualties high, and when one studied the score sheets, smacked of inefficiency. Something better was needed, and something better loomed with breathtaking promise in the form of the secret bionics and cybernetics laboratories resting on the flanks of the Rockies in Colorado. McKay had always envisioned a super-agent, but more than a foot soldier, an artillery man, or any combat veteran was needed. McKay wanted the very best and he bided his time.

Steve Austin was his reward.

Today was delivery time. Precisely at ten A.M. Goldman came into his outer office with Steve Austin and Dr. Wells. 'Send them right in,' McKay told his secretary. He heaved himself from his seat to greet them. McKay was delighted. Something seemed on fire inside Austin.

He glanced to the side of his desk. A green light glowed. Good. The team for Project Aquila was gathered in the next room. They could wait for a while. His gravelly voice banged through the room. It was upsetting and it was supposed to be.

'Sit down, sit down,' McKay told them. 'Colonel Austin?' The other man turned a hard face to him. 'Colonel, how much do you know of this organization?'

'Next to nothing.'

'Any conclusions on your own?'

Steve's face remained frozen. 'This is silly, McKay,' Austin told him. 'You didn't bring me all the way here, or—' he gestured to Rudy Wells, 'this man either, to play guessing games. So let's stop cocking around and get to it.'

McKay's smile was less forced than Steve expected. 'Very good. Better, in fact, than I expected.'

'Stop patronizing me,' Steve told him. 'One question, though. Did your outfit foot the bill for the program?'

'You mean the project we call Steve Austin?'

'Thanks for the answer,' Steve said. 'And at the same time, I appreciate the confidence you've expressed.' He looked up and smiled humorlessly. 'I don't mean confidence in me,' he went

154

on. 'The confidence you have in your own decisions is what I mean. And since you've paid out all that good money, McKay, why don't you start putting it to work and tell me why I'm here.'

'You're here because we plan certain operations for which your special talents are necessary. In many ways they are critical.'

'Indispensable is more like it.'

'You seem sure of that, colonel.'

Steve leaned back in his chair. 'I wouldn't be here otherwise. And I'd like to get one more thing very clear among us.' He glanced at both McKay and an attentive Oscar Goldman. 'I am not personally grateful to any one of you for being here. I know something about the operation of outfits such as you represent. There's no room in it for personal gratitude. You have a job to do. It's serious, in many ways it's dirty, in some ways it stinks, but,' he shrugged, 'having worn the blue suit for a long time and having exchanged unfriendly volleys between myself and other people doing their best to kill me, I understand and even appreciate what you do. Not in terms of personal commitment, I want you to understand. That's just a professional opinion.

'You will receive my absolute cooperation. I assure you of that. But I am also a guinea pig in this. My personal involvement is with myself. To make everything clear, I don't much give a shit for your operation. I'm willing to go along as part of the great experiment. I just want you to understand that I don't owe you a thing.'

'Fair enough, Colonel Austin.' And suddenly McKay was also all business. 'For the record, you will retain your Air Force rank as colonel with appropriate pay and expenses. Your orders will read that you are on detached duty to the Office of Special Operations for the purpose of testing various types of avionics equipment. However, you will have no further contact with the Pentagon or any other authority, except this office or the facilities in Colorado and, outside of Dr. Wells here, you will never discuss your assignments with anyone beyond a specific list of names which will be provided for you. In the event of my absence when certain crucial decisions must be made, Oscar Goldman will function in my capacity and with full authority.

'The operation we have in mind, colonel, appears to be tailored to your unique qualifications. We are carrying out this mission for the Defense Department. More specifically, a combined request from Air Force and Navy. I want to make something clear. This is not an undercover assignment as that phrase is so often misused. It will be a field assignment, rather unprecedented. You are an excellent swimmer. You were an excellent swimmer before your accident. I would like this on a personal basis, colonel, since I have been informed you have also spent much time in underwater work. I find that surprising, considering how little time has been available from your duties as an astronaut and test pilot.'

'Obviously you have my records,' Steve said. 'If I would add anything to what you know, it would be that I managed the underwater program for weightless tests at the Marshall center in Alabama. We developed equipment for the Skylab station there, and I logged a few hundred hours underwater. Comparison of weightlessness in the water and zero-g states, that sort of thing.'

'That fills in what I needed,' McKay said, openly pleased. 'It will save time for this operation we have in mind, and time is not in our favor. One more point, colonel. I said this would not be an undercover operation. We wouldn't dare turn you loose in that business. Despite your unusual advantages in many ways you wouldn't last twenty-four hours against the pros. You will need know-how, language nuances, certain expertise and techniques.'

McKay watched Austin's face.

'Underwater operation,' Steve said slowly. 'Different from what you may have done before. Got to be or you could use any really good UDT men. So you're talking about endurance and a situation one man or a dozen can't fill. No time for the special training you were talking about, so it's pretty much a one-man operation. And you're not expecting me to get involved with direct contact.' He looked up. 'How many pushups before I qualify?'

In answer, McKay gestured to the door by his left. 'The team for Project Aquila is waiting for us in there. You will be given a full briefing on the assignment. After that we would like to run a test here—'

'What kind?' Steve broke in.

'Hand-to-hand combat,' McKay said. 'I said before, we do not expect personal contact on this assignment. It may, however, take place. There is no other way to evaluate your ability to protect yourself, to escape certain situations, until we see what you can do. After that, we can better plan your equipment.'

'It sounds as if you have quite a party planned for me.'

'We do,' McKay confirmed. 'You will not be playing with amateurs.'

'We expect you to be here two days,' McKay went on. 'Then you will return with Dr. Wells and Mr. Goldman to Colorado, where the necessary modifications will be carried out to your – to your person. I don't wish to seem callous but—'

'But you are,' Steve told him. 'Don't sweat it, McKay.'

McKay nodded, dropped the subject. 'You will be in Colorado several days, which is what Oscar tells me will be the time required for the alterations we have in mind. After that, back here for final, specific training for the operation, and then we commit.'

'I can hardly wait,' Steve said quietly.

No one could walk directly into an OSO briefing room. You walked through a door, closed it behind you, and discovered you were in a trap. Steve knew without asking that the doors were steel-lined beneath the wood, worked by electronic locks. He glanced at Oscar Goldman, who nodded without saying a word. Wells was more interested in OSO's gimmickry. 'Ultraviolet and electronic scan?' he asked. Goldman nodded again, started to reply when a loudspeaker came to life. 'State your name, please. Colonel Austin first.' Steve felt foolish but did as the invisible voice requested, followed by Wells and Goldman.

'Voice ID,' Goldman explained. 'Your characteristics are already on computer file. Better than carrying a badge.' As he spoke the second door opened and Goldman ushered them into the conference room. It was much as Steve expected. He'd been in and out of conference and briefing rooms for years, and this one had all the earmarks of a major combat-operations planning center. Large wall maps and charts, reference manuals, stacks of photographs, projectors of all types, the long, center table and chairs. There was one immediate difference. At the center table stood two men. Another half a dozen men and women were seated at a second table against the far wall, members of the Aquila team. They would remain silent unless needed to answer questions in their respective specialities. Goldman introduced them to the two men at the table. The first was Marty Schiller, whose huge, calloused hand engulfed Steve's own. The pressure was firm, controlled, and a toothy grin appeared on his face. Schiller had skin that gave the impression of torn sandpaper – weathered, leathery, crinkled. He was rawboned, large and rangy, a man of endurance and strength, a UDT man with pararescue and other paramilitary experience.

The second was Dick Carpentier, a swarthy fellow who looked as if the five o'clock shadow on his face could never be removed. He was especially impressed by Steve's credentials as an astronaut who had walked on the moon.

Goldman took a seat and motioned for the others to do the same. The room darkened and a projection screen brightened with a detailed topographic chart of a coastline. 'The area you see is part of the northeastern coast of South America,' Schiller announced in the darkened room. 'The references are six degrees north and fifty-four degrees west, or approximately along the Surinam border, which is Netherlands Guiana, and to its east, French Guiana. The river delta is the mouth of the Maroni, which serves as the border.' The map snapped out and a detailed color photograph appeared in its place. 'This oblique view, taken by an aircraft flying due south toward the shore line, gives some indication of the hills along the shore. As you move southward you get into the steeper hills and rather deep valleys of the Guiana Highlands, which constitute the northern border area of Brazil. You won't, however, be concerned with that.' Again the screen flickered, and the still photograph gave way to the point of view of a pilot flying at no more than a hundred feet above the water. 'Again,' explained Marty Schiller, 'approach is due south, altitude approximately one hundred feet, speed about six hundred knots. Please pay attention to the number of boats that will appear in a moment.'

Steve watched in silence as the photo aircraft continued its rush over the water. A boat appeared to the left of the screen, and then another, and within seconds, at that speed, he had several dozen vessels in sight. 'Most of these ships are fishing vessels, yet there are not any worthwhile fishing grounds in the area.' The coast line appeared as a faint smudge on the horizon, rushed toward them with dizzying speed. The hills focused clearly and Steve saw excellent harbors, steep hills jutting from the water to form deep bays and anchorages. A flash of orange appeared suddenly, then another, and the screen seemed to be burning up along the shore line. The film stopped. 'Take a good look, colonel. What's your guess?'

Steve stared at the screen. 'Back it up thirty seconds,' he told Schiller. The screen went dark, came to light again thirty seconds earlier in the film. Steve waited until the flashes appeared again along the horizon. 'Hold it,' he said. The screen stopped and he looked at the single frame held on the screen.

'There's no mistaking that,' Steve said. 'Antiaircraft.'

'Right,' Schiller said. 'As we can see more clearly now,' and as he finished his words the film rolled again. The flashes were more brilliant and glowing balls drifted toward the camera. More flashes; Steve watched a battery of small rockets erupt away from his point of view. The rocket swept ahead in a spreading fan.

'ECM?' he asked.

Schiller confirmed it. 'Right. Electronic countermeasure decoys.' A moment later the shore line vanished and they were looking at clouds. They remained for perhaps twenty seconds, and then brilliant blue sky appeared as the camera plane ripped its way for altitude. 'What type?' Steve asked Schiller. 'A-5, modified Vigilante. Three engines.' Navy reconnaissance. Steve knew the ship. The screen went dark and the lights came on again.

'To the west of where this film was shot,' Schiller went on, 'is the river city of Nieuw Amsterdam. A bit further west is the Surinam capital of Paramaribo. We can still get people into the capital, but anything east of there is sealed off completely.' The map came onto the screen again and arrows picked out the points mentioned by Schiller. 'To the east, just across the French Guiana border, is the riverport town of Mana. It, too, is

159

closed off completely. You'll have the opportunity to go over these charts in more detail. What you will really want to study, however, are the films of one major river channel, the Maroni.'

Schiller paused, nodded to his associate. 'Ricardo?'

French and Spanish, Steve thought. But Cuban, or what? Just the touch of that accent. Carpentier leaned forward, his muscular forearms on the table, his hands toying with a pencil.

'We have clear evidence,' he began, speaking slowly and carefully, 'that the Russians have moved a group of submarines into a secret new base in the area you have just watched on this film. They are of two types, colonel. The first is their SSBN-Y class, which compares to the category of the Navy's *Ethan Allen*. It is every bit as good as our latest submarines that carry sixteen Poseidon missiles. It has somewhat more power, and it accommodates sixteen Sawfly ballistic missiles with a range of perhaps twenty-two hundred miles. The second type is their SSN-V, or Victor, class, which is an attack submarine without missiles. Those are used to trail our own missile submarines, for obvious reasons.

'Now the submarines themselves are not our concern. The Navy is paid to worry about such things. It is the base that has our attention, and it is the base that has brought you here. We are almost certain this base is deep water. To handle the number of submarines we believe to be involved, it must include a major facility that is above the water line, but that is concealed completely from us. We believe Castro elements are involved but we cannot be sure. It does not really matter. Only the base and what it contains are important, and our evidence adds up to a deep underwater facility, perhaps a mountain hollowed out naturally or even artificially, in an area of jungle coast line about which we know less than we would like. It *appears* that the submarine approaches also are through deep water. We have not been able to get close enough with our own submarines, or even with aircraft, to get decent photography and soundings.' Carpentier shrugged. 'They cover themselves very well.'

'That antiaircraft fire,' Steve said. 'How do they get away with shooting at us? I would think there would be some repercussions from that.'

'Not really,' Schiller added. 'They have declared the area a training base. They've posted it for international charts. A restricted area. Testing or training or what-have-you.'

'Including some pretty heavy AA,' Steve said.

'Very heavy,' Schiller confirmed. 'Latest stuff from Czechoslovakia. Radar controlled. As good as anything we have. Makes it rough getting in there.'

'That Vigilante seemed to make out pretty good,' Steve observed.

Schiller nodded. 'That he did. Two others didn't.'

'Also,' Carpenter said, 'we are in the anomalous position of technically being trespassers to prove a large international illegality. The Surinam government is cooperating fully with the Russians. They are a poor people. The Russians, from what we understand, have made some very large gifts to the right people. Since they do have local cooperation they break no laws. There is the argument that the Russians are violating certain agreements of the Organization of American States. The OAS does not agree, and one wonders if some additional gifts have also found their way to the right people.'

'We must *prove* that there has been such violation, as well as a violation of the historic Monroe Doctrine,' Schiller added.

'It is a dangerous situation,' Carpentier said. 'You see, they use this base for supplies and crew changes. It lets them establish a deepwater nuclear patrol in a southeastern perimeter to the United States. One of the ways they cover themselves, besides the area being marked off for training, is with an oil-exploration program. On the surface it is sponsored by cooperative funds from Russia. This means they have a valid reason for their presence. An *open* presence. They bring in boats, floating derricks—'

'I didn't see those in the films,' Steve interrupted.

'They weren't in the shots you saw,' Schiller told him. 'They were brought in afterward. You'll see them in high-altitude recce film.' He nodded to his partner.

'They have derricks, all sorts of surface and hydrographic activity going on,' Carpentier explained. 'They have also brought in a great deal of oil.'

'Brought it *in*?' Steve showed his surprise.

Carpentier nodded. 'In the shallower waters near the shore

line and along the river they release quantities of oil at different temperatures. The infrared patterns we use for tracking are then made worthless. We also believe they use iron filings, well magnetized, mixed in with the oil. This makes our magnetic anomaly detectors work very poorly.'

'The White House completely agrees with our evaluation, as does Defense's military intelligence,' Schiller said. 'They consider this base to be evidence of Russian duplicity, violating the agreement that came out of the so-called Cuban crisis. Now we've got far worse on our hands. We just can't bull our way in there because we'd be interfering with the sovereignty of Surinam *and* French Guiana, and God knows what else, and we could precipitate all sorts of crises.'

'It is all much worse,' said Carpentier, picking up the theme, 'because now the Russians, they have the missiles, right, but they also have perhaps fifteen to twenty Y-class submarines, *each* with sixteen missiles, and they are never in one place long enough for us to—'

'What about the Victor-class boats?' Steve asked.

'Perhaps a dozen,' said Schiller. 'Fast, maybe forty knots submerged. They're playing cat-and-mouse games with our subs. They're out in such numbers we know they've got to be resupplied. The Navy covers everything out at sea, so we know they're not resupplying at sea. It's all coming out of that base.'

'And where does this leave us?' Steve asked.

'Like I said,' Schiller said, 'we need objective, convincing proof. *Photographs.* Pictures that leave no doubt, pictures that let our people walk into the meetings of the OAS and literally slap them down on the table. Same thing with the United Nations. We need the kind of proof that lets us act swiftly and decisively, that gives the White House the edge in telling the Russians to get the hell out – or else, and not appear arbitrary and provocative. We must demonstrate with this proof that our interests are also the interests of the international community – especially as represented in this hemisphere by the OAS. That's a speech and I apologize.' Schiller shrugged. 'What it comes down to is we've got to get inside that base and get some pictures.'

'And,' added Carpentier, 'get them out again.'

'Who,' asked Steve, 'is "them"?'
Schiller looked at him.
'You are, colonel.'

CHAPTER SEVENTEEN

Ricardo helped him to polish his Spanish in case he might be forced ashore and need to get out on foot. They made three-dimensional models, courtesy of the cartography people, of the coastal area for him to study. He went to the mat, literally, with Ricardo for some karate, took his considerable bumps, and then found what he could do with his remarkably powerful limbs in hand-to-hand encounters. McKay watched it all, delighted with the tight, fine edge Steve was obviously developing. There was more than one way to program a man.

Then came the special adaptations for the mission. They equipped him with new knee joints that reduced friction by nearly ninety percent and in which the heat rise was negligible after the equivalent of some four hours of steady swimming. Next was an immersion test, in which they lowered the water temperature to what could be expected below the surface of the ocean off the Surinam coast. Steve wore a special insulating swimming garment to keep his body warm in the ocean. Wire hookups, laced in a back-and-forth pattern through the suit, drew energy through one of the small nuclear-isotope generators. The same reduction in friction and lowered operating temperature that characterized his new knee joints were built into his feet, so that he had better fore-and-aft ankle movement. The bottom half of his feet now contained a sliding compartment. Steve could release a safety catch and a folded web of woven metal slid forward through an opening just behind his toes. The folded web hinged back and was locked in place, and the fins then opened to full size so that he was 'wearing' swim fins that greatly increased his speed and maneuverability either on or beneath the surface of the water. If he needed to leave the water and move across land, he had only to unhinge the fins, snap the webs closed, bend the unit forward, and slide it back into his foot.

The capacity of the oxygen cylinder inside Steve's left thigh, just above the knee of the bionics limb, was supplemented by a

164

unit strapped to his body that could provide another thirty minutes of oxygen. The installation was repeated on his right.

He was given a camera, but in case he lost it, a miniature camera was inserted in the false eye. To activate the camera, Steve pressed against the side of his head, where a trip switch was embedded beneath the plastiskin that had been built around his once-shattered eye socket. This released the shutter mechanism. To take a picture he merely blinked his eye. The muscles still worked. His eye-camera had a capacity of twenty exposures.

If the way *back* from the underwater approach to the submarine pen were blocked, he could try to swim north or even south along the coast and they'd find him through a homing transmitter. But they also equipped him with weapons in case he had to fight his way overland through jungle and swamp – when the transmitter might not pick him up and he'd be entirely on his own.

His left hand, the bionics hand, was modified so that the outer side was provided with a bottom layer of silastic, over which went a strip of steel, extending from the wrist down to the end of the fifth finger. Plastiskin camouflaged steel. The outer covering of the hand when clenched into a fist received the same treatment. Properly braced he could punch his way through heavy wood or light metal. The middle finger gave him a weapon with reach beyond his body. Fanier's technicians disconnected and removed the finger and replaced it with a digit built to Schiller's specifications. When he extended the finger straight out and snapped a presslock, the curving cylinder that formed the finger became rigid. Once he rigidified the finger it became the barrel of a needle dart gun. It activated with a small CO_2 cartridge and a revolving chamber that contained a swift-acting poison. The darts were designed to penetrate skin, dissolve with impact, and spread the poison into the system to take its effect within six seconds.

Getting information back was the primary purpose of the operation, even if they couldn't get Steve and the photos back. A miniature wire recorder powered with two mercury-cell batteries was inserted into Steve's right leg. He could tape up to ten minutes through a small microphone extractable from the limb. He would have to be back on the surface for this action. When he completed taping his message he could twist a control on the microphone to rewind the wire. Then, using the radio transmitter built into his right leg, he could burst-transmit the recorded message. It was a system that had been in use for years aboard scientific satellites – compressing long periods of data into a single-burst message sent out in only minutes. In the case of Steve's recording equipment, ten minutes could be burst-transmitted in fifteen seconds.

There would be no great trouble picking up the transmission. The network of military communications satellites meant that there would always be two or three of those birds in position. If there were a problem in transmission power, the Air Force would have a U-2 or an RB-57B overhead at seventy thousand feet. One way or another they hoped to pick up whatever Steve sent.

They had required nearly a week for the modifications, for other equipment to be installed within his bionics system, for the equipment to be checked out and tested.

Now Dr. Wells stood before Jackson McKay's desk, ignoring for the moment the gestured invitation to be seated. To McKay's left, Oscar Goldman stood by his own leather chair. 'Where are they now?' Wells asked.

McKay pressed a button on the left side of his desk and the room darkened. A wall screen leaped into glowing life with a clear map representation of the northeast coast of South America. 'This is a replica of the chart being used at this moment in our situation room,' McKay said. 'The latest reported positions of Soviet vessels, surface and underseas, are shown there, and,' he pointed with a desk ruler, 'there. Of course there's a time lag in such reports. We gather these by satellite reconnaissance and aircraft reconnaissance. Now, over here,' he pressed another button and a glowing line snaked its way across the map, 'is the *intended* course of our force. But they are doing everything possible to avoid being tracked and they are very good at their business.

'Somewhere in this area, the submarine with Austin will ease to the surface. There will, of course, be considerable distraction through the entire area. That distraction will lead the Russians to assume, as we would, that some infiltration attempt will be made or is under way. A two-man torpedo sub will work its way into the defense zone, where it will be tracked by the Russians, and the two men aboard the sub will be killed – I'm sorry; the two men who will be "lost" at sea died accidentally in the twenty-four-hour period before the task force left port. A plane crash, in fact. We expect the Russians will be convinced when they find the bodies of two Americans and will not spend time looking for Steve.'

'The truth is you're a cold bastard, McKay. But I suppose you have to be in your line of work.' Wells sighed and leaned his head back against the chair. 'I really don't mean to be this antagonistic, it's just that Steve . . .'

'We understand,' McKay told him.

'Do you? *Really* understand? In every respect, no matter what has happened to him, what's been done to him, Steve remains a *man*. An extraordinary man, superior, marvelously flexible, but still very much and in many ways, a vulnerable human being. If his skull is crushed, despite the additional protection he now has, he will die like any other person. If his heart is pierced, the puncture will be just as fatal as for any other human being. If he bleeds excessively, he will die. He can freeze, burn, drown, suffocate. He feels pain, even though he can withstand more pain, and still function, than before. He's been in so many ways transformed into even more of an extraordinary individual than he was before, he's indeed superior, but by no means superhuman.'

Marty Schiller joined them. 'We've received the coded signal through the comsat net,' he said quietly. 'The Russians picked up the two bodies on the decoy sub. That means Steve is on his way.'

CHAPTER EIGHTEEN

The explosions came to them as distant, muffled booms, rolling coughs of sound from miles away. Steve Austin stood on the small platform of the submarine deck, listening to the sighing thunder, trying to hear details above the sound of water off metal. A light breeze came from the west. He ignored the rumbling sounds, the explosions brought on by the decoy maneuvering to draw attention away from them. Ricardo Carpentier tugged at his arm. 'They're almost ready,' he told Steve. 'Okay,' Steve replied, and turned to watch the mixed Navy and OSO crew at work.

The nuclear submarine was a modification unlisted in any public document. A teardrop in shape, with twin nuclear turbines, it could do fifty knots a thousand feet beneath the surface. It carried eight torpedo tubes forward and four aft. It was designed as a killer sub, but it had been modified for special operations such as the mission now under way. The sub rolled uncomfortably on the surface, a strange wallowing motion that reminded everyone she wasn't designed for stability anywhere except down deep. Steve ignored the motion and concentrated on the men working just forward of his position. A large hatchway had opened, and dim red lights showed the men moving two dull forms through the water in the open compartment. Steve glanced along the deck and noticed gray shadows, men with automatic weapons at the ready. He knew there were more at the stern. Above and behind him a sweep radar kept watch on the sea lost in darkness. Nothing within miles. It wouldn't stay that way for too long.

They were fourteen miles off the Surinam coast. Far enough to avoid immediate attention, yet the distance would not overly complicate what he had to do. He turned his attention back to the compartment. Several swimmers were moving the larger forms away from the submarine, and Steve saw that the securing lines were still in place before activation. A voice called from the water, 'They're ready.'

Steve turned to Ricardo. Another man held a shaded red lamp in position for Ricardo to make a last-moment visual check of his equipment. Ricardo went expertly over the scuba gear, the cameras, infrared equipment. He had performed this same inspection a hundred times before, was still edgy about the final examination. He nodded his head slowly and slapped his hand lightly against Steve's arm. 'It is time,' he said. Steve reached out and squeezed Ricardo's shoulder. They had become friends. Ricardo and another man helped Steve slip into the water. The fold-snap flippers were already in place, and Steve eased his way to the first of the two dark shapes rolling in the sea, still tethered to the sub.

These would be his way in and, they hoped, his ride back to the submarine.

They were Able and Baker, two most unusual porpoises. Dark-bodied, with wavy streaks of white along their flanks, their snouts glistening, eyes gleaming in the bare, red light from the submarine, they were strangely lifeless at this moment, rolling without any attempt to stabilize themselves. And they would remain so until Steve brought them both to life. Able and Baker were ingenious creations of the Naval Office of Scientific Research. At any distance over a dozen feet it would take another porpoise to distinguish them from the real thing. Once they were activated they moved through the sea with precisely the same motions as the living animals.

The naval scientists had labored for years to produce these mechanical electronic simulations. Flexmetal construction guaranteed a full articulation. They moved through the sea with their flukes duplicating the motions of the animals. Their flippers were fully articulated, and the long bodies themselves showed an outer skin that rippled in response to internal movement. Animals kept in huge artificial bays had been studied, and every movement registered was fed into a computer until the computer produced a mathematical readout of the engineering construction necessary to prepare the artificial equivalent of the animal. That meant artificial duplication of biological material, and it also meant developing a computer that would fit within the artificial porpoise and that would perform two tasks: assuring normal movement of the creature on the surface or within the sea, and, providing for input of new command material. The onboard computer had been developed originally for the Gemini spacecraft program, and modified to fit the needs of the porpoise effort. Directional control, or so-called position control, emerged from an old missile program that had been upgraded drastically through the years. It had begun with the original SM-64A Navaho ramjet missile of the Air Force when it was urgent to come up with an inertial-guidance mechanism. The Navaho had to cruise at two thousand miles an hour for five thousand miles, and then plunge with accuracy into its presented target. Along came the ballistic missile to shove the Navaho into a museum, but not its inertial-guidance system. That went into the ballistic-missile submarines of the Navy and into other long-range vessels and aircraft. As components were reduced in size, what had been the size of a large valise now went into a container the size of a softball. It was micro-miniaturization at its best, and with such manner of packaging, the porpoises became a reality. There was one final key – power. It came from the compact nuclear generators – dense, almost massive containers that ran for only two weeks before burning out, in order to deliver high power during that period. So the porpoises were born with their constant-energy source, their marvelous articulation and shape and movement. The outer skin did more than duplicate the visual appearance of the animal. It bounced along the exact wave length the reflections by radar from the real animal. The two porpoises in the water with Steve had functional blowholes and were programmed to emit the same high-pitched, sonarlike cries as do the real animals.

Steve eased his way to the first machine, code-named Able, slipped into a body harness that packaged him neatly within the porpoise, and placed his hands within reach of manual override controls. He was now within a complete miniature submarine that possessed the distinct advantage of being almost indistinguishable from a living creature. When moving along the surface, Steve would be able to see some distance ahead during darkness, thanks to an infrared scope powered by the single-point nuclear generator. If he went beneath the surface he would draw from the oxygen supplies of the porpoise, rather than draining his own limited supply that was packaged onto the harness he wore. If he believed himself free of surveillance, he could activate floodlights under the water or even use a limited-range sonar that would provide him with an underseas path through otherwise-invisible obstacles. Two-way radio equipment had been fitted into the construction framework. He had automatic transmitters to be activated in an emergency. In the belly of the machine was an array of small, silent-running, torpedo-like projectiles, carrying not explosives but a variety of devices to be used for diverting attention away from him if he should be under pursuit.

He studied the small control panel, the instruments glowing, feeding from the nuclear generator on standby. He flicked the control to bring the power flow to full on, depressed the inertial-guidance and display system. A circular glowscope brightened, and Steve studied a gridmap with glowing reference points. The coast line showed clearly, with indentations of rivers. A slowly pulsating light indicated his own position, and a second light, this one blue instead of orange, showed him the relative position of Baker, the fully robot porpoise. The computer, tied in with the inertial-guidance system, would always show him precisely where he would be in relation to the coast line and the particular bay he sought. Later, if he were still with Able – he smiled to himself, realizing he had already come to think of the machine as a living creature – he would be able to pick up a bearing and position reference of the submarine and go full speed to be picked up.

He turned to a second control panel, much simpler than the array for Able. This was his remote control for Baker, which had no provision for a passenger, internally or otherwise. Instead, the accompanying porpoise was an arsenal of electronic and ordnance equipment. Steve could guide Baker by working the small control stick inside Able, but he preferred to be free of such distraction, especially when he would be closer to the base. While Baker was on automatic, it would remain within a general distance of Able. Not a fixed distance at all, but a computer-directed variation resembling the actions of two porpoises at sea, moving closer and then a greater distance away, slipping beneath the surface and then sliding along the top with the dorsal fin exposed. Unless Steve hit the 'command' switch to take over direct control, Baker would maintain its fluctuating formation position with Able.

One final performance was built into the two machines. Each

171

was designed to 'die', when necessary, with a performance that would match a real animal in its death throes. If the porpoises were attacked and struck by gunfire to such an extent that no one expected them to survive, they – at least Baker – must 'die' with fully appropriate movements and sounds. And as a last resort, should there be the danger of the Russians or anyone else, for that matter, being able to capture one of the marvelous creatures, after a specified time interval the porpoise would destroy itself. The nuclear generator was programmed to over-extend itself and to release its energy in a violent spray of heat, consuming the generator and the entire porpoise as well. Should damage be excessive, the generator would 'blow' in three minutes. Not much time, Steve thought, but just enough.

He completed his checkout of both porpoises. Time to move out. For a while his movement would be straightforward. Get as close to the base as possible before encountering the de-fenses. He flicked switches to place the controls on auto, punched a position two miles from the harbor to the sub base as the destination, and felt the fluke behind him vibrate as it moved the porpoise forward.

He had a sudden moment when this whole thing seemed crazy, impossible. Here he was, inside this creature, moving through the sea, the same man who'd ridden a skittering angular metal bug through vacuum to the surface of a world that had never even *known* the first drop of water.

A direct course would have helped. With a speed of six knots along the surface he could have recovered the distance to the submarine base in just a little more than two hours. But fol-lowing a straight line would have been a dead giveaway that the porpoises were phonies, and so the computer was programmed to follow an erratic course, much as porpoises might have done. The Surinam coast had taken heavy rains for several days and there was a heavy water flow from rivers and streams into the ocean. This added to the current against which Able and Baker fought, a side current that required constant correction from the computer. It presented no operational difficulties, but it messed up the time allocated just to reaching the coast, and reduced drastically the hours of darkness on which they had planned. There was nothing to do but ride it out. The wind quickened and Steve found himself taking jarring bounces from wave action. It would be an awful time to become seasick. He activated the porpoise's oxygen system and that helped somewhat to offset the wave action, as well as the peculiar pitching motion of the porpoise through the movement of the fluke. He concentrated on the infrared scope, hoping it would reveal any vessel at sea. Nothing. He remained within his strange world, a modern Jonah in the belly of a small mechanical whale, watching the glowing pips of Able and Baker crawling across the surface of the gridmap.

He didn't need the map or the glowing points of light to tell him when he was within reach of the opposition. They announced their presence, still distant, through deep, pulsating waves of pressure that pounded through the sea and trembled through the structure of Able – random explosions about which he'd been briefed. Patrol boats moved lazily in crisscross patterns, trailing explosive charges that boomed and thudded through the ocean. The sounds reaching him were like those of a distant squall line, an intermittent barrage that set off its charges without pattern, that could catch you unawares by its very randomness.

Strangely enough, the explosions were a lure to sharks. It had taken a long time to understand the grim reality of this truth, but the lesson had been learned during and after the great sea battles of the Second World War. The thundering blasts that raced through the sea, the finned marauders seemed to learn, meant fresh meat in the ocean, and the sharks would congregate by the hundreds in response to the booming sounds. The Russians, and whatever locals worked with them, added to the shark presence by chumming the water with fresh meat and blood. It had meant hairy moments for men trying to swim into the base on their own, or even riding atop the two-man torpedo subs. But what had been an obstacle before could now be turned into an advantage. If the porpoises were sighted by their dorsal fins as these cut the water, they would fail to attract any particular attention. If the sharks sighted them they *might* consider them to be porpoises or, failing to pick up a familiar scent, the sharks might become overcurious. It could go either way, the sharks becoming a problem, or their very presence assuring Steve's continued anonymity in the water.

173

Three thousand yards out from shore, as indicated by the glowing pips on the gridmap, the chumming was so extensive the sharks had long since passed any period of feeding frenzy, when they went mad with bloodlust and would strike after anything that moved. No need to. They had more food than necessary, and they swam about in lazy groups, idly curious and content to snap when they desired at the food drifting down from the boats.

The distance to shore was just over two thousand yards when Steve decided to go deeper. Long hours had passed and the sun was already over the horizon behind him. By now he could see what was going on along the surface. Men in patrol boats, bored with the long hours of cruising – and touchy about being tested by their superiors with incessant mock attempts to penetrate the base during the night hours – had taken to shooting at anything they saw moving. Not with the intent of firing at an enemy, but for the sheer relief of the action. The sharks ignored their fellows struck with gunfire, but Steve could hardly afford such indifference. The slow-moving fins of the two porpoises were too promising a target. Time to go down.

He eased forward gently on the small control stick jutting upward from the panel, felt the slapping action of waves easing off. Several feet beneath the surface, he found visibility better than hoped for, the morning light slanting deep into the water. He had been told to expect a deep channel through which the Russian boats moved in and out of the sub base but to avoid, as long as possible, any movement within or over what would obviously be kept under careful study. The gridmap outlined the channel, and Steve maneuvered, now down to four knots, over the ocean bottom to the north of the channel. He kept up the wandering motion, always working closer to the shore line. Several times huge sharks drifted nearby, moving casually, eyeing Able and Baker, making no unusual moves.

The explosions pounded with greater force through the water. No longer were they distant muffled thunder. Now the blasts came as overpressure he could feel with his own body, jarring motions that rocked Able and blurred the instruments in front of him. He was able to see and to hear the patrol boats cruising the surface. Once a mess of bloody meat drifted at an angle before his path, sliding with a scraping sound along the

174

artificial porpoise skin. A huge white shark followed close behind, drifted to the side and stared directly at him. Steve worked the controls to thrash the fluke and the shark slid away.

One thousand yards. The water temperature was going up. During a period of perhaps thirty seconds he could feel the sudden temperature rise through his special suit. He knew what was happening even as the view blurred. Oil, a greasy layer oozing down from the surface, hotter than the water.

He cursed the oil as it left a thin film across the optical system of Able, seriously reducing his vision from the porpoise. Nothing to do about it now except continue in as straight a line as possible, compensating for the current pushing down from the north, to his right, working toward the entrance to the underground passage. Easier said than done. The current this close to the shore, fed by water pouring down to the sea by the rivers and streams, rocked the porpoise. Visibility worsened as he continued through layers of oil.

Four hundred yards to go. He slowed the forward motion of Able, knowing the Baker porpoise would maintain its speed and position along with his own. Slow down, he warned himself. Think. He felt his right arm trembling, wondered if holding it in the same position so many hours was bringing it on. That, he realized, and the energy drain. He barely drifted over the bottom and reached into a compartment for high-energy food bars and water. He considered several pills he carried for a jolt of energy, decided against the drugs at this time. It could be many hours before he would be able to come back this way, and getting the backlash from the amphetamines could do him more harm than good. He ate slowly, drinking through a tube from the storage compartment of Able. Within minutes he felt better and—

Something smacked against the side of Able. Steve went rigid, tensed himself to unplug from the porpoise and go to his own breathing system and get out. The porpoise rocked again, and he heard a harsh, scraping sound. It was one of several cables mooring the bogus floating oil derricks to the bottom. His attention had wandered. He had drifted instead of maintaining position over the bottom. He moved the stick forward, throwing more energy to the fluke. Able swerved sharply as a

175

fin caught against the cable. Then he was free, moving away from the cables.

Two hundred yards, perhaps less. The gridmap wasn't that accurate where such close range was involved. He'd have to play it now as best he could, commit to the deeper channel used by the subs. That had its own disadvantages. The explosions now thundered all around him. Close enough for the over-pressures to hurt. Several blows shoved Able hard to the side, made his ears ring. He hoped they couldn't keep this up *all* the time. The pressure waves would work their way along the sub-channel, clear through the underground river passage right into the base. It must have some thing to do, he realized, with the bogus attack during the night. The Russians had already stopped twelve men trying to infiltrate the base. Two more last night. They'd be edgy. Maybe not, he argued with himself. They might figure they'd mopped up pretty good. He cut short his self-debate, concentrating on what he would do next. Vision this close was lousy, a combination of oil and muck carried down by the rivers.

He checked his breathing gear. A regenerative system that created no telltale bubbles rising to the surface. He was glad the UDT, the underwater demolition teams, had used these for years, worked out the bugs from the system. But you played advantage against disadvantage. You couldn't go that deep with the regenerative system. It could raise hell with your lungs. He might have to get away from the porpoise, he realized. That need might come with shocking suddenness. Play it by the numbers, he told himself. While he had the time he checked out the camera, switched to his own breathing system. No more horsing around, he instructed himself.

His head ached from the explosions. Long hours locked within the porpoise, breathing tank air. He worked his way to the left, edging south, letting the current carry Able while he went another dozen feet down. Make it more difficult to be seen from the surface. He *hoped*.

The muck from the shore mixing with oil was destroying his hopes of decent visibility. He toyed with the idea of using the sonar. It would be a considerable gamble. The Russian defenses would be on the alert for such a move. There was no way to disguise the signals, even the weak pulses from Able, if he had to use the equipment. But if things kept up this way he wouldn't have much choice. The optical system for Able at best left something to be desired, and this was far from best. He shook his head. That last explosion ... they must have dropped a whole sequence of charges. Not one blast, but a staccato rumbling that slammed into the porpoise and threw him wildly against the harness. Like someone setting off a string of bombs. The pressure waves rolled and tumbled as they slammed into him, allowing no surcease between impacts. He breathed deeply, slowly. Danger here of hyperventilating if he started rapid breathing. Could knock him out easily. He shook his head again to clear the ringing sounds. He couldn't keep this up much longer. The going was getting dangerously slower and slower.

He increased the power slightly. A shaft of sunlight speared through heavy growth before him. He could slip beneath the billowing, swaying mass. Might be able to use the sonar then. If the men in the patrol boats had seen the porpoises, they might confuse the chattering, high-pitched squeal for real animals. It would be hard to tell the difference. His own sonar signal would be buried within the peculiar acoustics of the mammals. A real porpoise chattered away with an astonishing four high-frequency impulses per second, a cacophony of bleats, whistling cries, sonar clicks, quacks, and even the sound of squawking you expected to hear only from a seagull.

He eased beneath the heavy plant growth. Barely in time. Churning sounds grew louder. A boat overhead, moving closer to him. He wondered about the second porpoise, Baker. He'd forgotten for the moment that it was closer to the surface. Too close! They were on to something. He wished he could see, but the water was oily, and the screws from overhead were messing things up badly. Sunlight twisted and danced from the seething water overhead, mixing with oil and muck, and he knew he couldn't hack this much longer. He froze when he heard new sounds. Unmistakable. Automatic weapons and ... he listened carefully. The screws were pounding heavier now. A series of explosions. One blow after the other. Cannon shells. Had to be. But what—?

A red light flashed on the control panel. Baker ... the second porpoise. The light told him what had happened. The porpoise was taking hits. Its systems were being chewed to ribbons. Steve hit the controls for Baker, throwing full power to the reactor, ordering a reversal of course. He hoped they were still close enough for the sonic signal to be picked up. All that acoustic interference could drown the signal. He'd know soon enough. If it worked, Baker would be moving away from him, the fluke thrashing the water. He heard another sound above the booming explosions and boat screws. A shrill chattering at full power. Baker ... no question now that the porpoise was finished. It was going into its preprogrammed death throes. If the systems worked, a red chemical would be pouring out from the porpoise as it thrashed about wildly. Steve hoped the controls would operate long enough for Baker to lead its pursuers away from the immediate vicinity. He'd never have a better chance. The sea was almost boiling with sound. His own sonar should work, being limited to immediate range. He switched on the system, watched the scope glow with reflections of the passageway ahead. He moved the control stick forward, almost reckless now with the urge to move, to cover as much distance as possible during the tumult overhead. The porpoise cleaved its way through water and suddenly things went completely dark. Inside the tunnel now. Staying as close to the bottom as he could remain and still keep moving, he continued away from the uproar. When the blast came he was ready for it – the reactor in Baker, letting go as planned, sending out a violent pressure wave. It was far enough away not to hurt, but more than strong enough to cover his movement. They should be milling about on the surface, wondering what had happened. They were pursuing an animal and the animal had exploded. If the breaks stayed with him it would take them some time to figure things out, even longer to start looking for another phony porpoise, or something else.

The current began to fade. The sonar scope showed the sides of the underground channel broadening swiftly. He must be inside. He stayed close to the bottom, barely moving, trying to figure out what he might expect when he eased his way toward the surface. The sonar swept thirty degrees to each side and he had an impression of walls far to each side of his position. That meant there'd be no curving passage. Just the underground channel into a huge cave. He needed to know how far back it

178

went. He moved forward slowly, the thundering sounds now muted, far behind him. The scope picked up something new. No mistaking the shapes he saw glowing before him. Long, symmetrical. *Subs.* To his right, a line of them. The hulls of the Russian boats. Seven, then ... at least a dozen moored along the right side of the cave. Could be more. Should he move beneath the subs, using them for cover, or move to the opposite side of the cave, where there might be some growth along the bottom he could use for cover? The right decision could keep him alive. The wrong one could put him directly into the jaws of the defenses.

Whoever was running the defense system solved the problem for him. He squinted with the sudden pain of a shattering alarm signal. It pulsated through the water, hammering brutally at him. Far ahead of him lights began to stab through the water. Moving directly toward him. *Trapped.*

CHAPTER NINETEEN

Move.

No time to think. Do it instinctively, as he had planned it, as Carpentier and Schiller had rehearsed him for three days and nights. When the time came to abandon the porpoise there could be no waste motion.

His hand banged against a switch cover, snapped it away, pushed a toggle switch full forward. In the same motion he was out of the harness, shoving hard with both hands, making sure not to catch the thick cylinders strapped to his body against the structural rails of the porpoise. He had exactly ten seconds to free himself from the machine, ten seconds to get away from the fluke. He eased away carefully, kicking with his legs and swimming hard to get to the side. Not a moment too soon as the fluke seemed to go mad. At the count of ten seconds the nuclear generator went to maximum power. This close to Able, Steve heard the shrill whine of released energy as the fluke thrashed about, almost exploding the porpoise away from him. Steve went for the bottom, then struck out away from the bright lights that glowed through the water from the sub base, heading for the darker side of the cavern, where he hoped he could find weeds or some other growth. Behind and above him the porpoise went through several bizarre turns, then struck out in an erratic, weaving path. The thrashing sounds mixed with distant explosions and the churning of screws as patrol boats headed in the direction of the sudden turmoil in the water. There'd be more soon, and Steve knew Able was doing its last work in covering his presence. He heard the high-pitched squeal stabbing the water, then hissing sounds barely audible to his ears. These were small, gas-actuated cylinders fanning away from Able to create their own disturbance, emitting the same squealing noise. Anyone listening with hydrophones or studying a sonar scope would be confused, would judge that a school of porpoises had penetrated the cavern and then gone berserk. The cylinders shot through the water, hissing and squealing in wide,

180

random patterns. Whatever sea life present in the sea would be rushing about as well. It could be his chance. He swam with frantic energy, using only his feet, groping with his hands in front of him, starting up toward the surface now, hoping he could take advantage of the bright floodlights he was able to detect as he moved upward. The sound of screws was louder now. More ominous was the fact that he heard so many of them.

Something brushed his hand and he twisted violently to the side, reaching for a knife at his belt. In the same moment he knew he was moving within tall plant growth from the bottom. He slid gratefully into its midst, eased his body to the vertical and moved the flippers slowly to work to the surface. The higher he went the more he saw of the lights, rippling reflections of blue-white floodlights in spattering glows. Then he was immediately beneath the surface, the lights splashing from the oily water. He made certain nothing moved near him. The close-fitting, flat rubber over his head wouldn't reflect light but there was always the danger of the mask throwing back a reflection. No other way to go; he had to commit.

He broke the water silently, without a splash. He tried to accustom his eyes to the dazzling glare of lights several hundred feet away. A new barrage of sound above the surface came to him. Generators, engines, the sounds of men shouting, calling to one another. *Bursts of gunfire* ... of course; Abel, still tearing through the water, showing itself with a glistening hump and fin, calling attention to its presence. More firing. Automatic weapons, the flat crackling sound of clips being emptied. Above the thundering roars he heard the sharp whine of bullets ricocheting from the water.

He treaded water effortlessly, making sure to keep only the upper part of his head above the surface, turning slowly. The lights were no longer directly in his eyes and he could see more clearly now. The base was larger than he'd been told. He raised his eyesight and saw rock glistening wetly overhead, reflecting the blue-white floods. Wet rock ... of course; condensation would be an almost constant process here. Machinery would be throwing off exhaust fumes, but with the mask over his face he smelled nothing of the cavern. The roar of engines and continuing bursts of gunfire drowned out any machinery from the base itself. Far to his right he saw what he had come to confirm

181

on film. A line of dark shapes in the water, against a gangway of some sort built along the rock walls. He reached for the camera fastened to his waistbelt. His hand groped beneath the water. The camera was gone, lost somewhere when he was getting out of the porpoise. Well, that's why they sent along a self-contained camera, he told himself. He scanned the surface again, studying the position of the patrol boats. They were all about, milling, searchlights sweeping the water and—

A fast-moving cone of light sent him under. A dazzling glow swept immediately overhead. They were searching everywhere. He waited several seconds, came up again slowly, prepared to move underneath once more. But the light was gone, flashing along the walls far to his left. He reached up with his right hand, crossing across his chest, feeling for the trip switch embedded beneath the plastiskin. He pushed hard against the side of his head, near the socket, feeling the switch move. He turned to the end of the line of submarines, concentrated, blinked his eyes. *One*. He repeated the movement. 'Take two of everything,' Goldman had advised. He moved his head to the left, taking two more pictures. Then a view of the dock across the cavern. Maybe too far away to have it come out with any detail, but the photo people could worry about that. He took two shots of the boats in the water, dove for his life when a searchlight beam moved his way, came up once more. The boat was turning away, close enough for him to see the men on deck crouching down, holding their arms before their eyes.

Crouching down ... arms before their eyes ... What was—?
In that instant he became blind.

Instantly, reflex governing his actions, his hands pushed him beneath the surface. He wanted to cry out from the sudden agony in his right eye. He instinctively brought up his hand, trying to hold the eye, and discovered he was pawing ineffectively at the face mask. He drew in deep breaths, fighting the pain. For a long moment he fought vertigo, the waves of dizziness destroying all sense of balance. Stay still, he warned himself. Just hang on, don't move your head. Let it all settle down ... Vertigo could make him helpless here. If he were left with no sense of up or down or right or left ... nausea rippled his stomach and he fought down the bile that threatened to erupt from his throat. It wouldn't do to throw up into the mask.

182

He breathed deeply, evenly, trying to think, and then he knew what had happened. He opened his eye, saw streaks and spatterings of red. No vision yet, but it was coming back. Whorls and cartwheels of light as his eyes struggled to readapt.

They had one smart somebody protecting this place, a man who knew how to put himself in the mind of someone who would be trying to get in, for photographs or even to bring in explosive charges. You figure the intruders are going to be good; they've been trying for a long time. Fourteen men you know of have been lost. So you figure they're going to come in again, and there's every chance they'll send in underwater demolition teams. Maybe you won't see them, you won't have a chance to get to them before they tear up the place. Well, men must see in order to do their job. He had his warning and had been slow in reacting. The men on the patrol boat crouching down, covering their eyes. Because a flare bomb was about to go off, and whoever was looking at it when it detonated would be temporarily blinded.

He felt an alarm clamoring in the back of his head. He needed to think. He could see better now, but it was taking all his concentration. The signs were unmistakable but he couldn't put the pieces together. He blinked rapidly, realized he was wiping out the rest of the tiny film cartridge. He had enough. What he had come for. But unless he put himself into high gear he'd never get out. He stared with his right eye. Better than he expected. Normal vision was almost back, and—

He went cold with the realization of what was happening, what had happened.

The explosions had stopped.

It was a dead giveaway. Think ... figure there are UDT men inside the cavern. They set off the flare bomb. Maybe two or three or four. He couldn't tell, of course, after that first eye-stabbing agony. There could have been a dozen more, fired in rapid succession after he went back underwater. Then what? If they figure there are men caught unawares with the flare bombs, they also know they have them off balance. What next? They send their own men into the water after them. They send them after what they expect will be half-blinded, groping swimmers in the water.

The weeds had saved him. Now he could see the lights underwater, knew the lights had swimmers behind them. Swimmers who would be armed. Spearguns, most likely. Knives for the close work. Looking for him.

He stayed in the growth, pushed himself lower, went as far as he could get until he felt the flippers on his feet brush against bottom. He'd have to do something. The people looking for him had all the time in the world. He didn't. His clock moved with the flow of oxygen into his lungs, and he had perhaps an hour left in the tanks. Time was on *their* side. They could wait him out. He knew they'd have detectors ready to pick up any propulsion sound. Anything that used a screw or a hydrojet to move. They had men swimming around so they couldn't detect him through instruments. They'd have to find him directly. With the lights. Man to man.

That should have tipped the odds in his favor. Maybe not, despite his tremendous speed. He didn't know how many swimmers they had in the search. They'd be keeping a close watch where the cave narrowed down to the underwater passage. And the boats beyond that, outside on the surface. Waiting. A hell of a gauntlet to run. But now that he knew what was happening, at least he could make his move. And whatever it would be, hanging around while he sucked away his oxygen wasn't the answer. He hated to do it, but he'd have to surface again. Get his bearing and— No, he told himself sharply. You're against the wall. You saw where, how it curves coming into the cavern. He argued with himself. Stay along the wall. Work your way back that way. No one can get to you from one side. You can see them coming by their lights. . . .

It was the only sane way. He moved deeper into the weeds until he touched rock. Difficult to see. The wall was to his right. Okay. That's an established reference. He turned his head to the left. Lights. Many of them, moving through the water. Men behind the lights, moving in sweep pattern. He brought his watch closer to the faceplate. The dial glowed. Forty-five minutes of air left. Better to risk everything than be assured of getting creamed because he ran out of air and had to surface.

He started moving, his legs working in a slow, powerful beat that gave him good forward speed with the least possible disturbance of the water around him. It was rougher than he expected. He had to judge his distance by the shimmering pools of light to his left. Not good enough; the lights were moving, and he had no idea which sources paralleled movement, which moved away or closer to his own changing position. If he could see the wall to his right, the sloping, roughly shaped rock, it would help tremendously. But he couldn't. Several times he thudded into an outcropping of rock, stunning himself. Without the wetsuit he would have torn his shoulder. As it was he felt the material rip. A repetition of the scraping blow would flay open the skin.

It took nearly fifteen minutes of precious oxygen to reach the tunnel. Here he brought himself to almost a drifting movement. He felt the current, the different temperature of the water. More than that he saw the glow of lights ahead of him. Lights within the tunnel, lights above on the surface. To hell with those. The men underneath, at his level, were the danger. He started forward, stopped again. He was making a mistake and it came to him with absolute certainty. He was watching the lights, knew there would be men behind them. What about the others who might be lying on the bottom, looking up, waiting to see a form moving by them? That's when they'll move . . . The knife was in his hand. Wait. You may get in a worse tangle. He extended the middle finger of his bionics hand and snapped the presslock.

No more time to waste. The knife was back in his right hand, his left arm extended slightly before him as he maneuvered with his legs only. He went to the bottom, moving steadily, looking not for the lights but for shadows. He saw the first man almost at once. He was treading water, holding his position against the outflowing current, a speargun in his hand. Steve stayed low until he was directly beneath the other man, and when he came up it was with a savage thrust with his legs, his right arm extended ahead of him. The knife went in low in the belly, and Steve kept thrusting with his legs. He thought fleetingly of taking the speargun, but it was tethered to the other man's wrist and there was a thrashing paroxysm going on there. Steve curled his body, went for the bottom again, moved off to the side. As he expected, someone saw the sudden movement, came in to examine what was happening.

Steve kept moving over the bottom, trying not to attract attention. Lights were turning his way. Always try for surprise . . .

Ricardo had told him that over and over, and the words came back forcefully now. He had speed. Considerable speed.

He threw all his strength into his legs, felt them hammer the water behind him. In moments he was moving with great speed. They saw the form rushing through the water. Instinctively the men before him started moving to the side. Spearguns are for men, not whatever this was, moving at this speed. No one fired. He strained, driving as hard as he could, watched the lights sliding by. And forgot there might be others waiting on the bottom. Time enough for one man to see him coming. Steve saw the burst of compressed air, knew a spear knifed toward him. He arched his body, saw the spear race by, much too close. The man was right behind with a knife, moving the blade in a wide slashing motion. Steve doubled over, his own knife ready, ripped through an air hose. He didn't stop to see what was happening but kicked furiously again, into the tunnel. They had him spotted now. Something clamped onto his left leg. He didn't exactly feel the grip, knew what had happened more by the sudden dragging effect. He kicked violently, felt something soft yielding. The drag was gone.

A form clamped itself about his neck and a hand gripped his right wrist. Steve couldn't use the knife. He felt a hand tearing at his own hoses. He brought up his left hand. Something created pressure, then yielded slightly. He knew he was against skin. The bionics thumb pressed hard against the bottom of the extended middle finger. Compressed air rammed a frangible dart through the finger, directly into the skin. It took longer then he expected as he fought to free himself. The poison took effect with explosive reaction. Something thrashed wildly behind him, fell away.

Too late. Another form loomed in front of him, a knife sweeping unerringly toward his hoses. He sucked in air, held his breath, knew he'd lost his tanks. He didn't fight it. He hit the snap release on his chest, slipped away from the harness.

He pushed the tanks away. Oxygen bubbled in a hissing stream as the tanks wobbled through the water. Steve drove as hard as he could, straight ahead, where he could see light now. He swam fifty or sixty feet, went for the bottom, his lungs straining.

That's it ... they know you've lost the tanks. They've got you. They're convinced of it. You've got to come to the surface. They'll be waiting for you. He looked behind him. Sure enough, the lights were all ascending. This was his chance. They knew he couldn't go far. He'd have to surface to breathe. He moved by feel. The plug in his left thigh; there. He pressed it, felt the plug yield, pushed it aside. He knew he was running out of air. ...

His head pounded, but he had the mouthgrip out. He extended the flexhose, jammed the mouthpiece between his teeth, clamped hard, sucked in air. He felt his head clearing. *Move.*

He measured his strength, a fast, driving motion but with a sure rhythm to it. They were searching behind him for the man who'd lost his air tanks and *must* come to the surface. He could see now as he approached the open mouth of the tunnel. The current was stronger, helping him. Screws pounded overhead; they must have radioed to the boats for help in the search. But the boats were over him and they were moving *behind* him. Arms folded back along his sides, he rushed straight ahead, his legs flailing like pistons, moving him with steady speed through the water. He was much lighter now without the tanks and with less drag. He put more energy into his swimming. His only chance was open water. If he had to, he could rest there for a moment. Certainly not here where he could be trapped. He was out now, the shore line fading away to each side. He went deeper, his ears hurting. No other way. He drove his legs, pistoning.

He decided against an erratic course. He couldn't chance it, but he also couldn't move continuously in a straight line. He swam steadily, straining, hoping he was moving in a curving line away from the entrance to the tunnel. He suddenly realized something was different. No explosions. That couldn't last long. When they didn't find a swimmer back in the tunnel, or a dead body ... any minute now.

Shadows rippling before him. Again the mooring cables from one of the decoy oil rigs. *Decoy.* It wouldn't be occupied. He made for the cable, followed it to the surface, got beneath the rig over him. He had to take the chance no one would be looking here. He felt dizzy, realized at the same moment he was exhausting himself. He was running out of air. Had he really

187

been on the cylinder from his left thigh for nearly thirty minutes? It had to be. Then this must be one of the rigs more distant from the shore.

He came up slowly, lost in the shadows. He spat out the mouthpiece, sucked in long draughts of air. He clung to the cable to conserve his strength, to regain his wind. He studied the sea about him. Patrol boats were moving out from the shore under full throttle, already starting to fan outward in a wide search pattern. A storm had moved in during the late night hours and he saw heavy rainshowers in the distance. That might be to his advantage. He turned slowly to scan the distant surface. Even better. Dark buildups against a gray sky; if the cumulus got heavy enough . . .

He reached into the waistbelt, withdrew a sealed package. High-energy rations. He needed them now. He couldn't get caught by those boats. There was another danger, he realized. It was daylight now. Rain or not, they might bring helicopters into use.

Something else he needed to do. He could almost feel his body drawing energy from the rations. He reached down to his right leg, slid open a panel in the calf and withdrew a cylindrical container. He held in his hand a marvel of micro-miniaturization; in the one package was the wire recorder, antenna, buoy, and radio transmitter. He separated the components, glancing every few moments at the boats moving away from the shore line. None made any particular move in his direction. Not yet, anyway. He switched on the recorder, spoke clearly and slowly into the microphone. He pulled the wire connection free, let the microphone sink below him, then twisted the top of the recorder. He pressed a red button, and a small CO_2 bottle inflated a plastic buoy. An antenna unreeled and he released the unit. It floated away from him. In sixty seconds his message would be burst-transmitted. He hoped one of the high-flying planes or a communications satellite would pick up his message about his condition, which would be repeated every five minutes. The battery would last two hours, after which a small charge of acid would eat through its container and puncture the buoy, allowing the unit to sink from sight forever.

His strength had returned to him with the rest and the rations. Well, he'd done his best. Time to execute for himself and get the hell out of there.

188

Something else. The homing transmitter. The sub would be waiting to pick him up but they had to know he was free of the base and in open water. Of course, when the plane or a comsat, or both, picked up the automatic transmissions from the floating buoy, they'd know he had made it in, and back out. But they had to get a better fix on him to do something about it. He knew the sub would be patrolling on a bearing of zero seven zero degrees from the underwater tunnel. But could he maintain that kind of course? Impossible if he had to elude pursuers. And if he had the chance to get into the heavy rainshowers now moving through the area, well, to hell with the bearing. He had greater safety in concealment than simply plugging away in a straight line. His best chance was to start out and keep going. If the buoy kept the transmitter going long enough he knew the sub would be looking for him. And if his friends in the patrol boats got too close, well, they'd be perfect sonar and radar homing targets for the sub.

He slipped away from the cables, trying to keep the dummy oil rig between himself and the boats. Almost at the same moment he heard the explosions beginning again. They were taking no chances. The impossible *could* have happened and the man they sought had made it safely from the underground passageway. Or maybe there was more than one man. Better, from their viewpoint, to waste a few explosive charges.

He could make good time on the surface. He began swimming with a powerful, steady stroke. He still had that second oxygen cylinder in his right thigh, but he hated the thought of having to use it. Far ahead of him, maybe a mile or two, a cloud was dumping a wall of rain into the ocean. That was for him, he decided, accepting the risk of detection. He knew the sharks were still about but they hadn't been aggressive before and he counted on them still ignoring his presence.

The sharks ignored him, but not the Russians. Gunfire mixed with the booming explosions as they fired at anything that moved. Swimming steadily, he turned to scan the sea behind him and saw two boats, their prows out of the water, their wakes foaming behind, making high speed in his direction. At this distance they couldn't tell who or what he was, but they were angry and frustrated and they weren't taking any chances.

He felt the first light touch of rain, the windblown edge of the

189

heavy rainshower ahead of him. Lightning flashed between the ocean and the cloud. It could mean a thundering downpour within which he could disappear from sight. *If* he could make it. He put everything into his swimming, cutting the water like one of the sharks in the area. The rain was getting heavier and his hopes began to rise. He struck out even harder than before, and—

The horizon twisted crazily, and he knew he was tumbling through the air even before he heard the shattering *crack* of the exploding shell. He slopped crazily back into the water, hidden from sight for the moment by the spray all around him. He gasped for air, swimming wildly at a sharp angle from the line he'd been following. Sucking in air, he kicked his way beneath the surface, then turned sharply again, his legs pistoning him ahead with great speed. He knew they'd figure on his changing his direction, but they couldn't expect his speed, and that could give him an advantage. Each second counted now. Visibility was lowering steadily as he neared the rainshower. He stayed just under the surface, hammering ahead. He had to come up, his lungs threatening to burst. He gulped in air, then dove as explosions rattled the air and a line of geysers moved rapidly in his direction. They were throwing it all at him. Again he changed direction, and finally started using his head.

The oxygen line. For God's sake, get on the oxygen and stay under, stay deep. They won't expect that. He drifted, doubled over, fighting to get the plug from his right thigh, to get the mouthpiece gripped between his teeth. There; done. But he'd lost his bearings. The boats pounded the water with their screws; he was confused. He saw the shore line through heavy rain, turned and started down again. A sledgehammer smashed into him, burst the mouthpiece from his teeth. He grasped for it, clamped it again in his mouth. If he could get ten or fifteen good minutes of swimming he thought he could get away from them. He felt pressure waves pulsing through the sea. They were probably tossing hand grenades from the boats. Bad enough, but they had to be closer to knock him out for good. He stayed as deep as he could, the pressure driving icepicks into his ears.

The minutes dragged by as he pumped his legs with the steady piston movement. The boats were farther behind now, circling, covering the area where they figured a man could swim underwater. No one could expect what was happening and he knew he was outdistancing them as they milled about. But he couldn't keep this up forever. Where was the sub?

He eased toward the surface and was surprised to find himself moving in a curving line. Something was wrong. . . . He felt a strange tingling in his right leg. *In his leg.* He slowed just below the surface. Enough light to see. No wonder his course had become erratic.

His leg was mangled, plastiskin hanging in shreds, the steel alloys within showing a naked metal skeleton of a leg. That last explosion . . . something had torn into the leg. He didn't need the plastiskin to protect his wiring system, it was thoroughly sealed. But a piece of metal had flayed wires open and the sea water was now playing hell. The leg was twisted, bent at a crazy angle, useless to him. He turned again, grateful for the rain, using his left leg as a fluke to keep him moving. He went to the surface. Not enough air left in the cylinder to matter. He'd have to keep going, pace himself, swim this way for hours if necessary, hope the sub would find him.

Then the sky exploded. A shattering roar overhead, coming *from* the open sea . . .

They *had* picked up the explosions. Sonar pinpointed the blasts that nearly finished Steve. A KC-135 tanker was orbiting above the clouds at twenty thousand feet, two F-4C fighters in formation, picking up fuel from the tanker to stay on station. The sub moved toward Steve but its commander felt he might not get there in time. He played another card, spoke directly with the pilot in the lead fighter. 'Red Fox from Gray One, you read?'

'Go ahead, Gray one.'

'Are you homing our position, Red Fox?'

'Roger that, Gray One. We're locked on.'

'We'd like you people to come around to the east of us, home on us, and make a low pass on a heading of two nine zero. We'd like that as low as you can handle it in the soup. Over.'

'Roger, Gray One. We can take it down by radar to about three hundred feet. Do you wish immediate execution?'

'Affirmative, Red Fox. Execute immediately. And we'd

like all the noise you people can put out with these things.'

'Okay, Navy. Hang on to your hats. We'll be coming through in the Mach. Starting down now.'

The two fighters plunged toward the sea, pulling out by radar altimeters, dropping to just below three hundred feet over the water. As they came out of their dives the pilots went into full afterburner, sending a howling roar of thunder downward, accelerating the fighters past supersonic speed. Double shock waves ripped across the patrol boats with all the sound and fury of bombs going off nearby. It was at least enough to stop the pursuit.

Steve found himself nearly hysterical as the shock waves pounded over him. Still, he managed to recognize the swept-wing shapes overhead, realize what was happening. Relief also shuddered through his body and he moved slowly through the water, waiting. Not for long. The sensitive sonar had him dead center, and the sub was easing off its speed before he even saw the hull looming through the heavy rain.

Ricardo was in the rubber raft that reached him moments later to drag him from the water.

The crew pulled in the line swiftly, bringing the raft to the side of the hull. Steve looked up to see a white-faced sailor staring at the twisted, mangled leg. He exchanged glances with Ricardo as the sailor, instinctively, crossed himself at the sight.

CHAPTER TWENTY

'It's everything we wanted. That, and more,' Goldman was saying to McKay about the four glossy photographs spread on McKay's desk. 'The radio transmission was picked up by the plane we had orbiting the area, and then, we've got Austin's own report.' He shook his head in admiration. 'He's got an incredible memory for detail, Jackson.'

McKay studied the photographs, nodding slowly. No question but that Austin had carried out his tough assignment, had provided the hard evidence needed to make the OAS take action and force the Russians to back down and get out. Fine, mission accomplished, but it was only the prelude. Now that Steve had proved himself in a preliminary, he was ready for a main event. And the time was now.

'Oscar,' McKay said. 'How long to repair the leg?'

'It's up to Killian and the others.'

'Two weeks?'

'You're pushing pretty hard, aren't you? What's the big sweat?'

McKay swung his chair about, pulled a drawer from the desk, and rested his feet. 'Afsir,' he said.

'Afsir?' Goldman repeated. The desert. North Africa . . .

'It's heated up,' McKay told him.

'That hot? I mean, to use Austin so soon?'

'They need him yesterday,' McKay said.

Jean Manners couldn't wait. She threw her arms around his neck and hugged him tightly, tears on her cheeks. 'I really didn't think I'd ever see you again,' she said, kissing him. He tried to move, clumsy on the crutch, until she drew back and studied him at arm's length, smiling. 'I understand you've had enough swimming for a while.'

'Enough,' he agreed with a laugh. 'Got my old stall ready for me?'

'Ready.' She turned to walk by his side. 'I'd like just to sit with you for a while, Steve. You know, catch up on things.' She glanced at him. 'Maybe even hold hands for a while.'

He smiled at her. 'Best offer I've had all day.'

'Got a fresh pot of coffee up.'

'Great.'

She studied his walk. 'You're all tensed up, Steve,' she said. 'The crutch. You're pulling muscles. You're going to be all knotted up soon.'

He nodded. 'Can't help it. I'm forbidden to use a wheel-chair.'

'Who would—?'

'Private joke.'

'I might even be talked into giving a certain party an expert rubdown.'

'Look, Jean. I—'

'Shut up, Steve. *Please*. Just for once shut up and let someone do something for you and enjoy it. I promise I won't attack you.' A promise, she thought, but hardly a preference.

More than twenty-five men scattered throughout the Fort Carson obstacle course couldn't stop Steve Austin. They were tough veteran combat troopers. His leg had been repaired in a matter of days, and it seemed he was even faster and stronger now than before.

Watching him, Marty Schiller thought of a place known as Afsir. 'He's ready,' Schiller said to Carpentier.

Carpentier looked at him. 'I hope so,' he said, finally. 'Surinam was a piece of cake compared to Afsir.'

Dr. Killian looked up from the long charts he had been studying for the past several hours. He had gone over every line, every bend and squiggle and mark with painstaking care. He had compared the recorder charts with instrument readouts, with biomedical records. His staff had been on the grill through every moment. Earlier in the day he had put the records back on the long table, walked from the room straight to where Steve was undergoing electrical flow tests. Killian hadn't said a word, had exchanged no more than a brief nod with Steve. He watched the tests, suddenly straightened, nodded again to

Austin and returned to the charts. Then, finally, Killian pushed away the papers.

'Get me Goldman,' he said to Art Fanier. The OSO man was there in ten minutes, and Killian, who despite his aversion to all security people had grown rather fond of the sophisticated agent, greeted him with surprising warmth.

'Goldman, good to see you.' When Goldman received this with a startled glance, Killian smiled and gestured at the papers to his side. 'It's all there,' Killian said. 'You're prepared to send him out as soon as possible?' It was more a statement than a question.

'The moment you tell us he's ready,' said the OSO man, 'we'd like him in the home office.'

'For how long?'

'Two weeks, maybe less. It depends, doctor, on whether we can complete his briefings and special training here or ... where he's going.'

'Which is where?'

'I'm not free to say, Dr. Killian.'

'Nonsense. You are planning to send him to North Africa,' Killian said. 'Something about desert work. That much is obvious. You are also planning to have him fly again. Relax, Goldman. I'm hardly about to sell your precious secrets. But I want you to get something clear in your mind. We *are* co-operating with your office. So if you let us know where he's going, it's likely we can better prepare him for what you have in mind for him. Now, do you have a list of the modifications this assignment will require?'

Goldman tapped his pocket. 'I have it with me, Dr. Killian.'

'And the equipment?'

'It's here.'

'Very good. You're getting more efficient, I see. Now, how much time do we have?'

'We'd like to do it in three days, sir.'

'Let me see the list.' Goldman handed it to the doctor, who scanned it quickly. 'Is all this really necessary?'

'It is, Dr. Killian,' Goldman said. 'It's a rough job. And we'd like to have him back.'

She wore tight-fitting khaki shorts and halter. Her deep-brown legs carried her with a lithe movement that captured his eye. Her deep hue was a result of exposure to a burning sun. He stood absolutely still, watching her leave the room, and despite her back to him he couldn't shake the angular beauty of her face, the high cheekbones and startling red lips, the short, raven hair. She was incredibly *alive*. Energy seemed to coil within her like an electrical charge building for explosive release.

Marty Schiller had brought her into the room. Steve was finishing his familiarization tests with automatic weapons, firing a stubby submachine gun with a forty-round clip. He held the weapon in a firm but free grip, holding down the trigger and rotating the barrel slightly for a spreading field of fire. The chattering roar of the gun was deafening in the enclosed space, and for several moments he couldn't make out Schiller's words. Finally he turned from Schiller to the girl standing perhaps twenty feet away. Marty Schiller motioned her forward. 'This is Tamara Zigon,' he said. 'Tamara, Colonel Steve Austin.' She extended her hand and he took it gently, startled by the cool touch of her skin.

'It is my pleasure, colonel,' she told him, a slight but definite accent catching his attention. She glanced at the targets at the other end of the firing room. 'May I make a suggestion, colonel?' Her teeth showed brilliant white against her deeply tanned features. He nodded, not knowing what she meant. She walked past him, picked up the submachine gun, turned to the range officer. 'A full clip, please.' That man glanced at Schiller, who nodded. She slapped the clip into place, threw a round into the chamber, kept the barrel pointing at the targets as she turned to Steve. 'This particular weapon, colonel, is a Czecho-slovakian improvement on a piece developed for partisan work. Originally it was Russian. You will find it fires better, there is an angular motion to the recoil, if you hold it with the clip hori-zontal to the ground, like this, rather than the way you held it.' She turned sharply, dropped to one knee, and fired off the clip in short, stuttering bursts. Three targets were cut almost in two. She cleared the gun, handed it to the range officer. 'I will see you later,' she said, and walked from the firing room.

Steve stared until she was gone, then turned to Schiller. 'Who the hell,' he said firmly, 'is *that*?'

'Tamara?' Schiller looked at him closely. 'She's your partner,' he said.

'My what?'

'On your new assignment. You and Tamara. Starting the day after tomorrow.'

'But she's—'

'A girl. I know,' Schiller said. 'She is also a captain in the Israeli army, and one of their best secret agents.' He clapped Steve on the shoulder. 'C'mon, we need a final session with Fanier. I'll tell you all about her on the plane tomorrow.'

He eyed the ugly beast carefully, and the big, humped animal swung its long neck about, a matted stovepipe with a lumpy head and snickering, drooling lips on the end. The stovepipe extended suddenly and big yellow teeth clicked barely an inch from his arm as Steve leaped nimbly out of the way. He glared at the camel as it shivered its matted hide to shake off a horde of buzzing insects. 'Tamara, I'm warning you,' he said to the girl standing at his side, convulsed with laughter, 'if this monster tries that again, I'll—' He let the threat hang as he and the camel exchanged malevolent stares.

'What will you do? You cannot even ride him. Here is a man who has been to the moon and he cannot even ride a camel! Any little Arab boy can do what you cannot!'

'I'll ride him, just as soon as I figure how to climb up—'

'Use the saddle, my hero.' She moved to the side.

'You call that thing,' he said with a gesture of contempt, 'a saddle? That's a piece of wood with some wool over it, for God's sake. And what about the stirrups? Where—?'

'That's a Tuareg saddle. Didn't they ever teach you anything useful? And a real saddle for a camel doesn't have stirrups.'

'Why not?'

'I told you before. You use your toes to ride a camel. Get rid of your sandals,' she ordered. He glared at her, did as she told him. 'Now, surely you can remember what else to do.'

He turned back to the grotesque thing, determined to show the camel who was boss. She'd told him, all right. He'd watched the others do it and now he'd show this splay-footed nightmare – Tamara ran past him, brought the camel to the ground with its legs crossed crazily beneath the body. The animal lifted its head with mild curiosity. 'Come on, *now*,' Tamara urged him.

Steve grabbed the reins from her. He put his left foot on the left knee of the camel and quickly swung his right leg across the back of the saddle. Tamara stepped back as Steve wriggled his body to seat himself more comfortably, an impossible goal with the Tuareg saddle. He pulled on the reins. 'All right, you miserable dromedary, let's go,' he growled. And forgot, of course, that the riding camel doesn't follow the habits of other animals in climbing to its feet. The camel stays on its knees and heaves its rear end up first. Steve's butt slammed into the seat and his body pitched forward. He clung to the cross at the front of the saddle, trying for balance and then felt himself moving backward as the front end of the camel lurched upward. Swaying wildly, Steve tried to find a place to secure his feet, now flapping out from each side of the animal. He remembered what Tamara had shown him and swung his left foot upward to the camel's neck. The trick was to secure the skin of the neck between the big and the second toe, clamp the toes tightly, and use the hold for balancing on the neck ridge. He congratulated himself on his success, and then wondered what the hell to do with the other foot. He had no time to find out. He moved his foot along the neck for better leverage, but to a camel this means 'move out', and the beast lurched forward. Ten feet above the ground, Steve found the horizon swaying and bucking. He clamped harder with his toes, and discovered immediately that the digits of a bionics foot require careful control. His toes came together with the clamping bite of a pair of pliers, the camel let out a scream of outrage and took off with a wild lunge. Steve went up in the air and came down again as the saddle lifted to meet him with breath-shaking impact. The camel turned in a circle, its head twisting as it tried to bite Steve, who was already in midair, connected to the camel only by the pincers of his toes. The beast jerked to a halt and fell to its knees. Steve flew over the saddle to hit the ground with a crash. The camel stood again on all fours and eyed him disdainfully.

Steve walked away, looking neither left nor right.

He slammed the door shut, stripped off his clothes, and moved quickly into the shower.

'Give me the soap and turn around. I will do your back for you.' She stood just behind him. He had no need to turn around to know she was naked in the shower with him. Without a word he handed her the soap, felt her take it, then her hands scrubbing his back, working at his broad shoulders.

He stood quietly as she worked her strong fingers into his muscles. When she was through she held out the soap to him, still standing behind him. 'Leave the water running,' she said. 'I will shower as soon as you are out.'

He didn't reply, but moved under the spray, turning it to the highest temperature he could endure. Finally he had enough, moved from the shower stall to pick up his towel. 'It's all yours,' he called to her. She moved past him into the shower and he heard a gasp as the hot water hit her body. 'Tell me next time when you intend to scald me.' He didn't answer as he went into the bedroom, drying himself vigorously. He sat on the edge of the bed, not bothering to dress, taking the moment to think. He felt the heat stirring, and angrily drew on his shorts and trousers.

He had never known a woman remotely like Tamara, and he'd never known a week like the days that had just passed. She had him wildly off balance and he didn't know how to cope with her or this, to say the least, remarkable situation: sharing a house, a small bungalow, really, on the edge of a secret airfield in the midst of desert hills. This living together, sleeping in beds close to one another, Tamara casually naked but never flaunting or provoking him.

They had flown from Colorado to the complex of OSO buildings, the group assembling for his briefings and training. This time Jackson McKay and Oscar Goldman got down to cases immediately. They considered Steve Austin a full member of the OSO team, eliminating his previous special and, to him, irritating status. At OSO he would work, as before, with Marty Schiller and Ricardo Carpentier. There were also some new faces.

Tamara Zigon, for one. And a short man with a tremendous, barrel chest, muscled from head to toe, head set directly atop his shoulders with no discernible neck in between. Walid Howrani was a Jew from Turkey who had vowed to return to his native land only behind a gun. No one explained to Steve the reason for the fierce hatred, nor did he ask. His interest in Howrani was appropriately restricted to the role he would play in Steve's new assignment. Howrani had spent much time in the

Arab countries as a trader. He knew the languages and the customs and above all he had an uncanny memory for the land, its terrain, and characteristic landmarks. Especially the land between the Nile River and the Red Sea, between Qena on the Nile and the port town of Quseir to the east on the shores of the Red Sea. Howrani had personally traveled this area several times, and his knowledge would be combined with aerial reconnaissance photography.

There was also Major Mietek Chuen, a startling contrast to the thick mass of Howrani. Sandy-haired, with deep blue eyes and a slim and neatly muscled body, Mietek Chuen turned out to be much more than just another fellow pilot. In the war of six days in 1967, Chuen had led the first wave of French-built Mirage fighters into Egypt. Before the fourth day ended, with the Arab air forces battered, Mietek Chuen had personally shot twelve MiG-21 fighters out of the air. He was Israel's leading jet ace, and he had added another six kills since then in the brief disputes over the Suez Canal area.

Jackson McKay assembled them for the first full briefing. Steve noted that McKay personally would direct the briefings; a measure of the importance OSO placed on this operation.

'You'll get to know the face of Afsir as well as your own.' McKay stood before a large wall map of the eastern half of Egypt. He turned and ran a pointer along the map to follow a curving dotted line. 'Afsir is a bastard offspring of political convenience,' he continued. 'It's really not a country at all. Actually it's a territory the Egyptians carved out of their own land and arbitrarily declared it a political entity to be regarded as an independent sovereign state within the muddled customs and conventions of international law. The Russians and their allies, including, of course, Egypt, immediately gave it recognition – although their diplomatic representation was on the minor consular level. Militarily, it was something else. Afsir, as it's called, begins here,' the pointer touched at the Egyptian coast line of the Red Sea, just to the north of the port town of Hurghada. 'They picked a good point,' McKay acknowledged. 'As you can see, just to the west of Hurghada is the peak Gebel Shayib Al Banat, with a height of over seven thousand feet. They've got radar plastered all over the sides of that mountain, as well as along the peaks running down to the shore of the Red

Sea.' The pointer moved south until it stopped at twenty-five degrees north and thirty-five degrees east. 'You'll notice the so-called boundary of Afsir is directly south of Elath, the Israeli port on the north end of the Gulf of Aqaba. Now, the interior border runs slightly west northwest from here' – the pointer traced the dotted line as McKay continued – 'until we reach Isna on the Nile River. It follows the Nile northward to Qena, then works its way roughly northeast until we're back at a point just north of Hurghada.' McKay dropped the pointer on his desk and resumed his seat.

'Except for the area bordering the Nile, it's rough country, mostly mountains, arid and relatively hostile to life. But it's perfect for what the Russians and the Egyptians have wanted for a long time.' McKay paused, then went on. 'It amounts to a kept state, an outlaw country, where the Russians can, by invitation, move in their latest weapons for checkout and training without being exposed to the threat from the Israelis farther to the north, as well as the international community favorable to the United States, over directly provocative military operations in a tinder box such as Egypt. It's a thin deception, and fools hardly anybody, really, but it's a sop to world opinion – which the Russians *do* care about more and more these days. The so-called government of Afsir is serving them in much the same way Franco served the Nazis in 1939, when *they* used a whole country to test weapons and tactics before World War Two. Same idea, updated, is all. There's also been heat from elements of the Egyptian government who feel the Russians are crowding them, treating *them* like a kept state. They don't mind the Soviets pouring in billions of dollars worth of ordnance, but they're annoyed when the Russians insist on operating the equipment the Egyptians only manage to foul up.'

'Typical of them,' muttered Howrani, who held Egyptians in disdain.

McKay ignored the comment. 'The point is the Russians have been given their own little enclave from which to operate. They figured, of course, that by establishing the sovereignty of Afsir it would keep the Israelis out, while they could test their latest equipment from a modern airstrip they put up in the valley – here.' McKay turned and tapped the map with his finger. 'That's almost due west of Quseir. High hills. Treacherous

202

country, but it's got a twelve-thousand-foot strip. Which is infested, I should add, with antiaircraft, missile, and extensive ground fortifications. The guards are Arab, by the way. Sadat wouldn't give *everything* away.'

McKay toyed with a letter opener. 'The single most important reason for the airstrip in Afsir and Afsir's makeshift international status is for the Russians to test their new MiG-27 fighter. Are you familiar with it?'

Steve shook his head slowly. 'No, I know about the MiG-23, their Mach Three hardware. But I never heard of the '27.'

'Not surprising, it's still that new. As you well know, the Russians tried out their MiG-21 against us in Vietnam. On paper its performance is considerably better than the F-105 and slightly superior to the F-4, but they consistently come out second best in combat. No need for me to detail what you already know from your own experience. But just for the record, the Israelis, led by men such as Major Chuen, here, also managed to do in the MiG-21 fighters while flying the Mirage.'

Steve looked at Chuen and nodded. 'I know. They taught all of us something.' The major made no comment.

'Israel's pilots in the F-4,' McKay continued, 'have also managed to clobber the MiG-21 in almost every battle that's taken place. The Russian fighter is faster, has some other advantages, but the combination of excellent pilots and air discipline – again, I know I'm saying what you know, but I need to set the stage for this carefully – has kept the Israelis on top. Until now, that is,' he added.

'To get right to the point, Colonel Austin,' Major Chuen said in a clipped, almost British accent, 'the MiG-27 has wiped out our advantage. And to be blunt about the matter, we are very worried about the situation. We have managed to destroy no more than *one* of the new Russian machines. One of our pilots fired his entire complement of missiles – four Sidewinders, to be exact. One of them managed to contact the MiG, and the airplane exploded. Unfortunately it went down over the Red Sea and we have not had the opportunity to recover the wreckage. That way, we had hoped we might learn something about the machine.'

'But what's it got?' Steve asked. 'No matter what they've

come up with, major, it doesn't add up to sixteen for one.'

'Nevertheless, we have been unable to destroy more than one MiG-27 while losing sixteen of the F-4 fighters.'

'What's the speed?'

Chuen startled him with the answer. 'The Russian airplane can do better than Mach Two—' he hesitated, then went on, '—at sea level. At altitude our radar has tracked it at better than Mach Three Point Four.'

'That's over twenty-four hundred miles an hour,' Steve murmured.

'Precisely.' Chuen looked grim. 'We cannot touch the airplane in speed. Or climb, for that matter. Its speed is great enough, especially its acceleration, to render our missile attacks, almost worthless.' Chuen moved his shoulder in a shrug. 'Of course, we have tried to get in close where we might use the cannon of the F-4. But every time we try, well, the acceleration. The MiG leaves us flat.'

'From what the Israelis have told us, the MiG-27 is far ahead of our new F-15 fighter, and that ship won't go into operational service for another two or three *years*,' McKay broke in. 'Hell of a note; we're building what we hope is the best air superiority fighter in the world and it will be obsolete before it rolls off the production line.'

'There's another problem,' Chuen added. 'The Russians have not flown this new machine over any territory we control. Not even over the Sinai Peninsula. They are staying strictly over the area bordering the Red Sea. They seem eager to test the airplane, but are taking every precaution that we do not get our hands on one.'

'The Pentagon thinks it has some of the answers,' McKay said. 'Obviously they've got a remarkable engine in that thing. They may also be using something new in the way of fuel. We don't know. Major Chuen, and some of the Israeli intelligence people, believe they've equipped their new fighter with advanced electronics gear. Somehow they seem to have known each time the Israeli fighters have been behind them.'

'That's hardly new,' Steve said quickly. 'We were using tail-warning radar back in World War Two.'

'That's not the real point,' McKay argued. 'Whatever the Russians have, it not only provides adequate warning for their fighter to accelerate out of harm's way, it's also screwing up the ability of the air-launched missiles to track and home onto their targets.'

Major Chuen nodded his agreement.

'The Pentagon is in a panic,' McKay said. 'Not just because of what this airplane can do but because of what it represents. If they've really made that much of an advance in power, or fuel, the electronics systems, or whatever, it means the Air Force can't be assured of air superiority in limited-action situations in the future. It also means they might adapt this whole new package to a low-level supersonic bomber that could change, overnight, the concept of the Russians coming in against the United States with manned aircraft. As you know, some people feel our fighter defenses leave a lot to be desired.

'We've been working with Israeli intelligence and we've come up with a plan. A combined operation. It revolves around two people.'

Steve knew the answer.

'You, Steve – and Miss Zigon.'

Steve glanced at Tamara. Her face stayed impassive. He turned back to McKay. 'All right,' he said, 'let's hear it.'

'After your briefings and last-minute training by the Israelis,' McKay said, 'there will be a provocation of Israel by the powers-that-be in Afsir.

'Since they were nice enough to establish this new "independent state" of Afsir,' McKay continued, 'diplomatic inhibitions are minimal. We have never recognized any Afsir government, so as far as we're concerned it doesn't exist. It's the Egyptians, who insist it is a sovereign land, and the Russians and their bloc have gone along with the sham of diplomatic recognition. In effect, as far as diplomatic relationships are concerned, Afsir has become a convenient no man's land – but that now cuts two ways.

'As I said, the powers-that-be in Afsir will provoke the Israeli government. We've been trying to decide what would be best. The Israelis agree we should arrange for the Russians to shoot down – hopefully with surface-to-air-missiles – several Israeli planes.'

Steve couldn't help staring at McKay. 'Arrange to have some Israeli planes shot down?' McKay nodded. 'What about the pilots?' Steve said.

'There won't be any,' McKay said. 'We're shipping the Israelis a number of Ryan Firebee jet drones. Before they leave the States they'll be modified externally. They'll *look* like F-4 fighters. They won't be, but the Russians and the Egyptians won't know that. The drones, representing manned aircraft, will be released from a mother ship at high altitude, and will be directed toward Afsir. Russian radar will pick them up while they're still far out. The moment they get well within range of their SAM missiles, and still hold their course, the Russians will let go with everything they have. They're touchy about overflights, especially where Afsir is concerned.'

Steve nodded. 'Neat. The SAMs can't miss under those conditions.'

'Right,' McKay said; 'no electronic countermeasures of any sort. A guaranteed loss of two unarmed Israeli reconnaissance planes while they're still well short of the Afsir border. Provocation. Unforgivable. Attacking unarmed, helpless aircraft. The Israelis will protest. There'll be no question but that some response is in order.' He nodded to the Israeli officer.

Major Mietek Chuen didn't waste his words. 'We considered, naturally, a combined operation strike. Going in with large helicopters so that we might pick up one of these airplanes and just haul it back to Israel. But a number of things decided us against such action. The distance is too great for helicopters to carry that heavy a load. Also, the defenses in Afsir truly are formidable. We doubt that we could mount that much heavy covering fire for our helicopter people to get away with it. They would like to try, of course. Ever since they picked up an entire Russian radar system and all its missiles and brought them back to Israel, they are all for going in with their machines and stealing everything that they can unbolt or dismantle.'

'I remember the operation,' Steve said. 'It was a beautiful job.'

'Thank you. You will have the opportunity to meet some of these people and tell them yourself. They are also quite anxious to meet you. They would like to know if the moon can truly be more desolate than some of our own land.' He smiled. 'You will see that for yourself, as well.'

Again Steve held back from questions. Better to hear these people out, to look for the problems while they spoke, and then come back with what he might need to ask. Major Chuen turned to Jackson McKay. 'I must apologize,' he said quickly. 'I did not mean to interfere with your briefing.'

'No apologies necessary, major. It *is* your show, after all.' McKay turned to Steve. 'A good point to make clear, colonel. We're going along for the ride, so to speak. We'll support the Israeli forces, covertly, of course, but we will support them. Also, we've made a deal to replace whatever F-4 aircraft have been lost or will be lost against this MiG-27.' He nodded to the Israeli officer. 'Major?'

Chuen gave Steve his full attention. 'You already know that you and Tamara,' he glanced at the girl, 'Captain Zigon, will function as a team. Her knowledge of the country, especially with the help of Walid, is vital. She also knows every language and dialect spoken there. Including Russian.' He paused, then suddenly and unexpectedly threw a barrage of questions at Steve *in Russian*. To his pleasure, Steve's answers were immediate and comfortably within the language. He had spent nearly two years sharpening his control of the language by working with Russian cosmonauts and scientists on a cooperative effort for space-station activities. 'You would pass inspection of everyone, except perhaps a suspicious Russian,' Chuen said. 'I am very pleased.

'You and Tamara, starting tomorrow,' Chuen continued, 'must know each other as well as—' he hesitated, 'as well as sister and brother. You must be able to speak with one another fluently in the Russian language. You must know each other well enough so as not to be surprised by personality or other reasons, when such surprise could be to your disadvantage. During this time we will carry out an intensive training program in Russian equipment. There is an airfield in the Negev Desert that will be your base of operations. An isolated and extremely well-guarded airfield, by the way. There you will be able to fly a MiG-21 in the pattern – we don't see any need for more than that – to acquaint yourself with cockpit and other procedures of a Russian fighter machine.'

Steve had a hollow feeling in his stomach.

'We have obtained some photography, although the quality is rather poor, of the MiG-27. We believe the cockpit layout will be essentially the same as the MiG-21, because it is the Russian practice to standardize as much as possible between their different aircraft models. Easier that way for their own pilots to make the transition from one to the other. This will help greatly in your case, and since as a test pilot you have flown many different types of aircraft, you should have no difficulty in understanding the controls and the switches of a MiG-27.'

Steve's unease was building.

'Walid Howrani will assist you, and Tamara, in learning details of the area,' Chuen said, as if discussing a Sunday outing. 'He will have relief models of the area involved. This is strictly as an emergency backup, of course. Then, you will be equipped, I understand in your own apparently remarkable way, with special weapons. This is important. Outside of a hand weapon, a sidearm, you will not be able to carry anything visible. Your people will be with you at the Negev airbase to attend to that matter.'

Steve glanced at McKay. 'Art Fanier, Doctor Wells, some others,' McKay said casually.

'This will help meet any unforeseen situations,' Chuen continued, as Steve was now all but convinced of exactly what they had in mind. 'Women electronics specialists are not at all uncommon in Egypt,' said Chuen. 'Tamara, as I mentioned—'

'Major Chuen.'

The Israeli pilot waited.

'I think you'd better knock it off and tell me what you have in mind.'

Chuen showed honest surprise. 'Why, I thought you already knew. We're going to send you and Tamara into the Russian base in Afsir to steal one of the MiG-27 fighters.'

They flew to Israel, then moved by helicopter along a circuitous route to the secret airfield he knew only as Scorpion, deep in the Negev, surrounded by hills that bristled with Israeli gun positions and seasoned combat troops. He worked day and night until he was exhausted from the hours, the heat, the dry air, the relentless barrage of questions they threw at him and the answers they demanded. A man showed up one day in a Russian uniform. Shaul Arkham shouted in Russian at Steve, demanded immediate answers about insignia, rank, equipment, the heavily guarded base, where the living and working areas were; he was unnerving. He would appear without warning, disappear as quickly, show up in a different uniform, come at Steve with questions wholly unrelated to the subject he had previously introduced. When he heard Tamara and Steve talking with one another, in his presence, in any language except Russian, he cursed them both. It was effective.

Rudy Wells, Art Fanier, and two other bionics technicians from the Colorado laboratories set up a miniature bionics and modification center for Steve. Fanier worried and fussed over Steve like a mother whose child is about to start on his first trip away from home, and with his concern he fitted Steve with a variety of weapons concealed within his bionics limbs that just might save his hide, and thereby, his partner's. Major Chuen – and Tamara as well – insisted that Steve be tested for his ability in hand-to-hand combat. It wasn't as simple as he'd thought; Israeli commandos skilled in Arab fighting caught him by surprise the first few days. When he reached the point where he was no longer a stranger to their particular styles, he became too dangerous to continue the training. Rudy Wells and the airbase medical staff had their hands full with a steady flow of dazed and disbelieving commandos suffering an assortment of injuries from torn muscles to broken bones.

All this went well, as did the flying in the MiG-21, a beautiful machine that Steve flew through dangerously wild maneuvers at low altitude near the airfield. He found himself hammering the fighter to the very edge of its performance, and Tamara's place in the rear seat of the intercepter seemed only to goad him to more severe punishment. It was far worse for her as he wracked the MiG about in punishing high-g maneuvers that weighed her down and drained the blood from her head. She gasped for air, bore stoically his seeming rage in the airplane. Her only comment was that she hoped he would wait to kill himself until after their mission was ended.

Tamara.

He could cope with everything but this woman.

From the moment they arrived at the Scorpion base they had lived together. The situation unnerved him. The first time they were alone, when she stripped in the bedroom in front of him and he stared at her supple body, unable to resist looking at her breasts and her flat stomach, her swelling mound, she returned his stare, eyes level, her expression unclouded. 'I will shower first,' she said, and walked from the room. He sat in a daze on the edge of his bed until she returned, where she looked at him with curiosity. She dried her dark hair with vigorous movement.

He knew she was *not* flaunting, not teasing, but it drove him crazy, at once aroused and frustrated him.

She sat on her bed. 'Steve.'

'What is it?'

'Look at me.'

He did, turned away again.

She was still on the edge of the bed, eyeing him frankly. 'We are soldiers together,' she said quietly. 'You and I, Steve, very soon will be risking our lives. We will depend upon one another to survive. There can be no surprises between us, nothing hidden. Do you want me to hide from you? Here,' she gestured with her arm to take in the cottage, 'in this small place? That would be foolish. Better to be completely free with one another.'

'Anything you say.'

'Good,' she said, her voice light and comfortable. She went back to drying her hair. Slowly she stopped, again gave him her full attention. This time there was something different in her voice. 'You have an erection, don't you, Steve?'

He didn't believe it.

'If you are ashamed,' she said, the voice softer, 'I will not look at you.' She placed her hand on his arm. 'I am sorry,' she said suddenly. 'Perhaps it is . . . your limbs. Forgive me if I have offended you. I will go into the other room.'

'No,' he said quickly. 'You saw all that when they were working on me.' She nodded, not speaking now. 'That didn't bother you. I could tell that.'

'It did not bother me,' she said. 'I have collected the pieces of children's bodies, Steve. Including my own baby brother.'

He nodded, not knowing what to say.

'And please remember I have lived with our soldiers in the field. There were times when privacy was impossible. But respect is privacy. I have been like this, nude, before the soldiers. There are times to close off one's mind.'

'I suppose so,' he said, still dazed.

'Besides, an erection is hardly something to be ashamed of.' She smiled. 'I am pleased. Now, hurry, or we will be late for dinner.'

He undressed and went numbly to the shower.

It was like that the entire week when they were alone, but they never again mentioned the subject.

The last three days were the only time he accepted the relationship on her terms. There wasn't much choice. They were in final training.

Then they sweated out the ghost mission of two jet drones modified to resemble Phantom reconnaissance fighters. A Hercules transport hauled the Firebees to 30,000 feet, where they were dropped free. The drones accelerated to supersonic speed and raced directly for Afsir, climbing steadily to 50,000 feet. The Russians reacted precisely as the Israelis had planned. Radar locked onto the drones. A salvo of missiles burst upward from the defending sites and the 'Phantoms' were torn apart in the high, thin air of the stratosphere. Within the hour the Israeli government voiced its denunciation of the unprovoked attack against the reconnaissance aircraft. That was the signal they were waiting for.

The strike was on.

CHAPTER TWENTY-TWO

They went in with precise, split-second timing. The Israelis staged their fighters and fighter-bombers from a dozen different fields in Israel and scattered through the eastern half of the Sinai Peninsula. No large formations to give Russian radar the target on which they could concentrate their defensive fire. A group of fighters flew in darkness against the ever-ready defenses along the Suez Canal, the pilots using terrain-following radar that guided the planes unerringly close to the ground, lifting them through autoslaved controls to clear hills and other obstacles. The pilots swept in against the formidable missile defenses, launched missiles that soared high through the air at supersonic speed. Each missile was packed with an electronic device that registered on probing Russian radar and sent back the false echo of a full-sized aircraft. No warheads were carried, no targets were struck along the defense line west of Cairo. But the Russians, ears ringing to the Egyptian screams of a full-scale Israeli assault by air, unleashed *their* missiles in a devastating barrage. The night sky over the Suez exploded into an eye-stabbing display of powerful warheads detonating from sea level to 40,000 feet.

Other fighters raced over the Mediterranean Sea, swinging in wide, curving feints from the north toward coastal targets. No plane fired a shot against the Egyptian targets, but the desired effect was established. Egyptian and Russian defense systems were saturated. Fighters were assigned intercept missions, and within a quarter of an hour after the first register of targets on the Russian radar scopes the entire enemy system was in action – and pinned down to its assigned area of responsibility.

Far to the south, to the west of the Red Sea port of Hurghada, several Israeli formations began to join in the air. Split-second timing was essential to the strike, and two dozen fighter-bombers made their initial pass just beyond the mountains flanking the Red Sea. Again the decoy missiles were the first objects to be picked up on radar. Few defensive missiles were installed in the area, and these entirely within the sprawling Russian airbase complex near Qena. Sending back their radar returns of aircraft, the decoys did their job exactly as planned. Defensive missiles fired in batteries, the powerful rocket boosters blazing fiery trails in the night sky, followed by the brilliant winking flashes of warheads exploding high above the earth. A second wave of decoy missiles howled skyward, and the second defense line of Russian missiles on the ground were fired.

It would take the best of the Russian ground forces at least ten to fifteen minutes to reload, set the guidance systems, track, and fire. They were not given that time. The fighter-bombers raced up along the mountain slopes, then arced over in flight and hurtled close to the ground toward the Qena complex. Every pilot had his selected target to hit. The pilots followed the same procedures that had proven so successful in the Six Day War. the pilots throttled back to reduce their speed, then lowered their landing gear and flaps, and went back to full power. Moving at barely two hundred miles an hour, the airplanes rock-steady, the pilots sat atop superb gunnery platforms. First the rockets, waves of explosive warheads ripping into the missile sites, power plants, antiaircraft guns, fuel dumps, warehouses, barracks, truck depots, and other facilities. As the fighter-bombers swept in closer behind their devastating rocket assault they released their loads of bombs and napalm, their accuracy pinpointed in the glare of fires already started. The initial wave cleaned up the airplanes by bringing up gear and flaps, swept around in wide, low turns and came back for devastating strafing runs with cannon fire. Behind them came a second wave with full ordnance loads. It was a repetition of the classic strikes that had destroyed the Arab air forces on the ground. This time the Israelis added several new touches.

The Russian aircraft were hit hard in their sandbagged and concrete-walled revetments. Except for a group of a dozen fighters isolated near the far end of the runway, with a taxiway leading from the revetments right to the starting point for takeoff. Here the Israelis showed remarkably poor marksmanship, and the group of MiG-27 fighters survived the sudden holocaust. This particular point was, of course, completely missed in the frenzy of continuing attacks. Also missed was a single small plane that swept in to the south of the carnage, its run low over the ground unnoticed by the battered defenders. The pilot flew barely eight hundred feet over the local terrain, holding one hundred ten miles an hour. He held his course carefully, flinched when four fighters thundered by to his right, north of his patch of flight. The fighters brought the sporadic ground fire still sputtering from the airbase to bear on their roaring strike. And held the attention of almost everyone on the ground as they swept northward.

Far behind them two figures tumbled from the small, low, slow-flying aircraft. A static line snapped taut and black nylon blossomed immediately above the falling figures. Neither jumper wore an emergency chute; there would have been no time for its use had the main canopy failed.

Steve Austin and Tamara Zigon barely felt their chutes crack open when the ground rushed up at them. The jump, like everything else this night, was timed with split-second precision. They came to earth a quarter of a mile south of a perimeter road to the airbase, rolled expertly in the sandy ground and were on their feet at once. Steve gathered up his chute and ran swiftly to where Tamara waited. 'Any problems?' he asked anxiously.

She shook her head. 'Quickly. The chutes.' He slipped out of his harness, unfolded a trenching shovel, immediately began digging a deep hole. Tamara opened Steve's pack, removed their uniform caps that might have been lost during the jump. She dropped the pack in the hole with the chutes. Steve pushed in the shovel and used his hands to fill the hole. In the soft sandy soil it would be difficult, he hoped, to discover where the evidence had been buried.

The northern horizon pulsed with light. They took another moment to inspect one another. Their clothing was messed up and torn in several places; the uniforms showed signs of oil and smoke, and they each had facial bruises and cuts. Clear evidence of their having been in a truck that was strafed by one of the Israeli fighters. Evidence they had barely escaped with their lives. The truck? It didn't matter. If they were in the Qena complex long enough for that story to be checked out in the midst of the thundering fires and explosions, they would be in no position to go anywhere.

'Let's go,' Tamara urged. They started walking to the road

214

they knew lay several miles to the north. Steve checked his hip holster. The Russian automatic with the stubby silencer was in place. Using the silencer was a risk, but as they both knew, no one would stop to inspect their weapons unless that inspection were compelled by much more dangerous suspicion. Everything else on their persons, except the silencers, which could be twisted free and thrown away, was the genuine article. Their papers, undergarments, equipment, uniforms, wristwatches, all of it, *was* Russian, manufactured in Russia. Even the silencers had been obtained from a Soviet security office. 'If you're in the perimeter area,' Shaul Arkham told them, 'use the silencers. It will let you eliminate opposition while it is still not in direct physical contact with you. Use your advantage until you must resort to something else.' Good advice.

The road lay a dozen yards before them. Blood-red light glowed from the north, fires reflecting from low clouds, the flames punctuated with intermittent blasts and deep, booming thunder. They crouched behind a mound. The immediate visibility was poor but their main interest lay in what traffic might be on the road. The idea was to be spotted walking along the road, not entering it from a field. They had, by now, oriented themselves clearly. Relief maps, charts, reconnaissance photographs – all had contributed to this segment of their training. They moved quickly from the shallow ditch to the road. Steve bent down, felt it with his hand. 'Asphalt,' he said. 'Poor shape. Gets beaten up by the sun pretty bad. But it's what we were told to expect.'

They moved toward the northwest. They needed a lift, not only for speed but for its effect in getting them into the heavily guarded base complex, within the perimeter fences and guards. Their papers were in order; their identification showed them to be members of an electronic-maintenance and support organization. This gave them fairly ordinary working requirements, but it also provided them with freedom of movement throughout the entire Qena complex.

'Better have your torch handy,' Tamara reminded Steve, speaking in Russian, 'in case something comes along the road. Better to signal them than to have us appear out of the dark.'

'Good idea.' He held the Russian flashlight in his hand,

glancing occasionally behind them. They had walked nearly a mile, their concern mounting at the absence of traffic, when Steve heard an engine behind their position, around a bend in the road. They stepped to the side and Steve snapped on the flashlight, moving it in a slow, wide circle. Truck headlights brought their arms up to shield their eyes. Moments later the driver flicked his lights on to dim side-runners and coasted to a stop. He shouted to them in a tongue Steve found incomprehensible, but knew was Arabic. 'We're in luck,' Tamara said in an aside. 'No Russians with him.'

She shouted back, using her own flashlight to study the truck cab. Steve saw a look of surprise on the face of the driver as Tamara – identifying herself with her papers and by voice as Captain Nina Tsfasman, and Steve as Major Alexei Kazantsev – answered him rapid-fire in his own tongue. The surprise became a delight, and he turned to his helper with a sudden tongue lashing, sending that worthy to the rear of the truck to make room for the two unexpected passengers. They climbed aboard, the headlights went on again, and they were rolling down the road at nearly fifty miles an hour. Steve took every chance to study road features to the sides and ahead of them, confirming his memory of the area, anticipating specific structures or features coming up before them. Tamara spent most of the time talking with the Arab driver, whose pleasure at a foreign woman's mastery of the native tongue became almost embarrassing. Finally Tamara turned to Steve and spoke to him in Russian.

'Our friend here, his name is Hamad, tells me our cargo is a load of electrical supplies. Cables, solenoids, things like that. Does this give you any ideas?'

He thought quickly. 'What part of the base is he headed for?' She turned to the driver, conversed rapidly. 'Hamad says their authorization is to go directly to the central warehouse,' Tamara said. 'But he's worried because the warehouse may be in flames. He says the Israelis are devils in the dark and can see like bats. He's also afraid that if the attack continues the truck may be lost with its equipment and he will be in serious trouble.'

Steve nodded. 'Smart man, Hamad. I think he's going to be in more trouble than he imagines.' Tamara looked at him sharply, not replying for a moment as the truck swerved suddenly. Hamad had just missed a large piece of smoking wreckage lying on their side of the highway. Steve noticed that the glow in the sky was brighter, and now he could see the flames directly, with the sky waxing and waning in color as fires reflected from thick columns of smoke. 'Ask him,' Steve said, 'how far we are from the main gate on this road.'

She spoke quickly with the driver, turned back to Steve. 'Ten kilometers,' she said.

'That's about six miles,' Steve said. 'There's a bridge ahead of us, isn't there? Goes over a wadi that's dry at this time of the year?'

'There is. What about it?'

Steve kept his face straight ahead, seeming to concentrate on the road. 'Can you drive this thing?'

'Yes of course. But why?'

'We've got to get rid of Hamad and his friend before we cross the bridge.' He reached into his tunic pocket for a cigarette, Egyptian, and lit up after offering one to Hamad, who accepted with repeated sharp bows of his head. 'If we take the truck in ourselves, we can work our way closer to the planes. Otherwise, we could end up miles away from where we want to be, and no way to get where we want.'

There was mild protest in her voice. 'But how do we explain their absence?'

'We were strafed and they ran for their lives. It's our best chance, Tam – Nina.'

She sighed. 'You are right, of course.' He could feel her body hardening next to him. 'How?' she asked.

'Tell him to stop just the other side of the bridge. Be sure you know where he has the papers for the truck, though.'

'All right.'

'When he stops I want you to lean forward. Bend down as much as you can and—' A dull booming explosion that showered the air with fiery debris to their right interrupted him for a moment. They could hear Hamad cursing all Israelis. 'When you bend down, turn off the ignition. If the road is on an incline, the gears may hold it. Otherwise you'll have to find the brake.'

'I know where it is. I have driven several of these machines before.' He thought of the thousands of captured vehicles from the Six Day War.

'All right. I'll be leaning over you right after we stop. Just don't move for a few moments. Then I'll have to get the other one in the back.'

'What will you do?'

'Never mind. There's the bridge up ahead. Better tell him now.' Tamara turned to the driver, speaking rapidly and gesturing. Hamad shook his head, his protest clear to Steve even through the language barrier. Tamara's voice sharpened, and abruptly she changed from the woman he knew to a hard-nosed female Soviet officer, her tone even in Arabic unmistakable. Hamad's eyes widened, and finally he nodded agreement. They were across the bridge and slowing. No traffic ahead of them; Steve bent to look through the right hand mirror. No lights behind. The truck stopped.

'Now,' Steve said quietly, and Tamara bent down and leaned forward, reaching for the ignition key. The driver looked with surprise at her and Steve said his name sharply. 'Hamad!' The Arab looked up, facing Steve directly, and his left hand, the fist closed in a steel bludgeon, whipped forward. Tamara heard a sickening, wet *smack* and the form beside her slumped, the front of the skull caved in. Steve was immediately out of the cab, moving to the back of the truck. He banged on the side of the vehicle and the second Arab leaned out. Steve held the fingers of his bionics hand extended and stiffened, and his hand slashed down, the metal edge striking the Arab expertly on the side of the neck. He fell from the truck with a broken neck, dead before he hit the ground.

Steve checked the road again. Nothing in sight. Quickly he dragged the body from behind the truck to the side of the bridge, tossed the corpse down to the darkness and the rocks below. He ran to the truck cab, heaved the bleeding Hamad from the vehicle. 'He's still alive,' Tamara said tonelessly.

'We can't take a chance on his surviving. If he talks . . ' He let the words hang.

'I know,' Tamara said. 'Do it quickly.'

The bionics arm flashed up and back down again, and Hamad was also dead of a broken neck. He followed the first body and Steve returned to the truck. 'You drive,' he told Tamara.

Ten minutes later they approached the first roadblock. 'If Shaul knew what he was talking about,' Steve said quietly, 'there should be one Russian sergeant and a few Arab guards. Let's hope he's right. Got the papers?'

Tamara nodded. 'I think I'd better do the talking. Act as though you've been hurt.'

Steve slumped in his seat, clasping his left shoulder, his face in a grimace of pain. The Russian sergeant snapped to attention when he saw the rank of the two officers in the cab. Tamara extended the authorization papers for the truck, and before the sergeant could express suspicion about officers rather than Arabs driving, Tamara launched a tirade about cowardly Egyptians who ran off into the desert at the first sight of Jews in the air. 'I need to get the major to an aid station,' she added. 'Be good enough to hurry.' A searchlight passed quickly across Steve's face and vanished. He heard the sergeant bellowing orders at the Arab guards and the gate swung open. They went through with the sergeant standing stiffly at attention and saluting.

'Now what?' Tamara inquired.

'This road continues about two miles,' he said. 'Then it forks left and right. The right road goes to the warehouse area. But I don't think we'll be expected there tonight.' They looked at a sea of flames in the distance. Huge clouds of smoke boiled skyward, and glowing coals spattered the air like countless angry fireflies. 'If we turn left at the fork,' Steve continued, 'we can work our way to the airfield.'

Tamara nodded. They saw men walking alongside the road, many of them dazed, helping the injured. Ambulances screamed by, rushing in the opposite direction. 'Headed for Qena,' Steve remarked. He looked again at the flames. 'They did a good job. It looks like they—' He paused, straining to define shapes silhouetted against the horizon. 'Can you make those out?' he asked, pointing.

For a moment she seemed surprised with his difficulty, then remembered the man with her had but one eye. 'I think they must be the missile batteries. What's left of them, anyway.' Steve began to make out more details. Tamara was right. The missile sites had been torn up badly. High-explosive bombs and then napalm to cover everything with great searing sheets of

219

fire. Twisted wreckage showed the radar installations. Again it was a follow-up of proven success from the 1967 war. Knock out the radar and the computers and you've blinded the missiles.

More vehicles passed, and they saw more Russians now mixed in with the Arabs. Ahead of them the road forked, and Tamara turned on the left signal light. Several Russians with submachine guns at the ready stood by the road, studying all approaching vehicles. One man stepped out into the road and signaled them to stop. Tamara glanced at Steve who had loosened his holster flap. He nodded for her to follow instructions. She felt the flap of her own holster loosened, and Steve moving the weapon to be certain it would be ready for her instant use.

The Russian guard saluted. 'Your papers, please.' Tamara extended the papers taken from Hamad.

'This truck is to go to the warehouse, captain,' the guard told her.

'There is no more warehouse,' she said caustically. She pointed behind her. 'Take a look, sergeant. Our orders were changed verbally by Colonel Popovich. We were told to deliver this cargo to the airfield without delay.' She glanced at the fires only a few hundred yards off. 'Of course, this is not our job. Major Kazantsev,' she nodded at Steve, 'and I are electronics specialists. I imagine,' she added drily, 'we will be busy with repairs for some time.'

'Where is your driver?'

'Where do all Arabs go when the Jews come?' Tamara said angrily.

'Into the desert as fast as they can run,' the guard replied, sharing her open contempt. He still held the papers. 'I will need the password, captain.'

Don't hesitate, Tamara, Steve pleaded silently. Whatever you do, don't hesitate . . .

'I have no idea what the password is,' Tamara said haughtily. 'We have just arrived from the port of Quseir with these parts. How could we know the password?'

The soldier stiffened. 'I cannot let you through without the password, captain.'

'That is out of my hands. Do you have a telephone in your

vehicle?' She pointed to the truck at the side of the road. 'If so, call Colonel Popovich at once in the command post and get your authorization from him. But whatever you do, sergeant, I would advise you not to hold us up much longer. I imagine this material is needed rather badly right now.'

The guard glanced again at the papers in his hand and hesitated. 'The telephone lines are dead.'

'That is your problem. Stop acting like an Arab. Make a decision, sergeant. I don't care *what* it is. We do not intend to remain in this truck all night. I do not mind if the responsibility for failing to deliver these supplies is yours. We are tired, and I don't care much anyway for doing anything to help these filthy people. They stink like goats.'

A responsive chord had been struck. The guard thrust the papers back to her, waved them through and held his salute rigidly as they drove away.

'Very good,' Steve said.

Tamara let out an explosive sigh. 'We can't keep doing that for too much longer. The closer we get to the planes the tighter will be their security.' She negotiated a steep turn, concentrating for the moment on her driving, and he looked ahead of them. 'There it is,' he said. 'The airstrip.'

For the first time since he'd known Tamara he heard her curse. 'What's wrong?' he asked. In answer she flicked the headlights to bright. Far ahead of them the lights reflected from a high cyclone-type wire fence.

'Oh, Jesus,' Steve said softly, 'Shaul never told us a thing about *that*.'

She nodded. 'What happens now?'

'Slow down,' he told her. He scanned the road as far ahead as he could. 'We'll either have to stay on this road until we get to a main gate, and then try to bluff our way through—'

'I wouldn't recommend that. I know how their security system works. They won't suspect us of anything *yet*. But someone will order us off at the gate and one of the people authorized to be on the field will take the truck.'

'Which leaves us on the outside.'

'Unfortunately, yes.'

'We'll have to find some other way. A guard gate somewhere along the line. Something like that.'

'I think we must find a dark place, Steve, and try to get across the fence. They have no lights on. We may be able to get to one of the planes at the edge of the field. We will have to kill the guards, but—'

'Ahead of us,' he gestured. 'See there? There's a hill and the road turns. If we can find a spot around that hill it could be perfect for us. We'll park the truck alongside the fence and —'

'It may be electrified.'

'Could be, but I doubt it. Not right now. The generator station was one of the primary targets,' he reminded her. 'It takes a lot of juice to keep—'

A jeep with a flashing red light approached from the other direction, a Russian soldier waving at them to stop. 'Do it,' Steve told her. He withdrew the pistol from its holster and kept it at the ready as Tamara slowed. The Russian called to them, excitement in his voice.

'Captain!' he shouted above the engines. 'Are you armed?'

Tamara hesitated and Steve nudged her. 'Yes, Sergeant. What's wrong?'

'We have reports that the Jews may be sending paratroopers,' the soldier called back. 'There were some Arabs to the south of here who reported parachutes.'

Tamara went rigid but kept her voice unchanged. 'The Arabs are always seeing paratroopers,' she said sarcastically. 'Usually under their bed. Any excuse to hold us to protect them.'

The soldier agreed and shrugged. 'But one never knows. Please be alert, captain.' He waved and the jeep sped away.

'Close,' Steve breathed softly. Tamara rested her head for a moment against the wheel. 'One could build up a case of nerves like this,' she said after a while.

'Yeah. Let's go.'

They drove around the turn. He was right. The hill shielded them from the glow of fires still burning in all directions. 'Against the fence, quickly,' he urged. She cut off the road to the fence, killed the lights, her hands tight on the wheel. 'Now what?'

He ran to the back of the truck, withdrew a length of cable, and tossed it against the fence. It fell to the ground harmlessly. 'It's not hot, anyway,' he said. 'One for our side.'

'We just can't go over the fence and leave the truck here,' she said. 'It would be a dead giveaway.'

'We don't need the truck.' He studied the road. 'The ditch there is pretty steep. Drive the truck toward it. Can you get out before it goes off the road?'

'You ask that of a woman driver?' she smiled. She climbed back into the truck cab, took off with a clashing of gears. She headed for the other side of the road. He saw the door open and she leaped from the truck, rolling over easily as she struck the ground. In a single flowing motion she was on her feet and back at his side. Behind her the truck rammed into the ditch and slowly toppled to its side, the upper wheels spinning slowly. 'Let's make it fast,' Steve urged.

'The fence,' she said, with sudden realization. 'It's at least fifteen feet with barbed wire. How—?'

'See those bushes over there? Grab as many as you can and bring them here.' He turned to the fence, knelt down, and braced himself. He hooked two fingers of his bionics hand in the thick crosswire and then jerked hard. The fence ripped open across a span of three feet. He tore loose another section, this time raking his hand downward. He pushed in to bend the fence out of the way, a form of jagged flap that cleared the way for them. He sent Tamara through the fence, went through himself, and turned to bend the wire roughly back in place. They stacked the bushes against the fence to conceal the torn wire.

'Keep moving. Alongside the runway, see? That drainage ditch. If we can get in there and stay low we can keep out of sight. Work our way closer to the—'

He froze as sirens wailed. They looked at one another. 'It could be an all-clear signal,' he said. Tamara shook her head. 'Look.' In the distance, near the pilots' quarters, lights were coming on, bright as day. They could see small figures moving quickly toward jeeps and trucks, turning on headlights.

'Move!' he snapped. They ran for the drainage ditch, dropped into its concealing space.

'Goddammit, we're like two rabbits out here. They'll flush us for sure. It looks like they figure that paratrooper report was true—'

She grasped his shoulder, pushing him down. Jeeps were

racing down the runway, one vehicle stopping every thousand feet, the men climbing out with guns at the ready.

'Great,' Steve said, 'they've got dogs with them.' They had the guns out, safety pins off. Within minutes one jeepload was near them, and they heard the sudden frantic barking of dogs that apparently had picked up their scent from their discovered chutes. Tamara's gun came up slowly. Steve knocked it down. 'Don't shoot. There's no possible way we can hold them off. And there's more where these came from.'

She looked at him with an incredulous expression on her face. 'Are you mad? Do you know what they'll do to us? Especially to me?' She moved her eyes suddenly, then turned as the growling animals began to move in on them. 'I'm Jewish and I'm a woman – their favorite combination.'

'They don't *know* what you are.'

'You're a fool,' she retorted. 'Do you think they have no intelligence? What about the attack tonight? When those animals are through with me,' she gestured at the guards moving closer, 'they will turn me over to the Arabs. No, thank you. I'd rather—' She screamed as a huge dog threw himself down from the embankment. At the same moment her gun sounded – three times. The animal fell, twitching and snarling at their feet. Seconds later, a German shepherd leaped, fangs bared. Steve reacted by instinct, firing from point-blank range. He staggered backward as the dog, its head blown open, crashed against him.

The animals stopped as a voice roared out a command in Russian. A searchlight blazed into the ditch. Steve could barely make out men behind the light, knew guns were trained on them.

A voice called in Russian. 'Drop your weapons and come out with your hands in the air.'

Tamara clawed her way from the ditch, began to bring up her gun. Steve lunged at her, knocked the gun flying from her hand. She turned a withering look on him, tried to move forward. He remembered to use his right hand as his fist went against her jaw.

CHAPTER TWENTY-THREE

Two of their Arab guards stood in a far corner of the room, submachine guns leveled at Steve and Tamara. Across from them, standing easily with his own submachine gun, was a burly Russian sergeant. There were four more Arabs, each loosely holding his automatic weapon, ignoring Steve and the others, suggestively eyeing a stony-faced Tamara. She bore their innuendos with a fatalistic stoicism, and a burning anger at Steve for not allowing her to choose the option of death over the known consequences of capture. The Arabs she regarded as beasts of the lowest sort; she knew first hand about their abuses. She had long been a soldier in the Israeli army. Jews had been captured before by the enemy. Far better, she felt, to die quick and clean than to suffer what she was certain must come: interrogation by the Russians. Then to be used by whatever Russians wanted her. It depended on the officers involved. Some were decent, others uncaring. And ultimately to be turned over to that wolf pack. Israeli girls had been captured before. Those who were rescued and managed to survive were usually completely out of their minds – their only means of merciful escape. And it happened not only to the women. Young Israeli males taken prisoner by the Arabs had also been subjected to perverse assaults. Uppermost in her mind was finding a means of killing herself. . . .

Steve wasn't sure, but he supposed he had reacted instinctively in deciding to surrender and hope somehow to find a way out rather than end it all for both of them by resisting. He cared very much that Tamara have that chance – and, more surprising, he obviously now had the same concern for himself. He'd come a long way since that day when he had tried to destroy himself. For all his unusual assets as a cyborg, he was very much a man, with an ordinary, overwhelming drive for survival.

Still, a man could bear only so much and Steve knew he had to try something. He decided on the needle.

'You're supposed to be a man,' he said to the Russian. 'A member of the finest army in the world. A Russian soldier. If you are a man, if these characters don't rule you, call them off the girl.'

No answer came immediately, but it was clear the Russian sergeant was embarrassed, that he had little stomach for his Arab allies. He was a young man, free from the horrors his elder generation had known from the Germans. And despite what had happened through political command in Hungary and Czechoslovakia, and elsewhere, Russian troops – under strict orders from their commanders – had conducted themselves with restraint. There was more involved, Steve realized. The Russian sergeant was in a room with six Arabs armed as heavily as himself. They had just taken another humiliating beating at the hands of the Israelis, and the Arabs were either convinced, or at least wanted to believe, that these two were Jewish spies. *Any* depravity committed against them was a justifiable measure of revenge for the attack, the results of which were still evident in huge fires and clouds of smoke, in wreckage, in intermittent explosions as fuel and warheads went off in shuddering blasts. The Arabs could just as easily turn, with provocation, on the Russian as on the two prisoners. Steve would have to prod this man to take the risk of restraining the Arabs, who now were actually so close to Tamara that they were brushing against her, laughing and clearly preparing to be even more direct in their attentions. If he clashed with them, it might also give Steve and Tamara a remote chance for escape.

The sergeant waited for his superiors to arrive. They would conduct the interrogation of the prisoners. They might do so in this room or remove them elsewhere. High command might want to get into the act, but only if the Russians believed the man and woman were something other than saboteurs dropped by parachute to finish the job started by the air strike. Well, to hell with that for the moment. What mattered was the time between now and when the officers would show up. No doubt they'd be heavily armed and might be accompanied by troops, if they believed the reports of paratroopers.

Again Steve turned to the sergeant, again he questioned his courage as a Russian soldier. It began to have its effect; not only Steve's words but also the looks of disgust the Arabs gave the sergeant for even talking to Steve – for permitting the Jew to speak without being hammered to the floor. Slowly the Russian sergeant moved across the room, stood close to the Arabs and ordered them to move away from the woman. They turned to stare at him with open contempt. Finally the leader of the Arabs answered by putting his hand on Tamara's breast. As he turned toward the Russian, he spat on the soldier's boots. Steve watched the sergeant. He started to speak, to goad him further. It wasn't necessary.

The sergeant went white. He stepped forward, and his knee came up into the groin of the other man. The Arab gasped as he doubled over. He was still falling as the Russian half turned to slam the butt end of the submachine gun into his face. They heard the bones snap. No one in the room moved. Then came a sharp metallic *click* as the sergeant slipped the safety from his weapon. He called to the others to drag their comrade away from the woman. Whether they understood the language or not there was no mistaking the fury on the sergeant's face, and instant death in the muzzle of his weapon. The Arabs dragged their leader to the far wall, where they clustered in a group.

Was this his chance? Steve ran through all the moves open to him, decided against sudden action. Only one man of the seven in the room with them was disabled. Five murderous Arabs and a touchy, fast, capable Russian on the other side of the room with a submachine gun. The other Russians might show at any moment. He would have to kill, disable, or hold under a gun the six men now intently watching him – without having Tamara killed in the process.

The door opened. A Soviet colonel stood in the entrance, studying the scene. Behind him were two younger officers, likely his guard. Steve strained to see if there were more, but through the doorway he made out only a single jeep. That made sense. With the attack having torn up the base, there wouldn't be that many men available for guard processions. Most likely many of the soldiers were also moving out from the perimeters in search of other men who'd been dropped by parachute. But that made ten men in the room with himself and Tamara. One half-dead Arab, five very live Arabs, and the four Russians.

The colonel came in slowly, his men standing behind and to the side. The colonel pointed to the Arab doubled over, a

227

bloody mess, and asked what had happened. He glanced at Steve, believing him responsible. The sergeant stood stiffly, explaining what had happened.

'Why didn't you kill him, then?' The colonel looked at the Arabs, spoke angrily to them in their language. Two remained, the other four left.

The colonel sat on the edge of a low table. Steve looked around the room. They'd left the door open. The two young officers were backed against a wall, observing. The two Arabs remained where they were, their guns still at the ready. The sergeant stood to the side, uninvolved now except as a further protection for the colonel. Tamara had sagged back against the wall, refusing to sit.

'What is your name?'

'Major Alexei Kazantsev, sir. From the 455th Electronics Support Detachment.' He gestured at Tamara. 'She is Captain Nina Tsfasman, also of the 455th. I do not understand, sir, what this is all about.'

'We really do not have that much time to waste.' He almost sounded regretful. 'If you insist on a charade . . .' He shrugged. 'Either way you will not leave this' – he paused and grimaced – 'beautiful country of Afsir alive. But you have a choice. We will put you both before a firing squad or we will make you available to the Arabs.' Without turning he extended his hand to the Russian sergeant. 'Papers,' he said.

They were put into his hand at once. 'Everything is in order here. A beautiful job, but then the Jews were always superb at forgery. Now' – his voice lost all pretense – 'I will save all of us time and, hopefully, pain. It's pure bad luck for you there is no Colonel Popovich anywhere on this base. Certainly, though, a reasonable name to use on the road guard. And the name you gave the road guard, despite these excellent documents, does not happen to be on any of our records here. More bad luck, Major Kazantsev, or whoever you are.'

He studied Steve and Tamara carefully and folded his hands in his lap. 'What *are* your real names and where are you from?'

Steve didn't answer. There wasn't much use, really. Not questions like that, anyway. He'd answer those that might buy them what he needed most of all. Time.

The Russian officer waited several seconds, then turned to his two younger officers. Gloves came out of pockets. As the two Russians slipped them on, the colonel turned again to Steve. 'As you must suspect, we found your chutes south of the base. A low-altitude drop, I assume.'

Stall, Steve told himself. Don't get him too riled too quickly. Only need another ten minutes or so ... 'That's right, colonel.'

The colonel nodded. 'Good. You have found your tongue. How many were you?'

'A small force, colonel.'

'How many?'

'About thirty.'

'What was your purpose here?'

'That should be obvious, colonel. The missile radar and computers.'

'Oh? Why so obvious?'

'Surely you know we're going to have to attack across the Suez. Tonight proved we can handle your new missiles without too much trouble.'

No reaction. Steve waited.

'Then why would you need to send in people on the ground?'

'Insurance.'

'Insurance?'

'Of course. When we commit it's got to be all the way. We'll send in people on the ground to – colonel, I'm not telling you a thing you haven't figured out already. When we go across the Suez the next time we're not stopping until we're in Cairo. We both know that. So it's worth the extra effort to be sure we knock out your computers. Without them the missiles are useless.'

'How did you two get into this base?'

'You mean through the guards?'

The Russian nodded.

'We both seem to make mistakes – I need to learn to dig deeper holes, and our intelligence people need a better checking system for phony Russian names. On your side, you could do with better internal security.' He paused and the colonel waited, studying him carefully. So far, so good. The clock is moving.

Keep it going . . . 'We had a group of Arabs who work inside this base set up to meet us when we came down. We—?'

'You have names, I suppose?'

'I only knew one of them by name. Hamad. He's a truck driver. He picked us up on the road south of here. We used his papers to get through the—'

'Where are your Arab friends now?'

Steve shrugged. 'I don't know. We weren't briefed on what they would do after we took over the truck.'

The colonel tapped the papers against the desk. 'Where are your explosive supplies?'

'Our what?' Keep it casual. He's on to you . . .

The colonel stood, his patience gone. 'You are not a very convincing liar,' he said. 'You, or part of your group, killed the Arabs on the truck. Our dogs found them quickly. They are good at the blood scent. Also, you did not come here to blow up any computers or radar or anything else. You were picked up on the airfield with nothing on your person. The area has been searched and you left nothing anywhere. *Why* are you here?'

It was time to go into his act. He asked the colonel to wait please before he did anything drastic. He clasped his hands in fear, and the Russians saw nothing unusual in the finger-clenching movement during which Steve twisted the middle finger of his left hand and locked the finger rigidly in place. He worked to release a plastiskin plug in his left wrist. When the time came he'd have to get into there quickly. He—

The larger of the two Russian officers that had come into the room with the colonel walked toward him, pulling his gloves tighter. Behind him Steve heard the colonel's voice. 'He hates Jews almost as much as the Arabs do. I'm afraid he's going to enjoy this. Igor, don't kill him, there are still important questions to be answered.'

Steve looked quickly about the room, a frantic expression on his face. The sergeant had his submachine gun ready. The two Arabs were more alert now, their weapons also leveled in Steve's direction. No one paid attention to Tamara, but Steve saw the sudden alertness in her eyes.

A gloved fist smashed into his stomach. Pain ripped through him and he doubled over to meet another fist coming up from far below. It snapped his head back violently, and Steve

230

pounded against the wall behind him. God, the sonofabitch knows how to hit! He reeled, spinning about as another blow came at him. He felt blood on his lips, and then he was taking the punches as best he could, rolling with them, crying out with the pain. Let the son of a bitch think he's killing me . . . Several more brutal punches to the head and, as he doubled over, a swift kick to the stomach that lifted him clear off the floor and dropped him, gasping, back to his hands and knees. He couldn't take much more because the Russian could suddenly do real damage, and he also knew he was getting into a daze where he would lash out instinctively. He couldn't risk that. When the move came it had to be all the way, with precision and complete execution. He cringed as the Russian moved in for more punishment. A hand jerked him up by the collar and he felt a fist crash into the side of his face. His vision blurred. The Russian was there again, and Steve clung to the other man, asking not to be hit any more, and at the same time managing to block many of the punches. He caught a glimpse of Tamara, who stared at him with wonder in her eyes. She looked at his bleeding face, heard his pleas for mercy. The same man who in training had been able to handle some of the best commando fighters of Israel. She followed every move like a hawk.

The Russian pushed him away angrily and swung a roundhouse. Steve took it on the shoulder, infuriating the other man. Another flurry of punches and Steve hung on, tying him up, hanging in. He was close, his left hand clenching the other's uniform, when he heard it. The distant sound of jet engines, and he knew they were back for the next strike. That was to cover their escape in the stolen plane. This was their chance.

He closed his left thumb and forefinger against the Russian's collar bone; steel-finger claws snapped the bone. The man's eyes bulged and he started to scream, frozen where he stood by the pain knifing through his system. The bionics leg came up into his midsection with wracking force. Before the others in the room could move he had the gun out of the holster from the Russian's belt. No one fired, could fire, because he kept the now unconscious form of the man between himself and the others. He tossed the gun to Tamara and in the same movement pushed the body at the sergeant, who was already trying for an open shot.

A submachine gun roared to the side; the Arabs, reacting in fear and surprise, firing at where Tamara had stood. But she was already diving for the floor, cocking the gun at the same moment, pumping bullets upward into the two Arab guards. Steve also dove for the floor, bullets tearing the wall above and behind him. He steadied his left hand, thumb pressing the release in the extended finger, and the poison darts were propelled into the sergeant. His muscles seized as the poison hit his system. Steve was rolling over the floor as both the colonel and the remaining officer went for their guns.

They had no time to use them. A string of bombs exploded outside the building, dazzling them all with the glare of the blasts, followed by a shock wave. Enough to throw them off stride. Tamara fired two shots into the younger officer as the bomb explosions made him hesitate for a moment. In that same instant Steve was across the room to the colonel, catching him with a savage blow across the side of his head. Dead or unconscious, the Russian fell like a stone. Steve got to his feet, groggy from the punches he had taken. Tamara was by his side at once, her hand going to his bleeding face. 'Steve, I—'

'Never mind that now; get those machine guns from the others. We may need them.' Outside the sounds of the second attack increased in violence. They could hear the shrill roar of the jets intermingling with explosions and the *whoomp* of exploding napalm. 'We've got to get to the runway *now*. The attack will last about ten more minutes and by then we've got to be in one of those planes.' He grunted with the effort of dragging the unconscious colonel from the floor. 'We'll put him in the back of the jeep. Tell anybody that stops us we're taking him to a doctor. While the shooting's going on – we'll explain later. Let's go. You drive.'

They went outside, the Russian slung over Steve's shoulder. He dumped him in the back of the jeep, got into the front right seat, made sure the submachine gun he'd grabbed was cocked and had a shell in the chamber. 'Let's go!' he shouted above the din. Tamara released the clutch with a screech of gears and they took off for the airfield.

At the gate the guards were frightened but determined to let no one pass. Security had been tightened, despite the clamor about them as the jets swept in low, releasing bombs, rockets, napalm, and cannon fire. 'Can't you recognize the colonel?' Steve shouted above the noise. 'He's hurt. We've got to get him to an aid station at once.'

The guards hesitated. Steve half turned, then dove from the jeep, firing as he moved. He heard Tamara's weapon chattering. He rolled again, looked up. Four guards. Dead. He climbed back into the jeep and they were on their way again. If no one had seen the incident, the guards would appear to have been killed in a strafing burst from one of the Israeli jets. All they needed was time. Just a few minutes more.

There was a last guardpost to get through. They rushed toward it, Steve ready to fire. No need. The small building was gone, bodies strewn about. 'Good job,' Tamara muttered, and swung the wheel down a narrow perimeter road toward the fighter revetments. 'Tamara, when we get there you talk to the guards. Ask for their help with the colonel. I'll come around from the other side. And no firing if you can help it. It's not just the noise. If someone sees the muzzle flash we've had it.'

The jeep screeched around the side of a revetment, out of sight of the main buildings a quarter of a mile distant. Before they came to a stop, Tamara was shouting to the guards. They came running as Tamara explained that the colonel had been hit. Steve stepped down from the jeep, ran around the side, drawing no attention in his uniform. He killed the first guard with a hammering shot to the side of the skull. The second took a straight-edged blow to the forehead that laid bare the bone beneath. Steve turned to Tamara as the colonel stirred groggily. Tamara stepped to his side, shoved the pistol deep into his stomach and fired the last rounds in the clip.

'C'mon,' Steve shouted. 'That third plane down, it's on alert. That means it'll be ready to fire up.' They ran to the plane – and almost into the arms of two ground crewmen. 'Start the engines,' Steve called to them. 'We have orders to take off at once!'

He boosted Tamara into the rear cockpit, hit the ladder and climbed quickly into the front seat. The crewmen glanced at one another, then moved swiftly to the powercart. One didn't question an officer at a time like *this*.

In the cockpit, all the training in the MiG-21 paid its dividends. The basic cockpit arrangement of this MiG-27 paralleled its predecessor. It came back to him swiftly, and he had the help of a checklist beneath the gunsight. He looked for a helmet, cursed when he saw none. That meant no communication with the ground crew. He looked down and to his right, signaled with his hand. Moments later he heard the powercart speed up. He went through the starting process carefully and quickly. It seemed forever for the two engines to come to life, for the gauges to register proper fuel flow and pressure. There'd be a problem without the helmet – no oxygen mask, and he wasn't sure of the pressure levels of the cockpit. He could always stay below twelve or fifteen thousand feet. No problem with the Israeli interceptors. The pilots had been warned not to fire on any MiG-27 that made it into the air, to leave the enemy aircraft strictly alone.

They were ready. He had the belt and shoulder straps on, glanced in the mirror to his left. Tamara was strapped in. He signaled her to move her hands away from the edge of the cockpit. The fighter had a single clamshell canopy that would come down along a pneumatic strut and lock into place. He ignored the ejection seats and other equipment. No time. He turned again to the ground crew, signaling them to remove the chocks, and—

Headlights, coming fast. Those sparkling lights ... they're firing at us! Oh, babe, it's now or never ... To hell with the chocks ... move out!

He was doing things simultaneously now. His left hand went full forward on the twin throttles, and he hoped he wouldn't overload the engines with too rapid a throttle movement. Thunder exploded behind him as the ship rocked wildly against the chocks. Not enough! He went full forward, past the detent and into afterburner. The thunder was a constant explosion now as flame streaked from the jets. His right hand hit the canopy bar and the big plexiglas shell came down with hard authority. The fighter lunged against the chocks. He went to emergency power, and she rocked and pitched wildly, climbing over the restraining chocks on raw power. Canopy lock; he hit the bar for that as the fighter careened forward. He didn't bother with the runway. No time. The lights were closer from the right. With the canopy closed, the ship accelerating, he could now hear Tamara trying to get through to him. He glanced into the mirror, saw her

234

pointing to the left. More vehicles. He told her to get down, low into the cockpit, bent down himself as the jet pounded from bullets hitting the tail. They'd move the fire forward. He went down the taxiway, slamming his fist against the throttles, imploring the MiG to pick up the speed he needed. No way to take it off prematurely; he had to wait. One jeep was on the runway, racing after them, but they had speed now and were pulling away. At a hundred and fifty knots he rotated, came back gently on the stick and in the same motion hit the gear handle.

They were off. He watched the airspeed, holding her down for a few seconds more, wanting the speed to throw the ship high, to take her up steeply. *Now.* He came back on the stick and moved it sharply to the right for a steep climbing turn to throw off their aim.

They almost made it away clean. They were about two hundred feet up when someone got dead aim on them, leading with his fire, and the bullets started along the top of the nose, coming back. It was only a burst, barely enough, but the plexiglas to his right began to shatter before his eyes and he felt something hot stab into his right arm.

That wasn't so bad, he thought. The sudden coughing rumble behind him was far more frightening. One of the engines was going.

CHAPTER TWENTY-FOUR

An airplane always tells you when it's ready to die. The MiG beneath his hands was no exception. He lowered the nose, trying to ease off on his need for power by climbing away from the Qena airbase at a much shallower angle than he'd planned. Without even thinking about what he was doing, he had shifted his left hand to the stick between his knees, leaving the throttles full forward. It was a bitch of a job, flying a strange fighter at night, for the moment flying strictly by instruments with the nose raised above the horizon. That, plus his need to keep scanning the instruments from the flight panel to the engine gauges, where red warning lights flashed off and on to report some emergency within the bowels of the big airplane. He knew what was wrong without consulting the gauges, but the rising temperature, fluctuating fuel pressure, and coughing rumble that shook the entire airplane pinned it down. The right engine could keep running for a while with a lowered thrust. It *could,* but he didn't know. All he knew was that he must gamble on its operation for some time yet, and he must try to coax it along for as long as possible.

To reach the Sinai Peninsula, and Israel beyond, they needed altitude. There were mountains between them and their destination. The Scorpion airbase lay some three hundred forty-five miles away, if he flew an absolutely precise course (which he knew was impossible) and found the base in darkness in the midst of the high and dangerous Negev hills. The more immediate obstacles were the mountains that rose from the west banks of the Red Sea. If he flew the shortest route toward the Sinai they would run into peaks topping seven thousand feet. No way there, he told himself. If he flew due east he had a range of from three to four thousand feet. Flying to the south meant peaks at six thousand, as well as flying *away* from their destination.

There was another nasty little problem. Keeping the engines in afterburner was absolutely necessary at the moment, for they were running on partial thrust from the right engine and he needed everything the left engine would provide. But that meant sucking fuel from the tanks at a disastrous – in fact, prohibitive – rate. He had to cut back on the power to reduce their fuel consumption, but he also needed that power to climb.

Another problem: His right arm felt as if a hot poker had been stabbed into the muscle, and a hundred tiny devils were twisting the poker with agonizing effect against the nerves. Normally he flew with his right hand, but now it was only an extension from his body that wracked him with pain. No time to see what had happened, how bad it was, how badly he might be bleeding. Not much use in stopping bleeding if in the process you fly into a mountainside.

He kept the MiG in a right climbing turn, watching the gauges, talking to the engine to keep going, to keep running. If he could get to altitude then he could not only clear the mountains but he might also fly this beast on only one burner. It would be limping home, but what the hell, if it made it.

The long sweeping turn to the right helped him with his bearings – settlements and communities along the Nile River provided a long, twisting ribbon of speckled lights. The lights of river traffic also helped. He completed the wide climbing turn and eased in left stick and a touch of rudder as he came around to three hundred forty degrees. But not *too* long for that because that was taking them straight toward Cairo, and by now they must be very nervous up there—

The airplane shuddered violently throughout its length. Needles trembled. Instinct brought the nose down to reduce the power requirements. He glanced at the altimeter. Eight thousand. More than enough to clear anything this side of the Red Sea or the Strait of Jubal. He didn't dare fly any farther north; he'd be sliding into range of defensive missiles, and the radar nets could bracket him easily for interceptors. No doubt they'd be scrambling by now. When the Russians in Cairo got word that one of their precious MiG-27 fighters had been heisted by a couple of Jews who wandered in from the desert, there would be dedicated action to bring down the plane. He began a sweeping turn to the right, rolling out on forty-five degrees, to take them north of the Gebel Katherina peak that dominated the lower Sinai at nearly nine thousand feet above the Negev.

His world was a bank of glowing instruments, and lights on the horizon to his left, far to the north, where Cairo still cast a clear spray of light into the sky. But there was other light now and he vacillated between pleasure and disappointment. They were flying generally into the east, and the first pink touch of dawn showed before them. Well, it took away some of the sting. He wouldn't need to fly her strictly by the gauges; he could eyeball their way now with that horizon reference. It would also make it easier for pursuers to catch sight of him. To hell with that; it was the least of his problems. Keeping in the air was first, running so long as they had fuel. He didn't know the capacity of the tanks in the MiG, but flying at nine thousand feet in an airplane designed for efficiency at much greater heights was a sure way to suck the damn tanks dry.

The MiG shuddered badly again, the instruments dancing in wild vibration before his eyes. He felt no strain flying with his left hand; the bionics limb gave him more than enough strength. But the right arm ... in the dim cockpit light he saw the glistening reflection of his blood. It wasn't too bad, and he attempted to move his hand. It hurt but he was able to flex his fingers. Moments later he was moving the entire arm, wincing from the pain but grateful nothing had been broken or severed. He toyed with the idea of a tourniquet, but it would be a clumsy job at this moment. It would wait.

Again the shuddering of the machine throughout its length, and then a low, booming thunder. The engine was going. If the thing exploded, it could tear the entire ship apart. He had enough altitude and – he hadn't thought of Tamara all this time. He looked into the small mirror, saw her face, tense, her lips pressed tightly together. She was taking all of this in silence, not bothering him, but knowing they were committed to the MiG, that they lacked even the option of ejecting.

No chutes. Either they made it back to an Israeli field or he'd have to put her down somewhere in the desert. And wouldn't that be a job in a fighter that probably stalled out at a hundred and twenty or so? A vision of a silvery lifting body slamming into the flat surface of the California desert came to him with stunning clarity, and he shook his head to throw it off.

Another booming sound and he had no choice now but to shut down the right engine. He studied the panel, trimming just

238

a hair nose-down pitch. The gauges again followed the basic pattern of the earlier MiG fighter. He held his breath and began flicking switches, then brought the throttle all the way back to cut-off. There wasn't much yaw. This was a beautiful machine and he corrected the slight tendency of the nose to veer with the trim.

He took the time to study their position. No charts. He was doing it all by memory. They'd crossed the Arabian Desert; no doubt of that, because there was the Strait of Jubal which, to his left, the north, became the Gulf of Suez. Ahead and slightly to the right he barely made out in the morning haze the high reaches of the lower Sinai mountains, capped by the dominating peak of Gebel Katherina. They moved across the water beneath them. Then the shore line of the Sinai Peninsula slipped beneath the wings and he began to have new hopes that—

A red warning light flashed at him. The fuel warning light. Maybe five or ten minutes left. He'd never have time to figure out the fuel cross-feed situation. That meant getting down *now*. He dropped the nose to pick up some more speed and eased off on the left engine throttle. Even a minute could make a tremendous difference at this point. He knew he must land while he still had power. That would give him the chance to dodge anything unexpected. He could maneuver with power; otherwise they'd be dropping down into the desert with a lead sled on his hands that couldn't get out of its own way.

He turned as much as he could in the seat. 'Can you hear me?' he shouted to Tamara. She nodded. 'We're going down. Low on fuel.' She nodded again. 'Put on the shoulder harness,' he ordered. He did the same, realizing for the first time he'd never bothered to fasten the shoulder straps. It was a bitch of a job and he grimaced with the pain of slipping his right arm through the strap. But when they hit ... without those straps tight, their faces could go slamming hard into the panels.

The red warning light was now blinking furiously at him, and a warning buzzer sounded. There couldn't be more than five minutes of fuel left. The west shore of the Sinai was far behind them now; that could help. They faced the prospect of *walking* out of the Sinai. Knock it off, he told himself. Get this thing on the ground while you can. ...

The low horizon light helped, casting long shadows. He

wouldn't slam into a gully or a rise that was being washed out by a bright overhead sun. Just like setting her down on the moon. He almost laughed aloud at the image.

He figured they were well up into the Plateau of Eltih, in the midst of the Sinai Peninsula. The deathlands of the Egyptian armies ... remember how it went? The Israelis slashed the roads, forced them out into the open desert, the plateau, and the depressions, and left them there. ... He did some swift calculations, computing speed and time to determine distance, and as the desert moved up to meet them, they were beyond most of the Plateau of Eltih, moving into the huge depression beyond. That should put them just north, he didn't know how far, of thirty degrees latitude. He ran the charts through his mind. Port Suez lay just below thirty degrees and ... and they were going down into pure hell. He glanced up for a moment as the bright morning sun faded to gray and was startled to see a low, dark cloud cover obscuring the entire sky. He thought of it barely a moment, concentrated on the rugged terrain hurtling toward them. The flashing light and buzzer faded away to distant annoyances as he concentrated on what had to be done. Flaps down, try and drag her in with the last remaining dregs of fuel. He'd left the gear up – it wouldn't do any good here; it could snap and send them hurtling over the rough desert floor at a crazy angle that would end in a shattering blast of exploding fuel vapors. Full flaps, the nose high, working the best angle of attack for the wings. Full lift, full drag, balance them out. Now he flew with his right hand on the stick – to hell with the pain; his left was on the throttle quadrant, and he knew that at any moment she would quit on them and the bottom drop out like a stone.

A wadi ahead of them. Like the dry river beds back in the Arizona desert. He knew what they were like. Seemingly smooth, but roughened up with grooves and dips. Still, it was the best they had, their only real chance, because to each side of the wadi there were grotesque formations carved from the hard desert floor. No sand here, a hard, baked surface, and that could help. He held the nose off, saw the ground rushing by through his right peripheral vision. It screwed things up but experience helped, and he tried to see through the lower side of the canopy. The nose was high, he wanted full lift and drag at the same time, playing one against the other with the power, a delicate balance of wings rocking gently. There, they should make it right over—

The power went without a sound. No rumble or vibration or anything. He felt is through his whole system, the sudden sighing away of thrust to push them, and he knew they'd had it because—

Lower than he thought. He braced himself as the flaps scraped the ground, vibrating the airplane with a thrumming sensation that went through their bodies. He had just enough time to shout to Tamara to hang on when the nose slammed down and they were on the deck, the world a blur, their bodies hammered as they shot across the desert at more than a hundred and thirty miles an hour. Instinct kept his feet slamming against the rudder pedals, but there wasn't anything to respond. Wasted reflex motion, but he tried, and then she began to slew around. He knew pieces were tearing away but the pieces were from the flaps and the wings and the belly tanks.

A tremendous blow jarred his body. He felt helpless as he was thrown against the straps. A stinging sensation, blood. He realized he had bitten the inside of his cheek. The noise crashed against them, a crescendo of tearing metal. A sharp lurch came, and quiet. Shocking quiet. His ears rang, and Tamara flashed into his mind. He jerked the canopy release and the strut extended, lifting the plexiglas shell, bringing in the sounds of metal cooling and the smell of oil and kerosene mixing with sand.

'Tamara!' He struggled to release himself from his harness. Those crackling sounds ... they could be only metal or they might be the first warning sounds of fire. He heard her call his name. He was free, climbing from the seat, standing on the wing. She had a bloody right cheek but that was all. She was simply stunned by the crash landing. He loosened her harness, half lifted and dragged her from the fighter to the wing, then to the ground. He forgot the pain in his arm as he lifted her and stumbled away from the wreck. A hundred yards off, on the other side of a rock outcropping, he lowered her to the ground, studying her face.

'How do you feel?' He didn't know the strain showed on his face.

'I'll ... be fine in a moment,' she said quietly. 'As soon as I get my breath back.' She breathed deeply several times, closing her eyes. When she opened them she smiled. 'I'm fine, really, Steve.' She reached out to his right arm. 'It looks like it's stopped bleeding. I thought it was broken.'

He shook his head. 'Flesh wound, I guess.' He stood up and looked around, helping her to her feet. 'Where are we?' she asked.

Around them stretched desolation. Despite its desert conditions, much of the Sinai, like most deserts, was formed by the channeling of water. The surface was a wild mixture of sand, rock, and gravel, baked claylike material, all of it convoluted along hillocks and depressions. 'The best I can make out,' he said, 'we're slightly north of Suez. Maybe sixty miles to the east.'

She nodded slowly, thinking. 'If we continue straight east, the Israeli border is perhaps seventy miles from here.'

'That's straight-line distance. You can add ten to thirty miles for moving around this stuff. And that's if *we* move straight, which I don't think is too likely.'

She looked around them, spoke slowly and carefully. 'This is dangerous country. We will never be able to walk out of here to safety. As you say, it means walking a distance of perhaps a hundred true miles. In this desert we would never make it.'

'Those clouds will help,' he said.

'You didn't let me finish. *You* could make it. With ... with your legs, you could make it before your body became dehydrated.'

He didn't answer for a moment, but he'd gotten her message. 'Are you suggesting I just take off, leaving you, and try to save myself.'

She looked down at the ground and nodded. 'What we went for is more important.'

'Are you crazy?' He pointed to the MiG. 'Look at that twisted hunk of metal. We went to get an airplane and *bring it back* to Israel. Well, we didn't,' he said, 'because somebody had better aim than they deserved and because I never had a chance to find out enough about the plane to know if it had other capacities even on reduced fuel to get us home. We sure used up the juice – even the belly tank.'

242

She turned to her left, studying the surface. 'Is that the tank?'

'Yeah,' he said with a sour tone.

'Strange.'

'What's strange?'

'Would a fuel tank have fins at the end?'

He shrugged. 'Some of them do. Stabilization, that sort of thing.'

She started walking. 'Let's take a closer look at that tank.'

'What the hell's the matter with—?' He hurried to catch up with her. 'We're wasting time, Tamara,' he said as he walked beside her. 'We—'

His voice fell away as they neared the tank. It had been torn loose from the MiG in the landing and sent hurtling over the desert floor, breaking up before it came to a stop. He bent down, examining the inner mechanism. He looked up at her. 'It's not a fuel tank,' he said. She waited. He moved about, examining more material. '*It's an atom bomb. A big one.*'

'We thought so,' she whispered. 'Major Chuen, our intelligence people, we thought the Russians might be doing this. Moving these . . . these *things* into Afsir.'

He rose to his feet. 'Well, no more questions about it. That,' he pointed, 'is at least a one megaton warhead. It didn't go off because we didn't set the release mechanisms.'

'You've got to get back with this information.'

'*We've* got to get back,' he amended. 'Well, first things first. Move back a bit, will you?' She watched in fascination as he found the release beneath the plastiskin near the outer rim of the eye socket. He pressed in, felt it click into position. He judged the sun angle for the best light, and moved slowly around the remains of the MiG, blinking the eye muscles for the pictures. He took a dozen shots of the wrecked bomb, went back to the MiG-27, shot pictures of the bomb shackles, aircraft numbers, cockpit interior, and three exteriors of the machine from different angles.

'The camera is in the left eye,' he told her. 'If anything happens to me, remember that.'

'What are you saying?'

'For God's sake, Tamara, if I'm dead I won't feel a thing. It's a ceramic. You know, plastic. You'll have to twist a bit to tear

243

the muscle connections at the back of the eyeball, but—'
'Stop it!'

He was tired, irritated, touchy from the pain in his right arm. Maybe he was being sadistically graphic. Still, she had to know ... 'Look, you're the one who's always telling me how much blood and gore you're used to, goddammit, so why should one stinking plastic eye bother you so much?'

When finally she had back her control, her voice was a whip. 'You are not only unfeeling,' she said, 'you are also stupid.'

She turned and stalked off to the wreckage, climbing into the bent wing to regain entry to the cockpit. He ran after her. 'Just what do you think you're doing?'

She looked back over her shoulder. 'You are supposed to have a fine brain. Use it. We can't stay here forever. They'll be tracking down this machine. I saw a first-aid kit back there. We'll need it.'

She was right, and instinctively his eye went to the sky above them. The clouds were thicker, sweeping across the heavens, and he could smell the winds already lifting dust and sand. She glanced at him. 'Don't count on rain,' she told him. 'All we'll get is wind.'

'It wasn't the rain I was thinking of,' he said. 'No sun or stars if this keeps up.' He shrugged. 'Well, we've got a compass, anyway.'

'Get in here, *please*. We must be on our way soon.'

The first-aid kit was all they found. Steve had hoped the fighter would contain at least one survival kit in the seats, but apparently the Russians used the seat-pack arrangement, with the kit attached to the parachute. And there weren't any chutes, either, which meant no canopy for sun protection if they had to travel for several days. As he searched the wreckage the wind moaned louder around the torn edges of metal. 'Steve! We *can't* wait any longer.' He nodded reluctantly, climbed down, then looked up again. 'In this stuff we'll be out of sight in no time at all. We can—'

'Listen!'

He froze, but only for a moment. He grabbed her by the wrist and ran from the MiG, half dragging her behind him. He didn't need to listen any longer. He knew the sound of helicopter turbines. They had taken this long because of the weather. The fast turbine choppers could stay low. The MiG probably had an automatic crash locator beacon. Anyway, they were there. *But they were passing over. They had missed their target.* Of course; the sand billowing all about them. They'd find the MiG, no two ways about that. When they did, in a few more minutes. they'd be in there like sharks. In a few minutes the wind would obliterate their tracks. If he could slow down that chopper . . .

'Tamara, stay here,' he said quickly.

Her hand grasped his wrist. 'What are you going to do?' she asked.

'No time now. Just wait here for me, and be ready to move out fast.'

He pulled free and became no more than a wraith in the blowing sand. Visibility was terrible, but that was to his advantage. He heard the turbine chopper overhead, following a grid search pattern. He dropped to the ground, waited until the sound diminished, then was on his feet and running to the wrecked MiG. He ducked under a wing, pulled up his left sleeve. The plastiskin plug he had started to release before, back in the Afsir camp. He reached in with two fingers of his right hand, withdrew a plastic cylinder, twisted it open. Two containers fell into his hand. He tried to remember the time exactly; six seconds, no more. He tried to listen above the wind for the Russian helicopter. Still seemed far enough away. There was a fuel tank cap recessed into the top of the left wing. He climbed the wing, pried open the cap, held one of the containers over the fuel tank opening, twisted it suddenly and released it. In the same moment he hurled himself from the wing and ran from the MiG, his legs pistoning against the ground. He was ten yards away when a sudden glare washed over him. Twenty yards off when the small flare bomb he'd dropped into the tank exploded the trapped kerosene vapors.

An explosion shattered the MiG as he dropped to the desert floor, hugging the ground. Chunks of metal went over his head. he waited a few more seconds and was up again, running to where Tamara waited.

'Let's go,' he shouted, taking hold of her wrist and running again into the thickening sand. Behind them flames stabbed through the billows of windblown sand.

245

'You're crazy!' Tamara shouted. 'They're certain to find it now!'

'Save your breath. Sure they'll find it. They'll have just enough time to know the ship blew up. They won't have enough time to see if we survived it. Not in this wind. They'll take a fast look and be on their way home as fast as they can go. Without ever knowing we made it safely out of that thing.'

I hope, he thought as they ran.

CHAPTER TWENTY-FIVE

Tamara demanded that they stop after two hours of plodding through the increasing wind.

She had been walking close behind Steve, using his body as a buffer against the ceaseless howl of driving wind and sand. Still, the protection he provided was minimal. The air drove across the desert not with a steady flow, but a swirl, capricious in its pattern, remorseless in its strength. One moment she might feel relief from the wind, but this was only because of the changing direction of air. The next instant the wind curled around Steve's moving form, the pattern of air visible in the finer sand, driven so that when it slammed, scorching hot and raspy, it seemed to strike her with doubled fury. She stumbled now against his back, her hands clutching at his clothing to keep herself upright. Steve turned, his back to the wind, as Tamara buried her face hard against his chest.

'This is stupid,' she told him, her voice muffled through the cloth bands torn from their shirts and knotted across their faces. 'We're making hardly any distance at all. I don't think we've come more than three or four miles.' She put her arms about him. 'Steve, we *must* rest. This is madness. The wind, the heat . . . we'll wear ourselves out before we've hardly started.'

He nodded, hating to agree with her. No question but that she was right. He had removed one of his uniform buttons, unscrewed the false cap, and had been guiding them through the howling wind by the compass, trying to move steadily to the east. He knew they had wasted many steps. No way to avoid it. The wind howled steadily, not a full-blown storm, but enough to rake them with its enervating heat and sand that was already deposited throughout their bodies. As much as he remembered from his survival schools he was still no match for Tamara's hard experience in the desert. She used the knife from one of her boots to cut their shirt bottoms into makeshift but excellent face masks that kept sand from clogging their nostrils and getting into their mouths. But their eyes were taking a beating, and she was right about the wind. It dried them out with appalling swiftness, and he thought more and more about what lay ahead of them. No wonder Tamara had brought up the subject of his leaving her to go on by himself. No false heroics there. She spoke as an Israeli soldier, a damn good one. His film had information vital to her country. It had to get back so that critical diplomatic – and possibly military – action could be taken before the Arab-Russian coalition could pull off at least a gigantic piece of blackmail. Those nuclear bombs and secret weapon emplacements in Afsir might well win for the Arabs what their Russian-supplied military efforts were impotent to do – the territory lost in the Six Day War and, ultimately, the destruction of Israel itself.

He'd thought about that as they plodded along, picking their way carefully, faces down, Tamara staying as close behind his body as she could without impeding his own progress. Once this damned wind fell off, and Tamara thought it might die down by late afternoon, he knew he could start out with a steady running pace that would eat up the miles. Much faster than she could move. Okay, Tamara *was* right by her lights. Not by his. He'd risk his life, had been doing just that, but for his own country, for the mission, for the damned challenge it provided him because of what he'd become and what he was. Something else, too: Call it quixotic, old-fashioned, whatever, he simply could not deliberately abandon Tamara to this hellish country. Put another way, her survival was more important than the rest of the mission. More important, he was astonished to realize, than his own. He doubted Mr. McKay would approve of such an unprofessional scale of priorities, and he was ever surer the Israeli high command would censor him, but they were there and he was here, and that was that. Maybe it was the cyborg overcompensating to be human. The hell with it, he'd listen to no more from her – or himself – about it.

Finally it became too difficult to speak, to be heard over the hollow, booming thunder of the wind and the constant hiss of sand racing over the surfaces. It was even more difficult to walk. They had to quit, and they started searching for a windbreak. They found it beneath the sharp cut-off of a high slope, and Tamara and Steve sank gratefully to the ground, their backs huddled to the wall of hard-packed earth.

For several minutes Tamara was content simply to rest, to give her tortured lungs the chance to breathe without dragging dust and sand through her throat. She leaned against Steve, her head resting against his shoulder, her eyes closed as slowly she regained her breath and her strength. Steve took the opportunity to look around them. It must have been a wash of some kind, he realized. Either wind or water had sliced a deep furrow in the ground to create the sheer earthen wall and overhang above them, shaping it into a cupped arch that effectively took the wind and blowing sand away from them. Seated quietly, away from the direct, booming cry of the wind, he heard the sand as something new, making a sound surprisingly like dry, powdered snow racing over the frozen surface of the Arctic. To his left and right the sand arched almost straight out from the curving edges of the natural cupola, sand etched against what was left of the sun, a glowing half-light, yellowish in color, unreal, appropriate for the unfriendly world outside. They were in a pocket surrounded by fury, sand racing overhead and to each side of them, but reaching them only as particles sifting or trickling down the embankment against which they were resting.

If they had winds on the moon this is what it would be like, he thought. That fine powdery surface, whipped up and cast ahead – he remembered his own hours of slow movement on that cindery, dusty surface. Not like this sun-baked hell. No air, nothing to move the dust. ... Mars, that's another matter. They've got the granddaddies of all dust storms, cover the whole damned planet, like that one back in November of seventy-one. Winds of two hundred miles an hour and more. Miles high. A whole world wrapped in dust. Dust, but there wouldn't be much sound to it. Couldn't be. That's real dust there. Not sand. Sand comes from water eroding rocks down to the size of grains and—

He brought himself up short. Danger there. He was drifting, letting himself slide away down into the back of his mind, escaping from the moment. You've been in this sort of business before, he told himself, enough to know that if you can't cope with reality you hide in memories, escape. ... He wondered why his body seemed to be shaking, and turned to realize Tamara was prodding him. She smiled and shook her head.

'Give me your jacket. I've already asked you for it three times.'

He wondered at her request but slipped from the uniform tunic and handed it to her. Quickly she removed her own tunic, opened another button to release thin, hard fishing line. She handed him the knife. 'Cut a series of holes about an inch apart along the edge of each jacket,' she said. When he was through, she pulled the fishline through the holes, knotting each one until the two tunics together formed a makeshift shelter over their heads and shoulders. She cuddled as close to him as she could move, then, suddenly startled, pulled away, still hooded by the makeshift cape. 'What's wrong?' he asked.

'Your arm. It needs attention now.' She cut away the shirt sleeve. The blood had long before caked. She moved her face close to the wound and made a hawking sound. 'I'm trying to raise spit to wash away the blood so I can see beneath it.' She was already dry and her saliva greatly reduced. Nevertheless she managed to remove the covering of dried blood. She held the first-aid kit beneath the cape, broke the iodine and swabbed the wound. He gritted his teeth. Then she rubbed penicillin ointment over it and wrapped it tightly with gauze and tape.

'That thing have a mirror in it?' he asked. She searched the kit and handed him a small mirror, three by four inches. 'We could need this, to signal a search plane – hopefully a friendly variety.' He slipped the mirror into his shirt pocket. She put the kit on the ground next to him and returned her body to his, slipping beneath his arm and resting her face against his chest. For several minutes they were content to sit and regain some of their strength.

'Tamara?'

'Hunh?' She was almost asleep.

'That Russian chopper. The Israelis control the Sinai. How come they were so free and easy flying after us?'

She shook her head, still buried close to him, now with her arms about his body. 'No one controls the Sinai,' she told him. 'Only small parts of it. The rest is worthless, like where we are. We don't occupy this area, just patrol it every now and then.'

'That means they'll be back.'

'I've been trying to tell you that. That's why I want you to go on by yourself.'

250

'No way,' he said.

'Please. I wish you to be serious.'

'I'm listening.'

'The information about the atomic bombs.'

'Thermonukes, by the looks of them.'

'Even worse, then. Steve, that information *must* get back. The . . . pictures. *Listen* to me. By tomorrow morning, by noon-time at the latest, I will be dried out. We have no water; there is none here in the Sinai. I will not be able to walk and I do not crawl very quickly. You also will be dehydrated. But it will affect you less than me. You are stronger. If you push on, sleeping by day, you possibly can make it, Steve. *Please.*'

'Really, Tamara, knock this off right now. The answer is no. We move together.' He glanced up. 'Besides, those clouds are helping more than you think. It may not rain but the humidity level is up. We won't be losing body water as fast as before. So will you shut up and get some sleep? We're going to be moving all night.'

She stared at him, shook her head sadly and moved close to him again. He felt her breasts against the side of his chest. Firmly against him. His arm moved around to hold her, to bring her tighter. She murmured quietly, moved his hand to her breast, and fell asleep.

They awoke to a deep orange moon, low over the horizon. Steve was awake first, careful not to move. He listened. For the sounds of engines, voices, anything. Silence. Even the wind was gone. He glanced at his wristwatch. After midnight. They'd slept longer than he'd planned. He called Tamara. A croak was his only sound. Startled, he swallowed – or tried to. His tongue was swollen, his throat sandpaper dry. He moved his tongue about his mouth, feeling it raspy against his teeth, his palate. He managed to produce some saliva, moved it from tongue to teeth, to the sides, then to his lips. This time his voice came through. 'Tamara. Wake up.' He expected what might happen and he held her. For a moment she shuddered, grabbing him tight. Finally she sat up, removing the cape from over them. Sand fell in a shower about their bodies.

She'd been in binds like this before, he realized. No attempt to speak. She worked her mouth slowly and carefully, building

251

moisture, wetting her lips. He waited until she was through. She had a ghostly smile on her face as she looked at him. 'How do you feel?'

'Lousy.'

'This is the best we will feel until we find water.' She stretched slowly, climbed to her feet. 'By tomorrow night at this time . . .' she shrugged, as if she knew the futility of resuming their argument. She looked about her, studied the moon, coppery and huge, low on the horizon. 'That will help as it climbs,' she said. 'The desert reflects light well.' She turned to him. 'I imagine you have not come to your senses.'

'Let's go,' he told her. He slung the improvised cape over his shoulder and hooked the first-aid kit to his belt. He checked the compass and they started out to the east.

They walked in silence, sometimes apart, sometimes Tamara taking his hand without comment and matching his stride. The free air temperature was down to . . . he didn't know how cool it was but it helped, as did the relative humidity. He recalled the deserts of Mexico and Arizona at night, remembered that during his survival training even in the worst deserts the relative humidity would climb to forty or fifty percent. That would cut down the loss of body water. Still, he figured they'd lost anywhere from three to five percent of body water. That was enough dehydration to make them acutely uncomfortable, and it was only the beginning. He brought to mind the old military trick of finding a smooth pebble to put in your mouth so you could suck on the rock and activate your salivary processes. Great, except that your body had to have nearly its full complement of water to begin with. All a pebble would do when you were dry was to rattle around on your teeth. He remembered the salt tablets. Same damned thing. One gram of salt helped to retain eighty grams of water in the body, but once again you have to have the body water from the start, and if you didn't the salt could make you crazy with thirst. Leave it alone, just keep going, keep moving.

Several times he heard the distant sound of engines, and stopped to scan the sky. Tamara's vision was far superior to his own, especially at night. She saw like a fox in the desert and pointed out distant lights in the sky when all he detected was sound. Nothing in the air was coming close to them. In fact, their closest visitor was a good twenty miles off. Not friendly, either. There were four of them, flying fairly low in a grid search pattern, dropping parachute flares. He and Tamara watched as they walked along, trying to be on the alert for anything that might approach from another direction. When it did their hopes rose and were promptly shattered. Two Israeli jet fighters, Phantoms, by the sound of them, thundered from out of the east and raced for the enemy planes. Radar picked them up well in advance, however, and the Russian or Egyptian planes, or whatever the hell they were, raced for the other side of the Suez Canal. Steve came to his senses after the Israeli fighters had disappeared. The small flare bombs. He had one in his pocket, another four still in the left wrist container. He could have twisted the fuse and thrown them as high as possible. Hard to miss that at night in the desert. But he hadn't. The loss of body water obviously was screwing up his thinking. He tugged at Tamara's hand and she stumbled after him. 'Come on,' he said roughly. She didn't answer and he wanted to hold her in his arms when he saw the cracked, darkening lips.

At three in the morning he called a halt for another rest. He needed to relieve himself; despite the desperate need for water his body still functioned and he had to urinate. He had the passing thought that he should walk away from Tamara but he was too numb, and such civilities at this time, especially after their living together (now he began to understand the foresight in that arrangement), seemed rather pointless. He turned to the side and his hands fumbled with the zipper.

'Don't!'

'What the hell's wrong? I'm sorry, but the facilities aren't quite what I'd ordered—'

'We can't afford to waste any *liquid*.'

He looked at her with open disbelief.

'You don't understand,' she said, forcing the words through a parched mouth. 'Not drink. Dangerous. Salt from kidneys.' The words came out slow, spaced carefully. 'Wash out mouth, gargle. If not the tongue will swell, impossible to swallow.' She breathed deeply and looked up at him. 'Old trick of desert. Many Arabs ... Israelis have lived because of this.' She motioned weakly. 'Need a container.'

She searched about frantically, then pointed to his waist.

'First-aid kit. Save ointment for burns, our lips. Rest useless to us. Use that.'

He hesitated and her expression was one of weary exasperation. 'Don't be a fool. Do as I say.'

He opened the first-aid kit. It was a box that sealed tightly, made to resist the penetration of water. That meant it would hold liquids as well. But he still couldn't accept what she was saying, even though it clearly made sense. He emptied out the box, gave her the ointment, threw away the rest. He hesitated once more, and she gestured angrily for him to get on with it. He did, and to his astonishment, when he used the results as she directed, the cruel parchness of his mouth and throat ebbed away.

He brought her the container for her to do the same. She protested weakly that it was more important for him, that he needed his strength. He remembered what he had felt like, the cottony swelling in his mouth, barely being able to swallow. 'Take it, dammit,' he told her, and she did, repeating the process she'd taught him. Then with him supporting her, she provided what she could for the container. He sealed it off and returned the kit to his waist.

She spoke more easily now. 'Soon our bodies will dry up. It's important to contain all we can. Rinse out your mouth and throat as often as possible. Use it freely. Otherwise it will evaporate and do nobody any good. You cannot save liquid out here in the desert.'

She rubbed first-aid ointment against his lips and nostrils, then stood patiently as he did the same to her. He put away the ointment tube. 'We've got three more hours of night,' he said simply. There was nothing else to say. He held her hand firmly as they started out toward the east again, crossing the cruel floor of El Arish.

With the first light of dawn he found a depression in the side of an embankment, a half cave of sorts. He arranged her within the overhang, and suspended the makeshift cape to provide them some measure of shade to cut the savage heat of day. For the clouds were gone and the sun stalked the desert with malevolent fury.

He awoke with some of his strength restored by the long rest.

No time to waste. He roused her from a comalike slumber, waited until her head cleared and she had her bearings about her. 'Let's go,' he said, his voice toneless. They started out again to the east, and the whisper of a memory taunted him. She had explained there was no oasis near them, that farther to the east, closer to the Israeli border, was the first of these, and there would likely be military detachments there. 'Bur Um Hosaira is to the north,' she had said. 'The most northern one of the four. Then there is Agerud, Thamilet Suweilma, and closest to us, if we go straight east, El Kuntilla. They are all in low hills.'

An oasis. That meant that before the war they had been occupied by the Egyptians, and that meant Egyptian military forces. It also meant, his tired brain told him, that when the Israelis struck westward, they would have gone straight for the enemy encampments. At the first sign of a massive attack by the Jews, the Egyptians would have fled in a wild route to cross the Sinai. He racked his brains to recall the details of some of those pursuits. ... Speeding Israeli armored columns, led by spotter planes, had raced across the desert to cut up whatever Egyptian columns they found, and then sped on to hunt for fresh game. That meant ...

'Were there any major battles, Tamara,' he pressed her, 'in this area?'

She nodded. 'Between El Arish and Gerario, the dry beds,' she said slowly. 'Maybe twenty-five or thirty miles east of El Kuntilla. I remember ... I was a radio operator in one of the teams that went into the Sinai.'

'What happened?'

She shrugged. 'We destroyed a column. Many vehicles.'

'And?'

'We sent back the prisoners with a few guards and kept moving to the east.'

'So the battle would have been to the east of us, maybe some ten miles from here?'

She nodded, then fell silent, exhausted. But he had at least a goal, now. He had to find one of those columns of wrecked vehicles. In the desert things remained intact for years. The name *Lady Be Good* flashed into his mind. An old B-24 bomber from World War II. Crashed in the Libyan desert. The crew died. Fifteen years later someone found the wreckage and the skeletons. *But the water in the canteens was as good as it had been the day the plane took off on its mission.*

He pulled, dragged, supported her through the night, stumbling, sometimes falling, sometimes wandering in wide circles. But he pounded his hand against his skull, shouted and yelled to keep himself even partially alert. He had to keep moving. Their only chance now was finding one of the wrecked military columns.

The hours fell away into a staggering numbness. Several times Tamara collapsed, finally could go no farther. He laid her down on the desert floor, unconscious. He balanced himself carefully, lifted her up and placed her across his shoulders in a fireman's carry. He was surprised to discover it was far easier to walk with her as a burden than it had been before. Now he could set his own pace, not hobble himself with her erratic gait. He picked up his speed, moved along in a fast walk, leaning forward, his legs moving with the least effort he had known in many hours. It was the movement of an automaton. He thought of the bionics legs supporting him, carrying Tamara, legs he had once cursed. Now they were proving just how marvelous they truly were. No muscles to tremble, no nerves to go slack, no tendons to pull and hobble him. Still, as he moved at a steady pace, the weight of Tamara on his shoulders increased steadily, numbing his shoulder muscles.

The moon had slipped to just above the horizon and he cursed the increasingly longer shadows. The desert floor he walked over was a mixture of clumps of sand, hard rock, stones, and God knew what else. Sometimes his foot stabbed into an obstacle and he stumbled forward, reeling as he fought for his balance. His legs propelled him forward, tireless, pacing his steps, but the rest of him was being drained. A man can't walk like this without burning energy, and the body needs its water to compensate. He knew he had lost between ten and fifteen percent of his normal body weight, that Tamara also suffered. She was alive only because of her superb physical conditioning. He could move with the girl's weight across his upper body only because of the limbs that generated his movement, and for the first time, hoping he might continue on long enough to reach safety and save their lives – *her* life – he was grateful that he was no longer the man he had been before his crash in the California desert. . . . A man could lose everything in one desert and find it in another. . . . His thoughts dwelled on Tamara. He moved by rote, by the memory of cells. He could no longer think rationally of their immediate position. Moving on with Tamara, getting her to safety, dominated. He realized that if he were the same Steve Austin who had been an astronaut and a test pilot, he might still be alive and crawling on his belly rather than walking with this sustained pace. Most men who lose ten percent of their body weight through dehydration die quickly. At fifteen percent, those who are alive are crippled and raving. He raved, all right, but he could still feel and he kept moving, and he felt an unaccustomed and growing affection for the very things that had once made him curse himself as less than human. His feeling for Tamara was nothing if it wasn't human. He thought of the little girl whose life he had saved in the flaming bus, and realized with a shock that penetrated his be-numbed mind that he had been cured of this obsession with that moment.

He had a fleeting image of Jan Richards, somebody from a hundred years ago in a world a million miles away. He had the eerie sensation that no matter what happened this night, or in the hours to come, he was going through rebirth and that a new, a different Steve Austin was emerging from the figure plodding grimly through the Sinai. He knew, deep inside, that if he sur-vived she *must* survive, and that afterward they would some-how never be apart.

The sun's impact staggered him. My God, how long have I been walking? I don't even remember dawn, the sun . . . He felt the heat baking him, already starting its slow roasting of his exposed skin, no perspiration anywhere on his body. Not enough water left in him. But the sun . . . he must find shelter, get into shade. The sun could kill them both. He looked around, squinting his one eye in the painful glare, saw nothing to con-ceal their bodies from the heat mounting savagely with every moment. His tongue was swollen, protruding slightly from his lips, and he thought of the first-aid kit with the precious liquid. Balancing himself carefully with her body across his shoulders he removed the kit and brought it up to his face. *Dry as a bone.* He threw it from him, realized he must keep it, use it. He staggered after the kit, bent carefully, held it before him with one hand, fumbled for himself with the other. He was shocked to discover that urine now dripped involuntarily, that he had no control over his bladder, that he had been dripping away the last vestiges of body fluids during the night. For the second time in a few minutes he tossed away the container. He had to find shelter or Tamara would die even while she lay across his shoulders. He stood quietly, forcing himself to think, and rather than plod straight ahead into the blinding sun, he turned slowly to see if—

Twisted metal.

A long-barreled gun jutting against the sky.

The wrecked armored column.

He went ahead, a shambling run, the adrenalin going through his system. A few hundred yards away, up the side of a long slope. He went up it recklessly, throwing away his energy, clawing with his left hand at the ground for leverage and support, holding Tamara with his right. He made the top, moved into the shadow of a shattered, burned hulk of a weapons carrier, brought Tamara's limp form painfully from his shoulders to the sand.

He staggered back, unbalanced by the sudden change in pressure on his muscles. He stumbled into the vehicle, hoping to find a canteen. Nothing. Then to the next. Into a tank blazing with heat, to a jeep, another, and another, and nothing. He sat on the ground, numb, trying to curse and only a croaking sound coming out. The thought hit him suddenly that he was being a fool, that he wasn't thinking. He lurched to a jeep standing upright, its tires shot away. *Standing upright, the engine compartment untouched.* He dropped to the ground, crawled under the front bumper, searched for the petcock. There. Frozen in place. He twisted, ignoring the pain. He couldn't move it. If he had body water left he would have shed tears in frustration. Think, you bloody fool, his mind railed at him. He stared at his hand, the cut fingers that had failed him, the blood that barely oozed into sight. Use the other hand, the left hand. . . .

Steel-clawed fingers closed on the petcock, ripped it completely away. He shoved his body closer and an acrid flow of water from the radiator splashed on his face. He couldn't believe the incredible sweetness of its touch. He scrambled about, tore off his left shoe, held it under what was now a trickle. He tried for some self-control, dabbed water against his lips, sucked in a mouthful, and worked it around his mouth and tongue. He managed a few swallows, felt better, startled with his well-being. He was thinking clearly now, and he went to a second vehicle, managed a cupful of the radiator water. Holding the precious fluid in his shoe he started back to where he had left Tamara.

She was gone.

CHAPTER TWENTY-SIX

He looked frantically around, calling her name from his swollen throat. The only answer was the sound of the wind, the gliding sound of sand between the shattered vehicles behind him. It was impossible . . . could they have been followed by an Arab patrol? This close to Israel? But he would have heard engines, he would have heard something. He forced himself to think, to look down. Then he saw it. What had happened. He saw their footprints, and the depression in the sand where he had placed her, his own prints leading away, coming back. But there was another trail, a ragged disturbance leading away to the left, moving down the slope up which he had carried her. He managed to hold the shoe with its precious contents balanced carefully, a dawning suspicion compelling him to move as quickly as he could without spilling a drop. Then he saw her and he understood what had happened.

She had regained consciousness after he put her on the ground. Somehow a final spark of clear thought. She knew the desert, had lived with its menace most of her life. She *knew* Steve could not survive with her as a burden. Regaining consciousness, alone on the sand, she had seen him off in the distance. This was her chance. She crawled on her stomach, dragging herself down the slope by her hands and elbows, seeking some depression in which she might conceal herself. Anything that would hide her from him, leave him free to move on by himself.

He found her face down in drifted sand, her hands outstretched, clawlike, to drag her still farther. Panic grabbed him as he thought she might have suffocated with her face buried in the sand. He placed the shoe carefully by his side, knelt down to turn her over and hold her in his arms. He stared at her. Tamara's face had become blackened by the terrible dehydration of her body. Her skin had tightened her lips and gums until they pulled back to give her a death's head pallor. Against the darker mask of skin her teeth had become a vivid white. He was stunned to notice that even her nose had shrunk, her eyelids had shriveled so badly that her eyeballs seemed protruding, marblelike. His right hand felt the parchment surface of what had been lovely skin. He reached to his right, moved the shoe closer, dipped his fingers into the water. He remembered to be careful, to touch her lips with only drops. He tilted her head back, let water drop from his fingers into her mouth, sucked instantly into her body. He kept transferring water to her until the shoe was dry. Thank God it was having its effect. Her tongue moved and she moaned, a rasping sound.

He lowered her gently to the sand. He knew he needed more water himself, more water for her. There was only the brackish, metallic liquid he had found in the vehicles. But there were others, and he stumbled and ran back to the scattered remains of the convoy. He looked for a better container, jerked a gasoline can from the rear of a tank, unscrewed the cap. Bone dry. It would do. He went from truck to jeep to tank to every piece of metal, tearing open radiators, searching for water. He had emptied the radiators of at least half a dozen jeeps and trucks when he found it. A five-gallon water can lying in the sand, the cap sealed. He picked it up, shook it. It was perhaps a quarter full.

He returned to where she lay on the sand, her eyes staring vacantly. Again he knelt by her side and opened the water can, transferring the liquid to his shoe. He continued to apply water to her mouth and tongue. Perhaps fifteen minutes later she made her first feeble swallowing motions. He continued to wet her lips and drip water into her mouth. Swallowing at this point could produce a violent reaction. As the water took its effect, he opened the gasoline can, poured the brackish water into his other shoe, and began rubbing the liquid against her face, massaging firmly but gently.

Before another hour had passed she was fully conscious, though not yet coherent. He had carried her to the side of a truck and spread the makeshift cape for shade. He remembered that it's always cooler several feet above the desert floor than on the floor itself – cooler by twenty to thirty degrees. He tied the cape to a jeep windshield post and placed her carefully in the vehicle, where he resumed his water treatment. She swallowed slowly, with decreasing pain. He waited for the inevitable rejection. It came violently, her system rejecting the water. It would be better now. She managed to keep down another two cups.

The continued massaging had worked wonders as her skin softened from the water and began to soak in the liquid, just as rawhide softens when exposed to rain. Finally she slept, and he turned his attention to himself, drinking slowly and deeply. He thought about the mirror in his pocket and withdrew it to study himself. For a long moment he remained frozen where he stood, staring at the skull face that reflected back at him. He rubbed his face, massaging steadily, drank again. He shook Tamara gently, forced her to drink again, then drank another cup himself. The survival school had imprinted a warning in his mind. Never save water in the desert when your body suffers from dehydration. Replace the water at every opportunity you have. The cardinal law. You're liable to lose what you're carrying around. Have your body soak up every available drop. But for the moment neither Tamara nor himself could absorb more. He climbed into the jeep to cradle her in his arms, and fell fast asleep.

He awoke stiff and cramped. The sun had dropped to fifteen or twenty degrees above the horizon. This would be the final night, he knew. He had already made up his mind what had to be done. There might be pursuers. It didn't matter any more. Now was the time to gamble. First, he brought water to her lips. She swallowed with relative ease, following his movements with her eyes. Her skin had regained some of its resiliency although she still remained in terrible physical condition. More massaging, more drinking for himself. The water was gone.

He went quickly to work. He had never used the homing beacon from his right foot, out of fear of detection by the Russians or the Arabs. Now, closer to the Israeli border – how close he didn't know; it could be anywhere from twenty to fifty miles; they could have wandered around in wide circles – he would risk everything. He withdrew the emergency homer, extended the slim wire antenna from its case and stretched it between two of the wrecked trucks. He snapped the switch. The battery should operate for from four to six hours, broadcasting on 121.5 and 243 megahertz, the international distress frequencies. It was VHF transmission, which meant its surface range was limited, but it could be picked up in direct line of sight for fifty miles or more by something in the air – *if* somebody were listening to either or both frequencies.

The water had revived him, brought him unexpected strength, but he knew it would not last much longer. He climbed into a tank, kicked open the driver's viewing slit for better light, and used his knife to cut free whatever webbing harness he could find. He returned to Tamara, adjusted the harness about her. She seemed to be in shock.

Back to the vehicles. He tore pieces of wreckage loose, walked a dozen yards to the side of the convoy and laid down the metal in the form of a huge arrow that pointed due east. At the vehicles again, a wrecking bar in his hand taken from a truck, lugging the empty cans. He went from one vehicle to the next, pounding holes in fuel tanks until one can was full. With the can resting against what seemed to be the least damaged truck, he drained oil systems until the other can was half-filled with the sluggish fluid. He poured the gasoline and oil over the tires and inside the engine of the truck, stepped back a safe distance. He removed a flare bomb from his wrist, twisted the fuse, and threw it against the fuel-saturated tires. He had barely enough time to turn his eyes away from the ignition flash. He watched the flames lick through the engine, around the tires, and along the truck bed. The tires were what counted. If they could be made to burn they would throw off a tremendous pall of smoke, and that would bring someone in a hurry. Maybe, he warned himself. Better count only on yourself, Austin. He was already tiring from his exertions, and he knew the water had revived him for only a limited time. He hurried back to Tamara, helped her to her feet.

'I'm going to carry you with these straps,' he told her.

She nodded dumbly, then shook her head and tried to push him away, beating her fists against his chest with the force of a child. He held her wrists, spoke quietly to her until she subsided. He went to his knees, urging her to climb onto his shoulders, her arms hanging forward, her body fully supported in the webbing. Slowly he stood up, adjusting her weight with the webbing about his own body. Black smoke rolled heavily into the air, but it was too late; the sun was now below the horizon, and night swept in with the familiar swiftness of the desert. Someone

263

would see that smoke only if they saw it by moonlight. He checked the compass and started walking. He was still muscle sore and stiff from sleeping in the jeep, from the unaccustomed exertions, and he could already feel his body demanding additional liquid.

Well, there isn't any, he told himself. And there isn't going to be any. So let's see just how good you really are. . . .

He was committed now. His heels jarred into the sandy slope as he worked his way down from the height, stumbling in the sudden darkness, wishing the moon were higher. Several times he adjusted Tamara's weight on his back until his shoulder muscles accepted the burden and moved with the unexpected pressure. He had no time to set a leisurely pace. He would keep walking until all movement ceased in his body. Simple as that. Ten or thirty or fifty miles. It didn't matter. If someone picked up the homing transmitter signal they would send helicopters to the scene. No question what they would find there. Smoke pouring into the sky. The arrow on the ground pointing along his direction of travel.

The temperature had already fallen and he was grateful for a cool breeze. He needed that and all the help he could get. He knew his internal systems were wearing out, that only medical attention, rest, and vast quantities of liquid pouring through his system would bring his body – and Tamara's – back to health.

He glanced at his wristwatch. He had been walking four hours and his shoulder muscles were cramped into numbness from her weight. He leaned forward, taking more of her weight across his back. Several times, crossing a low area strewn with rocks, he stumbled badly, once collapsing to his knees, his hands outthrust to absorb the shock of striking the ground. A sharp pain knifed through his right hand as it stabbed into a jagged rock edge. He eased himself to his knees, gasping for breath, afraid to lower his body all the way to the ground, aware that he would never be able to force himself back to his feet. In the dim light of the waxing moon he looked at his hand. He had gashed it badly and for a moment he wondered why there was so little blood. His skin was leathery. No matter that the cut was deep. The water he had absorbed was already mostly consumed by his expenditure of body energy, and he had taken in only a fraction of what his system demanded. His blood had thickened. It was now sluggish, unable to flow easily. It crawled, oozed as a thick, viscous mass, to the surface of the deep gash, welling up slowly, drying even as he looked. Well, at least he could cut himself and he wouldn't bleed to death. Blood is mostly water and he was back again to cruel dehydration. He pushed himself to his feet, stood quietly, taking in deep shuddering breaths. He forced himself to think. Left foot forward. That was all he needed. No more than that fleeting thought. No forced straining of muscles, the wild effort of moving a limb leaden with exhaustion, the muscles cramped, the tendons taut, the arteries and veins and capillaries sluggish and drowning in their own viscous substance.

Not these legs. Just tickle 'em with a little ol' thought and whammo! Off we go, into the wild, blue yonder . . . His right leg jerked on him, a spasmodic twitch that sent him reeling to the side.

'Whoa! You summbitch, whoa there!' He heard the croak of his voice, brought his hand to his mouth, felt the now shapeless tongue that rested against his teeth. He pushed the tongue back into his mouth, forcing his teeth closed. Wouldn't do, wouldn't do at all to have ol' tongue hangin' out like that, now, would it?

He wondered why he had reeled so severely to the side. It wasn't the leg. He knew that. Finest you could buy in the supermarket. Comes wrapped in plastic, right? All shiny and neat and the ol' motors whirring away like crazy in there. It's your head, Austin, he scolded himself. Ol' head is fulla cotton and sand and squirrel shit, that's what. Gotta think. Gotta think if gonna walk. . . . Walk, you son of a bitch, Austin, WALK!

You do it like the manual says for the new cadets. Tha's how. Move your left foot. Now, before it stops, move the right foot, and then the left, and that's it, boys, Hup hup hut harrup threep fourp, dress it up in those ranks, chest out, get that gut in, your left, your right, your left, your right . . . and the long-forgotten voice of a drill sergeant hammered at his ears, and he started out, left foot, right foot, slowly starting to lean once again into his walk, and he heard the brass of the band and the big drums booming through his mind, sending out the commands, the shooting trickles of electricity coursing through his system, electrochemical nerve processes becoming electrical signals in wires, the nuclear generators working the articulated joints, and he marched, stumbling and lurching across the desert, hour after hour, but by God, he *marched*.

He got into the rhythm of it, and once started he was like the pendulum of a clock. His subconscious seemed to take over, and he kept walking, moving when he should have been dead hours before, huddled on the sand or amidst the rocks, but the legs, needing only that whispering urge from his brain, propelled him on and on and on. Time fled, there was no time, and his body worked for him, and he knew that Tamara was a ghostly figure strapped to his back, and he could not stop, he *must* not stop. . . .

Even then, even the massive numbness of body and mind could not disguise the horizon bouncing crazily up and down because . . .

Because he was running.

And how long he had been running he didn't know, the webbing straps around Tamara cinched tightly so she wouldn't be hammered by his pounding, thrusting motion, and he felt her arms slapping against his chest and against his arms. He knew he should not be able to walk but he was running, by God, he was *running*. His breath sounded like a barking, gasping cough. No matter. The fire in his lungs didn't matter either.

It was storming out there now, the thunder crashing in the sky, roaring in his ears, and he could hear the *rain* beating down, hissing against the sky, hissing against the ground, and his right leg dropped into a deep hole and twisted savagely and he felt or heard something rip, tear itself loose from something else. It didn't matter, the rain, he was falling face first into that wet ground, and the dry sand came up and smashed into his face.

He lay there, stunned, unbelieving. *Dry . . . the sand is dry . . . then what . . . what's that rain . . . that noise?*

There was no liquid for tears or spit or anything, and he choked on sand and tried to spit, but he sounded like a frog, coughing, and he tasted something, a blood taste. He managed to get his arms free of the webbing straps and crawled out from beneath the weight of Tamara's still form. He lifted himself up on his elbow and stared with his one eye into the dark night above, where strange ghost shapes danced. Now he heard again that roaring-hissing-thunder sound. He knew what it was. Turbines. Turbines and helicopter blades. Jet choppers. Had to be Israeli, this close to Israel. He yelled. No sound came from his mouth, only a spray of sand. There was still a spark left in his mind.

He reached into his left wrist, where his fingers fumbled with the spheres. He was on his knees, twisting with club-thick fingers at the small sphere. There, he'd done it, and with his left arm, that once-hated bionics limb, he threw it as high as it would go.

The flare burst like a star through the dark desert night.

Again. Another sphere, twist, throw!

The dazzling light exploded silently.

He reached for the third, but he was blinded from the light stabbing down from above into his eye. There was nothing left to do. He was inert, frozen, a statue of what had been a man, a blinded statue on his knees. Which was how the helicopter crews found him, frozen on his knees, conscious but his mind blanked out, his left arm extended, and the girl unconscious in the webbing, sprawled on the sand behind him.

'How are they, doctor?'

Dr. Rudy Wells looked up from his seat between the hospital beds at Major Mietek Chuen. 'They're going to make it,' Wells said. 'The human body is a marvelous organism. They were literally more dead than alive, but they're both,' he smiled, 'rather splendid human beings.'

'Incredible,' said the major.

'Yes,' the doctor agreed, there being nothing more to say. One does not enlarge on a miracle.

Chuen shifted his feet uncomfortably, not wanting to intrude further. But Wells deserved to know. He could tell Steve and Tamara later. 'The films are excellent,' Chuen told him. 'Proof that the Russians have brought nuclear weapons into what is, in effect, Egyptian territory. By flying out that airplane, Steve also made it clear they were on alert status. Israel, backed by your government, has already warned Moscow to remove immediately every nuclear device. There's no question they'll comply. We still don't know about the special qualities of their MiG-27. Next time ...'

Wells didn't give a damn.

He turned from the major to study first Steve's face, then Tamara's. He wanted to know what had happened out there in the desert. He suspected, though, that he already knew what was really important.

These two had found one another.

And Steve Austin had found himself.

A selection of bestsellers from Mayflower Books

Novels

DELIVERY OF FURIES	Victor Canning	35p ☐
THE DEVIL AT FOUR O'CLOCK	Max Catto	35p ☐
MURPHY'S WAR	Max Catto	30p ☐
FANNY HILL (unexpurgated)	John Cleland	40p ☐
THE STUD	Jackie Collins	35p ☐
BLACK STAR	Morton Cooper	50p ☐
THE PRETENDERS	Gwen Davis	60p ☐
GROUPIE (unexpurgated)		
	Jenny Fabian & Johnny Byrne	40p ☐
STORE	Alexander Fullerton	40p ☐
CHIEF EXECUTIVE	Alexander Fullerton	40p ☐
THE MEDICAL WITNESS	Richard Gordon	40p ☐
LIKE ANY OTHER FUGITIVE	Joseph Hayes	50p ☐
THE DEEP END	Joseph Hayes	45p ☐
I, A SAILOR	Morgen Holm	40p ☐
I, A PROSTITUTE	Nina Holm	35p ☐
I, A WOMAN	Siv Holm	35p ☐
I, A TEENAGER	Tine Holm	35p ☐
LAST SUMMER	Evan Hunter	30p ☐
BUDDWING	Evan Hunter	40p ☐
THE PAPER DRAGON	Evan Hunter	60p ☐
LITTLE LOVE	Herbert Kastle	50p ☐
THE MOVIE MAKER	Herbert Kastle	50p ☐
ALL NIGHT STAND	Thom Keyes	35p ☐
BANDERSNATCH	Desmond Lowden	35p ☐
PUSSYCAT, PUSSYCAT	Ted Mark	35p ☐
THE NUDE WHO NEVER	Ted Mark	35p ☐
THE COUNTRY TEAM	Robin Moore	40p ☐
THE SEWING MACHINE MAN	Stanley Morgan	35p ☐
THE DEBT COLLECTOR	Stanley Morgan	35p ☐
THE COURIER	Stanley Morgan	35p ☐
COME AGAIN COURIER	Stanley Morgan	35p ☐
TOBIN TAKES OFF	Stanley Morgan	35p ☐
TOBIN ON SAFARI	Stanley Morgan	35p ☐
COMMANDER AMANDA NIGHTINGALE		
	George Revelli	35p ☐
RESORT TO WAR	George Revelli	35p ☐
AMANDA'S CASTLE	George Revelli	35p ☐
THE CHILIAN CLUB	George Shipway	35p ☐
THE GADFLY	E. L. Voynich	40p ☐
THE BANKER	Leslie Waller	60p ☐

THE FAMILY	Leslie Waller	50p ☐
THE AMERICAN	Leslie Waller	50p ☐
STRAW DOGS	Gordon M. Williams	30p ☐
THE CAMP	Gordon M. Williams	35p ☐
THEY USED TO PLAY ON GRASS		
	Gordon Williams & Terry Venables	35p ☐
PROVIDENCE ISLAND	Calder Willingham	60p ☐
ETERNAL FIRE	Calder Willingham	60p ☐
END AS A MAN	Calder Willingham	50p ☐
THE GOD OF THE LABYRINTH	Colin Wilson	40p ☐
A COLD WIND IN AUGUST	Burton Wohl	35p ☐
THE JET SET	Burton Wohl	40p ☐
GOAT SONG	Frank Yerby	50p ☐
THE MAN FROM DAHOMEY	Frank Yerby	50p ☐
THE DEVIL'S LAUGHTER	Frank Yerby	40p ☐
THE SARACEN BLADE	Frank Yerby	50p ☐
MY BROTHER JONATHAN	Francis Brett Young	40p ☐

War
SEVEN MEN AT DAYBREAK	Alan Burgess	35p ☐
RICHTHOFEN (Illustrated)	William E. Burrows	40p ☐
HUNTING THE BISMARCK	C. S. Forester	25p ☐
SURFACE!	Alexander Fullerton	35p ☐
HOUSE OF DOLLS	Ka-Tzetnik	35p ☐
THE LIEUTENANT MUST BE MAD		
	Hans Helmut Kirst	40p ☐
FIVE CHIMNEYS	Olga Lengyel	35p ☐
PATROL	Fred Majdalany	30p ☐
'HMS MARLBOROUGH WILL ENTER HARBOUR'		
	Nicholas Monsarrat	35p ☐
THREE CORVETTES	Nicholas Monsarrat	35p ☐
AUSCHWITZ	Dr. Miklos Nyiszli	30p ☐
ALL QUIET ON THE WESTERN FRONT		
	Erich Maria Remarque	35p ☐
THE HILL	Ray Rigby	35p ☐
CAMP ON BLOOD ISLAND		
	J. M. White & Val Guest	30p ☐

Romance
DANCE IN THE DUST	Denise Robins	35p ☐
BREAKING POINT	Denise Robins	35p ☐
MY LADY DESTINY	Denise Robins	30p ☐
BRIDE OF DOOM	Denise Robins	30p ☐
GOLD FOR THE GAY MASTERS	Denise Robins	30p ☐
TIME RUNS OUT	Denise Robins	30p ☐

Mayflower War Books for your enjoyment

Fiction

WOMEN'S BATTALION	W. A. Ballinger	35p	☐
FROM THE CITY, FROM THE PLOUGH			
	Alexander Baron	35p	☐
BRANDENBURG DIVISION	Will Berthold	30p	☐
CASTLE KEEP	William Eastlake	50p	☐
THE WAITING GAME	Alexander Fullerton	35p	☐
A WREN CALLED SMITH	Alexander Fullerton	35p	☐
SURFACE!	Alexander Fullerton	35p	☐
THE LIEUTENANT MUST BE MAD	H. H. Kirst	40p	☐
PATROL	Fred Majdalany	30p	☐
MAQUIS	George Millar	50p	☐
'H.M.S. MARLBOROUGH WILL ENTER HARBOUR'			
	Nicholas Monsarrat	35p	☐
THREE CORVETTES	Nicholas Monsarrat	35p	☐
THE HILL	Ray Rigby	35p	☐
VERDUN	Jules Romains	60p	☐
THE CAMP ON BLOOD ISLAND			
	J. M. White & Val Guest	30p	☐

Non-Fiction

SEVEN MEN AT DAYBREAK	Alan Burgess	35p	☐
RICHTHOFEN (Illustrated)	William E. Burrows	40p	☐
PATTON: ORDEAL AND TRIUMPH			
	Ladislas Farago	50p	☐
HUNTING THE BISMARCK	C. S. Forester	25p	☐
A THOUSAND SHALL FALL	Hans Habe	35p	☐
HOUSE OF DOLLS	Ka-Tzetnik	35p	☐
FIVE CHIMNEYS	Olga Lengyel	35p	☐

All these books are available at your local bookshop or newsagent; or can be ordered direct from the publisher. Just tick the titles you want and fill in the form below.

Name...

Address ....

....

Write to Mayflower Cash Sales, P.O. Box 11, Falmouth, Cornwall TR10 9EN. Please enclose remittance to the value of the cover price plus 10p postage and packing for one book, 5p for each additional copy.
Granada Publishing reserve the right to show new retail prices on covers, which may differ from those previously advertised in the text or elsewhere.